Jack of Kinrowan

Jack of Kinrowan

Charles de Lint

A TOM DOHERTY ASSOCIATES BOOK
NEW YORK

For Mary Ann and Terri

and dedicated to the memory of K.M. Briggs (1898-1980)

also for Donna Gordon

This is a work of fiction. All the characters and events portrayed in this book are either fictitious or are used fictitiously.

JACK OF KINROWAN

Grateful acknowledgment is made to Robin Williamson for permission to use a portion of "By Weary Well" from the album *A Glint at the Kindling* (Flying Fish, FF 096); copyright © 1979 by Robin Williamson.

This book was originally published by Tor Books in July 1995.

Book design by Victoria Kuskowski

An Orb Edition
Published by Tom Doherty Associates, LLC.
175 Fifth Avenue
New York, NY 10010

ISBN 0-312-86959-2

Printed in the United States of America

D 20 19 18 17 16 15 14 13 12 11 10

Contents

Jack, the Giant Killer

Red is the colour of magic in every country, and has been so from the very earliest times. The caps of fairies and musicians are well-nigh always red.

—W.B. Yeats, from *Fairy and Folk Tales of the Irish Peasantry*

Rowan and I and I   am sister to the Red Man
my berries are guarded   by dreamless dragons
My wood charms the   spells from witches
and in the wide plain   my floods quicken

—Wendlessen, from *The Calendar of the Trees*

Though she be but little, she is fierce.

—William Shakespeare, from *A Midsummer Night's Dream*

One

The reflection that looked back at her from the mirror wasn't her own. Its hair was cut short and ragged like the stubble in a cornfield. Its eye make-up was smudged and the eyes themselves were red-veined and puffy. She hadn't been crying, but oh, she'd been drinking. . . .

"Jacky," she mumbled to the reflection. "What've you done to yourself this time?"

Five hours ago she'd numbly watched the door of her apartment slam shut behind Will.

"You're so goddamn predictable!" he'd shouted at the end. "Nothing changes the routine. It's just night after night of burrowing away in this place. What do I have to do to drag you away from your books or that glass tit? This place is a prison, Jacky, and I'm not buying into it. Not anymore. I'm tired of going out on my own, tired of . . . Christ, we've got absolutely nothing in common and I don't know what I ever thought we *did* have."

He'd stood there, red-faced, a vein throbbing at his temple, then turned and walked out the door. She knew he wasn't coming back. And after that outburst, she didn't *want* him back.

There was nothing wrong with being a homebody. There was nothing wrong with not wanting—not *needing*—the constant jostle and noise of a party or a bar or . . . whatever. Maybe it was better this way. She didn't need what Will offered any more than he seemed to want what she had. So why did she feel guilty? Why did she feel so . . . empty? Like there was something missing.

She remembered going to the window, reaching it in time to see Will disappearing down the street. Then she'd gone into the bathroom and stood in front of the mirror looking at herself. What was missing? Could you see it by just looking at her?

Her waist-length blonde hair hadn't been cut in twelve years— not since she was, God, seven. She was wearing her favorite clothes: a baggy plaid shirt and a comfortable pair of old Levi's. When she walked down the street, did people turn to look at her and maybe . . . laugh? Did they think she was some kind of hippie burn-out, even though she'd barely been out of diapers during the sixties?

She wasn't sure what had started it, but one moment she was just standing there in front of the mirror, and the next she had a pair of scissors in her hand and the long blonde tresses were falling to the floor, one after another, while she stood there saying, "I'm not empty inside," over and over, trying to find some meaning in what she was doing. And when she was finished, she was more numb than when Will had walked out the door. There was a stranger staring at her out of the mirror.

She remembered fumbling with her make-up, smudging it as she put it on, smearing it some more as she knuckled her eyes. Finally she bolted from the apartment herself.

The October air was cooling as it got dark. The streets of Ottawa were slick from the rain that had been washing them for the better part of the afternoon. She walked aimlessly, stunned at what she had done, at how light her head felt, at the touch of the wind on her scalp.

She had gone into a bar and had a drink. Then had another. Then lost count. And now she was here, in some grimy bathroom, the sound of the bar's sound system booming through the ceiling from upstairs, some strange-looking punk-rocker staring back at her from the mirror, and she was too lost to do anything.

"Get out of here," she told her reflection. "Go home."

The door opened behind her and she started guiltily as a pair of young women entered the washroom. They were sleek, like *Vogue* models. Styled hair, high heels. They regarded her curiously, and Jacky fled their amused scrutiny, the washroom, the bar, and found herself on the streets, stumbling, because she was far from sober; cold, because she'd forgotten to bring a jacket; and empty . . . so empty inside.

She took Bank Street south from downtown, leaving behind the unhappy mix of old-fashioned stone buildings and new glass-and-steel office complexes that looked more like men's cologne containers when she walked under the Queensway overpass and into the Glebe. Here stores still fronted Bank Street, but the blocks running east and west on either side were all residential. When she crossed Lansdowne Bridge, she turned east by the Public Library, following Echo Drive down to Riverdale, crossed Riverdale and walked down Avenue Road until she eventually reached Windsor Park.

Her route took her in the opposite direction from her apartment on Ossington, but she liked the peaceful mood of the park at night. The Rideau River moved sluggishly to her left. The grass was still wet underfoot, soaking her sneakers. The brisk walk from downtown Ottawa had warmed her up so that her teeth no longer chattered. The night was quiet and she was sober enough to indulge in one of her favorite pastimes: looking in through the lit windows of the houses she passed to catch brief glimpses of other people's lives.

Other people's lives. Did other people's boyfriends leave them because they were too dull?

She'd met Will at her sister Connie's wedding three months ago. He'd been charmed then, by the same things that had sent him storming out of her life earlier this evening. Then it had been "a relief to find someone who isn't just into image." A person who "valued the quiet times." Now she was boring because she wouldn't do *anything*. But he was the one who'd changed.

When they first met, they'd made their own good times, not needing an endless tour of parties and bars. But quiet times at home weren't enough for Will anymore, while she hadn't wanted to change. Had that really been what she'd wanted, she asked herself now, or was she just too lazy to do more?

She hadn't been able to answer that earlier, and she couldn't answer it now. How did other people deal with this kind of thing?

She looked in back yards and windows, as if expecting to find an answer there. The houses that fronted Belmont Avenue and backed onto the park where she was walking were mostly brick or wood-frame, dating back to the fifties and earlier. She moved catlike in the grass beside them, not going too close to the lit windows, not even stepping into their back yards, just stealing her glimpses as she moved slowly by. Here an overhead fixture lit a huge oil painting of a Maritime fishing village, there subtle lighting gleamed on two marble statues of birds — an eagle and an owl, the light behind them hiding their features, if not their profiles, and making soft halos around their silhouettes.

She paused, smiling at the picture they made, feeling almost sober. She moved on, then tensed, hearing a sound in the distance. It was a deep-throated growl of a sound that she couldn't quite place.

She looked around the park, then to the house beside the one with the two marble birds. Its windows were dark, but she had the feeling that someone was standing there, looking out at her as quietly as she was looking in. Catsoft. Silent against the rumble of sound that was getting louder, steadily approaching. For a long moment she returned the gaze of the hidden watcher. She swayed and shivered, sobriety and warmth leaving as she paused too long in one spot. Then she caught a glimpse of movement at the far end of the park.

It looked like a young boy — no more than ten or twelve, judging from his size, though she knew that could be deceptive in the dark. He ran under a pool of shadows thrown by the trees near the river, came out of them again, disappeared into another splash of darkness. And then the sound was all around her. She stood stunned at its volume.

It was the roar of an engine, she realized. No. Make that engines. Her gaze was drawn back to the far end of the park where the boy had first appeared and she picked out the source of the deep-throated roaring.

One by one the Harleys came into view until there were nine of the big chopped-down machines moving down the concrete walkway that followed the river. Jacky gasped when they left the concrete. Their tires ripped up the wet sod. They were coming towards her, the thunder of their engines unbelievably loud, their riders black featureless shapes.

She stumbled backwards, looking for a place to hide, and came up short against a cedar hedge. Her heart drummed a sharp tattoo in her chest. Then she saw that they weren't after her. It was the boy. She'd forgotten the boy. . . .

He was running across the grass now, the nine bikes following in a fanned-out half-circle, engines growling. Jacky vacillated between fear for the boy and her own panic. She shot a glance at the window of the house behind her and saw the hidden watcher clearly for a moment. A tall man, standing there in the safety of his house, watching . . .

She turned back, saw the boy stumble, the bikers closing in. They were frightening shapes in the dim light, not quite defined. Growling beasts with shadow riders. They circled around the fallen boy, a grotesque merry-go-rounding blur with whining engine coughs in place of a calliope's music, until something snapped in Jacky.

"No!" she cried.

If the bikers could hear her above the roar of their machines, they gave no notice. Jacky ran towards them, slipping drunkenly on the grass, wondering why there weren't lights going on all up and down the block behind her, why there was only one man watching from his window, a silent shape in his dark house.

Around and around the bikers rode their machines, tightening the circumference of their circle, until they finally brought their machines to skidding halts. Sod spat from their rear wheels as all nine Harleys turned to face the boy. The riders fed gas to their machines so that they lunged forward like impatient dogs, hungry for the kill, held back only by the leather-gloved grips on the brake levers.

The boy rose in a crouch, speared by the beams of nine headlights. And it wasn't a boy, Jacky saw suddenly. It was a man—a little man no taller than a child, with a tuft of white hair at his chin, and more spilling out from under a red cap. He had a short wooden staff in his hand that he brandished at the bikers. His eyes glowed red in the headbeams of the Harleys, like a fox's or a cat's.

She saw all this in just one moment, the space between one breath and the next, then her sneakers slipped on the wet grass underfoot and she went sprawling. Adrenaline burned through her, bringing her to her feet with a grace and speed she wouldn't have been able to muster sober, that she shouldn't have at all, drunk as she was. She saw the little man charge the bikers.

A spark of light leapt from the leader of the black-clad riders. It made a circuit of each biker, crackling from hand to hand until it returned to the leader. Then it arched out and the staff exploded. Not one of the riders had moved, but the staff hung in splinters from the little man's hand. A second spark made its circuit, darting from the leader to the little man. He stiffened, dancing on the spot as though he was being electrocuted, then he crumpled and fell to the ground in a limp heap. Jacky reached the closest biker at the same time.

As she reached out to grab the black-leather clad arm, the man turned. She looked for his face under his helmet, but there seemed to be nothing there. Only shadow, hidden by the smoked glass of a visor. She stumbled back as the rider twisted the accelerator control of his bike. The machine answered with a deep-throated growl and the bike pulled away.

One by one they moved out, the roar of their loud engines dwindling as they drew away. Jacky watched them return the way they'd come. She hugged herself, shaking. Then they were gone, around the corner, out of sight. The sound of the machines should have remained, but it too was cut off abruptly as the last machine disappeared from view.

Jacky took a step towards the little man. His head lay at an impossible angle, neck broken. Dead. She swallowed thickly, throat dry. She looked at the backs of the houses. There was still no sign that anyone in them had heard a thing. She hesitated, looking from the houses back to the broken body of the little man.

His cap had fallen when he'd collapsed, coming to rest not far from her feet. She picked it up. A man's dead, she thought. Those bikers . . . She remembered what she'd seen behind that one visor. Nothing. Shadow. But that had been because of the smoked glass. That had been just . . . her own fear. The shock of the moment.

She swallowed again, then started for the house where she'd seen the tall man watching. He'd be her witness that the bikers had been there. That she wasn't just imagining what had happened. But when she reached the back yard of that house, the building had an empty look to it. She looked to her right. There were the two marble birds. She looked back. This house was deserted, its yard overgrown with weeds. No one lived here. There hadn't been anyone watching. . . .

She shook her head. It was all starting to catch up with her now. The drinks. The shock of what she'd just witnessed. Her stupidity at just rushing in. It was all because of the weird head-trip she'd fallen into when Will had walked out . . . about being empty . . . and cutting her hair. . . . She ran her fingers through the uneven thatch on her head. That much was real. Slowly she made her way back to where the little man's body lay.

There was nothing there. No dead little man. No tracks where the Harleys had torn up the sod. There was only the splintered staff and what looked like. . . . She knelt down and reached out a hand. Ashes. A scatter of ashes. That was all that was left of the little man. Ashes and a splintered staff and. . . . She brought up her other hand and looked down at the cap. And this.

Two

Jacky stayed home from work the next day. She was too hung over to go in, too embarrassed by her ragged hair, too exhausted after spending a night on her couch, dozing fitfully, waking from dreams filled with faceless bikers driving machines that were like wheeled dragons, who were looking for her. . . .

She spent the day going from her mirror to cleaning the apartment; from the mirror to stare at the strange red cap; from the mirror to force some toast and coffee into a queasy stomach; from the mirror to the toilet bowl where she lost the toast. She took a shower, but it didn't help. Finally, late in the day, she slept, not waking until midnight.

This time the toast stayed down, so she made herself some soup, ate it, and it stayed down as well. She stayed away from the mirror, hid the cap on the top shelf of her hall closet, and sat up watching Edward G. Robinson in *The Last Gangster* on the late show until she fell asleep again. But when she woke the next morning, she still couldn't face going to work.

It wasn't just her hair or the dissatisfaction that Will had awoken in her. She wasn't even afraid of what she'd seen—imagined?—the previous night in the park. It was a combination of it all that left her realizing that things just weren't right with her world. She'd often seen herself as a round peg that everyone was trying to fit into a square hole. Her parents, her sister, Will, her co-workers . . . maybe even herself. Now she realized that she was more like a bit of scruffy flotsam, not moving against the flow as she'd liked to think privately, but just going wherever the flow pushed her. The path of least resistance. And it wasn't right.

She phoned in to work and put in for some time off that was owed to her. Her boss wasn't happy about giving it to her—things were behind schedule, but then things were always behind sched-ule—but he gave it to her all the same. She had three weeks. Three weeks that she could use sitting in her apartment waiting for her hair to grow while she tried to decide what was important in her life, important to her, at least, if to no one else, something that could be articulated so that she didn't have to have that helpless, hopeless feeling again that she'd had when Will tore into her last night.

She meant well, but her energy level was simply too low. It was all she could do to just sit on the sofa and alternate staring at mind-less soap operas and game shows with gazing out the window. The phone rang a few times, but she ignored it. By the time the doorbell sounded around five, she felt so lethargic that she almost left it unan-swered as well, except that the doorbell was followed by a sharp rapping which, in turn, was followed by a familiar voice shouting through the door's wooden panels.

"If you don't open this door, Jacqueline Rowan, I swear I'll kick it down!"

Jacky started guiltily and jumped up from the couch. Forget-ting how she looked, with her cornstraw hair poking up at odd an-gles from every part of her head and her eyes still swollen and red, she went to unlock the door.

"I swear," Kate said as she came pushing in, "someday you're going to give me a—oh, Jacky. What have you *done* to your hair?"

Kate Hazel was Jacky's oldest and best friend. She was a small woman with a narrow face and a head of short dark curls who al-ways seemed enviably slim to Jacky. At a few inches taller than Kate's five foot one, Jacky carried at least ten more pounds than her friend did—"All in the right places," Kate would tease her, but that didn't make Jacky feel any better about it. They'd met in high school, shared their first joint together in Kate's parents' garage, lost their virginity at the same time—the week before their high school graduation—gone to Europe together for one summer, and stayed fast friends through every kind of scrape to the present day.

Jacky moved back from Kate until there was a wall behind her and she couldn't go any further.

"I was worried sick," Kate said. "I tried calling you at work, and then here, and . . . " She paused for a breath and stared at Jacky's short unruly spikes of hair again. "What's happened to you, Jacky?"

"Nothing."

"But look at your hair."

"It just . . . happened."

"Just *happened*? Give me a break. It looks awful—like someone hacked away at it with a pair of garden shears."

"That's kind of how it happened."

Kate steered Jacky into the living room and onto the sofa. Perching beside her, back against a fat cushioned arm, legs pulled up to her chest, she put an expectant look on her face and asked, "Well? Are you going to give all the sordid details or what?"

Jacky sighed, half wishing that she'd never answered the door, but she was stuck with it now. And this was Kate after all. Clearing her throat, she began to speak.

She left out what had happened in the park the night before last, telling Kate only about Will's walking out on her, about standing in front of the mirror, about getting drunk—("Well, I don't blame you," Kate remarked. "I'd do the same if I saw that looking back at me from the mirror.")—and how she hadn't been able to go to work for the past two days and probably wouldn't until she'd done *something* about it.

Kate nodded sympathetically through it all. "You're better off without Will," she said at the end. "I always thought there was something glossy about him—you know, all shine, but no substance."

"You never said that to me."

"And you were all set to listen? Honestly, Jacky. When you get those stars in your eyes you don't want to hear anything but sweet nothings—and you don't want to hear them from me."

Jacky reached up a hand to twist nervously at her hair, but the long locks weren't there. She dropped her hand to her lap and covered it with the other. She knew Kate was just trying to kid her out of feeling bad, but she couldn't stop her lower lip from trembling. She didn't dare say anything more, didn't want to even be sitting here, because in another minute she was just going to fall to pieces.

Kate suddenly realized just that. "I'm sorry, Jacky," she said. "I was being flippant."

"It's not that. I just ... when he ... "

Words dissolved into a flood of tears. Kate held Jacky's head against her shoulder and murmured quietly until Jacky stopped shaking. Then she pulled a crumpled Kleenex from her pocket and offered it over.

"It's not really used," she said. "It just looks that way."

Jacky blew her nose, then wiped her eyes on the sleeve of her shirt.

"I didn't know you were that big on Will," Kate went on. "I mean, I knew you liked him and all, but I didn't think it was this serious."

"It ... it's not really Will," Jacky said. "It's everything. I don't do anything. I'm not anybody. All I do is go to work and then hang around the apartment. I see you, I saw Will, and that was it."

"Well, what is it that you want to do?" Kate asked.

"I don't know. Something. Anything. Can you think of anything?"

She looked hopefully at Kate, but Kate only sighed and leaned back against the arm of the sofa again.

"I don't know what to say," Kate finally said. "Are you sure you're not just overreacting to what Will said? I mean, *I* always thought you were happy."

"I don't know if I was happy or not. I feel so empty now—and it's not from Will's leaving me. It's like I just discovered I have a hole inside me and now that I know it's there, it's going to hurt until I fill it."

Kate pulled her oversized purse from the floor beside the sofa. "At the risk of sounding facetious," she said, "I bought some sticky buns on the way over. One of them with a hot tea could help to fill up at least an empty stomach, dearie."

The last part of what she said was delivered in a quavery old lady's voice that tugged a smile from Jacky.

"Perfect," Jacky said. "I'm worrying about how I look, and all you can think of is fattening me up."

"This is food for the soul," Kate insisted in a hurt voice. "I thought you were speaking of soulish type things. I didn't realize that you were just hungry."

"I suppose if I became a blimp, no one would notice my hair."

"What a romantic notion: my blimpy friend, floating through the night skies in search of—what? More sticky buns? I say you, nay! She searches for the perfect hairdresser—one who combines aerobics with hairstyling."

That lifted a genuine laugh from Jacky and soon they were in her kitchen, drinking tea and finishing off the sticky buns. As it got close to seven, Kate had to beg off.

"I promised my mom I'd stop by tonight—but I won't be staying late. Come by later if you don't want to be by yourself. In fact, come along. Mom'll be so shocked by your hair that she'll totally forget to nag me."

"Not a chance," Jacky told her.

"You're probably right. You sure you'll be okay?"

Jacky nodded. "Thanks for coming by."

"Anytime. And listen, Jacky. Don't try to take on everything all at once—okay? One thing at a time. You can't force yourself to get new interests. They've just got to come. I guess the trick is to stay open to them. Maybe we could look into taking some courses together or something—what do you think?"

"That sounds great."

"Okay. Now I've rally got to run. Promise me you won't cut off anything else until you've at least talked to me first?"

Jacky aimed a kick at her, but Kate was already out the door and laughing down the stairs.

"I'll get you for that!" Jacky called after her.

She closed the door quickly to make sure she got the last word in, but her satisfied grin faded as she turned to confront the apartment. In the space of a moment, it seemed far too small, now that Kate was gone. The good feelings that Kate had left with her went spiralling away. The walls felt as though they were leaning towards her, closing in. The ceiling sinking, the floor rising.

She had to get out, Jacky realized. Just for some fresh air, if nothing else.

Opening the door to her hall closet, she reached up to take her blue quilted cotton jacket from its peg and the red cap she'd found three nights previously fell into her hands. She turned it over, fingering its rough cloth. She hadn't told Kate about this. Not about the empty house with its hidden watcher. Not about the bikers. Not about the little dead man. Was it because she still wasn't sure if anything had really happened?

But the cap was here, in her hands. No matter what else she might or might not have imagined, there was still the cap. It was real.

"I don't even want to think about this," she said, shutting the closet door.

Stuffing the cap into the pocket of her jacket, she went down the stairs and out into the growing night. She tried hard to just enjoy the brisk evening air, but the mystery of last night's odd little scenario played over and over again in her mind no matter how much she tried to ignore it, intensifying with each repetition. It had to have been more than a drunken illusion. There *was* the cap, after all. But if it was real, then she'd seen a murder. Bikers killing a little old man. Bikers without faces. A corpse that disappeared.

Finally she turned her steps in the direction of Windsor Park. Whatever had or hadn't happened there, she had to see the place again. It was that, or accept that she was going completely off the deep end . . .

Three

Windsor Park had none of the feel of otherworldly menace tonight as it had had three nights ago when her fears and—vision? Drunken hallucination?—had sent her fleeing from its shadowed boundaries. There was still a mystery in the darkness, but it was the same mystery that could be found in any night—the stars up high, the whisper of a wind, the dark buildings with their lighted windows and the glimpses of all those other lives through them.

She paused in front of the deserted house. As she looked at its dark bulk, the flood of the night before last's images that had been troubling her washed away. God, she could be so stupid sometimes. Bad enough she'd hacked off all of her hair and then went out and got drunker than she'd been since she and Kate had celebrated their first pay cheques. Or that she'd let Will get her so worked up about what she did with her life. But then she'd had to manufacture this whole . . . weirdness involving men staring at her from empty houses, biker gangs and little men . . .

She pulled the cap from her pocket and investigated it, more by feel than by sight. But there was still this cap, she thought. She had to talk to Kate about it. Right. And she had to get on with her life. First thing tomorrow she'd go to the hairdresser's and have something done about this mess she'd made of her hair. When people asked her why she was wearing it short now, she'd just tell them it was because she wanted it this way. It had been time for a change, that was all. Time to find some . . . meaning.

That brought a frown. She brushed the short stubble with her fingers. She wished Will had kept his opinions to himself.

Still fingering the cap, she stretched it between her hands, wondering if it would fit. It would hide the ruin of her hair. She put it on, then blinked. A quick sensation of vertigo almost made her lose her balance. When she recovered, the night had changed on her again.

The otherworldly feeling was back. The silence. The catsoft sense of something waiting. She turned to look at the empty house and saw him again, the watcher, standing at his window, studying the night, looking at her, beyond her. She turned to look out at the park where he was looking.

It had either grown lighter, or her night vision was sharper tonight. She could see straight into the heavy shadows under the trees by the river, see the splayed branches, each leaf and each bough, and there . . . She sucked in a quick breath. Sitting silent on his Harley was one of the night before last's riders—a black figure on his black and chrome machine, a shadow watching her as well.

There was a connection between the riders and the man in the house. She knew that now. She didn't quite dare approach the rider—the night before last's wild plunge from her hiding place had been an act of bravado that she wasn't prepared to repeat sober—but the watcher in the house might not be beyond her. She could call to him, talk to him through the windows. She started to push her way through the low cedar hedge.

"Hssst!"

She turned quickly, looking left and right. Nothing. A pinprick of fear snuck up her spine. Before she could move again, a low voice sounded almost in her ear.

"Don't be so quick to visit the Gruagagh of Kinrowan—there's some say he owes as much loyalty to the Unseelie Court as he does to his own Laird."

This time she looked up. There was a small man perched in the branches of an oak tree that grew on the border of the park and the back yard of the watcher's house. She could see him very clearly, his blue jacket and the red cap on his head like the one she was wearing. He had a grim sort of face, a craggy expanse between his beard and cap, nose like a hawk, quick feral eyes.

"Who . . . ?" she began, but her throat was too dry and the word came out as a croak.

"Dunrobin Finn's a name I'll answer to. Here. Take my hand." He reached down a gnarled hand, veins pronounced, the knuckles knobbly.

Jacky hesitated.

"Quick now," Finn said. "Or do you want to be the Big Man's supper?" He pointed in the direction of the rider as he spoke.

"Do . . . do you mean the biker?" Jacky managed.

Finn laughed mirthlessly. Before Jacky knew what he was up to, he was down on the ground beside her. He hoisted her up under one arm and scrambled back up the tree. She was shocked at his speed and his strength, and clung desperately to the trunk of the tree when he set her on a perch, her legs dangling below her. It was a long way down.

"That one," Finn said, "is one of the Wild Hunt, and you don't have to be afraid of them until all nine are gathered." He pointed again. "There's the Big Man — Gyre the Younger."

Jacky's gaze followed his finger and she drew in a sharp breath. Standing with his back to them, facing the river, was a man who had to be at least eighteen feet tall. He was close to the trees that rimmed the riverbank and she'd taken his legs for tree trunks, never looking higher. Dizzy now, she clung harder to the tree she was in.

"Where . . . where are we, Dunrobin?" she asked.

It still looked like Windsor Park, but with giants and little gnome men in trees, it had to be a Windsor Park in an Ottawa that wasn't her own.

"Dunrobin's my clan name — it's Finn you should be calling me. That's the way we hobs pair our names — at least our speaking names. And this is still your own world. You're just seeing it through different eyes, seeing how you're wearing a hob's spellcap and all."

"It doesn't feel like my world anymore," Jacky said slowly.

"There are Otherworlds," Finn said, "but they're not for the likes of us. We're newcomers, you know. The Otherworlds belong to those whose land this was before we came—same as our own Middle Kingdom in the homeland belongs to us. Now that cap you're wearing—it belonged to Redfairn Tom. I know him, for he's a cousin, on my father's side. Where did you get it?"

"I. . . . "

She didn't know what to say. What she'd seen three nights ago . . . If she'd tried telling anyone about it, they'd have looked at her like she wasn't playing with a full deck. But this little man . . . He'd believe. The problem was, she wasn't all that sure that he was real himself. God, it was confusing.

"Give me your jacket while you're telling the tale."

She looked at him. "What?"

"Your jacket. I'll stitch a spell or two into it while we're talking. Walking around like you are, anybody can see you plain as day. The Host is strong now—getting stronger every day. They see you wearing a hob's redcap and they'll just as soon spike you as ask you the time of day. Come, come. You've a shirt on, as I can plainly see, and it's not so cold. Best give me your shoes while you're at it."

"Please," Jacky said. "I don't understand what's going on."

"Well, that's plain to see, walking about in the Big Man's shadow with never a care. Planning on calling in on Kinrowan's wizard and not a charm on you but a redcap and while that'll let you see, it won't mean a damn if he decides to find out what sort of a toad you'd make—do you follow my meaning?"

"I . . . No. No, I don't."

"Well, what don't you understand? And do give me that jacket. All we need now is for the Big Man to turn around and see you sitting here, like a chicken in its roost, waiting for him to pluck it."

"I don't understand anything. This Kinrowan you're talking about—my name's Rowan, too." She took off her jacket as she spoke, warily balancing herself on her branch, and passed it over.

"Is it now? That's a lucky name, named for a lucky tree, redberried and all. Red berry, amber and red thread—now that's a charm that would stop even a bogan, you know. Do you have just the one speaking name?"

She shook her head. "It's Jacqueline Elizabeth Rowan—but my friends just call me Jacky. What's a speaking name?"

"They're usually boys," Finn said to himself.

"What?"

"Nothing." He had just produced a needle and thread and was stitching a design on the inside of her jacket, the gnarled fingers moving deftly and quick. "A speaking name's the one you'll let others speak aloud, you know? As opposed to your real name that you keep hidden—the one that a gruagagh can use to make spells with."

"I don't have a secret name—just the one I told you."

"Oh? Well, you best keep the rest of your name to yourself in future, Jacky Rowan. You never know who's listening, if you get my meaning." He looked up from his work and fixed her with a glare that, she supposed, was meant to convey his seriousness. What it did do was succeed in frightening her.

"I . . . I'll remember that."

"Good. Now let's start again. The cap. Where did you get Tom's cap?"

Watching him stitch, Jacky told him all that she'd seen—or thought she'd seen—three nights ago. Finn paused when she was done and shook his head.

"Oh, that's bad," he said. "That's very bad. Poor Tom. He was a kind old hob and never a moment's trouble. I didn't know him well, but my brother used to gad about with him." He sighed, then looked at her. "And it's bad for you, too, Jacky Rowan. They've marked you now."

Jacky leaned forward and lost her balance. She would have tumbled to the ground if Finn hadn't shot out a gnarled hand and plucked her from the air. He set her back down on her branch and gave her a quick grin that was more unhappy than cheerful. It did nothing to set her at ease.

"Who . . . who's marked me?"

"The Host—the Unseelie Court, who else? Why do you think I'm talking to you, girl? Why do you think I'm helping you? I'd sooner take a crack in the head from a big stick before letting anyone fall into their clutches."

"You've mentioned them before. Who or what are they?"

Finn tied off the last stitch on her jacket and passed over. "Put this on first and give me your shoes."

"What did you do to my jacket?" she asked.

"Stitched a hob spell into it. Now when you're wearing it, mortals won't see you at all, day or night, and it will be harder for faerie, both the Laird's folk, and the Host." He took her sneakers as she passed them to him, one by one and went on. "Now the Laird's folk—those who follow Kinrowan's banner here—are sometimes called the Seelie Court. That comes from the old language, you know, and it means happy or blessed. But the Unseelie Court is made up of bogans and the sluagh—the restless dead—and other grim folk.

"We followed you here, followed your forefathers when they first came to these shores. Then we shared the land with the spirits who were here first, until they withdrew into their Otherworlds and left this world to us. We live in the cities mostly, close to men, for it's said we depend on their belief to keep us hale. I don't know how true that tale is, but time has played its mischief on us and we dwindle now—at least the Laird's folk do—while those of the Unseelie Court—oh, there's scarce a day goes by that doesn't strengthen them."

"But I don't know *anybody* who believes in any of you," Jacky protested.

"Now, that's where you're wrong. There's few that believe in the Laird's folk, that's too true, but the Host. . . . I've seen the books you read, the movies you see. They speak of the undead and of every horror that ever served in Gyre the Elder's Court. Your people might not say they believe when you ask them, but just their reading those books, watching those movies. . . . Jacky Rowan, every time they do, they strengthen our enemy and make us weak.

"We're few and very few now, while the Host has never been stronger. They're driving us from the cities and you've seen the Big Man yourself, just standing there, waiting for Kinrowan's Gruagagh to fall, if he hasn't already sold his soul to them. It's a bad time for us, Jacky Rowan. And a bad time for you, too, for now they've marked you as well."

"Marked me as what?" she asked.

"As one of us."

He was stitching designs on the insides of her sneakers now, first one, then the other, reminding her of all the stories that her mother had read to her of fairy tailors and shoemakers.

"But I'm not one of you," she said.

"Doesn't make no differ—not to them."

"Then the bikers . . . they'll be after me?"

Finn shrugged. "I don't know. These'll help," he added, holding up a sneaker. "I'm stitching swiftness into them. You'll run so fast now that even a Big Man'll have trouble catching you. But the Wild Hunt? I don't know. Not yet. But soon, perhaps."

"They're part of the Unseelie Court, too?"

"No. But Gyre the Elder has the Horn that commands them, so when he bids them fetch, they fetch. When he bids them kill, they kill. They must obey the Horn."

He was quiet then, concentrating on his work. Jacky peeked at the biker through the leaves, but she wouldn't look at the bulk of the giant keeping silent watch on something across the river.

"There's seven of those giants in this Unseelie Court," Finn said suddenly, "and each one's nastier than the one before. Just the two Gyres and Thundell are here now, but the rest are coming. They want the Gruagagh's Tower first, for there's power in it. And then they'll want the Heart of Kinrowan. And then—why then, they'll have it all, Jacky Rowan. You and me and every seelie one of us there be, damn their stone hearts!"

"But can't . . . can't you stop them?"

"Me? What am I to do? Or any of the Laird's folk? We're weak, Jacky Rowan—I told you that. We're not strong enough to stop them anymore. Now we must just hide and watch and hope we can stay out of their way. Pray that they don't find the Laird and spike his heart. But we don't have much hope. The time of heroes is long gone now."

"But what about the Gruagagh?" she asked, stumbling over the word.

"Well, now." Finn finished the second of her sneakers and passed them over to her. "He's a queer one, he is. A Kinrowan as well, on his mother's side, but there's not a one of us that trusts him now, and there's nothing he can do anyway."

"Why? What did he do?"

"No one knows for sure, but it's said he turned the Laird's daughter over to Gyre the Elder."

"Did he?"

"I don't know, Jacky Rowan. He was escorting her home to the Hill, just the two of them, you know, and the next thing we know, she's gone and we find him on the road, hurt some, but not dead. Now you tell me: would they let him live if he wasn't one of their own?"

"I . . . I don't know."

"No one does."

"What happened to the Laird's daughter?" Jacky asked.

"No one knows that either. Some say Gyre the Elder ate her. Others say he's got her locked away somewhere, but no one knows where. The Wild Hunt could find her, but Gyre the Elder's got the Horn, so only he can command them."

"You should get the Horn then," Jacky said. "Couldn't the Gruagagh get it for you?"

"The Gruagagh can't leave his Tower," Finn said. "That's the only place he's safe. And he must be protected for the way to the Laird is through him, you see."

Jacky didn't and said so.

"In peaceful times," Finn replied, "the Gruagagh sees to the welfare of Kinrowan itself. He sits in his Tower, weaving and braiding the threads of luck that flow through the earth by the will of the Moon—ley lines. Do you know what I mean?"

"Vaguely. I mean, I've heard of leys before."

"Yes. Well, his Tower . . . Think of it as a great loom that he uses to gather the luck we need, the luck that he weaves into the fabric of the realm. When there's a snag or tear in the luck threads, it's the Gruagagh who solves the problem, sometimes by a simple spell to untangle a knot in the thread, other times by directing the hobs and brownies of the Court to remove the obstruction. The luck gave us life and sustains us, you see, while the tides of your belief strengthens or weakens what we already are—at least that's what I heard the Laird say once. He said that without the lines of luck, we would be wholly dependent upon your belief and soon gone from this world.

"So the Gruagagh sees to the physical realm and its boundaries, while the Court itself and its people are looked after by our Laird and his family. The Laird rules and settles disputes, while his lady and her daughter hold in trust the songs that sow the seeds deeper, make the harvests more bountiful, keep the Host at bay on Samhaine Eve—the day-by-day magics that make life better. Only now our Laird is widowed and his daughter's gone . . . "

Finn's voice trailed off and he looked at Jacky. He seemed surprised by her attentiveness. "Are you sure you want to hear all of this?" he asked.

"Oh, yes," Jacky said.

It was like being caught up in a fairy tale, she thought. She imagined this Laird's daughter, maybe captive somewhere—if she was still alive—and all that was keeping her going was the hope that her father, or one of his people, would rescue her. And the Gruagagh—he was already a tragic figure in her mind.

"Well," Finn said. "Things being as they are—with the Laird widowed and his daughter lost—there's no one but the Gruagagh to do both jobs, to protect both the realm and its people so he has to stay in his Tower. The Host can't breach the Tower, but the Gruagagh must remain in it, for if he ventures forth again now and they catch him, then Kinrowan's fate is sealed and the Seelie Court will rule here no more."

"I don't understand why no one trusts him," Jacky said. "It sounds to me like he's doing his job."

"There's those who think he's only waiting until the time is right, and then he'll hand us all over to the Host—as he did with the Laird's daughter."

"Then why don't you get a new gruagagh?"

Finn sighed. "Because he's all we have—there's no one else to be had. But it's hard to trust a man who keeps so much of himself to himself."

"So what you really need is to get the Laird's daughter back," Jacky said. "Would he know what to do?"

"Would who know?"

"This Gruagagh of yours—would he know how to find the Horn?"

Finn started to answer her, then shook his head. He gave a quick look to the deserted house behind them. When his gaze returned to her, his eyes were troubled.

"I don't know," he said. "No one's asked him."

"Why not?"

Finn looked away then, refusing to meet her gaze.

"Why not?" she repeated.

"Because," he said finally, "there's few that would chance a talk with the Gruagagh—after what happened to the Laird's daughter, even the Laird avoids him. And there's no one who'd dare go looking for the Horn." His gaze returned to hers and he flinched at the look in her eyes. "Would you?" he demanded.

"Me? Why should I? She's not *my* Laird's daughter."

"But you're kin—you said so yourself. Your name's Rowan."

"Finn, until tonight, I never heard of *any* of you."

"Well then, you see," he said. "You're no different from the rest of us. You won't go, and neither will we, and all for the same reason no matter what we say. It's because we don't have the courage."

Now it was Jacky's turn to flinch. For one moment she was back in her apartment and Will was slamming the door.

"This is stupid," she said. "None of this is even real."

"Oh?" Finn asked, glaring at her. "Then why don't you waltz over to yon' Big Man and give him a kick in the toe. See what he has to say, before he swallows you whole!"

"The Big Man isn't even there and neither are you. I'm just seeing you both because of this stupid cap."

"It's because of the cap that you finally do *see*. We're all around you all the time, Jacky Rowan. Though in a few years time, it'll be only the Unseelie Court that walks the twilight shades of your world. Wear that cap long enough and you won't need it to *see* anymore. But then... oh, then... Merriment will have fled and all the wonder. There'll be nothing left but the Host and I wish you well in that world!"

She matched him, glare for glare; then before he could make a move she was sliding down the tree and running for the house that Finn had called the Gruagagh's Tower. She moved so fast, thanks to whatever magics that the hob had stitched into her sneakers, that she was at the back door before he was even down the tree.

"I'll show you!" she cried to him. Turning, she hammered on the door.

"Jacky Rowan, no!" Finn cried.

He knew what she couldn't, that the Gruagagh was quick to anger; that he had real power, not the small skilly stitcheries of a hob; that if he was roused in anger she would regret it for all the short minutes that remained in her life. But he was too late. The door opened and the Gruagagh was there, tall and forbidding in the doorway. Finn saw Jacky take a half-step back, then square her shoulders and look up at him.

"Mr. Gruagagh," he heard her say. "Can we talk?"

Finn sped across the yard, but the door closed behind them before he reached it. He lifted a hand to knock himself, hesitated, then let it fall back down to his side. For a long time he stared at the door's wooden slats, then slowly he returned to his perch in the oak tree. He sat there, staring out over the park, at the Big Man and the solitary member of the Wild Hunt. He thought of his cousin, Redfairn Tom, of what had happened to him, and he shivered.

"It's all gone bad," he muttered to himself. "Oh, very bad."

Four

Jacky followed the Gruagagh inside. Moonlight came in through the window looking out on the park, throwing a vague light on what appeared to be a kitchen, only its furnishings seemed vague and insubstantial, shifting and changing as she looked around. One moment the shadowy bulk of a refrigerator was by the door, the next it was over by the sink, and then it didn't exist at all. Ghostly stoves, kitchen tables and chairs, cupboards and counters came and went, never present long enough to quite focus on. In the darker corners where the moonlight didn't reach, there were rustlings and stirrings, as though small hidden creatures were disturbed by their entrance.

The Gruagagh lit a candle with a snap of his fingers and the darker shadows vanished. There was nothing in them. There were no ghostly furnishings. The room was empty except for the two of them. Jacky swallowed thickly. Just a trick, she told herself. But now the flickering light banished the shadows from the Gruagagh's face, and she wasn't so sure if it being a trick or not made any difference.

If Finn had seemed a little grim at first, the Gruagagh radiated a forbidding power that made Jacky wish she'd stayed outside in the hob's tree. His eyes were a piercing blue and he would have been a handsome man except for the scar that marked the whole left side of his face, puckering the skin.

"They did that . . . didn't they?" she said, looking at the scar. "The Unseelie Court . . . "

He made no reply. Instead, he sat down in the window-seat that commanded a view of Windsor Park and gazed outside, into the darkness. There was no place for Jacky to sit. She shifted her weight from foot to foot, wondering what had possessed her to come here. The Gruagagh scared her without making a move, without saying a word—and he was one of the good guys. She hoped. She cleared her throat and he looked away from the window, back to her.

"Why are you here?" he asked.

His voice was gravelly and low, not cold, but not exactly friendly either. Jacky tried a quick smile, but the set expression of his features didn't change. He waited for her reply. He looked as though he could sit there and wait forever.

"I . . . I want to help," Jacky managed at last.

The Gruagagh smiled humourlessly. "What can you do?" he asked. "Can you command the Wild Hunt? Are you a giant-killer? Or perhaps you mean to spirit us all away to some safe haven?"

Jacky took a quick step back under the vehemence in his voice. She remembered Finn saying something about being turned into a toad and her knees began to go weak.

"I don't know what I can do," she said finally. "But at least . . . at least I'm willing to try."

The Gruagagh said nothing for a long time. He returned his gaze to the park, frowning.

"That's true," he said. "And one should never ignore aid when it's offered, even by such a—" He looked her up and down. "—such a tatterdemalion."

"I didn't know this was supposed to be a fashion pageant," Jacky began, then put her knuckles to her mouth.

She hadn't meant to come out with that. She flinched as the Gruagagh lifted his arm, but he only patted the windowseat.

"Don't be afraid," he said. "That's twice I've spoken out of turn, and twice I've deserved a reprimand. What do they call you?" he added as Jacky cautiously made her way to the windowseat.

She sat as far from him as the seat would allow.

"Jacky," she said. "Jacky Rowan."

The Gruagagh nodded. "I see now," he said.

"What? What do you see?"

"Why you've come, for one thing. You've a lucky name and are kin as well."

"What's your name?" she asked, then corrected herself. "I mean, what's your speaking name? Or does everyone just call you the Gruagagh?"

"No one speaks to me at all," he said. "Except for the night. And it whispers with the voices of the sluagh. But my friends, when I had them, called me Bhruic Dearg."

Jacky nodded. "Is Bhruic your clan name?" She pronounced it "Vrooick," trying to approximate the way he'd said it.

"You've been talking to hobs," he said. "No. My clan is that of Kinrowan, the same as the Laird, though he's not so likely to own to that as he once was. Bhruic Dearg is my bardic name—Dearg for the rowan's red berries. I was a bard before I was a gruagagh—but that was long ago now, too."

"What . . . what should I call you?" she asked.

"Bhruic, if you wish."

"All right." She tried a small smile but the Gruagagh merely studied her.

"How did you mean to help us?" he asked finally.

Jacky's smile died. "It's . . . " She paused and began again. "Finn told me about . . . about the Laird's daughter . . . " She glanced at him, saw his eyes darken with shadows. She went on quickly. "I thought if we could retrieve the Horn—the Wild Hunt's Horn—we could use them to find her and then, then we could rescue her . . . if . . . "

"If she lives." The Gruagagh finished the sentence where Jacky didn't quite dare.

"Oh, I'm sure she's okay," Jacky said. "She's got to be."

"There," the Gruagagh said, "speaks one who doesn't know the Unseelie Court as we do."

"But if she *is* alive . . . "

The Gruagagh sighed. "Even if she is alive, she might be changed. . . ."

"What do you mean?"

"When the Host catch one of the Laird's folk . . . if they don't kill them outright, they change them. They diminish their light . . . their goodness . . . and make them over into their own kind."

"Then we've got to try and do something!"

Jacky wasn't sure why she was so caught up with the fate of the Laird's daughter. She just knew it was important. Not just to the Laird's folk, but for herself as well. It held . . . meaning.

"Do you know where the Horn is?" she asked.

The Gruagagh nodded. "It will be in Gyre the Elder's Keep."

"Where's that?"

"I'll show you."

He tugged a fat leather shoulder bag from under the windowseat and took out a roll of parchment that he laid out between them. A startled "Oh" escaped Jacky as she bent over it. The map was of Ottawa, but all the names were changed. Parliament Hill was the Laird's Manor and Court. The Market area was the Easting Fair. The Glebe became Cockle Tom's Garve.

"This shows Kinrowan," the Gruagagh said. "Kinrowan proper—the Laird's Seat. And this is the countryside, showing the boundaries of our realm."

Everything was familiar, but foreign at the same time. The shapes of the streets and the placements of surrounding villages and towns were all as they should be, but reading the names Jacky felt as though she'd stepped through Alice's looking glass, and everything had been turned around.

"It's all different," she said.

"Just the names. We have our own. And the Court of Kinrowan is not the only Seelie Court either." He pointed to the area north of the Ottawa River where the Gatineau Hills began. "This is the Laird of Dunlogan's realm." Now he pulled out a second map and the finger moved down it, from Kinrowan towards Kingston. "And this is Kenrose. But there are gaps, you see. Here and here." He pointed out shaded areas between the various faerie realms.

"These are the Borderlands where the fiaina sidhe dwell—the wild faerie that have no allegiance to either Court. But because the fiaina take no side, the Unseelie Court can host against us in the

Borderlands—unopposed." He pointed to Winchester. "Here is a place where the Host has driven out a Laird's Court, taking it for their own. Such places grow almost daily now.

"This map's not so new now and some of the borders have changed, for as Gyre the Elder's people grow in strength, our own borders shrink. There was a time, Jacky, when you wouldn't see a bogan though you walked from the High Dales of Dunlogan down to Avon Dhu." He pointed to the St. Lawrence Seaway as he spoke. "But now . . . now Gyre the Younger stands outside my Tower, penning me in, and sluagh whisper on the winds that creep between the boards."

"Can't these other Lairds help you?" Jacky asked.

The Gruagagh shook his head. "They're as bad off as we are—if not worse."

"What about these wild faerie?"

"The fiaina are impossible to gather under one banner. They are a solitary folk and won't see the danger until it's too late. Since the Host has made no move against them to date, they appear content to remain uninvolved. It's an evil time, Jacky Rowan, and it's not getting any better."

She pointed to the first map. "It says 'The Gruagagh's Tower' here," she said, indicating the house they were in. On the map, Belmont Avenue had become Auch Ward Way. "Why does it say Tower? This is just a house."

"In the homeland, the gruagaghs all had Towers," he explained. "We're a folk that stick hard to tradition, so that even if the building's not a tower, we'll call it one all the same."

"Here's Tamson House," Jacky said, still poring over the map. She glanced up at him. "It's called that in our world as well."

The Gruagagh nodded. "That is an old magic place—a doorway to the Otherworlds of the spirits who were here before we came."

Well, there was certainly something odd about the block-long building, Jacky thought. It had always fascinated her when she walked by—especially the towers—but she'd never been inside.

"Where *is* Gyre the Elder's Keep?" she asked.

The Gruagagh opened the second map again and showed her. She had to think for a moment before she could find the proper name for the place—at least the name she knew it by.

"That's near Calabogie," she said at last. It was an hour west of Ottawa and she'd had a picnic at a friend's cottage near there just this summer. "But I don't remember seeing anything that looked even vaguely like a Keep." Then she smiled. "But it's not a Keep, is it? You just call it that."

The Gruagagh nodded. "The Giants' Keep is a cave—a well-guarded cave, Jacky. You'll find it hard to get near to it, little say inside, even with a hob skillyman's stitcheries to help you."

"But I have to try, don't I?"

The Gruagagh nodded again. "I suppose you must."

"If I get the Horn, will you help me call the Wild Hunt? We can set it on the giants and see how much *they* like it."

"I can't help you," the Gruagagh said. "And you must not return here. They have marked you now. Once in and out of my Tower and they may let you go—or just follow and watch; to see who and what you are. Twice in and out, and they'll know you for an enemy and they will kill you."

"Why can't they get into this house?"

"Because 'this house' is my Tower—a gruagagh's Tower—and I use all my diminishing powers to keep the Host at bay. To protect the Laird's heart, to protect the realm. It and the Laird's Court are the only safe havens in all of Kinrowan now. The only other safety is to tread softly so that they don't see you."

"That's why the hob was running across the park last night," Jacky said. "He would've been safe if he'd reached this place. And that's why you didn't go out to help him—you couldn't."

"Just as I won't be able to help you once you leave here," the Gruagagh said. "You can go back to your old life, Jacky Rowan, and no one will think ill of you, for this isn't your war, no matter what your name. But if you do bring the Laird's daughter back safe, you can ask anything of me, and it will be yours."

"I . . . I don't want anything. I just want to help."

"You're a brave lass, Jacky."

She smiled quickly, pushing down the panic that was demanding to be heard. She was trying to be brave, though she didn't really know why.

"If you do reach the Keep," the Gruagagh continued, "you will still have to find the Horn. It won't be lying in plain sight, nor will

Gyre the Elder keep it with him. He can use it, but it makes him uneasy, so it will be hidden."

"How do I find it then?"

"By your name."

"That doesn't tell me anything."

"Rowan," the Gruagagh said. "It will be marked by the berries of the rowan. No matter what Gyre the Elder has disguised it as, you'll know it by the berries. Like your name: Berryred. Which makes us closer kin than you think."

Jacky nodded. He'd told her earlier. His bardic name, Dearg, meant red.

"Bhruic," she said. "What's the name—the speaking name—of the Laird's daughter?"

"Lorana."

His features grew bleak and grim as he spoke her name. For a long moment silence lay between them until at last Jacky stirred.

"I'd better be going," she said.

The Gruagagh nodded. He rolled up the maps and returned them to their storage place, then rummaged about in the pack for a moment or two. When he found what he was looking for, he took Jacky's hand and pressed a small brooch into it. It was made of silver and took the shape of a tiny staff, crossed by a sprig of berries. Rowan berries, she knew. And the staff would be rowan, too.

"Take this," he said.

"What . . . what does it do?"

"Do?" The Gruagagh smiled. "It doesn't do anything. It's just to remind you of me—it's my way of thanking you for trying what my own people won't dare."

It was all those magic stitcheries that Finn had put into her jacket and sneakers, Jacky realized. They made her think that anything she got from faerie would . . . do something.

"I'm sorry," she said. "I didn't mean—"

"I know."

The Gruagagh rose and she stood quickly with him.

"Don't go searching out the Giants' Keep straightaway," he warned her. "The Host will be watching you to see what you do and if you set off immediately, your quest will be doomed before you even start. Go back to your own life for a day or two. Let the Host grow weary of your routine. And then go.

"Wear your hob coat—it will hide you from most eyes at night, if not so well by day. The cap will serve you well, too. It allows you more than sight. Wearing it is what lets you accept more easily all these new things you've seen these past few nights."

He took the brooch from her hand and pinned it to her jacket.

"How come I could see you the other night?" Jacky asked. "You and the hob and the riders and everything?"

The Gruagagh shrugged. "Sometimes your people stray into our realm. Grief will bring you—or strong drink. A sudden shock."

Jacky blushed thinking of strong drink. The Gruagagh turned and extinguished the candle by simply looking at it. Jacky shivered in the darkness, the reality of it all coming home again. There was a rider outside, watching, waiting. And a Big Man. . . .

The Gruagagh opened the door and stepped to one side. "Luck be with you, Jacky Rowan."

Jacky peered out into the shadows of the back yard and hesitated. Then she frowned at herself. She stole a glance at the Gruagagh and impulsively stood on her tiptoes to give him a quick kiss, then was out the door.

The Gruagagh watched her go, startled. He lifted a finger to his lips and the shadows in his eyes deepened. If duty didn't bind him, he thought, then sighed. But duty did. And so Lorana was captured or worse, and this Jacky Rowan was going out to tilt with giants, and he was trapped, bound to his duty. By his oath. By the need of the realm.

"Luck," he said again softly and closed the door.

"Finn?" Jacky whispered at the foot of the garden.

She started to look up into his tree, but then she saw that the rider on the far side of the park was no longer alone. She froze against the cedar hedge, her voice caught in her throat. There were two of them now. She bit at her lip. Would they go away if she took off her redcap? Or would they still be there, invisible? She glanced back at the Gruagagh's Tower, wishing she hadn't left its safety.

"Finn?" she whispered again and shot a look up his tree.

She saw the hob sitting there, clutching the trunk. He turned to look down at her, a finger to his lips. Jacky followed his gaze and saw that he wasn't looking at the riders, but at the Big Man.

Gyre the Younger. An eighteen foot high giant. Here in the middle of Windsor Park. He shouldn't exist, but he did. And he was turning to look in their direction.

Frightened in earnest now, all Jacky could do was crouch by the hedge. She felt the ground tremble slightly as the giant lifted one foot, put it down, lifted the other, turned. Then he started across the park towards her.

H e was big, this giant. Bigger than any creature Jacky had
ever seen. His head alone was more than two feet high, almost a foot and a half wide. Legs, three yards long, supported the
enormous bulk of his torso and carried him across the park. He was
going to be right on top of her in moments and she didn't know what
to do. She was too petrified with fear to do more than shake where
she was crouched. Her fingers plucked nervously at the hem of her
jacket and she chewed furiously on her lower lip.

Run, she told herself. Get up and run, you fool. Find some
place too small for him to follow. Be a fieldmouse to his cat and find
some hiding place to burrow into.

But she couldn't move. Then Finn dropped from his tree with a rus-
tle of leaves and was crouching beside her.

"I'll lead him off," he whispered urgently. "He doesn't quite
know what's here, I'm thinking, so if he sees me run off, he'll give
chase to me. The stitcheries in your coat will keep you hidden so
long as you don't move!"

"B-but . . . what about you . . . ?"

"He won't catch me. Only the Hunt could catch me, but they won't follow. There's only two of them. They need their full ranks for a proper hunt."

"But—"

"Stay!" His gaze fell on the Gruagagh's brooch and he frowned, then quickly shrugged. "I'll find you," he added. "As quick as I've lost him, I'll find you. Stay till he gives chase, then go as quick as you can to a safe place."

The only safe place Jacky could think of was the Gruagagh's Tower behind them. But before she could say anything, the giant was looming over them.

"Hey-aha!" Finn cried at the top of his lungs. "Laird, but you're an ugly creature, Gyre the Younger!"

And then he was off with the same speed that had astonished Jacky earlier. She pressed against the ground, close to the hedge, trying to make as small a target of herself as she could. She expected to feel those great big hands lifting her, squeezing the life from her.

The ground trembled under the giant's tread, like an echo of the shivers that fear sent through her. She peeped open an eye to see the giant turning and heading in the direction that Finn had taken. Relief went through her for one long blissful moment, then she thought of Finn with that monstrous man on his heels. If the giant ever caught hold of him . . . She shuddered.

She stayed hidden by the hedge until the rumble of the giant's footsteps faded before slowly getting to her feet. Her bones were all watery, but she knew she had to go now, or she'd never get away at all. She glanced at the Gruagagh's Tower, but Bhruic wasn't at the window. A second glance went across the park to where the two riders sat on their gleaming machines. Then she gathered the tattered remnants of her courage and crept away, following the hedge to the back yard of one of the neighboring houses and from there onto Belmont Avenue.

Just as she was congratulating herself on her escape, the sound of a big Harley starting up came from the direction of the park. She reminded herself that the Hunt needed its full ranks to be dangerous, but that didn't do much to ease her fear. For someone like her, they probably didn't need more than one of the riders.

She took to her heels and ran, the hob stitcheries in her sneakers lending her speed that she could never have managed on her own. From the park, the sound of the motorcycle grew louder.

Finn led the giant for a merry chase, up streets and down the back alleys where the earlier residents of the cities had once kept their horses and buggies. He made sure to always stay just in sight of his monstrous pursuer so that the giant wouldn't give up the chase until Jacky had had time to make good her escape.

Gyre the Younger moved more quickly than one might have supposed from his initial lumbering pace across the park. He took steps of three yards or more at a time, and it was only the speedy stitcheries in the hob's own brown leather shoes that kept Finn ahead. Where the hob darted between parked cars, Gyre the Younger stepped over them. Where Finn squeezed through fences and dove under hedges, the looming giant continued to merely step over each obstruction.

They passed a couple, out for a late night stroll with their dog. Neither human noticed the faerie, but the hackles of their pet rose as Finn brushed by. The dog began to growl and bark after the fleeing hob, but then the giant was there and it whined, trying to hide between the legs of its master.

"Damn dog," the man said. "I don't know what's gotten into him."

Finn never heard the woman's response. He was already out of earshot, barely dodging a car on Riverdale. The driver never saw him, invisible as the hob was, but Finn gave him a curse anyway as he ran on. The car had come too close for comfort. Behind him, Gyre the Younger gave a booming laugh.

That was enough for Finn. He judged that he'd given Jacky enough time to make her escape, so he put on a new burst of speed, finally losing the giant in the trees up behind Perley Hospital. He stood and listened to the night, but it was quiet now. When he was sure that the giant had given up, Finn made his way to the convenient back steps of a house and sat down. There he let loose the string of curses that he hadn't had the breath to mouth earlier.

"Damn him, and damn his brother, and damn all his kin," he finished up with. "May he lose his head in a bogan's arse, looking for nits. May he feed on sores. May he fall asleep and let me stitch his mouth and nose fast shut, and then I'll watch him choke, and I'll smile, oh yes. Won't I just grin? Oh, damn!"

It was not so long ago that only the Laird's folk held Kinrowan and the Host kept to its own reaches. He could still remember when it was safe to have a gathery-up of hobs anywhere you pleased, and never have to worry about bogans or the restless dead. But times had changed, and were still changing, and none for the better.

"Oh, damn," he muttered again, scowling at his feet.

Gyre the Younger had this hob's smell, yes he did. And if he wanted, he could set the Hunt on him—just like he'd done to poor old Redfairn Tom. Finn's anger turned to sorrow, thinking of his cousin, and then he remembered Jacky. He sighed and rose silently to his feet. He supposed he had better fetch her.

What he'd told her was true: he wouldn't let anyone fall into the clutches of the Host. Not if he could help it. But that didn't explain why he'd told her all that he had or why he'd gifted her with stitcheries. That was more than just help, but it had seemed right at the time. Just as his leading the giant away from her had been, and going to fetch her now was. They, too, seemed like things that must be done. It was poor Tom's cap, he supposed. That had made him feel kindly to her at first. And then there was her name.

He set off at a grumbling walk, hoping she'd had the good common sense to head off for a safe place once he'd led Gyre the Younger away. She was an odd sort of a girl, he thought. Brave and frightened all at the same time. Fey as his own kin sometimes, but then so bloody mortal it made him wonder that a stitchery spell would even work for her. Oh, but it took all sorts, now didn't it?

He didn't wonder too much about what had happened between her and the Gruagagh in the Gruagagh's Tower—at least not until he was on Auch Ward Way, with the Tower in front of him, and no sign of her anywhere around. He should have been able to trace the trail of his own stitcheries—a trail not one of the Host would sense, though perhaps the Hunt could. The Hunt followed the smell of your soul.

It was as he cast up and down the street, then finally snuck into the neighboring back yards to assure himself that she wasn't still huddled by the hedge, that he realized what had happened.

"What game's he playing now?" he muttered.

For he remembered the Gruagagh's brooch he'd seen pinned

to her jacket and knew that it was some spell of the Gruagagh's that was stopping him from following the lingering trail of his own stitcheries. He paused in the middle of the street, scowling through his beard. He debated going back to his lookout tree by the Gruagagh's Tower, but he knew that the Big Man would be watching it very closely now.

So he needed a new tree to perch in—and what? Should he follow the girl, or leave her to her own devices? He was partly responsible for whatever she was up to, that much was certain. He'd given her stitcheries and pointed the way to the Gruagagh's door. He wondered if the Gruagagh had told her where the Horn was and if she truly meant to go after it. Only what if it had been the Gruagagh who had set the giant after her?

"Oh, I don't like thinking," he told the empty street.

Cloaked with the stitcheries sewn into his own coat, he crept into the back yard of a house a few doors down from the Gruagagh's Tower and stole a quick peek out across the park. When he saw just the one rider on his Harley and the giant still gone, he knew trouble was brewing. The giant would be fetching his kin—or the Horn to call up the Hunt—while the missing rider would be following Jacky.

He had to find her first. He was the one who had filled her head with all that nonsense about asking the Gruagagh for help and rescuing the Laird's daughter. Scowling at the dark shadow of the Gruagagh's Tower, he made his way back to the street. Deciding to find her was one thing, he realized once he stood there. Only where did he begin?

"Oh, damn," he muttered.

Choosing a direction at random, he set off. But Jacky had gone the other way.

As the sound of the Harley grew louder, Jacky cut across a lawn, scrambled over a fence to run alongside the house and through its back yard. At the foot of the yard, she squeezed through a hedge and paused to get her bearings.

At least he won't be able to follow me through all that, she thought, looking back the way she'd come.

She was in between Fentiman and Belmont now. Still too far from her apartment on Ossington. Go to a safe place, Finn had told her—oh, don't let the giant have caught him! But what was a safe place? Some place with people. A restaurant or bar.

Oh, think! she told herself.

She could hear the biker on Belmont now. The nearest restaurants were on Bank Street, but that was too far for her to go right now. There were too many streets to cross—open spaces where the biker could spot her. Then she thought of Kate. Kate lived just up on Sunnyside. Was she back from her mother's yet? Would going there put Kate in danger, too?

The Harley was idling on the street in front of the house now, making it too hard to think. She could imagine the rider putting his machine on its kickstand, coming around back of the house to get her . . .

She bolted towards Fentiman, tore the leg of her jeans going over a low fence, and sprawled across the lawn, but was up and racing for the open street as fast as her legs could carry her. She heard the Harley roar on Belmont behind her. The dryness had returned to her throat and her pulse drummed. Crossing the street, she plunged down the first laneway she came to. The biker came around the corner at the same time, his headlight like a searching eye. Had he seen her?

Another back yard, another fence, and then she was on Brighton, just one block away from Kate's street. Again the Harley appeared around the corner, this time well before she was out of sight. The biker started down the street, catching her in his headlight as she dashed for the next driveway.

The sound of the bike was like growling thunder in her ears. She panted for breath as she ran. Adrenaline and Finn's stitcheries got her to the end of the lane before the rider reached it. She dodged around the garage, through another yard. Now she could see Sunnyside through the gaps in the houses in front of her. Again she had to pause to get her bearings. Kate's apartment was a ground floor— on this side of the street, thank God!—and it was—

She picked her direction and started off through the back yards, heedless of flowerbeds and small vegetable patches, hauling herself over fences. One back yard, another. A third. The roar of the Harley was a constant drone in her ears. It made her teeth shake. The bike was on Sunnyside now, pacing her. Any moment she expected it to roar down a driveway and cut her off. But then Kate's back door was in front of her and she was up the stairs and hammering on it.

Please be home, oh, please be home.

The Harley was idling on the street in front of the house. The slower rev of its engine was somehow more frightening to her than the sound of it coming down the street after her. She pressed her cheek against the door, still knocking on it. A light went on over the door, half-blinding her. When the door itself opened inwards, she lost her balance.

"Who the hell—" Kate began.

Jacky caught her balance and leaned against the doorjamb. She looked into her friend's angry face, saw the anger drawing away to be replaced by shock.

"It . . . it's just me," she said. "Jacky." But then she realized what she must look like, with the redcap on her head and her corn-stubble hair sticking out from underneath it like a scarecrow's straw, with her clothes torn and her face and hands smudged with dirt.

"My God," Kate said. "Jacky, what's happened?"

Her friend's voice was suddenly loud in Jacky's ears—very loud—and then she realized that she couldn't hear the roar of the biker's Harley anymore. He must have killed the engine on his machine.

"I . . . I've been having a weird night since you left my place," she said.

"No kidding? You look like something the cat dragged in. And where'd you get this?"

Kate plucked the cap from Jacky's head. Jacky blinked, vertigo hitting her hard. When the world settled down once more, it wasn't such a bright place anymore. It was as though taking off the cap had drained something from it—a certain vitality, an inner glow that was now washed away. She tried to smile at Kate, but she was having trouble just leaning against the doorjamb.

"Can I come in?" she asked.

Kate took her by the arm and led her inside, shutting the door on the night.

Six

If she could share her current craziness with anyone, Jacky thought, it would be Kate, but what had been happening lately seemed too off the wall to share even with her, best friend or not. So Jacky told her nothing about hobs or gruagaghs, stitcheries, giants or the Wild Hunt. Instead she described being chased by a biker, and how she hoped that she hadn't brought any trouble with her by knocking on Kate's door.

"Creepy," Kate said when she was done.

"Yeah, but if he's still hanging around . . . "

"Oh, I wouldn't worry about that. He's had his fun. He's probably back at some bar with the rest of his asshole friends, having a good yuk about it."

If he wasn't gathering up the rest of the Hunt, Jacky thought uncomfortably.

Kate turned from the kitchen counter where she was making some tea. "Hungry?" she asked.

"No—yes. I'm starving."

"I've got cake—or I could make you a sandwich."

"I'll take the cake."

Kate grinned. "I kind of thought you would."

Jacky stuck out her tongue and relaxed in her chair. The effects of her latest encounter with faerie were beginning to wear off a little now as she sat in the familiar comfort of her friend's kitchen. The table she was sitting at was in a little breakfast nook that jutted out from the rest of the house into the back yard, with windows on three sides. There were enough plants hanging in there to start a jungle, together with various and sundry postcards that were tacked to the window frames and little odds and ends that were perched wherever there was a spot for them.

Jacky watched Kate bustle about getting tea mugs, pouring the water into the kettle, cutting a generous slice of nutcake for each of them. If there was one thing that Kate was mad about, it was nuts of every size, shape and description which, considering her surname Hazel, left her open to a great deal of teasing.

Jacky knew that she should get up and wash her hands and face, but she just didn't have the energy. It was so much better just lolling here in the nook, and then Kate was loading up the table and, well, Jacky thought, it would be rude to get up just when Kate was sitting down.

The tea was hot and perfect. The cake was homemade, hazelnut—which brought a suitable comment from Jacky as she tasted it—and delicious.

"Maybe," Kate said in reply, with her chin propped up on her hands as she studied Jacky's hair, "we could hire you out as a sort of walking broom." She plucked the redcap from the floor where it had fallen. "And where did you get this?"

"I found it."

"I can believe it. I just didn't think you were the sort to go through dustbins." She scrunched up her face and lowered her voice. "It's a dirty job, but somebody's got to do it."

Jacky snatched the hat back from her, then sat turning it over in her hand.

"Hey," Kate said. "I was just teasing."

"I know."

Jacky looked inside the cap and traced the intricate stitches she found there with her finger. Hob stitcheries, she thought. The dead hob who had owned it flashed in her mind . . . the angle of his neck as he lay on the ground, the sightless eyes. And then she thought of Finn, leading off the giant . . . She glanced at Kate.

"Do you believe in . . . in faeries?" she asked.

"Faeries as in gay, or faeries as in Tinkerbell?"

"As in Tinkerbell—but not all cutesy like that. More like faerie as in the realm of Faerie, with gnomes and wizards and giants and that sort of thing."

"Seriously?"

"Seriously."

Kate shook her head. " 'Fraid not. Are you doing a survey?"

"No. What about ghosts? You know, vampires and the walking dead and spooks that come out at night?"

"Well, I don't know about *ze* Count and his friends, but ghosts . . . maybe ghosts."

"Really?"

Kate sighed and poured them both some more tea. "Well, not *really*. But sometimes when I'm alone at night and the house's creaking—you know. You get that feeling. Would *you* stay overnight in a graveyard?"

"I suppose not."

And there it was, Jacky thought. The first person she asked confirmed what Finn had told her. People believed in the darker creatures of Faerie, in ghosts and the undead, far more readily than they did in gnomes and the like. She was sure that if she asked anybody she knew, they'd come up with pretty much the same answer as Kate had given her.

"What's with all this talk about spooks?" Kate asked. "Have you been reading Stephen King again?"

"I wish I was just reading about it."

"What?"

Jacky frowned. "Nothing," she said.

"Come on, Jacky. I know something's bothering you." She looked at Jacky, then shook her head. "God, what am I saying? First Will walks all over you, and then some lunatic on a motorcycle chases you all around Ottawa South. I wouldn't exactly be jumping for joy either. This guy didn't hurt you, did he?"

"No. But what if I told you I'd seen a gnome tonight?"

"I'd say 'That's nice.' "

"No, seriously."

"I am being serious—it's you that's not making any sense."

"What if I could prove it?"

Kate laughed. "Please don't pull out some clipping from the *National Enquirer.*"

"No. I mean, what if I could show you what I meant?"

"You're really serious?"

Jacky nodded.

"Oh, jeez. Now you're scaring me."

"Look," Jacky said. "This biker that was chasing me—"

"He was a gnome? Hell's Gnomes? Come on."

"No. He's not a gnome. He's a part of some kind of Wild Hunt. Remember in Caitlin Midhir's book *Yarthkin*, when those riders are chasing the girl and one of them's got these big antlers? It's like that. Except they're riding motorcycles."

"Antlered men riding motorcycles?"

"I didn't say he had antlers," Jacky said a little crossly.

Kate held up a hand. "Time out. This is getting too weird for me, Jacky. And it's scaring me because it's not like you at all."

"Is it because you've never seen anything like it before?"

"Well, that's good for starters."

"Well, you've never been to Japan before either. How do you know *it* exists?"

"I've seen pictures. I know people who've been there. I saw it in a movie."

"Well, I saw *Gremlins*, but that doesn't mean those little things are real. But this rider is, Kate. And I can prove it."

Kate sighed. "Okay. For the sake of argument, prove it."

"We have to go to the front of the house," Jacky said standing up.

As she led the way, the redcap dangling from her hand, she was of two minds. On the one hand she wanted to prove to Kate that what she'd been experiencing was real, just to have someone else who could see it, someone to be there to tell her that she wasn't going crazy. Because that was scary. But on the other hand, if the rider was there, that was even scarier.

She didn't know what she was hoping for, but by then they'd reached the living room. Standing by the front window, they looked out at the street. There was no one there. Just some parked cars. A cat was lying on the hood of one—the engine was probably still warm and it was stealing what heat it could before the metal cooled down.

"So now what happens?" Kate asked, peering up and down the street.

"You don't see anything out there, right?"

"Right. So therefore your gnomes are real?"

"Kate!"

"Okay, okay. Tell me what to do. Do I stand on one leg and squint out of the corner of my eye, or . . . " She let her voice trail off at Jacky's frown.

"Just don't do anything for a moment," Jacky said. Then she put on the redcap, bracing herself for the sense of vertigo that was going to come.

It wasn't so bad this time—more like a subtle shifting under-foot—and then a gauze seemed to have dropped from her eyes so that she could see everything clearly again. The redcap alone should prove it, she thought, but looking out the window she saw him, the chrome of his machine gleaming in the streetlights, the black leather swallowing light, the featureless shadow under his visor. She stared for a long moment, shivering, then stepped back.

"Jacky," Kate began worriedly.

Jacky shook her head and took off the redcap. She kept her balance by holding on to the windowsill, then handed the cap to Kate.

"Put it on and look out the window," she said. "Down there to-wards the house where that guy was working on his car almost every day last summer."

Kate stepped closer to the window and looked.

"Put the cap on," Jacky said.

Kate turned. "But there's nothing there."

"Please?"

"Okay, okay."

She put the redcap on and Jacky stepped in close to steady her as she swayed dizzily.

"My God," Kate said softly. "There *is* someone out there." She turned from the window. "We've got to call the cops . . . " Her voice faded as she looked at Jacky.

"What's the matter?" Jacky asked.

"I don't know. You look different all of a sudden. It's like I can see you better or something."

Jacky nodded. "Look at the biker again," she said. "Is he still there?" she added, once Kate was looking in the right direction.

When Kate nodded, Jacky pulled the cap from her head and then steadied her again. Kate swayed, looked out the window, then back at Jacky. Without saying anything, she moved slowly to a chair and sat down.

"It's a trick, right?" she said when she was sitting down.

Jacky shook her head. "No. It's real. The cap lets you see into Faerie."

"Faerie," Kate repeated numbly. "Now they're going to take both of us away in nice little white jackets."

"We're *not* crazy," Jacky said.

Kate didn't say anything for a long moment. Then she asked, "Where did you get that . . . that cap?"

"From a gnome."

"From a . . . God, I'm sorry I asked."

Jacky started to frown, but then she saw that it was just Kate's way of dealing with it.

"Let's go have some more tea," she said, "and I'll tell you all about it."

Kate pushed herself up, using the arms of the chair for leverage, and followed her into the kitchen.

"The floor's yours," she said.

Kate tended to frown when she concentrated on something. By the time Jacky was finished her story, her forehead was a grid of lines.

"You shouldn't do that," Jacky said.

Kate looked at her. "Do what?"

"Scrunch up your face like that. My mother used to say when I was pulling a face, that if I didn't watch out, the wind would change and leave me looking like that forever."

"Or until the wind changed again," Kate added.

She put her index fingers in either side of her mouth and pulled it open in a gaping grin, then rolled her eyes. Jacky burst into laughter.

56

"Of course," Kate said when they'd both caught their breath, "I suppose we've got to take all that shit seriously now, don't we? Black cats and walking under ladders—the whole kit and kaboodle."

"Oh, I don't know," Jacky replied. "But . . . you *do* believe me now, don't you?"

Kate looked at the redcap, then at her friend's face. "Yeah," she said slowly. "I guess I do. And now—like I said before. What happens? You're not really going to this Giants' Castle to look for the Horn, are you?"

"I have to."

"Why?"

"I don't know. Because of Bhruic and Finn, I suppose. Because no one else will and this is finally something I can do that'll have meaning."

Kate shook her head. "Will was full of it and you know it. What the hell kind of meaning do you call his way of living? I still don't know what you ever saw in him."

"Well, he had nice buns."

"Woman does not live by buns alone."

Jacky smiled.

"So how are you getting out there?" Kate asked.

"I hadn't really thought about it. By bus, I suppose. Do you think a bus goes out there?"

"We could take Judith." Judith was Kate's Volkswagen Beetle that had surprisingly survived God knew how many Ottawa winters.

Jacky shook her head. "No way."

"Why? You don't think she'd make it out there?"

"It's not that. I don't want you to come. This is something I've got to do, but I'm not going to drag you into it."

"Then why did you tell me about it? Why point out that geek on his bike to me?"

Jacky sighed. "I just wanted somebody else to know. I wanted to see if somebody else could see him too. So that I wouldn't have to keep wondering if I was just crazy, you know?"

"Well, you are crazy, but that's got nothing to do with this. I'm going, and that's final. A woman's got to do what a woman's got to do and all that."

"But it's not your problem."

"It wasn't yours either, Jacky. But you've made it yours—just like I'm making it mine."

"I couldn't stand it if something happened to you."

"Hey, I'm not all that big on sitting around here wondering if I'll ever see you again either, you know. We're pals, right? So what do pals do but stick up for each other? I'm going. If you don't want to come with me in Judith, then I'll just meet you there."

"But you didn't see them kill that little hob, Kate. And the giant—he's *so* big."

"We'll be like that little tailor in the fairy tale—remember? 'Seven with one blow.' No! I'll be the valiant tailor. And you . . . you'll be Jack the Giant-Killer."

"It's not funny, Kate. And I don't want to kill anybody."

Kate reached out to hold Jacky's hand. She gave it a squeeze. "I know, Jacky. I'm scared too. I'm just shooting off my mouth so that I don't have to think about it. You're sleeping here tonight, aren't you?" When Jacky nodded, she added, "Well, then let's hit the sack, okay?"

"Okay."

Jacky lay awake for a long time after she went to bed. She kept wanting to get up to make sure that the biker hadn't come any closer to the house, that the rest of the Hunt hadn't joined him. She worried about Finn, and about Kate coming with her to the Giants' Keep, and was of half a mind to sneak out right now, but she knew it was too late. Kate would just drive out to Calabogie herself and be sitting there waiting for her.

She listened to the wind outside her window. It was making a funny sound—almost breathing. She thought of what Bhruic had told her, about how he heard the whispery voices of the sluagh, the restless dead, on the winds at night.

She turned her head so that she could see the window from where she lay. When she started to imagine that she could see faces pressing against the panes—horrible faces, all bloated like drowned corpses—she slipped from under the covers and went into Kate's bedroom. Kate stirred as Jacky crept into her bed, but she didn't wake.

Listening carefully now, all Jacky could hear was the sound of their own breathing, nothing more. She felt a little stupid for getting spooked — and what did that say about how she'd do when it came to their expedition to the Giants' Keep? — but foolish or not, she was staying right where she was and she wasn't going to budge until it was morning.

Seven

The rumour touched all of Faerie that night: there was a new hope in the Seelie Court—a small one, true, but a hope all the same—and she meant to free the Laird's daughter and would, too, except that if the bogans didn't get to her, then surely the Wild Hunt would. But whether she was doomed or not, the rumour of her ran from the heart of Kinrowan to the Borderlands. It was heard by the fiana sidhe in their solitary haunts, and by the Seelie Court and the Host alike.

Hidden in a tree from which he could view both Manswater and Underbridge (the Rideau Canal and Lansdowne Bridge, respectively) with equal ease, Dunrobin Finn listened to the rumours, listened hard to hear if the Unseelie Court was looking for a hob skillyman as well. It wasn't, not so that he heard, but he frowned all the same.

"Now she's done it," he muttered to himself. "She won't get five feet from whatever hidey-hole she's found, little say recover the Laird's daughter now—not with half the Host looking for her tonight. And the Hunt . . ."

He pursed his lips and studied the sky. The night was draining quickly into morning. Too late for the Hunt to ride tonight perhaps, but it would be out tomorrow night, and then Jacky Rowan would know what it meant to be afraid.

"And they'll be looking for her today," he added aloud. "Those that can abide the light of day."

He could see the troll who lived in Underbridge stirring, sifting through the rubbish he called his treasure. Looking for a sword, Finn thought. Looking for something with which to cut himself a piece of Jacky Rowan before he took what was left of her to Gyre the Elder.

"Oh, Jacky Rowan. You'd better learn or steal a greatspell damn quick if you want to live out the day."

Finn frowned again, fingers plucking nervously at his beard. Oh, she was in trouble, deep trouble, there was no doubt about that, and he'd as much as thrown her to the wolves himself. If he'd just left well enough alone. Snatched Tom's cap from her, maybe. Never told her about the Gruagagh, surely. Minded his own business like a good hob couldn't.

"And that's the trick, isn't it?" he said to the night. "To be a good hob, you've got to stick your nose into a place or two and play your tricks, or what are you? Not a hob, that's for damn sure."

In Underbridge, the troll had found a rusty old sword and was now rubbing it on the big stone supports of the bridge. The grinding noise was loud coming across the water of the canal and it set Finn's teeth on edge.

And they'll all be doing that, he thought. Sharpening their weapons—those that have weapons. He shivered, remembering all the sluagh he'd seen go by tonight. A troll's stupid face, with its crooked teeth and mismatched eyes, nose like a big bird's beak— that was nothing like the faces of the restless dead. They had a drowned look about them—pale and bloated.

From across the canal, the troll's grinding continued. Finn scurried down his tree at last, mind made up. He was looking for Jacky Rowan, so it was best he got back to it. Best he found her, before something else did.

"And that's one thing for rumours," he said as he set off at a quick run, south and east. "They tell you where to go."

Like following the thread of one of his own hob stitcheries, he chased the threads of the rumours. They led him through Cockle

Tom's Garve, back and forth across the Manswater, then down into Crowdie Wort's Bally, where he'd first met and then lost Jacky earlier that night. Here the rumours were too thick, the threads twisting in and out of each other, for him to locate exactly where she was.

"But she's here," he said as he found a perch in a comfortable old oak tree on Killbrodie Way, which is the faerie name for Sunnyside Avenue. "And close, too. I'll bide a bit, now won't I, Mistress Oak, snug in your arms. Then we'll see what the morning brings."

Three blocks east, the Big Man's sluagh were gathered around Kate Hazel's house, peering through windows, looking for a way in. But the latches were all latched, the doors locked, and there was no one awake that they could trick into letting them in. Then the night finally drained away and they returned to their marshes, the bogans to their sewer dens, the trolls to their bridges.

Dunrobin Finn lay fast asleep in the arms of a Mother Oak, and the black rider kicked his Harley into life outside Kate Hazel's house. The chopper coughed loudly in the still street, a sound heard only in Faerie, and pulled away from the curb.

Another night was only hours away and he could be patient. He would have his brothers with him then. Let the hope of the Laird's folk sleep for now, for tonight the full Hunt would ride and there would be no escape. Not any at all.

The Gruagagh of Kinrowan watched the sun come up, pinking the eastern skies. For long silent moments he stared out the window of his house, that in Faerie was his Tower, then he turned at last from the view and sighed. The rumours had touched him as well—from the swollen lips of the sluagh, on the airy voices of those gnomes that rode the wind.

A hope? he asked the silent room. He remembered too well the power of the Unseelie Court.

That girl, he thought. She had the name—both Rowan and Jack—so there was more than luck in her arrival at the Tower tonight. But the task was hard. She would need help and friends, and with the Host's ranks swelling more every day, where would she find either?

Better a small hope than none at all, the rumouring tongues of the wind gnomes whispered outside the Tower.

Unhappily, the Gruagagh returned to the window to watch the sunlight wash Learg Green with her light. The park glistened. The skies were a brilliant blue. But there was misfortune in the air. The Gruagagh could taste it. Like Finn, he knew he had pushed Jacky into danger, but unlike the hob, he couldn't follow after to try to help. The Tower protected him, but it kept him a prisoner as well. He could only listen to the gossip on the wind and wonder at the fate of the hope of Kinrowan.

Eight

When Jacky woke, the bed beside her was empty. She had time for one blind moment of panic, then she saw the note pinned to the pillow beside her, and relaxed. Stilling the thunder of her pulse, she pulled the note free. It said, in Kate's familiar scrawl that passed for her handwriting:

Wimped out, didja? Well, don't
panic. Mother Kate's just gone
to the store to get us some goodies.

Back soon,
K.

Jacky grinned. She supposed she'd never hear the end of this. But last night, she was sure there'd been something at the window, peering in. Something that called to her, to open wide the windows . . . Right now, all that made its way through the panes was a wash of sunshine.

Slipping out of bed, Jacky padded to the bathroom, wearing

the oversized T-shirt that she'd borrowed last night to serve as a nightie. By the time she was dressed and sitting in the kitchen, frowning over the long tear in her jeans, Kate was back and making them both a breakfast of sausages and pancakes. Two mugs of coffee steamed on the table in the breakfast nook.

"So, when are we going?" Kate asked. She drifted over to the table to take a sip of her coffee before returning to the stove to fuss with their breakfast.

"I can't even believe it's real anymore," Jacky said.

"Then why'd you crawl into bed with me last night?" Kate asked. "Or have you just given up on men?"

Jacky blushed. "No. It's just . . . "

"I know." Kate concentrated on pouring a new batch of batter without spilling any of it over the sides of the frying pan into the burner. While she was waiting for airholes to appear on the tops of the pancakes so that she could flip them, she turned back to look at Jacky. "But what are we going to do?"

Jacky ran a hand through the stubble of her hair. "I thought maybe I'd go to the hairdressers' and see what they can do with this."

"Jacky, *nobody'll* be able to do *anything* with that. If you ask me, you should dye it a few different colours. You know, a bit of pink, some mauve, maybe a black streak . . . "

"Thanks a lot."

"No problem. Want to get the plates out of the oven?"

"Sure. I thought I'd go home and change first," she added as she took out the plates. There were three sausages and two pancakes on each one.

"Want me to go with you?"

"I don't want to be a pain . . . "

"Hey, what are mothers for?" Kate grinned as she put another pair of pancakes on each plate and took them over to the table. "Look, it's no problem," she said as she pushed one of them across to Jacky. "I might be teasing you about all this, but I wouldn't want you to go over there by yourself."

"Thanks."

They were busy eating for the next little while, but once the initial edge of her hunger had worn off, Jacky looked across the table.

"Last night," she said. "I was wearing that jacket that Finn stitched with his magics. You weren't supposed to be able to see me when I was wearing it, but you did."

"That's right," Kate said.

"Do you think it doesn't work?"

"We should probably check it out," Kate replied.

So after breakfast, Jacky donned her blue quilted jacket and buttoned it up. She stood in the middle of the living room with Kate watching her.

"Well?" she asked.

"I can see you."

"Shit." Jacky started to unbutton the jacket.

"Wait a sec," Kate said.

Jacky paused. "What is it?"

"When I don't look directly at you, you get all fuzzy—you know what I mean?" She stood facing away from Jacky and looked at her from the corner of her eye. "And now I can't see you at all."

"Maybe it doesn't work properly in the daytime or under a bright light," Jacky said.

"Maybe. But maybe it's just that I know you too well."

"What's that supposed to mean?"

"Well, to get all metaphysical about it, we're pretty close—right? Maybe it's just that I know your vibes so well that you can't be invisible around me. I *feel* you near and since I *know* you're there, it cancels out the magic."

"What if it doesn't work?" Jacky wanted to know.

"There's an easy way to find out," Kate said. She took her own coat from the closet and tossed Jacky the redcap. "Let's go to your place."

Jacky fingered the tear in her jeans, then straightened up and studied herself in Kate's hall mirror. God, she looked a mess. No wonder Bhruic had called her a tatterdemalion last night. She tugged the redcap on and tried to capture the various unruly locks that poked out from under it, then gave it up as a lost cause.

"Ready?" Kate asked.

Jacky nodded and followed her friend out the front door.

There was no way for them to check out people's reactions until they reached Bank Street, and then the reality of the hob's stitcheries were brought home with a very physical jar. No sooner were they standing on the corner of Sunnyside and Bank—after passing a certain oak tree with a hob fast asleep in its branches—than a woman ran over Jacky's toe with the wheels of her stroller.

"Oww!" Jacky cried.

The woman stumbled, almost overturning the stroller in her haste to back away.

"Jeez, that hurt," Jacky said to Kate.

The woman looked from Kate to where Jacky's voice was coming from, her eyes widening. Then her baby started to howl. As she bent over it, Kate quickly took Jacky's arm and hurried off across the street.

"Well, it works," she said.

Jacky looked back across the street to where the woman was still standing. The woman gazed across the street at Kate, then at the place Jacky's voice had come from until, shaking her head, she went on her way.

"This could be kind of fun," Jacky said. "Just think of the tricks you could play."

"That," Kate replied, "sounds suspiciously like what I've heard brownies and hobs are like, *not* my friend Jacky. You'd better watch yourself."

"Why?"

The answer was on the tip of Kate's tongue, but then she shook her head. She was worried that something in the hob's magic might soak through Jacky's coat and shoes and cap, that the stitcheries would change her friend, because that was the danger with Faerie, wasn't it? Mortals who entered it never came out unchanged. But she didn't have the heart to spoil Jacky's good mood just now.

Her friend stood in front of her, with her eyes all sparkling and her cheeks flushed, looking more alive than Kate could remember her being for a long time. Kate smiled. She was almost used to the unruly stubble that was all that was left of Jacky's hair now. It certainly gave her more of a mischievous air.

And who was to say that a little of the Puckish prankster in her wouldn't do Jacky a world of good? With all the weirdness going down—and with what they were going to be getting into when they headed out to Calabogie—maybe Jacky deserved to get something out of all this. Kate would just have to keep an eye on her, that was all.

"You know," she said finally. "I could get to like your new look."

"That's what I've got to watch out for?" Jacky asked. "Your bad taste?"

Kate laughed "Come on," she said. "Let's get moving."

They headed south down Bank Street, Jacky being careful not to bump into anyone, but keeping Kate in stitches with the faces she pulled at the passersby.

Jacky's apartment was the top half of a red brick duplex on Ossington Avenue, four blocks south of Sunnyside and a block and half west of Bank Street. Her downstairs neighbour was repotting plants on the porch as they approached and looked up when they arrived. His gaze went to Kate, since he couldn't see Jacky. This pleased Jacky enormously until he began to speak.

"Hello, Kate. I think Jacky's sleeping off last night's binge."

"Binge?"

Joe Reaves brushed some dirt from his hands and nodded. "You should have heard the party she was having up there last night. Didn't bother me too much—I'm off today anyway and I still owe her for the one I threw this summer—but I'm surprised Beekman next door didn't phone in a complaint." He paused suddenly. "Say, how come you weren't there? At the party, I mean."

"I . . . uh . . . couldn't make it," Kate said slowly.

Standing beside her, Jacky felt all the fun drain out of her invisibility trick. Her stomach was suddenly tied in knots.

"Well, it sounded like some bash," Joe said. "I didn't think she had it in her, you know? She always seems so serious—or quiet anyway."

"Yeah, well . . . I'd better see how she's feeling," Kate said and moved for the door.

She opened it, then stepped aside to let Jacky go in, covering up by pretending to listen to whatever it was that Joe was saying now. She could see his lips moving, but the words weren't registering. Dragging up a smile, she nodded to him, then followed Jacky inside and closed the door behind them.

"I was out," Jacky said in a tense voice. She unbuttoned her jacket and took it off, folding it across her arm. "All night, Kate. I wasn't here."

Kate nodded. She looked up the stairs, a feeling of dread catpawing along her spine. It was a beautiful autumn day outside, but that wasn't reflected in here. A dark, undefinable sensation crept down the stairs to meet them. Something awful was waiting for them up there, she just *knew* it. She wanted to run, but forced herself to take the first step, a second, a third. When she reached the landing, Jacky pushed by her, key in hand. Here, directly outside the door, the feeling of wrongness was stronger than ever.

"Maybe we should ask Joe to come in with us," Kate said.

"And tell him what?" Jacky asked.

Kate nodded. He'd wonder where Jacky had come from and if it hadn't been her in the apartment last night, then who had it been? It would just get too complicated to explain. As Jacky fit the key into the lock, Kate wished that they had a weapon of some kind, but all they had was her little trusty Swiss pen knife that she usually carried in her jeans. The key turned with a loud snick. They exchanged worried glances, then Jacky pushed the door open.

"Oh, God," Kate murmured, moving into the apartment beside a stunned Jacky.

The living room looked as though someone had let loose a small tornado in it. Sofa and chairs were turned over, upholstery cut open, the stuffing swelling out through the jagged slits. The coffee table was in two pieces. The curtains had been torn down and left lying in a corner. Jacky's books were all pulled from the bookcase and scattered throughout the room, most of them in two or three pieces.

They could see the kitchen from where they stood. The refrigerator door hung ajar. Milk and eggs were smeared across the counters and floor. Clouds of flour and spices and rolled oats had settled over everything. Frozen meat was unthawing in bloody puddles. Shattered plates and cups and saucers covered the floor. A sour, spoiled smell rolled through the apartment.

"The Host," Jacky said, tears swelling in her eyes as she took in the ruin. "That's who did this. The Unseelie Court."

"But what were they looking for?" Kate asked.

Jacky turned to her. "Me," she said in a small voice. "And . . . and when they didn't find me, they . . . they did this . . . "

The premonition of danger hadn't left Kate yet. "Let's get out of here," she said and gave Jacky's arm a tug.

Jacky shook off her hand and moved towards the bedroom. She was all empty inside—not the empty she'd felt when Will walked out, the empty that she had nothing important in her life, but an emptiness more akin to the aftermath of rape. Her most private place—her home—had been ravaged. Violated.

She tried to summon up an anger, but everything just seemed too bleak. As if nothing mattered anymore. All that was necessary now was to discover the full scope of the damage. Had the plush toys that had been her friends since childhood been destroyed? Had they broken the clock that had been the last Christmas present her grandmother gave her before she died? Was there anything left in one piece?

"Jacky!" Kate called softly, starting across the room.

Jacky opened the door to the bedroom. She had one moment to take in what she saw. The frame of her bed was broken into countless pieces and heaped against one wall. The dresser lay on its side, the drawers in a broken pile beside it. In the middle of the room, a huge nest had been made out of her shredded mattress, her blankets and sheets and her clothes. And rising from it, disturbed from their sleep and blinking slitted yellow eyes, were nightmares.

Their heads were wider than they were tall and their skin was brown, creased like wrinkled leather. Straw-pale hair hung in greasy strands. They weren't much taller than Jacky herself, but they were broad and squat, their heads disappearing into their torsos without the benefit of necks. Animal furs were tied about their waists, hanging to their knobby knees. Wide noses flared as they caught Jacky's scent . . . Kate's . . .

"Got her now, got her!" the foremost cried happily. His wide mouth split into a grin, revealing rows of pointed yellow teeth. "Got her, hot damn! Won't the Boss be grinning now?"

Bogans, Jacky thought.

She tried to evade the creature's grasp, but moved too late. A meaty fist closed on her arm, grip tightening until a moan escaped her lips. Her jacket fell from suddenly numbed fingers. The others were approaching. There were three of them altogether, but Jacky knew that one alone would be more than a match for her. But while they had her, they wouldn't get Kate.

"Run!" she cried. "Run, Kate!" With her free hand she snatched the redcap from her head and tossed it to her friend.

Kate caught the cap, but she didn't run. She saw the same ruin that the bedroom had become as Jacky did, but instead of a bogan gripping her friend, all she saw was a smelly old wino, gap-toothed and unshaven, with bloodshot eyes, baggy trousers, and a white shirt so dirty it was a yellow-brown. She didn't even think of what she was doing as she shoved the cap into her belt and picked up the nearest thing that came to hand. It was the brass base of a small table lamp. Three quick steps and she was in the door, her makeshift weapon coming down on the shoulder of the wino that held Jacky.

The bogan howled and Jacky pulled free of his grip. She dropped to the floor, grabbed her jacket and scuttled between the other two bogans, struggling to get an arm into the jacket sleeve. With the redcap gone, the bogans didn't look so clear anymore. She *knew* what they were, so she could still see their bogan shapes, but superimposed over them were the winos that Kate was seeing. Somehow they seemed more frightening because of that.

She got one arm in, wriggled the jacket around to get the other. She saw Kate whack the first bogan again, the base of the table lamp knocking the creature to the floor. The remaining pair had turned and were coming towards Jacky, but now she had her other arm in the jacket, pulled it on, and—

The two bogan/winos stopped in midstride as she disappeared. Jacky crept over to what was left of her bed and hefted a club-length piece of one of its legs. While the bogans stood there, trying to spot her with their day-dimmed eyes, she ran up and hit the closest one as hard as she could on its knee.

The creature cried out and stumbled to the floor as its leg gave way under him. The other bogan glanced at his companion. Before it could move, Jacky and Kate both hit it at the same time. It fell across the one that Jacky had brought down who was still clutching his knee. Jacky hit him with her club and then all three creatures lay still.

Breathing heavily, the two friends looked at each other. The moment of action had cut something loose inside them. The shock of the ransacked apartment and the attack faded before the self-sufficient feeling that rose in them. Going to the Giants' Keep and rescuing the Laird's daughter . . . it didn't seem quite so impossible now.

"Are they . . . are they dead?" Jacky asked, breaking the silence.

Kate shook her head as she still tried to catch her breath. "I don't know. Jacky, what the hell are a bunch of winos doing in your apartment?"

"Winos?" But then Jacky realized that Kate was seeing them without the benefit of hob stitcheries. "Stick the cap on your head and see what they really are," she said.

Kate worked the cap free from her belt and put it on. The lamp base fell from her hand.

"Oh, jeez," she mumbled. "What *are* they?"

"Bogans," a voice said from the living room before Jacky could answer. "And that was well-done indeed, though you're lucky it's day and not night, for you wouldn't have had such an easy time of it if they'd been completely awake."

Jacky and Kate turned, adrenaline pumping in a rush through their systems once more. Kate took a step back, but Jacky touched her arm.

"It's okay, Kate," she said. "This is Finn."

"At your service," the bearded hob replied with a small bow, "though you don't much seem to need it at the moment."

"What are you doing here?" Jacky asked.

"Following you. I chased after you all night, but couldn't find the right thread to lead me to you. Then the sun came up and I fell asleep. When I woke, my stitcheries told me that you'd passed right below me while I was snoozing. So I followed the new thread and it led me here—too late for the rescue that you didn't need, which is just as well, for I don't know if I would have been so quick to attack three bogans—even in the daylight." He regarded each of them admiringly. "Oh, yes. It's good to know there's still a hero or two left in the world."

"This is my friend Kate Hazel," Jacky said before she remembered that she should have thought up a speaking name for Kate, rather than giving away her true one. Jacky didn't exactly distrust the little man, but with that touch of feral slyness in his eyes, she wasn't sure if she trusted him completely either.

"Kate Hazel," Finn said. "Hazel—that's the Crackernut, you know. A wise tree—not so lucky as the Rowan, to be sure, but sometimes clever thinking will take you farther than ever luck could. It's more dependable, too. I'm pleased to meet you, Kate Crackernuts."

Kate looked at him, not really hearing what he was saying. She turned to Jacky.

"We have to get out of here, Jacky," she said.

Her gaze flickered to the bogans. The one she'd struck was definitely dead. Thick greenish-red blood was pooling around its head.

"I think I'm going to be sick," she added.

Finn nodded. "We'd best go quickly. Where there's a few bogans, likely there's more. No sense pressing our luck, even if we do have a Jack with us."

Jacky swallowed hard. She too couldn't look at the bogans for long without feeling queasy. But she felt no regret at what they'd done.

"Let's go," she said.

Taking Kate's arm, she led the way out of the apartment. On the stairs going down, she took the redcap from Kate's head, thrust it into the pocket of her jacket, then removed the jacket once more and carried it in her free arm.

"I believed you," Kate was saying as she let Jacky lead her down the stairs. "I *really* did. I mean, there was the cap and that biker last night who was there and then wasn't, depending on how you looked at him. But I thought it was . . . I don't know. Not real at the same time. Do you know what I mean?"

She paused at the bottom of the stairs and looked back up at the door to Jacky's apartment. Finn had closed it behind them.

"I guess I'm not making much sense, am I?" she said.

"Lots of sense," Jacky assured her.

"Not to me," Finn said, but Jacky glared at him so he shrugged and said no more.

Jacky opened the front door and stepped out onto the porch, tugging Kate along with her. Finn followed right on their heels. Joe Reaves looked up from his pots and plants, his eyes widening. Jacky had forgotten the way she looked, but she wasn't going back upstairs for new clothes now.

"What happened to you, Jacky?" Joe asked. "That *is* you, isn't it?"

"Oh, it's me all right."

"Going punk on us, are you? No wonder your party was so rowdy last night." He grinned, but his humour faltered when Jacky just looked at him. "Look, it's your hair. . . . " he began.

"It's okay," Jacky said. "I've just going through a bit of a weird time and I'm kind of in a hurry, Joe."

"Hey. No problem. See ya around."

Jacky nodded and led her two companions off down the street, leaving her downstairs neighbour on the porch, scratching his head. It was weird, she thought. She knew she should be scared, and she was, but not like she should be. It was more a cautious kind of being scared that would keep her from getting too cocky. But those things back in the apartment . . .

"Are you going to be okay?" she asked Kate.

"Yeah. I think so. But, jeez. Talk about wimping out."

"You didn't wimp out, Kate. You saved the day." Jacky found a grin for her friend. "Just like the valiant tailor."

Kate came up with a small smile. "I'm sorry about your place, Jacky."

"Me too. I think maybe we shouldn't wait the couple of days Bhruic told me to. We should take off now."

"What did the Gruagagh tell you?" Finn wanted to know.

"Oh, this and that. What will those bogans do when they find us gone and one of them dead, Finn?"

"They won't be so gentle with you next time," the hob replied. "None of the Host will."

"Great." Jacky glanced at Kate. "Are you up for Calabogie?"

Kate nodded, not quite trusting her voice. Jacky squeezed her arm.

"I know what you're feeling," she said.

"I'm still going," Kate told her.

"I know you are. And I love you for it."

Walking a couple of paces behind the pair, Finn shook his head. They were either brave or fools. What they had just undergone in Jacky's apartment could not begin to prepare them for what was waiting in the Giants' Keep. And yet, brave or foolish, they were going all the same. And he—knowing himself to be a fool—was going with them.

The Laird of Kinrowan's folk owed them that much and since

he was the only one of the Laird's folk present, since he'd put the burr in Jacky's cap and set her on the road, it seemed only right and proper that he be the one to see it through and go with them. But oh, he wasn't happy about it. Not one bit.

Nine

"You okay?" Kate asked.

Jacky nodded. Or at least as okay as could be expected, she
thought, now that the immediate need to be brave and sure of herself
had passed. When Kate had been falling apart back at the apartment, it had been easy to take on the leader's role. But now Kate was
more herself and Jacky was wondering where she'd find the
courage to go on. When she thought about those things in her apartment . . . the bogans . . .

"You and me," she said to Kate. "We're like a couple of yo-
yo's—first you're being strong for me, then I'm doing it for you, and
now we're back to square one again. I just hope that we don't ever
fall apart at the same time."

"There's always your friend Finn."

"I suppose."

The two of them were sitting in a window booth at Hitsman's,
a restaurant on Bank Street that was just a couple of blocks south of
Jacky's apartment on Ossington. They were trying to come up with
a plan of action. Finn was at the pastry counter, deciding what he
wanted to have with his tea. He looked like a small, but ordinary

man, rather than the hob Jacky knew, but that was a part of the—
what he called—glamour that he wore in the everyday world.

They had chosen the restaurant, rather than Kate's apartment,
because it was more public and therefore—they hoped—safer. The
Unseelie Court preferred to act in lonely places and at night, Finn
had assured them.

"It's past noon now," Kate said. "Do you think we can get to
Calabogie and do whatever we have to do before it gets dark?"

Jacky shook her head. "I've got a pretty good idea where the
Keep is from Bhruic's map, but I don't know how long we'll be inside looking for the Horn. Actually, I don't even know *how* we'll get
inside, or what we'll find there." She looked out the window and
watched a couple of cars go by. "Actually," she added as she turned
back to Kate, "it seems like a pretty crazy thing to be doing in the
first place. I mean, it's not like we're really the heroes that Finn
keeps talking us up to be."

"Maybe we should get a gang," Kate said. "We could call it 'the
Gang' and . . . " She was looking out the window and broke off as
Finn joined them, his plate loaded down with a half-dozen pastries.

"You're going to get sick eating all of those," Jacky said.

"Finn," Kate said before he could reply to Jacky. "There's a
guy standing there beside the Fresh Fruit Company—on the left, see
him? He's been there for about ten minutes now, not doing anything
except just hanging around."

"Where?" Jacky said, sticking her face close to the window to
have a look.

The man met her gaze from across the street, a half-smile on
his lips, then stepped back around the corner of the building and out
of sight. Jacky was left with a vague memory of a tallish man in
jeans and a jean jacket, clean shaven with tousled chestnut hair.

"Now you've done it," Kate said. "You've let him know we're
on to him."

"It's not so bad," Finn said. "That was Arkan Garty—one of
Crowdie Wort's foresters."

"Does that make him one of the good guys or one of the bad
guys?" Jacky asked.

"Crowdie Wort owes his allegiance to the Laird."

"Then why was his forester watching us?"

"I . . . " Finn looked from Jacky to Kate, then shrugged. "I don't know. The air is thick with rumours. Foremost is the fact that you mean to rescue the Laird's daughter, so the Laird's folk can only wish you well. But at the same time they know that you've been to see the Gruagagh, so those more devious-minded amongst the Seelie Court are suspicious that your rescue attempt is just a story and that your presence in the scheme of things spells yet another disaster for the Laird's folk."

"You're kidding, right?"

Finn regarded Kate seriously and shook his head. "With winter coming, the loss of the Laird's daughter is the worst thing that could have happened to us. Without her to sing the lockspells on Samhaine Eve, we could all lose our lives that night."

"You're not making sense," Jacky said. "What're lockspells? What happens on Samhaine Eve?"

"The dead walk. Not just the sluagh, but all the dead, and we have no power against them. They are jealous of our living, so on that one night we hide in places locked safe with spells that only the Laird's daughter knows."

"Well, she must have learned them from *someone*."

"She did. From her mother. But the Lady Fenella is gone and Lorana has no daughter yet to pass the knowledge on to. Without the lockspells, we are easy prey for the dead. They wouldn't kill us all, but enough so that we could not survive the winter being harried by the Unseelie Court.

"We were stronger once. We had revels on Samhaine—gathery-ups and all manner of fun. The Lady Fenella led us in the songs then and just the singing of them kept the dead at bay. But now . . . now we hide in safe places locked tight with spells and wait for the night to pass without a smile or a laugh passing our lips. For those that the dead catch on Samhaine Eve—they become the sluagh of the Unseelie Court. There is no afterlife for them, and no borning again."

"Bhruic said Lorana was the green soul of Kinrowan and he was its heart," Jacky said. "Wouldn't he know the songs, too?"

"No one knows what the Gruagagh knows or doesn't," Finn replied, "except for maybe the Laird himself. But Deegan is none too happy with the Gruagagh for losing his daughter, and there's few in the Seelie Court that would trust the wizard enough to let him lead us in the songs."

"I *like* Bhruic," Jacky said.

"He can glamour anyone to like him."

"It wasn't magic—it was just, oh, I don't know. I just *know* he's not evil." She hoped.

"And I know that you're not evil," Finn said, "but there's still some that won't trust you simply because you've been the Gruagagh's guest."

"I'd like to meet this Gruagagh," Kate said before an actual argument broke out between Jacky and the hob. "Why don't we go see him now on the way to my place?"

"We can't," Jacky said. "He said I shouldn't return."

"Well, could you at least show me his Tower?"

"It's just a house," Finn said, shaking his head. "And Learg Green's too dangerous for us now."

But Jacky, feeling obstinate, disagreed. "Oh, we can look at it," she said. "We can go to Kate's place by following the river. It won't be dangerous just to walk by," she added to Finn. "There'll be lots of people in the park—jogging, playing ball, walking their dogs and babies."

"And how many of them will belong to Gyre the Elder?"

"Who knows?" Jacky replied with a shrug. "But you said yourself that they wouldn't do anything when there's lots of people around." She eyed his plate of pastries. "So eat up and let's get going."

Finn looked down at his plate. "I'm not hungry anymore."

"Maybe this wasn't such a good idea," Kate said while they were getting a bag for Finn's pastries. The hob was still sitting at their table, staring morosely out the window.

"It'll be okay," Jacky said. "I think he just likes to build things up."

"He didn't build up those guys back at your apartment."

Jacky frowned. "No. But we've got to wait until tomorrow morning to leave anyway and it doesn't matter which way we go back to your place—there's the chance that the Host'll be watching us no matter how we go. It's tonight at your house that's worrying me—not getting there. Thanks," she added as the red-haired girl behind the counter gave her the bag with Finn's pastries in it.

"We could have a party," Kate said.

"What?"

"A party. Tonight. We'll invite all the bruisers we know and have all sorts of protection."

Jacky laughed. "We don't know any bruisers."

"Then we'll just have to meet some."

"I think you're almost serious."

Kate winked. "Maybe I am," she said as they returned to their table to collect Finn.

By day, the park across from the Gruagagh's Tower was a different place. There were no bikers, no giants. The Rideau River moved slowly along the south side of the green. Dried reeds rustled in the breeze. The swans were gone now, but flocks of ducks floated close to shore, hoping for handouts. There was a football game in progress as they entered the park's Bank Street entrance. The teams were short—only five men to each side—but what they lacked in numbers, they more than made up for in enthusiasm. On the path by the river two women with strollers were walking. A jogger moved around them onto the grass as he passed and soon left them behind.

"That's the Gruagagh's Tower," Jacky said, pointing it out. "The one with the back yard all overgrown."

"It looks deserted."

"I think it is—except for him." A big shout came from the football players as one team scored a touchdown. "And there are your bruisers," Jacky added with a grin.

"I think I'll pass," Kate said. "Can we walk closer to the house?"

"Sure. Only don't expect to see much from here because . . . " Jacky paused as Finn plucked at her shirt sleeve. She shifted her jacket from one arm to the other as she turned to him.

"We can't stay," he said urgently.

"Why? What's wrong?"

"I don't know. I just feel it in my bones. There's a glamour lying thick and deep here, just waiting to snare us."

"A glamour . . . ?"

Jacky looked around as she spoke. The day, the park and the people in it, all seemed so ordinary. But then she remembered what had been waiting for them in her apartment, and last night's mad flight from the biker flooded her mind. God, she could be so stupid. What was she doing, bringing them all here when she knew—she *knew*—how real the dangers were? It was as though ever since the attack in her apartment, she'd decided that they'd won the war. But all it had been was one small engagement.

"Which way should we go?" she asked.

"Back the way we came," Finn replied. "Come. Quickly now."

Jacky nodded. But it all felt so normal still. Her pulse drummed, but there was nothing that she could see that she could even pretend was a danger to them.

The women with their strollers were almost out of sight. The football players had just begun a new play. The quarterback pumped his arm and the ball went spinning, a high, long pass in their direction. The ball was caught about twenty yards away from where they were standing, the man who caught it grinning with pleasure. His teammantes worked to block the tacklers that were coming in from either side. And then—

Then it was too late.

Before Jacky could turn, before she could put proper use to the swiftness stitcheries that Finn had sewn into her sneakers, they were upon her. At the last moment, their forms shimmered. They were college-aged men and bogans at the same time. The foremost man threw the football aside and hit her hard, scooping her up under his arm. Her breath went out of her in a whoosh at the impact. Her jacket, with the redcap in its pocket, went flying from her grip.

"Got her, got her, GOT HERRRRR!" her captor roared.

There was no more attempt at disguise as the bogans charged through the park, their captive held fast. They cheered and shook their fists in the air. Kate saw Finn go down as he tried to rescue Jacky, and then a bogan fist smashed into the side of her head and sent her spinning.

She tried to rise, the whole world turning dizzily around in her vision, but another of the creatures stopped long enough to kick her in the stomach. She buckled over, bile rising in her throat. When she finally pulled herself up to her knees, the park was eerily empty except for herself, Finn who lay a half dozen paces away from her, and the blue jacket that Jacky had dropped.

Kate crawled towards Finn. Every movement of her head

brought tears of pain to her eyes. Her stomach felt as though something had ruptured inside. When she finally reached Finn, it took all her strength to turn him over. A trickle of blood escaped the corner of his mouth and he was so pale that she was sure he was dead. His face had a greyish cast to it and he lay so still . . .

She brought her cheek down to his face and held it there until she was sure that what she felt on her skin was his breath. So he was alive at least. But Jacky . . . She looked despairingly in the direction that the bogans had taken her friend.

What in God's name could she do now? She looked back at Finn, but he was in worse shape than she was. There was no one she could think of that she could go to with a story this weird. The police would think she was nuts. God, *anybody* would think she was nuts.

Slowly she got to her feet and stood swaying. She'd get the jacket. And then she'd—God, it was hard to think—then she'd what? Her gaze fell on the unkempt lawn of the Gruagagh's Tower. Then she'd make *him* help her. She started for the jacket when a voice stopped her.

"Fools."

She turned slowly to find Crowdie Wort's forester regarding her.

"Moon and stars!" he cried. "What possessed you to return here? Surely you'd at least guess that they were waiting for you?"

Kate decided to ignore him. Step by careful step she made her way to the jacket, picked it up. She saw the redcap sticking out of the pocket and plucked it out, putting it on as she turned back. Arkan Garty's glamour fled him as the redcap settled in place.

He was no longer tall and no longer . . . human. His skin was a reddish brown, his head narrow and more a fox's than a man's. The jeans and jean jacket he had been wearing had now become some weird tunic and trousers that looked as though they were just leaves and feathers and bits of fur all stitched together.

"Did they tear out your tongue, girl?"

Kate took a quick breath to settle the drum of her pulse. I didn't do much good. There was a weird light in the forester's eyes that seemed to say that he was capable of anything, but surprisingly, she wasn't afraid of him.

"What . . . what do you want?" she asked.

"I was charged to watch out for you."

"Well, you didn't . . . do such a good job, did you?"

The lights flickered dangerously in his eyes. "If you'd kept to safe ways—" he began, but Kate cut him off.

"Did you see where they took her? Where they took Jacky?"

He shook his head. "I lost them on the Laird's Road—but they left a trail that I can follow. It's not easy to miss the stink of a bogan and a pack that big will be easy to track. I came back to see if you needed help."

"And . . . now?" Kate asked, wishing her head didn't ache so. "Are you going after them?"

"That's for Crowdie Wort to say when I bring news of this afternoon's work to him."

Kate nodded, then wished she hadn't moved her head. She looked at the forester and thought of what Jacky had told her—how none of them would help the Laird's daughter. Instead they left it up to someone like Jacky who wasn't even close to their match in magics and strength. Anger boiled up in her.

"Well, go bring him your news," she said softly. "And then crawl back into whatever hole it was that you came from. You and your people seem very good at arriving after the fact. And then you talk the talk, real good. But me—when I look at you—all I see is a snivelling coward."

As she spoke the last words, she slipped on Jacky's blue jacket. From the look on Arkan's face, she knew that its stitcheries were working for her as well.

"Little hob spells won't help you against the Unseelie Court!" he cried. "Don't you think that we'd *want* to help our own Laird's daughter? But the Giants' Keep won't be breached by strength alone and the Wild Hunt will track down and kill anyone who tries. The luck's gone out of us—just as it's run out for your friend. Moon and stars, if there was something we could do, we would. But the Host outnumbers us five to one and they have the Hunt!"

"Screw you too!" Kate called to him as she started painfully across the park towards the Gruagagh's Tower.

"Come back! Crowdie Wort will want to talk to you."

Kate glanced back to see him testing the air with his nose, looking for all the world like a dog casting for scent. Scent! She pushed herself to move more quickly. The jacket might hide her from his sight, but it wouldn't do anything about her scent. And she didn't dare let him take her back to this Crowdie Wort—whoever *he* was—because the Host had Jacky now and if she didn't do something about rescuing Jacky, no one would. Arkan and his people would let her rot in the Giants' Keep the same way they did their own Laird's daughter. Clutching her stomach, she broke into a halting trot, aiming for the Gruagagh's Tower.

When she reached the hedge at the back of the Gruagagh's yard, she paused to look back again. Arkan had guessed her destination and was coming for her at a swift lope. She turned quickly and made her way across the overgrown back yard, reaching the Gruagagh's door at the same time as Arkan did.

He grabbed at the air around him, but Kate pressed close to the door and hammered on it, then dropped to her knees so that Arkan's arms cut the air above her head. Open, she told the door, but it was too late. Arkan's hand brushed her shoulder, returned and grabbed her, hauling her to her feet.

"You *will* come with me," he told her. "Moon and stars, girl! It's for your own good. The Gruagagh's not to be trusted."

Kate brought her knee up into his crotch and he doubled over, losing his grip on her. She hadn't been sure what kind of equipment a being like Arkan had between his legs and was happy to see that he had the same weakness as an ordinary man. She backed up against the door, flinching at the wild look in his eyes. His gaze raked back and forth across the small back porch, vainly looking for her.

"Damn you," he said from between clenched teeth. "I'm not the enemy."

Before Kate could reply, the door opened behind her and she tumbled backwards. Strong hands caught her and set her back on her feet. She looked up, and up, and there was Jacky's Gruagagh looking down at her from his height. Apparently the jacket's properties didn't work against him. He gave her a long considering look, then turned his attention to Crowdie Wort's forester.

"And who is the enemy?" he asked softly. "The untrustworthy Gruagagh, perhaps?"

The change in Arkan was immediate. Kate could see the fear fill him.

"Oh . . . oh, no . . . your reverence . . ."

For a long moment the Gruagagh simply stared at Arkan, then he said: "Bring the hob here to my door—and gently."

Arkan nodded quickly and backed away. When he reached the bottom step of the porch, he turned and bolted for the park. Kate was sure he was going to just keep on running until he'd put as much distance as he could between himself and the Gruagagh, but he surprised her. When he reached Finn's still form, he lifted the hob into his arms and hurried back.

"They mean well," the Gruagagh said to Kate as they watched Arkan return with his burden. "But these are hard times."

"I . . . I suppose. It's just . . . I don't know. I'm not really sure who's who and on what side just yet. Jacky's told me everything she knows, but that doesn't seem like a whole lot."

"Jacky," the Gruagagh breathed.

Arkan reached the porch just then and the Gruagagh took the hob from him, cradling Finn in his arms.

"Go back to Crowdie Wort and spill your tale," he told the forester. "And mark you don't forget to say a word or two against me while you're telling it."

"Oh, I wouldn't, your reverence."

"Not much you wouldn't," the Gruagagh said.

He turned and motioned for Kate to close the door and she did, getting a small sense of satisfaction out of seeing the fearful look that was still on Arkan's face as she shut the door in his face. But then she remembered why she was here, and where here was, and who here belonged to. Jacky said she'd liked the Gruagagh, but he seemed downright scary to Kate. Who was to say he *could* be trusted?

"Will . . . will Jacky be all right?" she asked.

Laying Finn down on the windowseat, the Gruagagh lifted the hob's eyelids, one by one, to examine the rolled-back eyes. Only then did he glance at Kate. He seemed to consider her question for a long moment, but rather than answering it, he turned back to the hob again, making no reply.

Ten

K ate found the Gruagagh's Tower to be just as strange as
Jacky had described it. Wherever she looked she got the
sensation of things sliding out of sight just as she settled her gaze in
their direction. Ghostly furnishings that were here and then gone.
And in the darker corners, there was movement of a different sort.
She thought of rats and spiders and moved closer to the windowseat
where the Gruagagh sat beside Finn. But when she looked at the
Gruagagh's grim features, she found little comfort there.

He had pulled a fat leather shoulder pack from under the windowseat and was now removing various vials, poultices and blankets. The pack, Kate thought, didn't look big enough to hold half of
what he was taking out of it. The first thing he did, once he pushed
the bag back under the windowseat, was mix up some concoction in
a small bowl which he then handed to her.

"Drink this."

"No way," she said, beginning to back away.

"It won't harm you," he said.

Kate hesitated for a moment longer, then gingerly took the
bowl from him. The liquid smelled awful, a sweet cloying smell.

"You came to me for help, did you not?" he said when she simply held the bowl, not drinking. His voice was mild, but his gaze was fierce.

"Okay, okay," Kate said.

Screwing up her face, she drank it down. Whatever it was tasted as foul as she'd imagined it would, but no sooner had she swallowed it, than a warm feeling spread from her stomach, easing her queasiness and clearing her head.

"What is this stuff?" she asked.

Rather than replying, the Gruagagh indicated that she should help him with Finn. While Kate held the hob's head and the bowl, the Gruagagh forced small amounts of the liquid between Finn's lips, stroking the hob's throat to make him swallow. Once some colour had returned to the little man's wan features, Kate stood to one side as the Gruagagh tended Finn's hurts. He rubbed a lotion into the bruises on the hob's torso and applied a poultice to the little man's brow. Then he turned to Kate.

"Your turn," he said. "Sit here and lift your shirt."

Kate felt uneasy again, pulling up her shirt in front of the Gruagagh, but he maintained a professional, detached attitude throughout the examination, gave her an ointment to rub onto the bruise, and pronounced her as fit as she could be after a run-in with a pack of bogans. He made a bed for Finn in the corner of the room, using the blankets he'd pulled from his seemingly bottomless pack, then brought out two mugs and a thermos which began to steam from its mouth as soon as he opened it and placed it on the windowsill between himself and Kate.

Kate looked at his grim face, then at the thermos. The blend of tea smelled delicious. She wanted to ask him where she could get a bag like his, but another look at his face froze the question in her throat. She turned instead to look out the window at Windsor Park — what Finn had called Learg Green.

"I take it you don't get many visitors," she said after a few moments.

"Few enough." He poured some tea, already mixed with milk in the thermos, and handed her a mug.

"Thanks."

It was far better tasting than the earlier concoction, but spread a similar warmth from her stomach as she took a sip. She looked around the kitchen. The sense of hidden movement and ghostly furnishings wasn't so pronounced anymore.

"What do you *do* in here?" she had to ask.

"Duty didn't always confine me to my Tower," he said. "Time was I was as free to roam as any of the Seelie Court. But times are hard and with the Laird's daughter gone, Deegan won't let me risk Kinrowan's Heart in rescue of her—for all that she's his daughter and her loss pains him deeply."

"What is this Heart?"

The Gruagagh smiled. "Why, it's myself. I'm the Laird's heart—the Heart of Kinrowan."

"I don't understand."

"You've been told how our glamours and magics have diminished, haven't you?"

Kate nodded, though from all she'd seen this past day, she had to wonder what those magics were like before they had diminished. They seemed to work pretty well so far as she could see.

"Well, diminished or not," the Gruagagh said, "what we have left is maintained by my focus. This Tower of mine is built on a crisscross of leys—straight tracks. Do you know the term?"

Kate nodded. "They're supposed to be lines that connect sacred sites, aren't they? So the Tower's like Stonehenge?"

"Exactly—but on a much, much smaller scale than that holy place. The ley lines are conduits of power—earth strength, moon strength, water, fire and air. I take those strengths and spread them through the Laird's land. They are all that keeps us from fading."

"Jacky said it has something to do with people not believeing in you anymore."

"That is an old argument that has never quite been resolved," the Gruagagh replied. "Many faerie, and some few mortals, have put forth the thought that we are sustained by your belief. All I know is that in this time of disbelief—disbelief that the Seelie Court exists, at any rate—we are diminished from what we were, I have also heard it put forth that the cause lies in the fact that we live in a borrowed land."

"In your homeland," Kate asked, "do the people still believe?"

"More so than here," the Gruagagh replied, "but I see your point. Our numbers are fewer there as well. The issue becomes more clouded, I think, by our willingness to accept that we depend upon mortals for our existence."

Well, she could see that, Kate thought.

"So you're Kinrowan's Heart," she said to change the subject, "and the Laird's daughter is its soul. Were you lovers?"

Something flickered in the Gruagagh's eyes, but Kate couldn't quite read what it was. Pain, perhaps. Or anger? But it was gone as quick as it had come.

"We have played the part," he said, "when the seasons demanded it. But mostly we are friends. If Lorana had a husband, then I would be freed of my duties. But until that day . . . "

Kate wondered what he meant by "when the seasons demanded it." It sounded too much like animals going into heat, but then she realized that he must mean holy times, like solstices, May Eve and Samhaine.

She stole a glance at him as he stared silently out the window, his face set in stern lines again. She remembered Jacky telling her about his scar, and how it didn't matter when he relaxed. But when he was tense like he was now, it made him seem so grim. It was probably time for her to go. But first . . .

"Are you going to help me find Jacky?" she asked.

The Gruagagh turned to her, his gaze looking into unseen distances. Then his eyes focused and he regarded her steadily.

"For that we must go upstairs," he said.

Kate glanced at the hob where he lay sleeping in his nest of blankets. "What about Finn?"

"Let him rest. Hurt as he is, he won't be much help in what you must do anyway. Now come. We've spent too long gossiping. The day's almost done."

Kate set her tea mug down and looked out the window. It was getting late. Fear pinprickled through her as she realized that she'd have to set off at night to find Jacky. The Gruagagh was at the door, his pack hanging from his shoulder by its strap. Turning from the window, Kate hurried to join him and followed him upstairs.

They went up one flight of stairs, then another. Around them the house was quiet. Kate still thought she saw sly movements in the darker shadows, but the small shapes made no sound. Their own footsteps echoed strangely in the empty halls and rooms as the Gruagagh led her into a third-floor bedroom. Except for the lack of furnishings, the house didn't look deserted. There was no dust. The plaster walls were clean. The wooden floors and trim were highly polished.

"How come no one lives here?" she asked. "Besides you, I mean."

"It's too close to Faerie. I have shared it with others from your world, but they always find the place too . . . unsettling, and quickly move."

"Why don't you just buy it—I mean in the real world?"

The Gruagagh turned to her. "Which is more real?" he asked. "Your world, or Faerie?"

"I . . . "

"But I do own this house—in your world as well as in my own."

"Well, why don't you furnish it, then?"

"You see only what you are meant to see. Come here now."

He motioned to the window and opened it as she came to stand by him. For a long moment she clung dizzily to the windowsill. She had expected to see the street below and the tops of the trees that lined it, their leaves all red and gold and stiff with autumn. Instead the entire city was spread out below her in miniature. From Britannia in the far west end all the way out to Vanier; from Parliament Hill on the Ottawa River to the north, all the way south to where Bank Street became Highway 31.

What she saw didn't seem possible. Vertigo counteracted the effects of the potion that the Gruagagh had given her earlier and her stomach roiled. The Gruagagh touched her arm, steadying her.

"Is . . . is this real?" she asked in a small voice.

"The city—or our view of it?" he replied with a touch of amusement.

"You know what I mean," she said.

The Gruagagh nodded. "Both the city and our view of it is real. We see it from a gruagagh's Tower, you see. A gruagagh must be able to view all of his Laird's land at once in times of need—a time such as this."

"There's my house," Kate said, pointing it out.

"Be still a moment," the Gruagagh said.

He leaned far over the windowsill. As the minutes ticked by, Kate shifted her weight from one foot to the other, but the Gruagagh never moved. Then, just as she was going to say something, he made a sound.

"Ah."

"Is that a good 'ah,' or a bad one?" she asked.

"That depends," the Gruagagh said as he pulled back from the windowsill. "Do you see that big building there in Cockle Tom's Garve?"

"In *what*?"

"Cockle Tom holds the area you call the Glebe in trust for the Laird, in the same way that Crowdie Wort holds this area where we are now."

"Oh. What building? That's the Civic Centre at Lansdowne," she said when he pointed it out again. "Is that where they took Jacky?"

The Gruagagh nodded. "Until tonight. Then I think they will move her to their Keep."

"In Calabogie—where Lorana is?"

"We know the Hunt's Horn is there," the Gruagagh replied, "but not where the Laird's daughter is. That was why Jacky was going to steal the Horn."

"Yes. But couldn't you just 'find' Lorana like you did Jacky?"

The Gruagagh shook his head. "They have the Laird's daughter too well cloaked with glamours for me to find her."

They were silent for a long moment. Finally Kate sighed and stirred.

"Well, I suppose I should get on with it," she said. "Do you have any ideas?" she added as the Gruagagh led the way back downstairs.

"Strength will do nothing, but slyness might. What you must do is steal in and find her, secret and sly, then make your escape as best you can."

Kate paused on the stairs. "Oh? Is that all? What a perfect plan. Now I wonder why I didn't think of it."

The Gruagagh looked back at her. "What do you want of me? Should I wave my hands and set all to right?"

"That'd help."

"My magics don't work that way."

"So how do they work?"

The Gruagagh sighed. "In secret ways—mostly. The time for greatspells has passed this world. Remnants remain—such as the

Wild Hunt's Horn and the moon dancing of longstones — but little enough that ordinary faerie may use."

"But you're supposed to be this mighty Gruagagh. Everybody's scared to death of you."

"What magics I have," he said, "cannot be used for such things. If I forsook my responsibilities, there are things I could try, but I dare not. Shall all of Kinrowan's faerie fail so that I might rescue your friend?"

"You're no better than the rest of them," Kate said. "You're just looking for saps like me and Jacky to do your dirty work for you."

"Not so."

There was a dangerous flicker in his eyes that Kate ignored. "Not so?" she began in a squeaky, mocking voice, but then she thought better of it.

There was more that she wanted to say. It lay on the tip of her tongue, but she bit it back. What was the point? She had Jacky to think of right now. And there was the Laird's daughter — she deserved better, too. So for them, but especially for Jacky, she'd go and do what she could. But not for Faerie, and certainly not for the Gruagagh.

She pushed by him. "See ya later, chum. I've got things to do."

She went down the hall until she found the room where Finn was still sleeping. There she collected the blue jacket and the redcap that had started it all.

"Kate," the Gruagagh said as she headed into the kitchen. "Jacky chose to go — no one made her."

"That's because no one else would go."

The Gruagagh shook his head. "Because no one else *can*."

"Okay," Kate said. "I understand you've got to stay here and, you know, be that focus and everything, but what about the other faerie? Why don't *they* do something?"

"Because of the Hunt. Contrary to your nursery tales, we do have souls. But those that are taken by the Hunt lose them."

"So it's okay for me or Jacky to lose ours?"

"Fear doesn't seem to paralyze you as it has my people, nor are you trapped by your duties as I am."

"You didn't answer me."

"No one forces you to do anything," the Gruagagh said.

"It's kind of late for that, isn't it? They've *got* Jacky now."

"It was not something I planned."

Kate thought about how Finn had warned them to stay away from the Gruagagh's Tower and nodded slowly.

"When you say the Hunt takes your soul," she said. "Does that mean you become one of the restless dead like on Samhaine Eve?"

"No. The Hunt feeds on the souls they catch."

Kate shuddered. "But still . . . "

"We've lost our heroes, Kate. All we have left are hobs and brownies, little folk that can't even stand up to bogans, never mind the Hunt of Gyre the Elder and his kin. They have had to hide and steal about for so long now that they don't know *how* to be brave. It will take new heroes to show them and our heroes have always been mortal."

"If you're expecting *me* to be their role model, you're in for a rude surprise. I'm not a hero."

"No? But still you're going to rescue your friend. I'd call that brave."

"Yes, well . . . " Kate flashed him a quick awkward smile. "I've got to go."

"Be careful, Kate Crackernuts."

Kate regarded him for a long moment, then nodded. Slipping on the redcap, she ducked out the back door. She stood in the back yard and looked up at the darkening sky. It would be full night before she even got back to her place to get her car. She was about to put on the jacket and head out, when a familiar figure stepped out of the hedge. Arkan Garty, Crowdie Wort's forester.

"Don't *you* start again," Kate told him before he could get a word out.

Arkan held his hands open in front of him. "I want to go with you," he said. "I want to help."

"Is that what your boss told you to say?"

Arkan shook his head. "I haven't left the Gruagagh's yard since you went in. I've been thinking about all you've said and I . . . I'm ashamed. . . . "

His voice trailed off and he looked so uncomfortable that Kate took pity on him. She wasn't really sure why she did what she did, because she only half-trusted him, but perhaps it had something to do with what the Gruagagh had said to *her* about heroes. She didn't feel particularly heroic, but it took some doing to admit you were wrong—she knew that from the times she'd had to do it herself. If Arkan Garty was willing to help, then she should be willing to give him the chance.

"Come on, then," she said. "Time's running out."

Arkan fell in step beside her and they hurried on down the park, making for her apartment.

"What do they call you?" he asked as they reached the spot where Belmont met the Rideau River.

That was a polite way of putting it, Kate thought, remembering what Jacky had told her about faerie and their speaking names.

"Kate," she said. "Kate Crackernuts," she added with a smile. She had to be nuts. "Welcome to my nightmare."

"What?"

The rock and roll reference was lost on him, Kate realized, but she didn't try to explain it. How did you explain Alice Cooper to someone from Faerie?

"Nothing," she said. "It's just something that Jacky and I say to each other when the going gets weird, and tonight, Arkan, let me tell you, the going's definitely gotten weird."

The foxish head nodded beside her. The gloom of twilight gave Kate the eerie feeling that she was hurrying through the dusk with a werefox. Definitely a weird night. And it was just starting. Hang in there, Jacky, she thought. The cavalry's on the way. All two of us.

Eleven

J acky was hanging in there—just.

When the bogans snatched her, she'd literally gone numb with panic. She saw first Finn, then Kate go down, and then the bogans' rush took them out of the park into a mad dizzying run through Ottawa South's streets.

Don't they *see*? she remembered thinking as the bogans swarmed by a man walking his dog, children playing in a schoolyard, two workmen taking a coffee break. But there was Faerie and her own world, she realized, and only with a redcap could you see into the former from the latter. A redcap or . . . She'd dropped both cap and jacket when the bogans grabbed her, but she still saw.

Touched, she thought. Touched by Faerie and I'll maybe always *see* now. I've gone fey.

The bogan gripped her so tightly, and the heavy reek of his body odour was so strong, their speed so dizzying while she bounced against the creature's rock-hard skin . . . it all combined into a frightening whorl that spun inside her until Jacky did something she'd never done before. She fainted dead away. When she finally came out of her faint, sick and feverish with its aftereffects, there was cold concrete under her and a pool of bogan faces spinning slowly around her, slowing down like a merry-go-round running out of steam until she could make out each hellish face with a clarity she wished wasn't hers.

She almost passed out again, but knew she couldn't afford to. She had to get OutOfHere. RightAway. As the dizzying feeling came over her again, she bit down on her lower lip and forced her eyes to stay open. Her stomach churned, but she remained conscious.

The creatures that surrounded her weren't all bogans, or at least they weren't all like the things that she and Kate had fought back in her apartment. Some were twins to those ugly squat creatures, but there were others . . . Something like a naked woman, emaciated and grey-skinned, her ribs protruding and the skin drawn tight across her features, snuffled close to Jacky's head. Pale eyes regarded her with a hungry gaze. When the creature leaned close and licked at Jacky's cheek, she choked on a scream and whipped her head aside. The bogans laughed at that.

"Don't like you much, Maghert, hot damn!"

The grey woman-like thing hissed. "Give usss a tassste."

A bogan gripped Jacky's head and held it while Maghert rasped her tongue across Jacky's cheek. Jacky moaned and that made the bogans laugh some more. Thick fingers poked at her stomach, squeezed her thighs, jabbed at her breasts.

"Plump enough to spit her, sure," one of the bogans said. "Don't need to stew this one, no, hot damn!"

Twig-thin creatures capered and danced just beyond the circle of the bogans. The grey-skinned hag's tongue felt like it was licking the side of her face raw. There was a trollish, slopebacked creature, its body festooned with shells that clattered as it bent close, a gap-toothed leer splitting its face. Jacky tried to curl herself into a ball, but the bogans just pulled her straight, poking and prodding. Saliva spilled from their mouths when they laughed. Their reek made the air unbreathable.

"I like mine raw," a rumbling voice announced to a new chorus of rough laughter.

A bogan pulled Maghert away from her, cuffing the hag across the head. "Leave a bit for the rest, you old whore," he muttered.

One of the tiny twig-thin creatures sidled close and began to pluck at her hand. "Just a finger," it moaned before it too was cuffed aside.

"Leave her be!" the large bogan who'd pulled the hag away roared, taking command. "Leave her alone, or I'll spike the lot of you, just watch if I don't, hot damn!"

A chorus of protests arose.

"Greedy!"

"Spike you, arsebreath, hot damn!"

"We'll stew *you*, Skraker!"

"She's for the Big Man," Skraker growled. He stood over Jacky, like a cougar straddling its prey, and slowly faced down the crowd of angry creatures. "She's for the Boss and maybe he'll share her and maybe he won't."

"We're hungry now!" a bogan protested.

"Give her to usss," Maghert whispered, creeping closer again.

Skraker leapt forward and began batting the creatures indiscriminately with his big fists until they all backed off. He spared Jacky a glance. When he saw she was still breathing, he paced back and forth across the concrete floor, glaring at his companions until they broke off into small groups of twos and threes and fell to arguing amongst themselves. Then he sat down near Jacky to keep guard.

The smell of her made his stomach rumble, but he knew better than to go against the wishes of the Big Men. Human prey was rare. Take too many, and the men were out hunting you, pretty damn fast. So the few humans that fell into the clutches of the Unseelie Court went first to the Big Men. But there were always scraps. And it was those that followed orders that got the scraps, hot damn.

For a long time after the creatures had stopped pawing at her, Jacky lay still, hardly daring to breathe. The sheer horror of her predicament had unnerved her to the point where it was all she could do to keep herself from fainting dead away again. The touch of the hag's tongue, all those hands and fingers, squeezing and prodding, and the talk of spits and stews . . . She shuddered.

She'd thought the worst thing that could happen would be to fall into the clutches of the Wild Hunt. Now she knew better. Anything to do with the Unseelie Court was a horror. She felt weak and sick, hardly able to lift her head. But slowly, as she was left alone, the terror was pushed back. She realized that she had to plan, she had to do something to get away. There would be no rescues. And now, with this first-hand experience, she understood the reluctance small hobs like Finn had about confronting the Host.

Think, she told herself. Remember all those fairy tales you read as a kid. If these things are real, then whatever the good guys used to destroy them probably worked too. Except they all had magic swords, or talking cats, or handsome princes to rescue them. All she had was herself. A very scared self. Against twenty or more monsters. She started to shiver again, then pinched herself hard. The pain was enough to help her focus on trying to think of something, instead of just curling up and dying.

She sat up, very slowly, stiffening when the big bogan nearby turned quickly around, nostrils flaring. Jacky thought her heart would stop as he stared hungrily at her. She lifted a hand to her face and wiped away the drying, sticky saliva that was there. Her stomach did a flip as she frantically wiped it off her hands. The bogan grinned.

"Try and run," he said, "and I'll take off one of your legs, the Big Man be damned!"

"I . . . I . . ." Jacky began, but she couldn't get anything out except for that one syllable, and it sounded like the kind of squeak a mouse made.

"Bet you taste good," the bogan muttered as he turned away from her. "Hot damn!"

Her sitting up had brought a circle of the other creatures around them that quickly dispersed when the bogan guarding her snarled at them.

She had to wait, Jacky told herself. Wait for the right moment. They'd left her with her sneakers and the hob magics stitched into them. If she could just get a little bit of a head start, they'd never be able to catch her . . . would they? But the waiting was hard. Time dragged, the way it always did when she was waiting for something. And then there was the bogan sitting so close to her, its body odour traversing the distance between them in sickly waves. And the other creatures that were snuffling about—the hag and the little feral twig creatures, the trollish thing with the clattering shells, and the other bogans. Not to mention the knowledge that one of the Big Men was on his way . . .

To try to keep her mind away from all of that, she studied her surroundings. This was the Civic Centre, she realized. An indoor rink that was also used for concerts. She'd gone to a zillion rock shows here. Was this the Ottawa home of the Host? Were they into rock and roll? When she looked at the creatures around her, she didn't think they'd be out of place in a heavy metal band's video.

An image popped into her mind of the bogans tying her to a spit while an announcer's voice spoke overtop, "And now, new from the Unseelie Court, here's 'Eating Out With Jacky' . . . " And there was the hag, singing lead, with bogans on guitars and that big thing with the shells on drums, looking like some psychotic's version of a Muppet . . .

She shuddered and knew that she couldn't wait for the right moment. She had to make it for herself. If she stayed here much longer, she was just going to wither away. It was bad enough that she kept feeling faint. If she kept that up, the next time she woke up it might well be in a stew.

She got ready to get up and run for it and damn the torpedoes. It was time for GoJackyGoJackyGoJackyGo. But then there came a commotion at the far end of the arena and all her resolve drained away in a rush. This was it. The Big Man was here for his dinner. Except it wasn't the giant. It was more bogans and they were dragging in a new captive.

Oh, God—they've got Kate, she thought, then knew a moment's relief when she saw that the short brown curls on the Host's new victim belonged to a man. At least she thought it was a man. She squinted, trying to get a better look, realizing at the same time that she was passing up her best chance of Getting-OutOfHere. The new captive seemed to be wearing some kind of feathered boa. Then wonder snared her completely and she couldn't move.

It was a man all right, only he didn't have a man's arms. In place of them he had two big black wings. They didn't give him the majesty of any angel, as she might have thought if someone had described a winged man to her. Instead the wings hung awkwardly from his shoulders, the feathers drooping. A kind of rough brown tunic covered his torso.

As his captors dragged him closer and the creatures already present began to howl, one of those old fairy tales she'd been trying to remember came back to her. It was the one about the seven brothers who were turned into swans. At the end of the story, after their sister had woven nettle shirts for each of them, they all turned back into men. All except the youngest. He was left with a swan's wing because his sister hadn't had time to finish one sleeve of his shirt.

This swan man was like that, she thought. Except his sister hadn't finished off either one of his sleeves. Then she had no more time to think, for the noise of the creatures became deafening as they howled and those howls rebounded from the lofty ceilings.

"Royal blood!"

"HotdamnhotdamnHOTDAMN!"

"Oh, give usss, give USSSSS!"

The bogan guarding Jacky lunged to his feet. He caught hold of one of Jacky's arms and hauled her up, dragging her with him as he went to meet the newcomers. With his free fist he batted away at the shuffling creatures that were trying to get at the swan man.

"Back off, shitheads!" he roared. "BACK OFF!"

When he reached the newcomers, he threw Jacky at the swan man and turned to beat off the snarling, howling crowd of creatures. Jacky fell to her knees, feeling the painful jar of the concrete floor all the way up to her jaw at the impact. Her face struck the swan man's arm—wing?—and she choked on the feathers. A bogan hand grabbed the short spikes of her hair and pulled her head roughly back.

"Hey, Skraker!" the new bogan leader said. "This thing of yours is trying to eat our boy!"

Jacky's captor turned with an evil grin. "I'll eat you, arse-breath, if you don't give me a hand with these shitheads."

Jacky and the new captive were unceremoniously hauled off to one side where the bogan remained on guard, while the rest waded into the excited creatures that were trying to get through Skraker. There was more of the Host here now, Jacky realized. A lot more. Their numbers seemed to have tripled. The fact of her doom pressed down on her like a heavy weight once more and she leaned back against the wall, fighting back tears. The noise in the arena made it impossible to think. The squabbling creatures, each more horrible than the next, just brought home her helplessness.

It was a good ten minutes before some semblance of order returned. Skraker came back to stand guard over Jacky, talking with the leader of the new patrol of bogans. They both kept an eye on the ever-growing crowd of the Unseelie Court.

"The Big Man better get here soon," Skraker said, "or I'm throwing both of them out to that crew—minus a leg or two."

"Hot damn!" the other bogan said. His own patrol was now lost in the crowd out on the floor. "A taste of Royal blood—now wouldn't that be something."

Skraker shook his head. "The Big Men don't eat those. Keep 'em for trade. But I'd eat 'em, sure would. You know, Gooter, sometimes I just . . . "

The two bogans drifted mercifully out of Jacky's earshot. She closed her eyes, but that brought no relief. Something touched her shoulder, light as a feather . . . She blinked her eyes open wide to see that it was a feather, or at least the tip of a wing. She almost laughed at the weirdness of it all. But she knew that if she laughed, that'd be it. GameOver and That'sAllFolks. Because she'd never stop.

"You're a mortal," the swan man said.

Jacky pinched herself again, waiting for the pain to bring her down to earth. At this rate, between the Host and herself, she wouldn't have an unbruised spot on her body. She managed to nod and then cleared her throat.

"You . . . you're not?"

He shook his head. "I'm Eilian Dunlogan." The look on his face said, Don't you know me? Then a half-smile, self-mocking and bitter, touched his lips, adding, And why should you? "I'm the Laird of Dunlogan's son," he said aloud.

Jacky nodded wisely, still in the dark, though there was something familiar about the name. "I'm Jacky Rowan," she said. "What did they do to your arms?"

"Do? They did nothing. All the Lairdsblood can wear the shape of a swan or a seal. They've just used one of their damned spells to bind me between shapes. They're not stupid, though you wouldn't think it to look at some."

"But can't you just . . . just fly away?"

Eilian shook his head. "These wings could never support a man's body. You see, with my wings, I can't get the nettle tunic off, and with the tunic on, I can't complete my change. It's a very clever trap—especially for such as these."

Jacky bit at her lip. This seemed a little too simple. Couldn't she just pull the tunic off? She started to move forward to do just that, when Skraker strode up behind her and cuffed her across the back of the head. She sprawled across Eilian, knocking the breath out of him.

"Don't you be getting no ideas, little smellsogood, or I swear I'll leave you less one arm, hot damn!"

Two black wings encircled her, trying to give what comfort they could. It was little enough, but it was something.

"And you too, you Royal shithead," Skraker warned. "I've got eyes in the back of my head and in the sides and up my arse. You can't chew snot without me seeing you—got that? The Boss'll be here soon and you can take up any complaints with him. He might spike your new little friend there, but you'll be safe enough. Until we get to the Keep. And then, oh hot damn, you better start worrying about then, for what's Dunlogan got that's worth trading you for? Royal soup's the better bargain, I'm thinking."

He strode back to Gooter, chuckling. Slowly Jacky sat up. She turned in her winged embrace to look at Eilian, trying hard not to cry or let her fear show. Surprisingly, it was getting easier. She wondered if she was just getting used to her predicament—they said people could adjust to anything—or if it was because she wasn't alone anymore. She wouldn't wish this on anyone, but she couldn't help feeling better for having company. And even if Eilian did have wings, he was still worth looking at. He was handsome in a rugged sort of way—which was odd, because his bones seemed very delicate. It was the warmth of his eyes, she decided, that helped most. That, and the laugh lines around his mouth.

"It . . . it was really bad being here by myself," she said.

Eilian nodded understandingly. "I'm glad to have met with you, Jacky Rowan, even in circumstances such as these." The wing tightened around her shoulders.

Jacky blushed. God, I'm such a mess, she thought. But then Eilian was just as disheveled as she was.

"How did they catch you?" she asked.

Eilian sighed. "They put up a sign that said, 'Fools wanted,' so naturally I ran over to see if they could use me." He grinned at her smile, then sighed again. "No, it wasn't as bad as that—though not by much. How much do you know of Faerie?"

"Not a whole lot."

"But you know of the two Courts? How the Seelie Court grows weaker, year by year, while these creatures grow ever more bold and strong?"

Jacky nodded. "Bhruic told me about that."

"Bhruic? Bhruic Dearg, the Gruagagh?" Eilian regarded her sharply, then shook his head. "Laird love a duck, I am a fool. Why, you're the reason I came south from my father's Court."

"Me? But you don't know anything about me."

"The whole of Faerie's a-buzz with word of you, Jacky. And by your name, I should have guessed who you were. You're the hope of Kinrowan, aren't you? The one who means to storm the Giants' Keep?"

Hysterical laughter started to bubble up in Jacky and it was only with a great effort that she kept it down. "Look at me," she said. "Do I look like I could storm anything?"

His warm eyes regarded her for a long moment, and then he said, "I think so, yes."

Jacky could feel another blush coming on, so she looked away and cleared her throat. "Does . . . ah, the Host have a weakness?"

"For flesh, mostly."

"No. I mean, something that can hurt them."

"Cold iron's best—sword or axe or knife—though it wouldn't do one much good with this lot. Faerie that dwell in the city have become acclimatized to the sting of iron over the years—though they give up something in exchange for that immunity. Their lifespans are shortened and they're no longer as hardy."

"Isn't there anything else?"

"Well, there's the wood, berries and leaves of the rowan—like your name—and the red thread sticheries of a skillyman hob. Salt, too. Running water slows them—they can't cross it easily. And if they're chasing you, turn your coat inside out and you'll lose them for a time."

"Oh." It was starting to come back to her. "What about using the name of God?"

"That, I'm afraid," Eilian said, "is a story passed around by your church and not based on truth." Jacky looked disappointed even though she wasn't an avid churchgoer. "Faerie," he went on, "are more like mortals now than we'd like."

As they talked, Jacky had been keeping an eye on the various creatures of the Unseelie Court, particularly on the two bogans, Skraker and Gooter.

"I've got magic sneakers," she whispered when she was sure neither of them was paying any attention.

"What?"

"My shoes—a hob made them magic."

"Ah." Eilian said with a nod. "Swiftness stitcheries."

"If I can get a bit of a headstart, I'll bet I could outrun them."

And then, she thought, I'll just take off my shirt in the middle of Bank Street and turn it inside out so that the Host can't find me. No problem.

"And you want me to create a diversion for you?"

Jacky shook her head. She was still watching the two bogan leaders. They were beginning to get into an argument.

"How tight's that nettle shirt?" she asked.

Understanding gleamed in Eilian's eyes. "Too tight for wings to loose, but not so bad for you."

Jacky bit at her lip, gauging the distance between the bogans and themselves. The argument between the bogan leaders was intensifying. She chose a moment when Skraker roared something at Gooter and then gave the other bogan a shove that sent him sprawling.

"Let's do it," she said.

Quickly she turned and grabbed hold of his shirt. The nettles stung and pricked her fingers, but she ignored that. She jumped to her feet and hauled the shirt free. Black feathers sprayed around her as though she and Eilian had just had a pillow fight.

"Go!" she cried.

Before her eyes, the son of Dunlogan's Laird became a black swan. The big wings, no longer useless, beat at the air, lifting him from the ground. Howls broke out all around the hall, but neither Eilian nor Jacky stayed to look. He rose high into the air, out of their range, while Jacky pulled herself over the balustrade that separated the rink from the spectators' tiered seats and took off at a run.

Feets don't fail me now, she thought.

The swan flying above her made encouraging noises. Her sneakers slapped the concrete floor. She was really moving, she thought. And thank Finn for that. Behind her and following on the main floor of the arena was the horde of the Unseelie Court's creatures, their growls and snarls raised in a cacophony. But she was GettingOutOfHere and adrenaline was pumping through her. She had magic shoes and no one was going to catch her.

She was almost to the closest doorway and well ahead of their pursuers. She started to pluck at the buttons of her shirt, feeling stupid, but willing to give anything a try if it would help. Eilian cried down at her. She didn't look up, just kept running.

GoJackyGoJackyGoJackyGo!

The door was near, and she was through it. There were stairs coming up. Don't trip, she warned herself. Behind her the Host was gaining on her. She tried to slow down as she neared the top of the stairs, didn't think she'd make it, then saw why Eilian had been calling to her. One of the Big Men was coming up the stairwell.

He wasn't as big as Gyre the Younger, but he still stood fourteen feet tall, with legs and arms like small tree trunks and a big barrel of a torso. The hair on his head was a grizzle of grey brown, his beard hung halfway down his chest. He looked up, grinning a big gap-toothed grin.

The thing with the shells back in the arena must be his little brother, Jacky thought, looking at that grin. She didn't have time to think anything else. Didn't have to plan. Didn't even know she'd do what she did until she was already doing it.

As she reached the top of the stairs, she launched herself right at the giant. He tried to bat her out of the air, but she was moving too fast. She hit him hard, toppled him, then rode him down the stairs, holding onto his beard for purchase. They hit the bottom of the stairs with a jarring crash. There was a sound like something splintering, but it was a wet splintering sound, then Jacky lost her grip and went rolling, skidding to an abrupt stop against a wall.

For a long moment she lay there, half-stunned. She looked back, seeing the Unseelie Court swarming at the top of the stairs. Right at the bottom, the giant lay with his head cracked open, blood and greyish brain matter splattered all around his head.

All she could do was stare, her stomach doing flip-flops. Then Eilian dove down at her, startling her with a sharp call and a brush

of a black feathered wing. Right, she thought. She was GettingOut-
OfHere. She was GoJackyGoing.

She got to her feet and started to run again, hardly realizing
that the only thing that had saved her during her moment of disori-
entation back there was that the Unseelie Court had been just as
shocked as she was by the death of one of the Big Men.

A giant, Jacky thought as she ran. Holly shit! I killed a giant!

There were doors up ahead. She reached them, coming to a stop
by running into them. Holding them open for Eilian to fly through,
she slipped out after him and was stunned by the fact that it was night
outside. Night! God, she'd been in there with the bogans for hours.

She undid the last button of her shirt and was tugging it off so
that she could turn it inside out—and wouldn't that just add to her
fashionableness—when something landed on her back. She
screamed, arms trapped by her shirt. Hot breath touched her neck.
Tiny twig-like fingers plucked at her hair and skin. Then Eilian dove
from the sky and knocked the little creature off with a blow of his
wings. Jacky took a few stumbling steps away and saw that the one
twig-creature wasn't alone. There was a great deal of rustling movement in the shadows behind its fallen form.

Hardly daring to breathe, she finished taking off her shirt,
backing up all the time. Eilian kept dive-bombing the creatures,
keeping them from her as she turned the shirt inside out, put it back
on, started to button it. She was mostly down the steps outside the
Civic Centre now.

"Eilian!" she cried.

Things scurried by her, but they didn't see her. Jeez, it works,
she thought. But then she realized that it probably worked on Eilian
as well. She tried to spot him, but the sky was too dark.

"This is getting stupid," she muttered as she started to undo the
buttons again. But she wasn't going to go on without him. If she had
a lucky name, then he was her lucky piece, because without him she
might never have gotten out of there. Nor killed the giant.

"Eilian!" she cried again, pulling the shirt free.

Suddenly there was scurrying all around her. Eilian dropped
from the sky and took his own shape by her side. The bogans and
other creatures from inside the Civic Centre were at the top of the
steps and still coming out of the glass doors. In the darkness around

Jacky and Eilian, the twig-creatures were gathering their courage, hissing and chattering among themselves.

"What do we do now?" Jacky asked her companion.

He turned to her, but then they both heard the squeal of tires and saw a car turn in from Bank Street. Its headlights caught them, blinding them both. Jacky heard the driver downshift a gear and the car leapt forward with a roar of its engine.

"Oh, shit," Jacky said. "They're going to run us down."

Twelve

It was dark by the time Kate and Arkan Garty reached Kate's apartment. The street was quiet. Up the block a couple of teenagers were just turning the corner, their voices loud in the still air. Kate and Arkan waited until the pair were out of sight, then approached the house, keeping to the shadows.

The darkness didn't trouble Kate half as much as the fact that the windows of her apartment were all lit up. For one moment she thought, maybe Jacky's there. But then she realized that if Jacky *was* there, it was in the company of the Unseelie Court.

"What's the matter?" Arkan asked.

Kate glanced at her foxish companion. "There's someone in my place."

Arkan's eyes narrowed as he studied the lit windows. He moved into the deeper shadows alongside her neighbour's house, pulling Kate with him. Softly they crept across the driveway, hugging the walls of Kate's building as they stole up to a window to have a look. One glance was all that was needed.

"Bogans," Kate said, seeing them for what they were with Jacky's redcap on. "Shit. Now what're we going to do?"

"We don't need to go inside, do we?" Arkan asked. "It's only your car we came for."

"But the keys are inside. I've only got my housekeys on me."

"Where is the car?"

"We *need* the keys to the car," she told him. "Or do you know how to hotwire it?"

Arkan nodded.

Kate stared at him. "You *do*?"

"Just because I'm part of Faerie, doesn't make me stupid."

"Yes, but you don't drive cars."

"Who told you that?"

"Well, no one. It's just in all the stories."

A foxish grin stole across Arkan's face. "There weren't many cars in Shakespeare's plays either."

"Yes. But they didn't have cars back then . . . "

Kate's voice trailed off. Right, she thought. And they didn't have them when people were putting together fairy tales either. Andrew Lang hadn't been much of a hotrodder and Perrault wasn't known for his skill in the Grand Prix. And when she thought of Jacky's Wild Hunt . . . black-leathered bikers on their Harleys . . . Well, who was to say what a denizen of Faerie might or might not know?

"Well, let's get to it," she said.

She led the way to where Judith, her VW, was sitting in the driveway. She cast a quick glance back at the apartment—that was her life the bogans were prying into now, *her* personal space—then she bit down the rising tide of resentment. Jacky was what was important now. Not her apartment.

They reached the Volkswagen. The driver's door opened with a small protesting creak. The interior light didn't come on, but that wasn't through any forethought on Kate's part. It had simply burnt out a few months ago and she hadn't bothered to replace it yet.

"Judith," Kate hissed. "Help us out and I'll get you an oil change as soon as this is all over—I promise."

Arkan regarded her with amusement, then slid in. He bent down to fiddle with the wiring under the dashboard, leaving Kate to stand nervously by the open door. She plucked at the quilting of Jacky's blue jacket that she was still carrying. Something caught her gaze, a rapid movement in the corner of her eye that was there and gone so quickly that she barely registered it. She started to put on the jacket.

"Arkan," she warned. "There's something out here."

When she had the jacket on—and it had better be working, she thought—she moved away from the car, looking for something she could use as a weapon. No pack of bogans was going to bonk her on the head again and leave her sprawling, thank you very much. The next-door neighbour's rake was leaning against his back porch.

All right, Kate thought as she made for it, going on tiptoes. There. She saw something move again. Just around the corner of her house. And she could hear whispering now. A dry, unfamiliar smell was in the air. Her fingers closed on the rake. The weight of it was comforting as she soft-stepped her way back to the car. She was about to call out to Arkan—just to ask what was taking the great faerie car booster so long—when she saw something big and bulking glide from the front of the house and move soundlessly towards Judith's open door.

Not feeling brave, just angry, the rake tight in sweaty hands, Kate moved in behind the creature. She let him get nice and close to the car, then swung the rake behind her and brought it around in a sweeping arc until it connected with the head of whatever it was that had been sneaking up on Arkan. The wet sound as it hit and the jarring blow that went right up her arms to her elbows killed satisfaction she got from her deed.

The big shape dropped like a felled ox. The rake dropped from Kate's hands. She saw Arkan jump at the double sound, knocking his head against the dashboard.

"It's . . . it's okay," Kate called in a loud whisper. "I got him."

Whatever "him" was. She bent to retrieve the rake just in time to see a collection of small lanky creatures come scurrying from around the back of the house. Oh, shit, she thought. There had to be fifteen or twenty of the things. They were small, shadowy shapes, like the silhouetted branches of winter trees come to life. As they scurried forward, that dry smell was in the air again . . .

"Look out!" she called to Arkan as she ran to meet them, trusty rake in her hand.

The VW's engine coughed into life on the heels of her words. Kate threw the rake at the foremost creatures and watched them go down. The ones immediately behind fell over their leaders as she bolted for the car. Arkan had it in gear and was backing down the drive while she was still opening the door.

"Wait for me!" she cried.

She hauled the door open and flung herself inside. Arkan floored the gas pedal and Judith lunged out onto the road, passenger's side door flapping. Pulling in her feet, Kate grabbed the loose door, kicked away a couple of over-zealous twig-creatures, and banged it shut. She braced herself as the VW skidded to a stop. Arkan slammed the car into first and Judith leaped forward, leaving rubber on the pavement behind her. The sudden movement thrust Kate against her seat. Arkan changed smoothly from first to second, into third. Looking out through the rear window, Kate saw that they were losing the little band of creatures.

"Nice timing," she said as she turned around to face front once more. "God, what were those things?"

"A kind of goblin."

Arkan shot her a foxish grin. The longer she was with him, the more he looked like good old Reynard, Kate thought.

"A kind of goblin," she said. "Lovely." Another thought came to her. "Can you see me?"

Arkan shook his head, concentrating on his driving. "No. But I can hear your melodious voice, so I assume you're with me."

Oh, he was a cool one, Kate thought. But she liked him better like this than as the penitent that had met her at the bottom of the Gruagagh's garden.

"So what kind of goblins were they?" she asked as she worked at removing the blue jacket in the confines of the car.

"Gullywudes. Tree goblins."

Kate stifled a giggle. She'd almost heard gollywogs. Then, jeez, she thought. Look at me. I just fought off a pack of these gullywudes, knocked a bogan for a loop, and I'm sitting here laughing about it all. Like it happens every day. Another giggle slipped out and she put a firm clamp on any more. This wasn't funny. This was being hysterical.

As she finally got the jacket off, Arkan gave her a quick glance.

"I know, I know," Kate said. "I shouldn't be, but I'm feeling giddy as a goose."

"It often happens when mortals mix with faerie," Arkan replied. "It's a natural reaction—no different from how you'd feel after a moment of stress. And you've just been going through both."

"So now you're a doctor?"

"It's a common fact—did no one tell you?"

"No."

Great, Kate thought. First I've got to worry about Jacky turning into a trickster, and now I'm turning into a giggly basketcase. And then she had something else to worry about.

They had just reached a red light at the corner of Sunnyside and Bank and Arkan took a sharp right without stopping. Kate grabbed for the handle hanging above the passenger's door. Okay. So it was legal to make a right on red in Ontario, but couldn't he at least have stopped and *looked*? There was a sudden blare of horns and screeching brakes behind them.

"It'd be nice if we made it there in one piece," she muttered.

Arkan didn't take his gaze from the road. "It'd also be nice if we didn't have the Hunt on our tail."

"The Hunt . . . ?"

Kate turned again and saw three Harleys coming around the corner, cutting off more cars.

"Oh, jeez." She turned back. Lansdowne Bridge was coming up fast. "I thought you had to be from Faerie or wearing a redcap to see them?"

"You do. I'm from Faerie and you're—"

"Wearing a redcap. Yeah. I know. But the other cars on the road aren't, and they can see 'em." She looked back. The three bikers were gaining.

"Take off the cap and you'll see what they see."

So she did. There were still three motorcycles back there, but now they looked like they were being driven by members of a biker gang like the Devil's Dragon.

"The last time I took off the cap they just disappeared."

"Were they in traffic?"

"No, there was just one of them, sitting on my street, watching the house."

"They occupy space," Arkan explained. "even when invisible. In traffic like this they must be seen or a car might run into them."

"So they can be hurt?"

"It would . . . delay them."

They were up the hill of Lansdowne Bridge and barrelling

down the other side. Still going fast. Very fast. Kate wondered if some hob skillyman had stitched a few spells into Judith's tires.

"What do you mean 'delay them'?" she asked.

"They would have to find new bodies."

"New . . . Right. Forget I asked." She leaned back to look out the rear window again. "I thought all nine had to be together before they attacked?"

"True enough. But there only needs to be one, if all they are doing is following us."

Kate turned to face front, swallowing thickly. "Turn here," she said as the entrance to the Lansdowne Park came up.

Arkan's response was instantaneous. They went around the corner on two wheels, tires screeching again.

"Jeez!" Kate protested. "Be still my heart."

But then the headlights picked out a small figure standing in the middle of the parking lot by the Civic Centre. It was Jacky! The head with its freshly-cropped stubble was familiar now. Only why was Jacky standing there in her bra, with her shirt hanging from her hand? Arkan put the gas pedal to the floor once more.

"Arkan!" Kate cried. "That's Jacky!"

"I know. But she's not alone."

Not alone? Kate fumbled for the redcap and stuck it back on her head. The scene in front of her leapt into a new focus. There was Jacky, as before, but there was a man standing with her as well. All around them was a whole forest of gullywudes. Down the steps of the Civic Centre a flood of bogans and other creatures were descending. Not to mention that behind the VW was a third of the Hunt. Perfect. All they needed was a Big Man or two and—

She braced herself, hands against the dash, when she realized what Arkan was up to. As he neared Jacky and the man, he suddenly hauled left on the wheel. The responsible little VW lunged at the nearest bunch of twig-creatures, mowing them down. And like bundled twigs, the gullywudes just seemed to come apart, spraying bits of wood everywhere. Arkan spun the wheel some more. The tires screeched on the pavement as he swept through a second, third, fourth grouping. He made three circuits, then brought the car to a shrieking halt.

This time Kate was prepared. As soon as the car stopped, she had the door open. She scrunched herself forward against the windshield, hauling the seat with her so that Jacky and her friend could get into the back.

"Kate!" Jacky cried. "Oh, God, am I glad to—"

"In, in, IN!" Kate cried.

For the first time Jacky seemed to be aware of the three members of the Hunt. The howl of their bikes was loud, drowning out the cries of the Unseelie Court as it rushed down the final steps of the Civic Centre. Without another word, Jacky crawled into the back seat, tugging on Eilian's arm until he followed her. The Laird's son was still getting in when Arkan pulled away again.

"Now where to?" he asked nobody in particular.

"Some place safe," Kate said quickly. She was leaning over the back seat, grabbing for Jacky's hands. "You're okay! How'd you get out?"

Jacky was a-glow with excitement. "I did it, Kate! I killed a giant. I really did. Just like you said I would."

"You *what*?"

"I killed . . . " Then the wonder of it all drained from Jacky's features as what she was saying hit home. She'd killed someone. Dead. Finito binito. "Oh jeez," she said.

A sick feeling came over her. She began to tremble, her eyes filling with tears, and she buried her face in the shoulder of the young man sitting beside her. Kate looked at him, wanting to know who he was and what part he'd had in all of this when Arkan demanded her attention again.

"Mistress Kate," he said. "*Where* safe?"

He was still going around in circles in the parking lot. The headlights kept giving them glimpses of hordes of gullywudes, bogans, hags, shelly-coats and goblins. And the three riders of the Hunt. As he drew near to the latter, Arkan suddenly dropped into a lower gear and tromped the gas pedal, twisting the wheel at the same time. The VW's fender clipped the nearest biker's machine. He went flying, his bike skidding across the pavement in a shower of sparks.

"I don't knoooow!" Kate wailed. Everything was just too wild.

"A restaurant," the stranger in the back seat said. "A place with lots of light and many people."

"Right," Arkan said. He straightened the wheel and aimed Judith for the gates of the parking lot.

Kate took a deep steadying breath, let it out. Too quickly, but it didn't matter. It had helped.

"That won't stop them . . . will it?" she asked.

"With Cormoran dead," the stranger said, "the creatures have no leader to tell them what to do. They naturally avoid the well-lit public places of man, even in a moment such as this — unless ordered otherwise."

"She really killed one of the Big Men?" Arkan asked.

"Wart-nosed Cormoran — and she did it all on her own."

"Damn," Arkan muttered. He brought the car out onto the road in a skidding turn, then immediately slowed down and tried to blend in with the sporadic traffic on Bank Street. "That I'd like to have seen."

"What about the Hunt?" Kate asked. "Won't they still follow?"

"They'll follow," the stranger said.

Kate sighed. "And they won't be happy. We hurt one of them back there."

Jacky's companion shook his head. "Discomforted him, perhaps, but the riders of the Hunt are not so easily hurt."

"Then what'll stop them?"

"The death of Cormoran for the time being. That will leave them without orders. They'll follow us, I think — the two that are still mounted, the third if his machine was not too badly damaged — but I doubt they'll do more for now."

He was stroking Jacky's head, comforting her as he spoke. Jacky's shirt was a bunched-up ball in her hands.

"Who are you?" Kate asked.

"My name's Eilian. Your friend rescued me from the Unseelie Court."

Kate shook her head, her lips forming a soundless "wow." *Her* Jacky had done all this? She reached through to the back seat, adding her own comfort to what Eilian offered, even if it was just a pat on the knee.

"Maybe you should get her shirt on," she said. Through the rear window she could see two of the Hunt following. "If we want to get into a restaurant, it'd help."

Understatement of the week. The way they all looked, she wondered where they'd all get into. And why wasn't Jacky wearing her shirt? She probably shouldn't even ask. There was so much going on that she felt left behind while everything spun past her in a dizzying whirl.

They were over Lansdowne Bridge again, past Sunnyside, going down the long hill that Bank Street made before it crossed the Rideau River at Billings Bridge. This was an odd strip—antique stores and bookshops side by side with bicycle and auto repair stores. Hillary's Cleaners came up on the left. The South Garden—a Chinese restaurant—was on the right, but it was too quiet.

"There!" Kate cried, but Arkan was already pulling into the parking lot.

It was a Dairy Queen. Lit up. Huge glass windows so that you could see all around. And even this late in October, it had lots of people in it. Kate leaned over the back seat as Arkan parked the car. Jacky sat up and squirmed into her shirt, looking the worse for wear with her rumpled clothes and the wild stubble of her hair. But she seemed to have a grip on herself again. A small smile touched her lips.

"Let's all go to the Dairy Queen," she sang quietly to the tune of its familiar advertisements.

"You ass," Kate said, but she could have kissed her.

She opened the door on her side and stepped out nervously. She looked around once, twice, then spotted the two black riders sitting on their Harleys in the lot of the gas station across the street. Arkan looked at her from over the roof of the car.

"Are you sure we'll be okay here?" she asked him.

Arkan shook his head. "No. But what else can we do?"

Good question, Kate thought. She stood aside as Eilian and Jacky disembarked, then led the way into the restaurant.

Thirteen

Jacky and Kate brought each other up-to-date over burgers, fries and thick milkshakes. They interrupted each other constantly with "You didn't!"s and "I would've died"s, much to the amusement of their faerie companions.

Hilarity sparked between them and Kate thought about what Arkan had said about how Faerie affected mortals who strayed into it. She worried, remembering snatches of old tales telling of poets driven mad by faerie queens and the like, but it was too hard to remain sensible with the way Jacky was carrying on and the giddiness that continued to bubble up inside herself.

There'd been no need to worry about how they looked. The mid-evening Dairy Queen crowd, while not quite as scruffy as the four of them, were hardly fashionable. Polyester and jeans were the order of the day. One man in green and yellow plaid trousers, mismatched with a red and blue striped windbreaker, set them all off again.

Double-dating at the DQ, Kate thought as she looked in the window and caught the reflection of the four of them in their booth. Then she saw the third rider pull up into the parking lot across the street. He put his machine on its kickstand beside the other two bikes, then walked over to where his companions stood under a billboard advertising Daniel Hechter sweatshirts.

What struck Kate first and foremost was that she wasn't wearing the redcap at the moment. It was sitting on the table beside the wrappers of the two burgers that she'd devoured.

"How come I can see them?" she asked, interrupting Jacky in the middle of explaining why she'd been standing with her shirt in her hand when they'd picked her up. "The riders," she added at the general collection of blank looks her question gathered. "I can see all three of them and I'm not wearing the cap."

"Each time you see into Faerie it becomes easier," Arkan said. "Not for all, mind, and quicker for some than for others. You see us don't you?"

"Yes, but—"

"Think of it as a painting that you've had for years. A nice landscape, perhaps. One day someone comes in and says, 'Look at that face in the side of the hill,' and from then on you'll always be aware of that face. Because you'll *know* it's there."

"It's that simple?"

"No," Arkan replied with a grin. "It's faerie magic."

Kate aimed a kick at him under the table, but missed.

"What're we going to do about them?" Jacky asked, indicating the riders with a nod of her head. "We won't be able to do anything with them following us around."

"We must lose them," Eilian said.

Arkan shook his head. "Easy to say, but impossible to do."

"The Gruagagh would know a way," Jacky said.

"But he told you not to go back."

"That was before, Kate. He was afraid they'd get my scent or something. Well, they've got it now, so what harm would there be in going to ask him for advice?"

"One does not go lightly against the wishes of a gruagagh," Eilian said.

"We're not really going to do that," Jacky insisted. "It's just that things have changed. Nothing's the same anymore. We can't go sneaking into the Giants' Keep, because with the Hunt following us we might as well just step right up and ring the front doorbell. We need a trick to get by them and the Gruagagh's the one to give it to us."

"We do need something," Eilian agreed.

"How did you know about Jacky?" Kate asked the Laird of Dunlogan's son, speaking as the thought came to her. "What brought you here looking for her?"

They all looked at him and even Jacky saw him as though for the first time. There was a look about him that set him a cut above the common. His hair was the black of the feathers she remembered, his eyes darker still. A Laird's son was like a prince, wasn't he? Eilian smiled as though reading her thoughts. Unfortunately, Jacky told herself, by that reckoning, the only princess around here was Lorana. Rescuing her could make this whole thing into a regular fairy tale.

"There is a story told in Dunlogan," Eilian said, "that was told before this time of trouble began. It foretold the fading of Faerie, both in Dunlogan and Kinrowan and all the new haunts of our people here in Liomauch Og; warned as well of how the Host would grow stronger in turn. When that time came, there a new Jack would arrive in one of the Seelie Courts, come to cast down the giants as the Jacks have of old."

"I'm not a Jack," Jacky said. "I'm a girl."

Eilian nodded. "Most assuredly, yet the spirits of the Jacks of old is in you. It's a lucky name—as the tales that your people still tell can vouch for."

"I've heard that before," Arkan said. "But where do you fit in?"

"I'm the third son of a third son of—"

"A third son," Arkan finished. "I see."

"Well, I don't," Kate said.

"It's like in the stories, isn't it?" Jacky asked.

Eilian nodded again. "The histories of Faerie tend to repeat themselves as much as your own do."

"You see," Jacky said, turning to Kate to explain it. "It's always the youngest son—not the eldest or the middle, but the third, the youngest son, that wins through in the end. It's in all the stories."

"Why?"

"Oh, Kate. I don't know. Because that's the way it works."

"But this isn't a story."

119

"It might as well be one." Jacky grinned. "Hobs and giants and bogans and all. It makes me feel light-headed."

"I shouldn't wonder. You've lost about ten pounds of hair."

Jacky turned to her reflection, lifting a hand to the blonde stubble. "Oh, God! Look at me! I'd forgotten how terrible I looked."

"That's the least of our problems," Kate said.

"That's easy for you to say."

"I just did."

Jacky tried out a fierce look on Kate but couldn't hold it. The two erupted in laughter leaving Eilian and Arkan shaking their heads. Arkan turned to the Laird's son.

"I think it's something about the air of Faerie," he said. "Even in a place like this."

"Either that," Eilian said, "or mortals *are* all mad."

Jacky finally caught her breath. "You were saying?" she prompted.

"Times have been bad," Eilian said after a moment or two, "and getting worse. When word came north of how Gyre the Elder was moving his Court into Kinrowan, our Billy Blind said it was time now for me to go and help as I could. Three knots he tied in my hair, one for each—"

"What's a Billy Blind?" Jacky asked, interrupting.

Arkan replied. "It's a custom we brought with us from the old country. Every Court has one—a man or woman who has been crippled or blinded. They can often see into the days to come and the old magics run strong in them—as recompense, some say. Even your folk had them in the old days."

Jacky's mouth shaped a small "O." Then she turned to Eilian. "And he tied knots in your hair?"

Eilian nodded. "One for each mortal danger I must face. Here, look." He turned his head so that Jacky could see two small braided knots of hair that hung behind his right ear.

"There's only two."

Eilian nodded again, adding a smile. "That's because one's come undone—after you rescued me from the Unseelie Court this evening."

"You mean you've got to go through that two more times?"

"That . . . or something like it."

"Oh." The prospect wasn't very pleasing to Jacky. "Well, at

least you know you'll be okay, won't you? I mean, something'll happen, and you'll pull through until both those knots are gone as well—right?"

"It's not that assured, unfortunately," Eilian replied.

"It's usually that way with augurings," Arkan added.

"Easy for you to say,' " Kate said, "seeing how you don't have knots in your hair."

Arkan smiled. "How do you know what I do or do not have in my hair?"

"The thing we've got to do," Jacky said, "is get out of here." She didn't like all this talk about hair and who had what in theirs. "I say we make our way to the Gruagagh's Tower and stay there tonight, then head out for Calabogie first thing in the morning."

"And the Hunt?" Arkan asked.

"I've got a plan."

Kate looked at Jacky and shook her head. "I don't think I'm going to like this at all," she said.

Over Kate's protests, Jacky took her jacket and went to the washroom. Moments later the door opened and Kate saw her friend come out, but knew that no one else would, for she was wearing the blue jacket now, with its hob-spelled stitcheries. She frowned at Arkan and Eilian, neither of whom had objected to Jacky's plan because they were both enamoured with the fact that she was "the Jack, after all. She killed a giant, didn't she?"

Jacky waited by the door until a customer was leaving, then winked at Kate and slipped out behind him. It took all of Kate's willpower not to stare out the window and watch Jacky's progress. Jacky might be invisible to the Hunt, but if Kate and her two faeric companions had their noses pressed up to the window, the riders would soon know that something was up.

Count to a hundred, Jacky had said. Staring daggers at the two faerie in the booth with her who had let Jacky go through with her plan, Kate began to count.

Once she was outside, Jacky's confidence, fueled by Eilian and Arkan's admiring agreement to her plan, began to falter. There were too many shadows around her. The wind rustled leaves and the odd bit of refuse up and down the street, effectively swallowing any tell-tale sounds that might have warned her of approaching bogans and the like.

A car pulled into the Dairy Queen's parking lot, almost running her down. She was about to shout something at the foolidiot-jerk, then realized that the poor sod behind the wheel couldn't have seen her. Not with the jacket on. She glanced back at the restaurant where Kate and the others were playing their part. Then, biting at her lower lip, she faced the three riders of the Hunt across the street from her.

This, she realized, might not be one of her brightest ideas. But it was too late to back out now. They had to do something. It was that, or dawdle around the old DQ until the place closed and they were kicked out. By then who knew how many of the Unseelie Court would be skulking around looking for tasty mortals to gnaw on.

She shivered, remembering her helplessness in the Civic Centre. But you got away, she told herself. And you did kill a giant. They'll be scared of *you* now. Right. Sure.

She started across the street.

Fifty-five, fifty-six.

Surely she could dare a peek?

Fifty-seven, fifty-eight.

Kate's nerves were all jangling. She should have insisted that she be the one to go out. At least then she wouldn't be stuck inside here worrying.

Sixty, sixty-one.

She glanced casually out the window, saw Jacky starting across the street, then just as casually stretched and looked back at her companions.

"I wonder what's taking her so long in there," she said to Arkan who obligingly turned and looked at the door to the washroom.

Sixty-nine, seventy.

He shrugged as he looked back at her. "Maybe she's looking for knots in her hair," he said.

Eilian and Kate laughed.

Seventy-four.

Kate wondered if Eilian's laugh sounded as hollow to him as hers did to her.

Seventy-six.

If I was a Huntsman, she thought, I'd *know* something was up, just by the way we're all sitting in this booth like a bunch of geeks.

Eighty, eighty-one.

As she passed by the Hunt, Jacky was tempted to grab something and whack one of them over the head, but all she did was go by as softly as she could, positive that they could hear her knees rattling against each other, her teeth chattering, her pulse drumming out: "HereIam, hereIam!" And then, just when she was as close to them as her path would take her, one of them lifted his head and looked around himself uneasily.

Oh, shit, Jacky thought.

Close as she was, she could see that the impression of emptiness under their helmets was caused by visors of nonreflective dark plexiglas. The one who had lifted his head now pushed back his visor and for the first time Jacky got a glimpse at what a Huntsman really looked like. His features surprised her. He seemed quite human—rough and craggy, but human all the same. He didn't have anything like the monstrous visage she'd imagined. Of course the way he looked wasn't going to stop him from giving the alarm once he spotted her. His gaze settled on where she was standing.

This is it, she thought. I'm doomed.

But then a truck went by on the street and she moved quickly with it, hob-stitched sneakers lending her the necessary speed, the truck's passage swallowing any sound she might make. When she reached the position in front of the Bingo Hall that she'd been making for, she looked back to see that the rider had dropped his visor once more, his attention turned elsewhere. Jacky glanced over at the Dairy Queen.

She hadn't been counting herself, so she wasn't sure how long she had to wait. Just a couple of secs, she thought, but time dragged. She peeked back down at the sidewalk at the three riders. She could tell just by looking at them that they knew something was about to happen, they just didn't know what.

Hang in there, fellas, she thought. The show's about to start.

She wondered why she was so thirsty. Her throat felt like somebody had rubbed it with sandpaper. Come on, Kate. How long can it take to get to—

A hundred.

This is it, Kate thought. She got up and knocked on the door of the washroom while Arkan went outside to the car. Eilian stood by the door waiting for her. She knocked again, looked across the street to see the riders moving to their bikes, then glanced at Arkan. His head was under the dashboard looking for the ignition wires. When Judith coughed into life, he sat up and grinned at them, then tromped on the gas. The VW leapt across the parking lot with a squeal of tires.

Jacky waited, her coat unbuttoned, until the VW started. Then she pulled off the jacket and stepped out from under the awning of the Bingo Hall and onto the pavement.

"Hey, bozos!" she cried.

The riders, moving for their Harleys, paused at the sound of her voice. She couldn't see the surprise register on their faces because of their dark plexiglas visors, but their indecision was plain in their body language.

Do it! she willed to Arkan.

At that moment the VW came tearing out of the parking lot. Jacky moved towards the riders, but slowly, making them hesitate. Then Arkan was aiming Judith at their bikes.

He hit the brakes as he neared the big choppers and the car slewed sideways. It hit the first bike and sent it crashing into the others. The riders leapt out of the way as the three machines toppled. Arkan brought Judith to an abrupt halt, backed up, popped the clutch back into first. The transmission shrieked. He floored the gas again, driving the bikes against one another and up against a streetlamp. Jacky didn't stay to watch any more.

She ran across the street for the front door of the Dairy Queen where Kate and Eilian were waiting. They watched Arkan back Judith away from the bikes and roar across the street to where they waited. The fenders and front trunk of the little car were a mess—crushed in, bumper hanging askew, one headlight dangling from the left side, the other shining straight up into the sky on the right.

"My car!" Kate wailed. "It's ruined!"

Arkan pulled to a screeching stop and Eilian opened the passenger's door. Grabbing Kate's arm, Jacky propelled her into the car. They both got into the back—Kate under protest. Eilian was half in when Arkan pulled away. He turned left at Riverdale, moving quickly through the gears up to third.

"It worked!" Jacky cried. She twisted around, peering out the back window. She could see the riders trying to untangle their machines. "We've lost them."

"I've had this car for seven years," Kate said.

"We'll get you another one," Jacky told her.

"You can't buy these anymore—not like Judith." She glared at Jacky. "How could you do this to Judith?"

"I . . . " It had been such a good plan, Jacky thought. And it had worked too. But she'd never really thought about what it would do to Kate's car. "Jeez, Kate. I wasn't trying to wreck her."

"God! Imagine if you had been."

"Well, you're the one who insisted on coming along."

"I . . . " Now it was Kate's turn to deflate. "I suppose I did. It's just that . . . "

Jacky gave her a hug. "We'll get her fixed up," she promised. "We'll make the Gruagagh put a spell on her."

"Do you think he would?"

"Your chance to ask him is coming right up," Arkan said from the front seat as he pulled into the driveway beside the house that was the Gruagagh's Tower.

The front yard was all overgrown as well, though not so badly as the back. A tall oak stood sentinel on the lawn, branches bare of leaves spreading overhead. A rundown garage, its door closed and the whole structure leaning a bit to one side, crouched at the end of the driveway. The house was dark. It looked, at that moment, more deserted than ever.

"End of the line," Arkan said.

Eilian got out first. As Jacky and Kate disembarked, he opened the garage door. There was plenty of room inside, so Arkan drove Judith in, then reached down and undid the wires, killing the engine. Eilian closed the garage door behind Arkan and they rejoined Jacky and Kate.

"Jeez," Jacky said, looking at the dark house.

Second and third thoughts were busily cluttering up her mind. Her stupid throat had gone all dry again. She swallowed with a grimace.

"I hope he's in a good mood," she said as she led the way to the front door and knocked.

Fourteen

When subsequent knocking, and even a few well placed kicks against the Gruagagh's door elicited no response, Jacky tried the doorknob. To her surprise, it turned easily under her hand and the door swung open. Shadows fled down the hallway, banished by the vague illumination of the streetlights behind her. But some of them seemed to move in the wrong direction. For a moment she thought she saw a coatrack against the wall by the door, but as soon as she looked at it, it was gone. There were vague sounds, creakings and stirrings that seemed more than just an old house settling in on itself.

She could remember Bhruic telling her that this was the best protected place in Laird's lands. Oh, really? Then how come it was so easy to get in?

"Bhruic?" she called down the hallway. It was still filled with shadows, but now they lay motionless. The creaks and stirring quieted. "Are you there, Bhruic?"

Her voice echoed through the house. The stillness that followed was absolute. A horrible feeling began to rise in her. She remembered her first visit here. It was hard to forget the tall, forbidding Gruagagh, the sly movements spied in the shadows and the ghostly furniture that never really seemed to be there when you looked straight at it. She started forward, but a quick brown hand closed its fingers around her arm and hauled her back.

"You *never* go unbidden into a Gruagagh's Tower," Arkan warned.

"I don't think he's here anymore," Jacky said, shaking her arm free.

"He has to be," Kate said.

Jacky's bad feeling grew more pronounced. Something was definitely wrong here. Either the Unseelie Court had found a way to breach Bhruic's defenses or . . . or he had left on his own. Either way, she felt betrayed.

"I'm going in," she said. "Whoever wants to can wait out here, but I'm going in."

She moved into the hallway and this time no one tried to stop her. Kate hesitated, then followed with Eilian. Arkan stood uncertainly on the stoop. He looked back at the deserted street, cars parked in neat rows along one side, houses spilling rectangularly-shaped yellow lights from their windows onto their lawns. Swallowing once, he faced the Tower again and went inside.

A feeling of certain doom made his chest go tight as he crossed the threshold and he found it hard to breathe. His faerie senses could see deeper into the shadows, could hear far more clearly. There was a feeling of *otherness* all about him. But as he closed the door and followed the others down the hall, and still nothing happened—no lightning bolts, no angry Gruagagh roaring at them—his initial fears quieted a little. But only to make room for new ones.

If the Gruagagh *wasn't* here, what hope was left for them? The Gruagagh held the heart of the Laird's kingdom in trust. If he had betrayed them . . . The rumors that had abounded when the Unseelie Court stole away the Laird's daughter returned to haunt him. Oh, moon and stars! If the Gruagagh was in league with the Host . . .

"Where could he be?" Jacky whispered. "He promised— promised!—me he couldn't leave the Tower."

"Maybe he doesn't know we're here," Eilian said. "He could be upstairs, out of earshot . . . "

"Look," Kate said.

She was standing by an open doorway, pointing in. The others joined her. They could see Windsor Park through the room's windows. Phantom furniture came and went as they looked about, then the room appeared to be empty, except for a small figure lying on a huddle of blankets in a corner.

"It's Finn," Jacky said, crossing the room.

She knelt by the little man and touched his shoulder. His eyelids fluttered at her touch. His eyes opened to look, first at her, then over her shoulder where Kate and the other two members of their small company stood.

"Where . . . where am I?" he asked.

"In the Tower," Jacky said.

The little man's features blanched. "The . . . the Gruagagh's Tower?"

Jacky nodded. "Where is he, Finn?"

"Where . . . ?" The hob sat up, a hand rising to rub at his temple. "The last thing I remember is the bogans grabbing you and then something hitting me harder than I ever care to be hit again . . . " His voice trailed off as his fingers explored his scalp. "At least I thought I was hit on the head. But there's not even a bump."

"The Gruagagh fixed you up," Kate said.

"And now he's gone," Jacky added, trying to keep the hurt from her voice.

Why did he lie to her? Finding Finn here, alive and unhurt, proved that the Host hadn't stormed the place. So where could the Gruagagh have gone? And why?

"I'm going to look around some more," she said. "Kate can you show me that room upstairs?"

Kate nodded, but it was Arkan who spoke.

"We should go," he said. "It's bad enough we're in his Tower without his leave; it'll be worse if we go poking and prying."

"The Gruagagh is gone?" Finn asked. "And you're spying on him? Jacky Rowan, are you mad?"

"Angry, maybe, but not the kind of mad you mean. Come on, Kate."

The two women left the room with Eilian and began to explore the other rooms. "This is bad," they could hear Finn mutter behind them as they started up the stairs. "This is very bad."

The halls and rooms upstairs were all dark, free of dust and unfurnished, and there was no one there. There were no ghostly furnishings anymore, no sense of sly movement in the deeper shadows. Jacky had an eerie feeling moving through the deserted house. She felt like a ghost, like she didn't belong here or anywhere anymore. With the Gruagagh's disappearance she had to wonder how much of anything that he'd told her was true.

Why did he want her to go to the Giants' Keep? What if Lorana wasn't there? Or if she was already dead? If he was in league with the Unseelie Court, he might have been setting her and Kate up for . . . well, God knew what. When she thought of the bogans and their prodding fingers, the hunger in their eyes . . . She didn't plan to end up in a stew, that much was certain.

"I can't find it," Kate said.

They were on the third floor now and had been in and out of every room at least a half dozen times.

"A room can't just disappear," Jacky said.

"A gruagagh's can," Eilian said. "Our Billy Blind has places he can sit and never the one of us can see or find him until he suddenly steps out—as if from nowhere."

"A Billy Blind's like a gruagagh, isn't he?" Jacky asked. "Sort of a poor man's gruagagh?"

Eilian nodded. "My father's Court is not so big as some—not so big as Kinrowan, that's for certain. And we have no gruagagh to spell the Samhaine charms—only a Billy Blind."

"Well, what do you do on Samhaine Eve then?"

"Hide and hope."

"Hide and hope," Jacky repeated. She looked around the third floor landing where they were standing. "Can you hear me, Bhruic Dearg? Are you hiding somewhere near? Well, come out and talk to us, dammit!" She stamped her foot on the wooden floor, but its echoes were the only sound that replied. "Was everything he told me a lie?" she asked no one in particular.

Eilian shook his head. "There *is* a Horn that rules the Hunt and the Laird of Kinrowan's daughter *was* stolen by the Unseelie Court—those weren't lies. And you, Jacky. You are the only Jack we have now."

"I wish you'd stop calling me that. I'm a woman. You make me sound like a sailor."

"It's a title," Eilian said. "Like 'Billy Blind.' Our Billy Blind's not named Billy, nor even William."

She forced a small smile to her lips. "I guess we might as well go back downstairs. Do you think this place'll be safe enough for us tonight? I don't see us going to Calabogie tonight, but the way we all just waltzed in here . . . I don't know."

"So we're still going?" Kate asked.

"What else can we do?" she asked. "With or without the Gruagagh, we've still got the Host to contend with. The only idea worth following through on is the one we started out with — get the Horn and use it to find and free Lorana. The Laird's folk will rally around her and, if we've got the Horn, then we control the Hunt. After we use it to find Lorana, we can turn the Hunt on the Unseelie Court and see how they like being on the receiving end for a change."

"This is still a gruagagh's Tower," Eilian said. "I think we'll be safe here — from Gyre the Elder's people at any rate. But if the Gruagagh returns and decides he doesn't care to guest us . . . "

"If the Gruagagh shows up," Jacky said, "he'll be too busy answering a question or two that I've got for him to be bothering anyone. Believe me."

"Getting real fierce, are we?" Kate said to her as they started down the stairs.

"Oh, jeez, Kate. Am I getting too weird?"

Kate shook her head. "With bogans and gruagaghs and men that turn into swans running around? I don't think so, kid. It's about time you got a little fierce."

Jacky sighed. "Can you just see Will's face if he could see us now? And he thought I was too predictable."

"Maybe we should stop by his place tonight," Kate said with a grin. "We can see how he likes standing off a bunch of bogans for us while we get a little sleep."

"Oh, wouldn't I just!"

"Who's Will?" Eilian asked.

Jacky glanced at him. "Just somebody I never knew," she said.

Very fierce, Kate thought approvingly. Whatever else this madcap affair left them, at least it had finally brought Jacky out of her shell. Not that Kate had ever agreed with Will. His idea of bar-andpartyhopping as the means to having a fulfilled life wasn't exactly her concept of what Jacky had needed. All Jacky needed was some confidence in herself. With some confidence, Kate knew Jacky could do anything. And she was proving it now.

Fifteen

When Kate left him, her recriminations still ringing in his ears, the Gruagagh of Kinrowan returned to the third floor room with its view of the city in miniature. He marked the various positions of the riders of the hunt, the gathering of bogans and hags, gullywudes, trolls and other creatures of the Unseelie Court. Of the Laird's folk there were few and, of those few he could see, all save the odd forester were hiding.

Not so the Host.

As night fell, he watched the sluagh rise from their marshy beds. The trolls under their bridges grew bolder. Packs of gullywudes and spriggans and other unwholesome, if minor, members of the Unseelie Court ran up and down the city streets, chasing leaves and the pets of humans, and sometimes humans as well. They never showed themselves. Instead they teased with fingers like wind and voices like wind, awaking fears that didn't settle even when the humans were safe within their homes and the doors closed on the eerie night.

He could not see into the building where the bogans held Jacky captive, but he could imagine what went on in there. The greedy faces pressed close to her, feeding on her fear as much as the smell of her. If the giants didn't want her for their own, the stew pots would already be heating. She would be despairing . . .

"Use your wits, woman," he whispered into the night. "Why do you think the powers that be gave them to you, if not to use?"

But then he saw the new captive that the Host brought into the building. The swan wings would have told anyone what the new captive was, but even without them Bhruic would have known. He had not served Lairdsfolk for so long as he had without recognizing them; by sight, by sound, by smell, no matter what shape they wore. He recognized who this young Lairdling was, too. Dunlogan's son. His third son. Eilian. The Giants' Keep would ring with celebrations tonight. A new Lairdling to add to their bestiary, and a Jack as well.

He closed his eyes, not to shut away the sight of what lay in front of him, but to seek council inside. He let his inner turmoil rise and fret, caught each fear and loosed it from inside him like so many freed birds until only silence lay there, deep and soothing. And filled with possibilities. They lay like threads in front of his closed eyes, going every-which-way, unraveling into pasts and presents and times yet to come. He couldn't work them, couldn't weave them, that was for other hands more skilled than his, but he could take one thread, one possibility, and tie his need to it, then send it forth from his silence like a summoning call.

For a long time he stood by the window, motionless, sightless as Eilian's Billy Blind, which was to say he saw not the world around him, but the worlds within. He stood and waited, without expectations, but open to what might come; not hoping, but neither did he feel hopeless. And the first inkling he had that his call was answered was a sound that appeared to rise up from inside him, it seemed so close. A rhythm like hooves drumming on long hills, a winding call like a horn sounding, a melody that was fiddling, piping, harping—all at once.

"I hear you, Gruagagh," a voice said softly. "Has the time come for you to set aside your spells and come with me for good?"

Bhruic opened his eyes. Before him, lounging on the windowsill, was a slender man who wore trousers and a jacket that looked to be made of heather and twigs and leaves all woven together; whose feet were unshod for they were hooves; whose red-gold hair fell in curls around an old-young face; whose eyes were too dark and too deep and too wise to be the eyes of mortal or faerie. He held a fiddle loosely in the crook of his arm, an instrument of polished wood with a head carved into the semblance of a stag's. He reached out and tapped Bhruic with the end of his bow.

"Well?" he asked.

Bhruic shook his head. "I need a small favour."

The stranger smiled. "I doubt it's that simple."

"It never is," Bhruic agreed.

"You play your hand too much in shadow," the stranger said. "But you know that already, don't you?"

The fiddle went up under his chin and the bow licked across its strings. The melody he played was both merry and sad and he didn't play it for long. When he was done, he studied Bhruic for a time.

"You were a poet first," he said finally. "A bard. You could have been the best poet we had. Do you still remember what it was like before you let wizardry rule your life?"

"There was no one else to do what needed to be done, Kerevan. Kinrowan had no gruagagh."

"And were you truly the man for the task? Will all the music and song you never played or wrote be worth it?"

Bhruic made no reply.

Kerevan smiled. "So be it. What small favour do you need, Gruagagh of Kinrowan? And ask me not again to look for the Laird's daughter you lost, for you know I can't."

"It's the one called Jacky Rowan," Bhruic said.

A fiddle string rang out as Kerevan plucked it. "Ah," he said. "That one."

He leaned back so that the Gruagagh could look out the window. Bhruic saw the tiny figures of Jacky and Eilian in the parking lot of Lansdowne Park, surrounded by bogans and gullywudes, saw Kate's Volkswagen pulling in off Bank Street.

"But the giant . . . ?"

"She killed it. She's a Rowan and Jack—haven't you said so yourself? What she doesn't win through pluck, she wins through luck. That was always the way with Jacks—even in the old days. She'll be cannier than even she knows herself, that one."

"It's still a long road to the Giants' Keep."

Kerevan nodded. "That it is. And a great deal can happen to

one upon the road these days, if you take my meaning," he added with a sly wink. Then he frowned. "You shouldn't meddle with the Host, Bhruic. Nor with the Laird's Court either. Our kind were not meant to strike bargains with either—you know that."

"Do I have a choice?" Bhruic asked.

"You always have a choice—no matter who you bargain with. But speaking of bargains, what will ours be? What's its worth? Will you go with me?"

Silence lay between them as Bhruic hesitated. Then finally he sighed.

"On Samhaine day," he said. "If all goes well."

"On Samhaine day no matter how it goes," Kerevan returned.

Bhruic hesitated again.

"Don't you trust your luck?" Kerevan asked.

"On Samhaine day," Bhruic agreed.

"Done!"

Up went the fiddle again, under Kerevan's chin, and down went the bow. The tune that spilled forth was a mixture of three or four reels that he tumbled together willy-nilly, but with great feeling. Laying aside the bow, he grinned.

"But mind," he said. "You're not to talk to Host or Seelie Court till my return—I'll not have you making new bargains on top of the one we have ourselves."

Bhruic nodded.

"Now what's this small favour you'd have in return?" Kerevan asked.

The Gruagagh sat beside him on the windowsill. "This is what I'd have you do," he said.

When they were done making bargains, Kerevan picked up his fiddle again. Hopping about on his cloven hooves, he sawed away at his fiddle until the room rang with the sound of his music. Bhruic could feel his own blood quicken.

"Until Samhaine, Kerevan," he said.

He closed his eyes. The threads were there once more, moving and weaving in time to Kerevan's reels. Bhruic unravelled the one that had brought the fiddler. The music faded and when he opened his eyes he was alone once more.

He meditated for a long time in that room that looked out on more views than it should. When he heard Jacky and her companions arrive, he spoke the necessary words that would hide him and the room from any but another gruagagh's sight, in the same way that a Billy Blind will speak a word and sit unnoticed in a corner of his Laird's hearth, forever and a day if that was what he wished. Bhruic meant to keep his side of the bargain, just as he knew Kerevan, capable of mischief as he was, would keep his.

He heard Jacky and Kate and the Laird of Dunlogan's son stomping about on the third floor, looking for him, looking for this room, but the sounds came as though from a great distance. When he gazed out the window once more, the grand view of Ottawa was gone.

In place of the panorama of the Laird's holdings, he saw only the street below. There were gullywudes down there, sniffing and creeping about on twig-thin limbs. Bogans, sluagh, and a troll too. At the far end of the street, a Huntsman sat astride his motorcycle, featureless in the shadows that cloaked him from all eyes but those of sacrio. Then he saw Kerevan wandering down below as well, fiddle under his chin and playing a tune.

The music of Kerevan's fiddle drove them all away. The gullywudes scurried away and hid. The bogans snarled and made threatening gestures, but they too finally retreated. The sluagh hissed and whispered, faded like mist. Last to go was the troll, snuffling as he wandered aimlessly down the street, hitting the concrete with a big wooden club as he went. A forester from the Laird's Court happened by then, but he too was sent off by the spell in the fiddler's music.

Then only Kerevan was there, hooves clicking, fiddle playing. And the rider. Motionless in his shadows. And that was the way it remained for the rest of the night.

Sixteen

"I dreamt I heard a fiddle play — all night long," Jacky said when she woke the next morning.

They had slept in the room overlooking Windsor Park, the five of them sharing the blankets that the Gruagagh had left for Finn, the hard wooden floor for their mattress. They woke in various moods of discomfort. Finn and Arkan were nervous about their surroundings. Kate hadn't appreciated the meager sleeping arrangements and felt a bit grumpy, while Jacky was still fuming about the Gruagagh's disappearance. Only Eilian was cheerful.

"I heard it too," he said. "And I thought I knew that music — or at least who played it — but it's not so clear now that the sun's up and I'm more awake."

"Unseelie musicians, that's who played outside this Tower last night," Finn said. "Who else would be abroad in Kinrowan? Only the Unseelie Court . . . and gruagaghs. Oh, we're in for a bad time, I just know it."

"The Host has gruagaghs too?" Jacky asked.

"Every court has wizards of one sort or another," Arkan said. "Even your own folk."

"Can't trust them either," Finn added. "Not one of them. And the Gruagagh of Kinrowan himself is in league with Moon knows what."

"He fixed you up," Kate pointed out.

"For what?" Finn asked. "For why? No good'll come of it — mark my words."

Jacky looked away from the window. She'd been standing there, watching the sunlight fill the park. She felt better now, with the night gone. She hadn't just heard music last night. She'd heard the whispering sound of sluagh around the Tower, the restless dead calling out in their mournful voices. Not close, not as close as the fiddling, but too close for comfort.

"We'll just have to make our own good," she said. "And we'll start by going to Calabogie. Now, while the sun's up and the Host's not so strong. Unless anyone's got any better suggestions?"

Kate looked up from where she sat, cleaning her nails with her little Swiss penknife. "Breakfast?" she tried.

"We can stop for it along the way."

"I'm ready to go," Eilian said and one by one the others nodded, even Finn.

"Don't we make a grand company," the hob muttered as they followed Jacky to the front of the house. "We've got Gyre and all his kin just shaking in their boots, I'm sure."

"She did kill a giant," Arkan said, nodding ahead to Jacky.

"There's that," Finn agreed.

Jacky had reached the front door and flung it open. Standing on the steps, arms akimbo, she looked up and down the street. October sun was bright in the crisp air. The grey pavement of the sidewalks and streets was ablaze with the colour of dried leaves that scurried and spun down their lengths. With her redcap on, though she didn't really need it anymore, Jacky studied every possible hiding place, and a few more besides, but could see nothing. Not anything dangerous. Not anything at all. They could easily be alone in the world, the street was that quiet.

"They're not here," Arkan said wonderingly. "I knew we could lose the Hunt for a while, but I thought sure they'd have tracked us down by now. Yet there's not a soul to be seen."

Jacky nodded, though she still sensed something watching them. She couldn't spot whatever it was. "It'll be a tight squeeze — five of us in Judith," she said to Kate.

"I'm still going," Kate said.

"Of course you are. I'm just saying it's going to be cramped, that's all."

"Kerevan," Arkan said suddenly.

Jacky gave him a strange look. "What?"

"Last night—the fiddling you heard. It was Kerevan playing."

"Who or what is Kerevan?" Kate asked.

"No one's all that sure," Finn explained. "There's some say he was here when the first faerie arrived, others say he's of mixed blood—that of Kinrowan and that of the native faerie."

Eilian nodded. "That's right. I've heard that story. And he's mostly seen in Kinrowan's lands—if he's seen at all. But that hasn't been for many years."

"What does it matter?" Jacky asked.

"Well, before the Gruagagh of Kinrowan became the Gruagagh, he was prenticed as a bard. He went into the Borderlands between Kinrowan and Dunlogan and prenticed himself to Kerevan, who learned his own craft from the old Bucca, Salamon Brien. There was a great to-do about it—especially in those days when we didn't have the Host to worry about so much—because the Bucca's one of the fiaina sidhe, you see, those faerie who bow to no Laird."

Finn nodded in agreement with what Eilian was saying. "There's always been a strain of something strange following the Gruagagh of Kinrowan," he said. "If it's not prenticing himself to Kerevan, it's becoming the Gruagagh in the first place. If it's not being the best of both—poet and wizard—it's losing the Laird's daughter to Gyre the Elder and suffering no more than a few hurts himself."

"But what's wrong with this Kerevan?" Kate asked.

"Why, he's dead," Arkan said. "He's been dead for a hundred and fifty years."

"So it was his ghost we heard last night . . . ?"

"Oh, great," Jacky said. "That's all we need. I think it's time we hopped to it. We can exchange all the ghostly stories you want on the drive up, but let's get going."

She led the way to the garage, as she'd led the way out of the Gruagagh's Tower. Taking the lead was coming naturally to her— which was odd enough in its way, she thought. But odder still was the way the others were deferring to her. It came, she supposed, from killing giants. This morning she didn't feel weird about that. It was as though she'd seen an exciting, if a little bit overly gruesome, movie the night before and, while she could remember what had happened, the gory details weren't so clear anymore.

Arkan lifted the garage door and they all stared at the car.

"Judith!" Kate cried. "Look at her!"

"She's never going to make it," Jacky said.

"Oh, we'll get her running," Arkan said.

With Eilian's help, and Kate fussing about over their shoulders like a concerned mother, Arkan managed to bang the VW's fenders into a semblance of their proper shape. A piece of wire pulled taut around each of the lights had them pointing straight again. The dent in the bumper they banged out with a rock from the Gruagagh's garden.

"Well, what do you think?" Arkan asked, finally, stepping back to admire his own handiwork.

"We'll get her fixed up properly as soon as we're back," Jacky promised, cutting Kate off in the middle of a rant about what exactly was wrong, everything was wrong, were they blind that the couldn't see that poor Judith was just so much junk now thanks to ...

Jacky squeezed into the back with Kate and Finn. Eilian and Arkan rode up front with Arkan driving. The car started smoothly as Arkan connected the ignition wires. He backed out of the garage and onto the street at a reasonable speed that bore no resemblance to last night's flamboyant ride. Jacky peered out the back window and all around as they drove off but, while the feeling of being watched persisted—they *were* being watched—she couldn't see by whom, or from where. Then they were on Riverdale. The Gruagagh's street was left behind, and with it, the feeling.

Hobs weren't the only beings that could stitch invisibility. Hidden through the Hunt's special magics, one of the nine riders watched and waited. As soon as the VW started up in the Gruagagh's garage, the rider kick-started his Harley. He waited until the VW was almost at the end of the block, then fed the bike some gas. But before it could pull away, the music started.

It came from all around him, catching him unaware. His hands went lax on the handlebars. The bike coughed and stalled. The rider slumped in his seat and the machine began to totter. Before it fell over, a lithe figure with cloven feet slipped forward and leaned his own weight against the bike, keeping it upright, all the while playing his fiddle.

The rider was firmly snared in the music's spell—something Kerevan had only accomplished by taking the rider by surprise. It wouldn't last long. He lifted the bow from his fiddle and slid the pair of them into the sack that hung from his shoulder. Then he took a firmer grip on the motorcycle and let the rider slide off it, onto the ground. He grinned down at the fallen Huntsman as he straddled the machine.

"Oh, my," he said, kicking the Harley into life once more. "Won't this be something."

He roared out of the rider's hiding place in time to see the VW turn onto Riverdale. Giving a jaunty wave towards the window where he knew the Gruagagh was watching, he fed the bike some more gas with a relaxed twist of his wrist and sped off in pursuit of the little car, humming a hornpipe under his breath. The tune was "The Tailer's Twist" and most appropriate it was too, he thought.

"It seems fairly straightforward," Jacky said. "We just take the Queensway out to Highway 7, follow that to Arnprior, down 2 until we reach Burnstown, and then the 508 to Calabogie."

She was reading their route from one of Kate's maps that was a part of the clutter underfoot in the cramped back seat.

"But that's just it," Kate said. "If it's that straightforward, won't they have some nasty surprises waiting for us along the way?"

"The other choice is to go down to . . . oh, Perth, say, then take Highway 1 up through Lanark to where it turns into 511—but 511's a pretty windy and hilly road. If we're looking for good ambush country, that'd be it. What do you think, Arkan?"

"We should take the quickest way," he replied. "There'll be enough of the Host around the Keep by day. Come nightfall, their numbers will easily triple."

"What did the Gruagagh suggest?" Finn asked.

Jacky frowned and folded the map with a snap. "What the Gruagagh does or doesn't suggest isn't our concern."

In the front seat, Arkan and Eilian exchanged glances. "Remind me never to get on her bad side," Arkan said in a loud stage whisper.

Jacky gave him a playful whack on the shoulder with the map. "I heard that," she told him.

Leaning forward, she turned on Judith's radio, switching stations until one came on playing the Montreal group Luba's latest single, "Let It Go."

"I like this one," she said with a smile.

She turned up the volume and squeezed back in between Kate and Finn as the lively song with its hint of a Caribbean dance beat filled the car with an infectious rhythm.

They reached the turn-off to Pakenham without incident, having decided to leave the main highway once they'd covered half the distance to Calabogie. The radio had long since been turned off, though Jacky was still singing "Let It Go" under her breath. The bridge in Pakenham was under construction and they had to wait a few minutes before their lane could move. The Mississippi River was on their right, bearing no resemblance to its American cousin except for its name. On the left was a big stone building that had been built in 1840 as a private home, but now housed Andrew Dickson's—a well-known craft and artisan gallery.

"I had a friend who had a showing there," Jacky said. "Remember Judy Shaw?"

Kate nodded.

"I have a cousin who lived there for a while," Finn remarked. "But he had to move because of Grump Kow."

"Now who's Grump Kow?" Kate asked.

"The troll who lives under this bridge they're working on."

"Lovely. I had to ask."

Their lane was clear now and Arkan steered across the bridge. He followed the road into Pakenham, then turned right onto 15. It turned into 23 before they hit White Lake, then they took Highway 2 into Burnstown.

"I'm starving!" Jacky said and insisted they stop at the Burnstown General Store.

It was an old brick building and, in honour of the approaching

Halloween, had pumpkins lining the concrete steps leading up to the front door, and a straw man in Wellie boots, jeans and a plaid shirt tied to one of the porch supports. They filled up on coffee, sandwiches and donuts, sitting on the porch while they ate.

"So far we're clear," Arkan said. "I'm not sure if that makes me feel good or not."

"Doesn't it mean that we've lost them for sure?" Kate asked.

"Not really. They know where we're going. I'm afraid the reason we're being left alone now is because they're preparing something really horrible for us in Calabogie."

Finn stared at his half-eaten donut. "All of a sudden, I'm not hungry anymore."

"Time we were going anyway," Jacky said with false jollity.

"Easy for you to say—you've already finished eating."

"Don't mind her, Finn," Kate said. "She's feeling terribly fierce these days."

Eilian laughed as he gathered up their wrappers and empty coffee cups and dumped them in a garbage barrel at the end of the porch.

"All aboard!" Arkan called.

They piled back into the VW, Jacky leaning into the front seats again as she tried to see just what it was that Arkan did with the wires to make the car start without a key. Judith coughed into life without Jacky being any the wiser as to exactly how it had been managed, and then they were off again, taking 508 on the last leg of their journey to Calabogie.

Cloaked in a spell that hid him far better than either a hob's stitcheries or a Huntsman's magics, Kerevan kicked his borrowed Harley into life and followed after them once more.

The lack of pursuit or any interest by way of the Host troubled him as well. He was of half a mind to speed ahead and spy out what lay in wait, but didn't dare risk letting the VW out of sight. If something happened to his charge while he was spying ahead, his bargain with Bhruic would be voided. And that he wouldn't allow. He'd waited long enough for Bhruic to shed his Gruagagh cloak. Too long, by any reckoning.

But he had a bad feeling about what lay ahead.

Calabogie, which was first settled in the early 1800s, could be considered the hub of Bagot & Blythfield Township. The Township takes up an area of 175.9 square miles, two thirds of which is Crown Land. Calabogie has a resident population of 1600 that swells to over 4000 in the summer when the cottagers descend upon it. The town takes its name from the Gaelic word "Calaboyd," meaning "marshy shore," of which Calabogie Lake, on which the village is situated, has plenty.

Jacky and her friends approached it from the east. Their first inkling that they were near was when they spied Munford's Restaurant & Gas Bar, on the corner of 508 and Mill Street. Behind the restaurant was a small trailer camp.

"Where to now?" Arkan asked, slowing down.

"We go straight," Jacky said, consulting her map, "until we see a gravel pit on our right, then we turn left on a sideroad."

"Are you sure you know where we're going?" Kate asked.

Jacky pointed to her roadmap. "This is the same as the one Bhruic showed me, except it's got names we can understand instead of faerie ones. Once we hit that sideroad, we're looking for a cliff face that overlooks the lake at"—she studied the map—"McNeelys Bay."

"The cliff face is the Giants' Keep?" Eilian asked, turning around to the back seat.

Jacky nodded.

"Then perhaps we shouldn't be in quite such a hurry to drive right up to it," Eilian said. "Is there a way we can approach it from the rear?"

"Not unless you want to hike over these mountains."

"Look at that," Kate said, pointing to a motel sign as they passed it. " 'Jocko's Motel,' I love it."

Everyone looked and made suitably appreciative noises except for Arkan who was watching the rearview mirror. A pickup truck was approaching them quickly—too quickly for his liking.

"Hang on!" he cried.

"What—?" Jacky began just as the pickup rammed them from the rear, knocking them all about in the confines of the small car. Arkan fought the wheel, trying to keep Judith on the road.

"My car!" Kate moaned.

"Is that guy nuts?" Jacky cried at the same time. She turned to look out the small rear window and saw, even before Arkan called out, who was in the truck.

"Bogans is what they are!" Arkan warned.

"Can't we go any faster?" Jacky asked.

"Not with this load."

The truck rammed into them again, this time slewing them along the highway, rubber burning before Arkan managed to regain control and straighten the car. As the pickup lunged forward for a third time, Arkan hauled left on the wheel. The VW's direct steering answered with frightening efficiency. Again Judith's wheels were squealing on the concrete. Arkan tromped on the brake. The pickup, trying to correct its aim after Arkan's abrupt maneuver, went sailing by. Then its brake lights flared. There was a small bridge coming up that crossed a ravine with a creek running through it. Arkan brought the VW to a skidding stop a half dozen feet past the bridge.

"Out!" he roared. "Everybody out!"

They scrambled to obey. Arkan had his door open and was hauling Finn from the back seat. Eilian, not so quick, was on the road a half moment later, helping Kate out. Jacky saw that the pickup had stopped ahead of them. Its reverse lights went on and she knew what it was going to do—ram them again.

She froze for a long second, then Arkan had a hold of her arm and was bodily dragging her from the car. Her blue jacket, tied around her waist, caught for a moment, then came with her as she fell to the ground, half supported by Arkan. The pickup smashed into Judith and knocked the VW right off the road into the small ravine. The little car hit the rocks at the bottom with a screeching sound of buckling metal.

"We've got to run for it!" Arkan cried.

He helped Jacky to her feet, then went to get Finn, who was sitting dazed by the road. The pickup was disgorging its load—three bogans from the cab, a half dozen more from its flat bed. Eilian and Kate ran to where Jacky and the others were. For a long moment they milled uncertainly, not knowing which way to run. Then the fields around them came alive with bogans and gullywudes, hags and spriggans, and an eighteen-foot-high giant who pushed his way out of a stand of small saplings to roar at them.

"Oh, Jesus," Jacky cried. "We've had it." She turned to Eilian. "Go! Fly Away! There's no sense in all of us getting caught."

Eilian hesitated.

"Do it!" she shrilled, her voice high with frustration and panic. There was no escape for the rest of them. The ambush had been too well-planned and they'd rushed right into it like a pack of fools. Black feathers sprouted all over Eilian. Arms became wings. Neck elongated. For a brief moment there was this strange hybrid creature standing there, then the black swan lifted up into the air with an explosion of his wings. He went up, out of range of the Unseelie Court, then circled to see if he could help. The other four bunched together as the bogans encircled them.

Jacky was so mad at herself that she didn't have time to be scared. She waited for the first creature to come at her, hands curled into fists at her side. She was going to hit them and kick them and scratch them and generally make it so hard for them to tie her up that they'd regret ever coming near her. Well, at least that was her plan. Except just at that moment there came a familiar roaring sound. The throaty engine of a big chopper. A Huntsman.

The bogans hesitated in their advance. Jacky and the rest stared as one to see one of the big Harleys suddenly pop into view in the middle of the road. One moment the pavement had been empty, in the next the big machine was thundering right for them. Only the being driving it wasn't a Huntsman—or if he was, he wasn't wearing his leathers and helmet. Red-gold hair blowing, tunic fluttering and looking like so many leaves and twigs and bits of this and that sewn together, he drove right at the bogans, scattering them. His left arm reached out and snatched Jacky up, swinging her behind him, then the chopper literally leapt forward, front wheel leaving the ground as the back one burned rubber.

"No!" Jacky cried.

She didn't know if this was a friend or a foe, all she knew was that her friends were being left behind while she was speeding away. She would have jumped from the bike, but it was going so fast she knew there was no way she'd survive the impact when she hit the ground. She clung to the weird rider's weirder coat.

"Please, stop!" she cried. "Those're my friends back there. Please!"

But the stranger just drove the big bike faster.

Seventeen

Kate saw the Huntsman grab Jacky and speed off with her on his Harley, then the Host was swarming over them and there was no more time to worry about her friend's fate. She clawed and bit at the creatures, kicked and punched, all to no avail. The gully-wudes danced out of the way of her ineffectual blows, then sidled close, tripping her, pulling at her short hair, at her clothes, pinching and striking her with sharp stick-like hands. Then the bogans had her.

They were great smelly brutes. The reek of them made her gag. The power in their hands made escape impossible. She saw Finn lose his own battle. She heard Arkan's sharp cries—like the barking and growling of a fox. He lasted the longest of the three of them, but soon he too was held captive. And then the giant was there, looming impossibly tall over them. Seeing the sheer bulk of the creature, knowing how much of Jacky's besting one of them had been luck, it still boggled her mind that her friend had been able to stand up against one, little say kill it.

All the fight went out of Finn as the giant stood over them. Arkan snarled, until a bogan cuffed him unconscious with a brutal

blow. Then it was just Kate staring defiantly at him, held fast by bogans, her heart drumming in her chest. High above, Eilian soared, as
helpless to help them as though he was caught himself. The giant
gave a swift nod to one of the hags.

The grey naked skin of the creature seemed to swallow light as
it stepped forth. It spread its arms where flaps of loose skin hung
batlike between arms and torso. Two, three more hags joined the
first. Up they went into the air, their take-offs awkward, but once
they were airborne they moved swiftly and surely after the black
swan winging high above them.

Standing near Kate, a gullywude took a sling from its belt and
chose a smooth stone from the roadside. Then the sling was in motion, whirring above the little creature's head until it hummed. The
gullywude released its missile and the stone went up, up, past the
hags. It struck Eilian's wing and he floundered in a cloud of black
feathers. Down he spiralled and Kate looked away, unwilling to see
his end, but the hags caught him. Screeching like harpies, they bore
him to where the Unseelie Court waited. A bogan thrust a nettle
tunic roughly onto the stunned Lairdling, and then they were all
captive. All helpless.

"OH," the giant boomed in good humor. "OH, HO! LOOK
WHAT WE HAVE NOW! TRUSSED FOR STEWING, EVERY
LAST ARSE-SUCKING ONE OF THEM. AND WON'T GYRE
BE HAPPY WITH ME NOW, JUST WON'T HE, HOT
DAMN!"

Bogans and gullywudes, hags and spriggans, all bobbed their
heads in eager agreement.

"Got 'em good, Thundell," a bogan cried above the growling
din of voices.

"YOU WANT A JOB DONE," the giant said, his voice carrying easily across the noise, "YOU GET A BIG MAN TO DO
IT!"

Choruses of agreement followed this statement as well. The
giant's huge face bent down to peer at Kate. A big finger poked at
her, knocking the breath from her. The frown on that face, almost
two feet wide, made her feel faint with fright.

"ARSE-BREATHING SHITHEADS!" he roared. "YOU
GOT THE WRONG ONE!"

The monster's breath almost knocked Kate out. She trembled

at the increased volume of his roaring voice, eardrums aching. The bogans holding her shook her fiercely as though she were to blame for Jacky's escape.

"One of the riders took her, Thundell," a reedy-voiced gully-wude piped up.

"Never saw a rider like that," another muttered.

"A RIDER GOT HER? GOOD, OH, HO! GOOD! TOOK HER BACK TO GYRE, I'LL BET, HOT DAMN!" He stared around at the crowd of creatures. "WHAT ARE WE WAITING FOR, TURDBRAINS? LET'S TAKE THESE ONES IN TOO!"

Kate was dragged to the back of the pickup and dumped in the flatbed along with the other captives. So many bogans crawled on to guard them for the ride that it was hard to breathe in the crush of bodies. Gullywudes hung from the sides of the truck, danced along the top of its hood, singing shrilly, songs about stews and what went in them. The pickup started with a loud roar, lurching into motion with a grinding of gears. She was pushed against Eilian and Finn.

"Bad," she heard the little hob mutter despondently. "Oh, it's gone very bad."

She could think of nothing to add to that.

It was hard to judge how long the ride took from the ambush spot to the Giants' Keep. The smell was so bad, the cursing voices of the bogans and shrill shrieking songs of the gullywudes, the press of the bodies, all combined to make it impossible to think. Kate felt like she was in a state of shock, but knew that couldn't be completely right because she was aware of her state of mind—as though she were standing outside of herself, looking in, mind you, but aware all the same.

Arkan had recovered consciousness by the time they finally came to a halt. When the four of them were hauled from the back of the truck and thrown down to the dirt road, it was almost a relief. Leather thongs bound their arms behind them—except for Eilian who, with his swan wings and man's body, needed no such bindings—and then they began a hellish ascent up a brush-choked rise.

There were creatures ahead of them, crawling through the brush like maggots on a corpse, and more behind, pushing and shoving, laughing uproariously whenever one of the captives lost their footing, which was often. Spriggans would dart in to trip them.

Beaten and weary, they were finally led in front of a great stone face near the middle of the rise. A portion of the wall swung back at their approach with a sound grinding stone. Torches sputtered on the rock walls of the tunnel they were now pushed and dragged into. The gullywudes' various songs had fallen into one that apparently everyone knew.

> *Chop in the fingers, joint by joint,*
> *smell that stew, oh smell it now;*
> *now a tip of a nose, now the ends of the toes,*
> *—better than sheep, ho! Better than a cow!*
>
> *Pop in the eyeballs, one by one,*
> *smell that stew, oh smell it now . . .*

The shrill voices rang in the confines of the tunnel, bouncing back from side to side until it sounded like hundreds of voices singing in rounds. The bogans kept up a "dum-dum-dum" rhythm that the prisoners were forced to march to. From what conversation they could make out amidst all the noise, they learned that while Eilian was bound for the Big Men's amusement, and Jacky as well, the rest of them were to meet another fate.

> *A slice of an ear and a shaving of spleen,*
> *smell that stew, oh smell it now;*
> *now chop up the entrails, just a tad, it never fails*
> *—better than sheep, ho! Better than a cow!*
>
> *Sucking on a marrow bone while it cooks,*
> *smell that stew, oh smell it now!*

The tunnel opened up into a well-lit area—a gigantic cavern that reeked like a raw sewer and was filled with capering creatures, grinning bogans, hungry-eyed hags, and other monsters they hadn't seen yet that day. Goblins and knockers, trolls and black-bearded duergar, all yammering and pushing forward to see the captives.

151

"BACK OFF! BACK OFF!" Thundell roared, swiping the creatures out of the way with wide blows of his big hands.

A space cleared around them. Breathing through her mouth, Kate lifted her head wearily. Every bone and muscle in her body ached from bruises. The place was a nightmare of sight and smell and sound. And there, sitting at the far end of the cavern on a throne cut directly from its rock wall, was the largest and ugliest of the monsters yet.

She didn't need anyone to tell her who this was: Gyre the Elder, greasy-haired, with a nose almost as big as the rest of his face. A hunch back that rose up behind his head. Hands, each the size of a kitchen tabletop. Chin and nose festooned with warts, some almost four inches long. If she had been at home and run across this creature in a picture book, she would have laughed. As it was, her legs gave way and she fell to her knees on the hard rock ground.

The two giants conversed, but it was like listening to thunder roaring in the confines of the cavern and she never did hear what it was they said. They could have been speaking Swahili for all she knew. She would have fallen full length on the ground, but a bogan snared his thick fingers in her short hair and pulled her head upright. The whole weight of her body hung from his hand. Then just as she was getting used to the thunder, to the pain, she was hauled to her feet and they were led forward.

Dragged in front of Gyre the Elder, Kate stared blearily at him, unable to keep her eyes from his ugliness. The worst thing about him—the absolute worst—was that his eyes were totally mad. But clever-looking too. Sly, like a weasel's, or a rat's.

Numbly, just as she was shoved past him and out of his sight, she saw the small ivory of a horn hanging on the wall behind him. She blinked as she looked at it, knowing it meant something, but no longer able to remember exactly what it was. It appeared to be discoloured with red dots, as though someone had splattered blood over it and not bothered to clean it. Then the bogan behind her gave her a shove that drove her into Arkan's back and the horn was gone, out of her view. She forgot it as she fought to stay on her feet.

They were pushed and prodded down a narrower corridor, then finally herded into a chamber cut out of the rock wall that had a great wooden grating for a door. The bogans threw them into the room where they fell on the damp straw strewn across the floor. The wooden grating closed with a jarring crash. A great beam of wood that took five bogans to lift was set into place, barring the door, and then finally they were alone. Blessedly alone.

It was a long time before Kate even had the energy, little say the inclination, to sit up. Then it was something snuffling in the straw near her that made her push herself rapidly away from the source of the sound, her rear end scraping the floor while she pushed with her feet.

"Moon and stars!" Arkan cried. "What is it?"

Creeping forward was a piglike creature. It was a dirty white, eyes rimmed with red and wild looking—mad eyes, not like Gyre the Elder's which were sly as well, but mad eyes of a hurt and broken creature from whom most sense had fled. It was trussed with a nettle coat like Eilian's. Belly on the ground, the creature moved slowly towards them, snuffling and moaning.

"No!" Kate shrieked as it came closer to her.

The thing backed away making whimpering noises that sounded all too human for comfort.

Beside Kate, Eilian gazed at it, horrified. "I . . . I think we've found the Laird of Kinrowan's daughter," he said.

"Th-that? But it . . . it's a pig."

"And once it had Laird's blood—why else bind it with a nettle coat?"

Bile rose in Kate's throat as she looked at the pitiable thing. "Why . . . why isn't it part swan, then?" she asked. "Like you?"

"Because they've changed her," Arkan said. "Their Gruagagh's changed her."

He moved closer to Kate as he spoke. Grunting with the effort, he tried to bring his bound hands around in front of him, but his hips were too wide for the maneuver. He backed up to her then, and began to work at the leather binding her hands.

"That wasn't a Huntsman that caught Jacky," he said as he fumbled at the knots with numbed fingers.

"How can you be sure?" Kate asked.

She couldn't take her gaze from the piggish thing that might once have been Lorana if the others were to be believed. It was emaciated, reminding her of the pictures she'd seen of starving people in Africa or India.

"That's what the giants were arguing about before they had us put in here," Arkan replied. "We've been spared for the moment because the whole Court's going out to hunt her down."

Suddenly Kate's hands were free. She brought them around in front of her, rubbing the chaffed wrists. Prickles of pain started up in her hands as her circulation returned.

"Why don't they use the Hunt?" she asked.

"They're missing a rider. Whoever took Jacky away had one of their motorcycles. Moon knows what her captor did with the rider. If he managed to kill it—which is very unlikely—she'll be safe from the Hunt. For awhile, at least. When one of their number's slain . . . They don't work as well unless all nine are alive and gathered."

It was taking Kate a lot longer to remove Arkan's bonds than it had taken him to undo hers. She kept starting at every noise she heard. My nerves are shot, she thought. Finished. Kaput. And whenever the piggish thing snuffled, she could feel her skin crawling. But at last she had Arkan free. Then she removed the nettle coat from Eilian while Arkan untied Finn.

"I knew it'd come to no good, talking to that girl," Finn muttered as he was freed. "All her talk about rescuing this and doing that, and here we all are, trapped in the Big Men's own Keep—damn their stone hearts—and where's she? Running free, is where. And far from here if she has any sense."

"That's unfair to say," Eilian said before Kate could voice her own sharper retort to the hob. "She led us, yes, but we followed of our own will. And it wasn't part of her plan to get snatched away while we were all ambushed."

"She had no plan," Finn said. "And that's where all the trouble began. Just pushing in here and pushing in there—oh, I admire her pluck, yes, I do—but there was never a hope. Just look at us now—ready for the stewpots if those gullywudes have us, worse I'm sure, if the Big Men decide they want us. And our Jack herself, out being hunted up dale and down by everything from Big Men to the Wild Hunt itself, I don't doubt. Oh, it's a bad time we're in the middle of, and the end'll only be worse."

Arkan had been investigating the grated wooden door while Finn was complaining. He turned back and shook his head at Eilian's unspoken question. "There's no way out through that—not unless we can match the strength of five bogans."

"I won't go easy this time," Eilian said. "They'll not do to me what they did to this poor soul. I'll hang myself first."

All gazes turned to their cellmate. The ugly head of the creature scraped the ground as it backed fearfully away from them, belly to the ground. Kate took a deep breath, let it out. She swallowed, then moved slowly forward.

"There, there," she said to it. Someone had to do something for it. "We won't hurt you. How could we, you poor thing? Come here. Don't be afraid of me. Kate won't hurt you."

It trembled as she approached, but no longer tried to back away. Forcing her stomach to keep down what wanted to come up her gorge, Kate reached for the creature, stroked the rough skin of its head as she worked at undoing its nettle coat. Her hands were already stinging from removing Eilian's and now the pain was worse—sharp, like hundreds of little knives piercing her skin.

She wasn't afraid of the creature anymore—not as she had been at first. And even her repugnance faded, now that she could feel it tremble under her hands. It wasn't its fault that it was in this predicament—any more than it was their own. But oh, what would the Gruagagh do if this was all that had become of his Laird's daughter? Samhaine Eve was just a couple of weeks away, and the lot of them all trapped anyway. Except for Jacky. And though Jacky had killed a giant and been lucky in everything so far, what could she really do against the hordes of the Unseelie Court that were out there looking for her now?

The last fastening came loose and she tugged the coat from the creature. Its shape began to change, the emaciated pig's body becoming a sickly-thin woman's. But the head—the head didn't change at all.

"Are there beings like this in either of the faerie Courts?" Kate asked her companions as she held the trembling woman with the pig's head against her shoulder. The creature burrowed its face in the folds of Kate's torn clothing.

Eilian shook his head. "She's been enchanted—evilly enchanted."

"By a gruagagh?" Kate asked.

"Or a witch."

Kate put her head close to the woman's. "Can you speak?" she asked. "Who did this to you? Who are you? Please don't be afraid. We won't hurt you."

"Ugly." The one word came out, muffled and low.

Kate forced a smile into her voice. "You think you're ugly? Haven't you seen that monstrosity lording it over his Court out there? Now that's ugly! Not you."

There was a long pause before the muffled voice said, "I saw ... your face. I saw my ugliness reflected in your eyes."

Kate stroked the dry pig skin of the woman's head. "I was scared then—that's all." She looked over at Arkan. "Give us your jacket, would you? The poor thing's got nothing on—no wonder she's scared. Bunch of jocks like you gawking at her." Arkan passed her his jacket and she wrapped it around her charge. "We want to help you," she said. "We're all in here together, you know, so we might as well try to get along. My name's Kate Hazel. What's yours?"

The pig's head lifted to look Kate in the eye. Kate steeled her features and refused to let any repugnance show. In fact, it wasn't so hard. She felt so bad for the poor woman that she didn't see her as ugly anymore, for all that it *was* still a pig's head. She schooled herself not to show pity either. Strangely enough, feeling protective for this poor creature, she'd ended up losing her own fears about being trapped here in the Giants' Keep.

"Make up a name," she said, "if you don't want to tell us your real one. Just so we can call you something."

The creature swallowed nervously. Its gaze darted to the others in the cell, then back to Kate.

"I ... I'm Gyre the Elder's daughter," she said finally.

Eighteen

Clinging to the back of what might be either her benefactor or captor, with the rough texture of his twig and leaf coat stickly against her and the wind rushing by her ears with a gale-like force, all Jacky could do was hold on for dear life. They were going too fast for her to dare jumping off. But as the ambush fell further and further behind them and, with it, her captured, maybe hurt—please, God, not dead—friends, her fear for her own safety got buried under a wave of anger. When the Harley began to slow down about a half-mile past the gravel pit, she dared to let go of a hand and whacked the stranger on the back.

"Let me go!" she shouted in his ear.

The motorcycle came to a skidding halt along the side of the road, so abruptly that they almost both toppled off. Jacky hopped from her seat and ran a few steps away from the machine. She wanted to take off, but after what had happened back at the bridge, and with this new as yet undefined being facing her, she wasn't quite sure what she should do. The stranger, for his part, merely smiled, and pushed the Harley into the ditch. Jacky swallowed nervously when she spotted his cloven feet.

"Who—who are you?" she asked.

"I have a pocket full of names," he replied, grinning.

Like most of the faerie Jacky had met so far, there was something indefinable in his eyes, something that she was never sure she could trust.

"I wonder which you'd like to hear?" the stranger added, thrusting one hand into a deep pocket. "A Jackish one won't do—you having a Jackish name yourself—but perhaps Tom Coof?"

He pulled something from his pocket and tossed it into the air too quickly for Jacky to see what it was. A fine dust sprinkled down, covering him, and then he appeared like a village simpleton to her.

"Or maybe Cappy Rag would please you better?" he asked. "A bit of a Gypsy, you know, but more kindly than some I could be."

Again the hand went into the pocket, out again and up into the air. When the new dust settled, he was wearing a wild coat that was covered with multi-coloured, many-lengthed ribbons, all tattery and bright. He did a quick spin, ribbons flying in a whirl of colour, dizzying Jacky.

"Or perhaps—"

But Jacky cut him off. When he'd done his little spin, she'd seen the bag hanging from his shoulder, recognized the shape of the thing it held.

"Or perhaps your name is Kerevan," she said, "and you play the fiddle as well as the fool. What do you want with me?"

Kerevan shrugged, showing no surprise that she knew his name. The ribbon coat became a coat of heather, twigs and leaves.

"I made a bargain," he said. "To see you to the Giants' Keep."

"A bargain? With whom? And what about my friends?"

"The bargain didn't include anyone else."

"And who did you make this bargain with?"

"Can't say."

Bhruic, perhaps? Jacky thought. Only why would he do this, why had he disappeared from the Tower . . . none of this made sense. And what if it hadn't been Bhruic? It was so hard to think. But she was sure of one thing: She didn't want anything to do with this—she glanced at the hooves again—whatever he was. She looked back down the road they'd travelled, but they'd gone too far for her to see what had become of her friends and the attacking Host. Then, before Kerevan could stop her, she slipped on her hob-stitched coat and disappeared from sight.

"Then think about this," her bodiless voice called out to him. "You didn't see me to the Giants' Keep and I'm not going with you, so your side of this bargain will never be completed."

Hob-stitched shoes helped her slip swiftly up the pavement from where she'd been standing.

"You can't do this!" Kerevan cried. "You mustn't!"

He tossed a powder towards where she'd been standing, but it fluttered uselessly to the ground, revealing nothing because she wasn't there.

"Who did you bargain with?" Jacky called, moving with magical quickness as she spoke. "And what was the bargain?"

By the time Kerevan reached the spot she'd been, she was away down the road again. She looked back, expecting him to at least be trying to pursue her, but instead he took his fiddle from its bag, then the bow. He tightened the hairs of the bow, but before he could draw it across the strings, Jacky had her fingers in her ears. She could hear what he was playing, not loudly, but audible all the same.

There was a spell in the music. It said, *Take off your coat. Lie down and sleep. What a weary day it's been. That coat will make a fine pillow, now won't it just?*

If she hadn't had her fingers in her ears, the spell would have worked. But she'd been prepared, cutting down the potency of the spell by cutting down the volume, as well as being mentally prepared for, if not exactly this, well then, at least something.

She moved silently closer, soft-stepping like a cat, watching the growing consternation on the fiddler's face. She was close to him now. Very close. Taking a deep breath, she reached forward suddenly, snatching the fiddle from his grasp, and took off again, with a hob's stealth and speed.

"This is a stupid game!" she called to him, changing position after every few words. "Why don't you go home and leave me alone? Go back and tell Bhruic that I *am* going to the Giants' Keep and I don't need fools like you getting in the way. And I don't need him, either."

"But—"

"Go on, or I'll break this thing."

"Please, oh, please don't!"

"Why shouldn't I? You've stolen me away from my friends— they could be captured or dead or God knows what and all you do is stand around playing stupid word games when I ask you a civil question. Thank you for helping me escape. Now get out of my life or I'll smash this fiddle of yours—I swear I will!"

Kerevan sat down on the side of the road. He laid his bow on the gravel in front of him and emptied his pockets. What grew in a pile beside the bow looked like a heap of pebbles, but they were all soft and a hundred different colours. There was magic in them, in each one, Jacky knew. She moved closer, still silent.

"A bargain," Kerevan said. "My fiddle for the answers to what- ever you want." When there was no reply, he pointed to the pile. "These are wally-stanes," he said. "Not quartz or stone, and not playthings, but magics—my magics. They're filled with dusts that can catch an invisible Jack or change a shape, or even a name. They're yours—just give me the fiddle and let me see you safe to the Giants' Keep."

"Why?"

"Why, why, why! What does it matter why? The bargain's a good one. The fiddle's no use to you, without the kenning, and I doubt you know the kenning, now do you? But these wally-stanes any fool can use, even a Jack, and there's a power in them, power you'll need before the night's through!"

Again there was a silence. Then Jacky spoke once more, this time from a dozen feet away from where her voice had come when it had asked why.

"This is the bargain I'll offer," she said. "Your fiddle, for my safety from you, for the wally-stanes, and for the knowledge of who you had your first bargain with—the bargain to see me safely to the keep," she amended quickly.

Kerevan's smile faded as she caught herself. His first bargain would have been easy. That was his bargain with life and with it he'd gotten born. Oh, this was no fool, this Jack, or the right kind of fool, depending on how you juggled your tricks.

"That's too much for an old fiddle," he said.

"Well, I'll just be going then," Jacky replied.

She was standing almost directly behind now and startled him with her proximity. Kerevan wanted—oh, very badly—to turn around and try to nab her, but he thought better of it. She was no fool, and she was quick too. But he remembered now, while he'd been looking for her, with more senses than just his eyes, he had sensed something he thought he could use.

"Let me show you a thing," he said. "Let me take you to a place nearby and show you something—no tricks now, and this is a promise from one puck to another."

How can I trust you? Jacky wanted to ask, but she was standing in front of him at the time, looking into his eyes, and knew— without knowing how, while thinking, oh, you're a fool, indeed, and not the kind Kerevan meant either—that she had to trust him. Yet she'd trusted the Gruagagh . . .

"All right," she said finally. "But I'm keeping the fiddle."

"Fair enough." He tossed the bag out towards her voice. "But store it in this, would you? There's a fair bit of my heart in that wee instrument and if you chip it or bang it, you'll be chipping away bits of me."

Jacky caught the cloth and stuffed the fiddle into it. Then before she slung it over her shoulder, she removed her blue jacket and stood in front of him on the road.

"What's this thing we're going to see?" she asked, worried that she was making a big mistake.

"It's a seeing one, not a talking one," Kerevan replied. "Come follow me."

He scooped up his wally-stanes and replaced them in his pockets, snatched up his bow, then took off into the woods at a brisk pace that Jacky, if she hadn't had her hob-stitched sneakers on, would have been hard-pressed to follow. They darted in and out between the trees, the ground growing steadily steeper as they went.

"Quiet now," Kerevan whispered, coming to a sudden halt.

Jacky bumped into him. "What is it?"

"We're close now—to bogans and gullywudes and all the other stone-hearted bastards that make up the Unseelie Court."

He crept ahead then, moving so quietly that, if Jacky hadn't known he was there, she would never have noticed him. And she, city kid though she was, found herself keeping up with him, as quiet, as slyly, as secret, with no great effort on her part. Hobbery magics, she told herself. Cap and shoes and jacket on my arm. But a voice inside her murmured, once perhaps, but no longer just that.

This time when Kerevan stopped, Jacky was ready for it. She crept up beside him, and peered through the brush to see what he was looking at. One fleeting glance was all she took before she quickly looked away. She wanted to throw up.

There was a clearing ahead, an opening in the trees where a cliff face was bared to the sky. There were bogans there, and a giant snoring against a tree, and other creatures besides, but it wasn't they who disturbed her. It was what was on the cliff face itself.

Once she might have been beautiful—perhaps she still was under the dirt and dried blood. But now, hung like an offering—like Balder from his tree, like Christ from his cross, like all those bright things sacrificed to the darkness—a swan-armed woman was bound to wooden stakes driven into the stone. She hung a half-dozen feet from the ground, her clothes in ragged tatters, but the nettle tunic, oh, it was new and tightly bound around her torso. The swan wings were a soiled white, as was the hair that hung in dirty strands to either side of her emaciated face. The flesh of her legs was broken with cuts and sores. Her face was bruised and cut as well. And she was—this was the worst—she was still alive. Hanging there, on the stone wall of a cliff that was stained with white bird droppings, many of which had splattered on her, surrounded by the jeering Unseelie Court that had had its pleasure mocking and hurting her for so long that they were tired of the sport.

She was still alive.

Acid roiled in Jacky's stomach. Tremors shook her. In another moment she might have screamed from the sheer horror of that sight, but Kerevan touched her shoulder, soothed her with the faintest hum of a tune that he lipped directly against her ear, then soundlessly led her back, away, higher, into the wilderness. She leaned against him for a long while before she could walk on her own again, and then they still moved on, travelling through progressively wilder country until they came to a gorge that cut like a blade through the mountainous slopes.

It was heavily treed with birch and cedar and pine, and Kerevan led her into it. The fiddler sat her down on some grass by a stone that she could lean against. He came back with water cupped in his hands, made her drink, went for more, returned. Three times he made her drink. At any time he could have retrieved his bagged fiddle and been gone, but there were bargains to uphold, and now a shared horror that bound them, not to each other, but to something that was almost the same.

"My bargain," Kerevan said suddenly, "is with the Gruagagh of Kinrowan. Did you know he meant to be a poet before he took on the cloak of spells he wears now? No other would wear it and it had to be one of Kinrowan blood, so he took it. He kept Kinrowan alive, shared the ceremonies with Lorana. Between the two of them they kept a light shining in the dark.

"But the time for light is gone, Jacky Rowan. That was Lorana we saw there, and that will be Bhruic too. That will be the Laird of Kinrowan, that will be every being with Lairdsblood, and probably that will be Jacky Rowan too. There is no stopping it."

Jacky couldn't drive the terrible vision from her. "But if we freed her . . . "

"That would only prolong what will be. The time of darkness has come to our world—to Faerie. They moved here from the crowded moors and highlands to their old homeland when the mortals came to this open land. But the Host followed too and here, here the Unseelie Court grows stronger than ever before. Would you know why? Because your kind will always believe in evil before it believes in good. There are so many of you in this land, so many feeding the darkness . . . the time for the Seelie Court can almost be measured in days now."

"I don't understand," Jacky said. "I know what you mean about the evil feeding on belief, but if Lorana was freed . . . "

"They have the Horn. They rule the Wild Hunt. Nothing can withstand the Hunt. For a while a power like Bhruic wields could, or my fiddle might, but when they are set upon the trail of some being, mortal or faerie, that being is dead. They *never* fail."

"So we have to steal the Horn."

"Listening to Bhruic, I thought so once, Jacky Rowan. But the Horn is too great a power. It corrupts any being who wields it. It corrupts any being who even holds it for safekeeping."

"But Bhruic . . . "

"Wanted the Horn to find Lorana. She was his charge; he was responsible for her."

Jacky frowned. "And you've known where she was all the

time and said nothing to him. How could you? She's been suffering for months! Jesus Christ, what kind of a thing are you?"

"I don't know what I am, Jacky Rowan, but I never knew she was there until we stood on the road, you and I, and I strained all my senses to find you. Instead I caught a glimmer that was her. They hide her well, with glamours and bindings."

"But now we know," Jacky said. "Now we can help her."

"You and I? Are we an army then?"

"What about your fiddle? And your wally-stanes?"

"They're tricks—nothing more. Mending magics, making magics—not greatspells used for war."

Jacky stared away into the trees, seeing the tormented face of the Laird of Kinrowan's daughter no matter where she looked, and knew that she'd do anything to help her.

"If I had the Horn," she asked, "could I use it to command the Hunt to free her?"

"You could. And then what would you command? That all the Unseelie Court be slain? That any who disagree with you be slain? You may call me a coward, Jacky Rowan, but I wouldn't touch that Horn for any bargain. Use it once and it will burn your soul forever-more."

"Bargain . . . " She looked at him then. "Tell me about your bargain with Bhruic."

"In exchange for what?"

"Tell me!"

Kerevan regarded her steadily. The fierceness in her gaze gave him true pause. Here was gruagagh material . . . or another wasted poet turned to war. But that was always the way with Jacks, wasn't it? They were clever and fools all at once. But the image of Lorana's torment had stayed with him as well, and so he made no bargains, only replied.

"I was to bring you safe to the Keep and then he was to come with me."

"Where to?"

"To where I am when I'm not here—that's not a question I'll answer, nor even bargain to answer for, Jacky Rowan, so save your breath."

She nodded. "This is my bargain then: I'll return your fiddle, for safety from you and for some of your wally-stanes."

"That's all?"

"That's all."

"And you'll let me lead you to the Keep?"

"I have to go to the Keep. My friends are there, if they're still alive. And the Horn's there."

"Girl, you don't know what you're talking about. That Horn is no toy."

"*Boy*, you'll take the bargain my way, or your fiddle will lie in pieces from here to wherever the hell it was that you came from in the first place."

They glared at each other, neither giving an inch, then suddenly Kerevan nodded.

"Done!" he said. "What care I what you do in that Keep or with that Horn? I want the Lairdlings to be safe—all of Lairdsblood—and whoever will come with me, by their own desire or if I must trick them, those will be saved. But not by doing what you do. Not by the Horn."

"Running away from what you have to face doesn't solve anything."

"And running headlong into it does? Willy-nilly, and mad is as mad does? Oh, I wish you well, Jacky Rowan, but I doubt we'll meet again in this world."

"I don't know," Jacky said. "You seem to do pretty good moving from one to the other."

"What do you mean by that?"

"I was told you'd died about a hundred and fifty years ago, but I get the feeling that, even if you *did* die back then, with you it's never permanent."

"I'm no god—"

"I know. You're Tom Coof and Cappy Rag and you're full of tricks and bargains. I think you might even mean well in what you do, Kerevan, but sometimes I think you're too damn clever for your own good—you know what I mean?"

Before he could answer, she stood up and offered him his fiddle. "Come on," she added. "I want to get inside the Keep before it gets dark."

"There'll be an uproar," Kerevan said. "They'll be scouring the countryside, looking for you."

"Well, then. If you want to keep your bargain with Bhruic,

you'd better start thinking about how you're going to get me in there in one piece, don't you think?"

Kerevan considered himself a manipulator, one who cajoled, or tricked, or somehow got everyone to follow a pattern that he had laid out and only he could see. It was worse than disconcerting to have his own tricks played back on himself. He took his fiddle bag, returned his bow to it, and slung it over his shoulder. Taking out his wally-stanes, he let her choose as many as she wanted. She took nine.

Three times three, he thought. She knows too much, or something else is moving through her, but either way he was caught with his own bargains and could only follow through the pattern that was unwinding before him now.

"Come along, then," he said, and he led her back into the forest once more.

Nineteen

"H is daughter?" Arkan said, staring at the pigheaded woman. "Oh, that's just bloody grand, isn't it?"

"Arkan, be still," Eilian said softly.

Kate, looking from the poor creature to the two faerie, was suddenly struck by what a difference Lairdsblood made. Arkan, brash and not easily cowed except by the Gruagagh, had immediately obeyed Eilian's quiet statement. She could see the distaste blooming in his eyes, but he said not another word as Eilian came to where she sat with the giant's daughter.

"If they're not born Big Men, and strong," Eilian said, "oh, it's a hard lot to be a giant's child."

The creature tried to hide her features in the crook of Kate's shoulder as he leaned closer, but he cupped her chin and made her look at him.

"You weren't born this way," he said. "Who set the shape-spell on you?"

"The Gruagagh," she said.

Kate gasped. "The Gruagagh?" Her worst fears were realized. Bhruic Dearg *had* set them up.

"I warned you," Finn muttered. "But would anyone listen?"

"Not so quickly," Eilian said. "There is more than one grua-gagh, just as there's more than one Billy Blind. It's like saying weaver or carpenter—no more." He turned back to the creature. "Which gruagagh? One in your father's Court?"

The creature nodded.

"That could still be Bhruic Dearg," Arkan said. "For all we know he—" He broke off as Eilian shot him a hard look.

"And what's your name?" the Laird's son asked the creature, gentling his features as he looked at her once more.

"Monster," she said gruffly and tried to look away, but Eilian wouldn't let her.

"We came here to help another," he said, "but we won't leave you like this when we go. We'll help you, too."

"And how will we do that, Laird's son?" Arkan asked, embold-ened by the fact that there was no way Eilian could make good such a promise. "Even if we had spells, you know as well as I that Seelie magic'll never take hold in this place. We can't help her. We can't even help ourselves."

"Be still!" Eilian cried, his eyes flashing with anger. "We have a Jack with us," he said to the giant's daughter, "loose outside the Keep and she'll help us. Don't listen to him."

"A Jack," Finn repeated mournfully. "And what can she do, Eilian? Didn't you see the Court Gyre's gathered here? All it needs is sluagh to make its evil complete—and they'll be here come night-fall."

"Our Jack's all we have," Eilian repeated quietly. "Let's at least lend the strength of our belief to her, if nothing else. What's your name?" he tried again, returning his attention to the giant's en-sorceled daughter.

There was no escaping the Lairdling's gaze. It penetrated the creature's fears, burning them away.

"Moddy Gill," she said.

"That's a nice name," Kate offered for lack of anything better to say. The creature gave her a grateful look.

"And a powerful one, too," Eilian added. "There was a Moddy Gill that once withstood the Samhaine dead, all alone and that whole night—do you know the tale?" Moddy Gill shook her head. "It was a bargain she made with the Laird of Fincastle. One night alone against the Samhaine dead and if she survived, she could have what she wanted from the Laird, be it his own child."

"What . . . what did she take?" Moddy Gill asked.

"His black dog," Eilian replied with a grin. "And with it at her side, she stormed Caern Rue and won free the princeling from the Kinnair Trow. Oh, it's a good story and one I never tired of hearing from our Billy Blind. They married, those two, and went into the west with the black dog. No one knows what befell them there, but do you know what I think?"

Moddy Gill shook her head. She was sitting upright now, just leaning a bit against Kate.

"I think that if they didn't live happily ever after, they at least lived happily, and for a very long time. And so will you, Moddy Gill. We'll take you with us when we leave this Keep."

"You came for the swangirl, didn't you?" she asked.

"In part," Eilian replied. "But we came to make an end of the Unseelie Court here as well."

"Is she your girl?" Moddy Gill asked.

"Who? Lorana?" Eilian laughed. "I doubt she knows I exist. I came here to help our dear Jack, not looking for swangirls to wed."

Kate gave him a considering look. There was something in his voice when he spoke of Jacky that made her think that he had more in mind than simply helping her.

"I know something," Moddy Gill said. Her pig's head was nodding thoughtfully, the tiny eyes fixing their gaze on Eilian. "I know where they keep the Laird of Kinrowan's daughter. They hang her out by day, but not at night. Then they put her in a cell—a secret cell—and I know where it is."

"When our Jack comes, will you help us rescue her?"

Moddy Gill sighed. The sound was a long wheezing snuffle. "We'll never get free," she said. "And the night's coming soon when they'll give her to the Samhaine dead and then they'll stew us for their feast."

"Well, at least someone's speaking sense here," Arkan said.

Kate frowned at him. "Why are you being like this?" she demanded. "I thought you were going to help."

"And I wanted to help, make no mistake about it, Kate. Your courage made me feel small, but moon and stars! I remember now why I had such a lack of it myself. We were helpless against the horde that ambushed us, and they were but a drop in the bucket compared to the size of the Court Gyre has gathered in this place."

"We've no magics here," Finn explained. "Not hob magics, nor Laird's magics—nothing sainly. Not even a gruagagh's spells will take hold in a place so fouled by the Host."

"Then we'll just have to depend on something other than magic," Kate said.

Eilian nodded grimly. "Until we're dead, there's hope."

Arkan looked as though he meant to continue the argument, but then he shrugged. "Why not?" he said. "I heard a poet say once that we make our own fortunes and if our future goes bleak, we've ourselves to blame as much as anything else. 'Be true to your beliefs,' he said, 'and you'll win through.' They're just words, I thought then, and I think so now, but sometimes words have power—when they fall from the proper lips. I'll mourn our deaths no more—not until the blade falls on my neck."

"Oh, they won't use axes," Moddy Gill said. "They like to throw folks in their stews while they're still kicking—for the flavor, you know."

"And have you tasted such a stew?" Eilian asked.

Moddy Gill shook her head. "I've no taste for another's pain, Lairdling. Not when knowing so much of my own."

Kate patted the girl's shoulder, then stood up to investigate the wooden grating that served for the door to their prison. The beams were as thick as a large man's thighs, notched together, then bound in place by heavy ropes that appeared to be woven from leather thonging rather than twine. The beam that lay across the door, held by a stone slot at either end, had taken five bogans to set in place. They didn't have close to that kind of brute strength in their own small company.

"Why did they just use rope?" she asked Eilian as he joined her.

"Faerie can't abide iron."

"And even steel's got a high iron count—big enough to make no difference," Kate said with a considering nod. She turned to Eilian. "But what about those bridges the trolls live under—and the buildings in the cities? There's iron in all of them."

"True enough. Faerie that live in or near your cities and towns come to acquire a resistance to it. Some can simply abide a proximity to it, but can't handle it themselves. Others, like our forester here, seem to have developed a total immunity—how else could he use your vehicle with such ease?"

Her car. Judith was dead and gone now. "And what about the Host?" she asked.

"They're a wilder faerie, not always used to urban ways. Against many, a penknife would be enough defense."

There was a long moment's silence, then Kate grinned and reached into her pocket. "Like this?" she asked.

She opened her hand to show her Swiss penknife. Opened, it had a blade length of two inches. She could have kicked herself for not thinking of it earlier when they were struggling with their bonds. But it didn't matter. They had it now.

"Oh, Kate!" Eilian replied. His eyes shone with delight. "Exactly like that."

"But these ropes are so thick . . . "

"They were woven with faerie magic. Even your little blade there will have no trouble cutting through them."

"All *right*."

She pried the blade out of its handle and began to saw away at the nearest rope. The others gathered round to watch the little knife cut through the first thick cord as though it were no more than a piece of string. Moddy Gill regarded Kate with awe.

"Moon and stars!" Arkan said. "When I find that poet, I'll gift him with enough ale to keep him drunk for a fortnight."

Finn nodded eagerly. "This hope's a potent magic all on its own," he said.

Arkan grinned. "And the next time you hear me whispering against it, Kate, just give me a good strong clout across the back of my head."

"With pleasure," Kate said as she continued to saw away at the ropes.

She didn't bother to mention that once they got out of their cell their troubles would be just beginning. There was no point in dashing their sudden enthusiasm. But they were going to have to come up with something more than a little Swiss penknife before they got out of this place. And then there was Jacky. Had the bogans caught her as well? Or was that strange being that had snatched her on the highway one of the Wild Hunt in another guise? She had the sinking feeling that the nightmare was just starting to get under way.

Twenty

"What's up now, Tom Coof?" Jacky asked in a whisper.

"Whisht—just for once," the fiddler hissed back at her.

They were hidden in undergrowth, high up in the forest and rough terrain that was, Jacky supposed, near the Giants' Keep. The land was certainly wild enough. The tree covering was mostly pine and cedar, with some hardwoods. Granite outcrops jutted from the ground like the elbows of buried stone giants. Roots twisted around the outcrops; deadfalls surrounded them. It had taken them the better part of the afternoon to get here from the road—Jacky in her hob jacket and Kerevan using his own spells. The forest was alive with the creatures of the Host, searching for her.

Jacky was just about to repeat her question when she saw what had driven them into hiding once more. As tall as some of the trees around them, a giant came, moving with deceptive quiet for all his huge bulk. He sniffed the air, a nose the size of Jacky's torso quivering. Jacky stopped breathing. Finally the giant moved on. Gullywudes and bogans moved in his wake. Not until they were five minutes gone did Kerevan speak.

"Do you see that small gap? There—just the other side of the deadfall?" he whispered.

"In the rocks there?"

Kerevan nodded, but neither of them could see each other, so the motion was wasted. "That's one of their bolt holes," he said. "Take it and follow it into the heart of the mountain and it will bring you straight to where Gyre the Elder holds his Court."

Jacky bit at her lower lip, which was getting all too much wear of late. "You're leaving me here?"

"This is the Giants' Keep. You *did* want to come here, remember?"

"Yes, but . . . " She sighed. Somehow she'd hoped that, once they'd reached the place, Kerevan would change his mind and offer to help her.

"A word of warning," the fiddler added. "Seelie magics are of no use inside—so your hob coat won't hide you, your shoes won't speed you, your cap won't show you any new secrets, and even the wally-stanes you took from me will do you no good. Not when you're inside."

"Is that why you won't go in?"

"It's suicide to go in there," he replied. "A fool I might be, but I'm not mad."

Jacky looked in his direction. If she squinted and looked very hard she could just make out the vague outline of his shape.

"I don't know what to do," she said. "Now that I'm here, I don't know what to do, or where to begin. Can't you give me some advice—or does that require another bargain?"

"This advice is free: Go home and forget this place."

"I can't."

"Then do what you must do, Jacky Rowan, and pray you didn't use up all your luck these past few days."

"And nothing will work—I mean, none of the magics?"

"Not one." Kerevan sighed. "There was a reason that no Seelie's gone to do what you mean to try, and now you know it. It's not so much a lack of courage—though the Seelies left are not so brave as once their folk were, and who can blame them? Once in that Keep, they would be powerless. You've seen the Big Men. You've seen their Court—the bogans and all. How could hobs and brownies and the like stand up against them, without their spells to help them? Even Bhruic would have no more than his natural strength in there."

"Okay, okay. You've made your point. I go by myself and it's kamikaze time."

Kerevan knew what she meant, that it was a suicide mission, but he said: "Do you know the actual meaning of that word? 'Divine Wind.' Perhaps you should call on the gods to help you."

"I don't believe in God. At least I don't think I do," she added, hedging.

"The desert god your people hung from a tree couldn't help you here anyway," Kerevan replied. "This is the land of the Manitou. But Mabon walks that Great Mystery's woods sometimes and the Moon is sacred everywhere."

"Is Mabon your god?"

"Mabon is the young horned lord."

Jacky gave him a quizzical look, but he didn't elaborate. "I guess that when I go down that hole," she said, "it's just going to be me and no one else."

"I fear you're right."

"Then I suppose it's time I got my ass in gear and got to it."

An invisible hand touched her shoulder and gave it a squeeze. "Go lucky as your name can take you," Kerevan said.

Jacky swallowed. "Thanks for getting me here," she said. "I know you were just fulfilling your bargain with Bhruic, but thanks all the same."

"I mean you no ill, Jacky Rowan, and I never have."

There was nothing more to say, so she moved ahead, past the deadfall to the gap in the rocks. There was a passage of some sort there. A familiar reek rose out of it. This has got to be the way, she thought, because nothing else could smell this bad. Breathing through her mouth, she squeezed between the rocks and forced her way in. The passage wasn't high enough to stand in, so she moved forward at a crouch, one hand on the wall to her left, the other brushing the ground ahead of her.

Kerevan sighed when she was gone. He touched his fiddle, felt the stag's head scroll through the cloth material of its bag. He was free to go now. He had done all that he'd bargained to do. Yet he stayed hidden in the underbrush, staring at the bolt-hole. After a long while, he sighed again, then began moving slowly up along the rocky mountainside, heading for the great stone gates that were the main entrance to the Keep.

There's fools and there's fools, he told himself as he went. And here I am, all these years old, and I never knew I was still *this* sort of a fool.

The smell intensified, the deeper Jacky went down the narrow tunnel. If this was a bolthole, she thought, it could only be one for little creatures, because a bogan wouldn't fit in and a giant would have trouble just sticking his arm into it. She'd never been one of those people that got nervous in an enclosed space, but this tunnel, with the weight of a mountain on top of it, had her shivering. Combined with the darkness and the stench, and with what she knew lay waiting for her at the tunnel's end, there were half a dozen times when she thought she would take Kerevan's advice after all. She was ready to just GoJackyGo right out of here.

But then she remembered the pitiful figure of Lorana, hanging from the cliff. Not to mention the fact that Kate and the rest were probably trapped down here somewhere. Not to mention that the Host was out to get her personally now. Not to mention . . . oh, it made her head ache just to think of it all.

Her watch didn't have a luminous dial so she couldn't even tell what time it was, or how long she'd been down this hole. It seemed like forever. It had been getting dark when she first crawled in—that time when shadows grow long but it's still not quite twilight yet. It could be midnight now, for all she knew. But the stench kept getting stronger, so she knew she was getting somewhere. And she'd begun to hear a noise—a booming sort of sound that rose and fell like speech, but didn't seem to be a voice. Unless it was a giant's voice . . .

An interminable length of time later she came to the end of the tunnel. The reek here was almost unbearable. Light spilled down the tunnel from the gap at its end—a sickly sort of light that flickered as though it was thrown by torches or candles. And the booming sound *was* a voice. A huge voice that had to belong to one of the giants. He was cursing the Court for their inability to find one Jack—"ONE

LITTLE SHITHEAD OF A JACK." Underlying his roaring was a constant chitter and rattle of other voices—bogans swearing, hags hissing, gullywudes, spriggans and other creatures all adding to the babble. Feeling as though her heart was in her throat, Jacky crept forward.

The end of the tunnel was blocked with boulders. When she dared her first peep over them, she realized that this wasn't so much a bolthole as an airhole, for she was looking down into an immense chamber. The floor was invisible, covered with a moving carpet of bodies. The Unseelie Court swarmed in that stone hall.

Jacky ducked quickly back. Lovely. Perfect. Not only were there more of the creatures than she'd ever imagined waiting for her down there, but unless she managed to grow wings, she had no way to get down. She leaned despondently against the wall of the tunnel. Who was she kidding? What could she do down there anyway, except end up in someone's stewpot?

The constant babble of noise, with the roar of more than one giant thundering overtop it as they argued with each other, was almost more than she could bear. It wouldn't let her think. The stench wouldn't let her breathe. Her helplessness made her want to scream with frustration. Or cry. It all seemed so useless.

Oh, she'd been filled with sharp criticism for the Seelie faerie who wouldn't dare storm the Giants' Keep. Oh, yes. It was easy to be brave and make brave noises then. But with the Court gathered below her now . . . when she knew their strengths, their sheer *numbers* . . . The voice of her panic was starting up its GoJackyGoJack-yGo chant inside her. Get out of here while you can. NowNowNow.

She frowned at herself. Well, she'd go all right. But not back up the tunnel. Not to safety. Not when Kate needed her help down there. Not when the Laird's daughter was suffering so.

She gathered up the ragged bits of her courage and peeped over the boulders again, this time taking a good long look. She saw the giants—five of them sitting along one wall, with a sixth, that had to be the biggest living creature she'd ever seen, sprawled on a throne roughly-carved from the face of the rock behind him. That one had to be Gyre the Elder.

Fearful of being spotted, but determined to spy out what she could, she studied the huge hall, looking for some trace of Kate or the other Seelie Faerie that had come to Calabogie with them, looking for Lorana, looking for . . . She saw the Horn then, hanging from the wall behind Gyre the Elder at a height that only a giant could reach. Even in the uncertain lighting she could make out the red dotting on it.

Rowans had red berries, she remembered, so that must be what Bhruic had meant about it being marked by the berries of her name. Except he'd also said it would be hidden. So what did it mean that it was just hanging there on the wall? Either Bhruic had his information wrong—and where would he have gotten it from anyway? she wondered with renewed suspicion—or there was a trick of some sort going on here.

She wished Kerevan was with her—that he'd stayed to help. He seemed up on all the faerie tricks, if you believed half of what he said. But if he was a trickster, well, he'd called her one too. *From one puck to another*, he'd said.

I need a trick of my own, she thought. I need to clear this place of the Host so that I can get my hands on the Horn. But she had nothing on her—and there was nothing in the tunnel that she could use. She studied the huge chamber once more, marking how, though it had been naturally formed, it bore the signs of toolwork as well. The throne, the stone benches along its walls, perhaps this very airhole, had been carved from what had originally been merely a naturally-formed cavern. Then she saw something she hadn't noticed before.

She'd been so busy looking down that she never thought to look about at her own height. There was a cleft running in the stone, at about the height of the top of the tunnel. Under it was a small ridge about five inches wide. She could just reach the cleft from the mouth of the tunnel—she was sure of it. That could take her around above and behind the giant's throne to where the Horn was—though how she'd hook it up into her hands from the precarious perch she'd be in, she didn't know. But the ridge also went to another opening about two thirds of the way around the hall. This one looked larger than the one she was hidden in. Perhaps it led down to the main floor. Or to wherever they kept their prisoners.

Jacky bit at her lip as she studied the cleft and the ridge below it. In some places the distance between the two would be a real stretch. She'd be in plain sight of anyone who chanced to look up. And it wasn't exactly going to be a stroll in the park either. If she fell . . . But it was that, or give up and go back the way she'd come.

GoBack! her panic told her. GoBackNowGoBack!

She shook her head. Below her, the giants' argument was getting ugly. There were thundering roars of "SPIKE YOU!" and "STEW YOU, ARSEBREATH!" and the Court itself was jabbering away, louder than ever. Arguing. Taking sides.

It was now or never, Jacky told herself.

She climbed over the boulders and reached for the cleft. The rock was firm at least—not crumbly as she'd feared. Taking a deep breath, she swung herself out, one foot still at the mouth of the tunnel, the other scrabbling for purchase on the ridge. There wasn't much room on it. But it would do. It would have to do. Closing her mind to the babble of fear that came bubbling up inside her, she swung completely out. Then refusing to look down for all that she was sure that every eye was on her, she began to inch her way along the ridge, making for the other opening she'd spied across the hall.

Twenty-one

The wooden beam that Kate was cutting free was the bottom horizontal one. When it fell, and if they could roll it away, they'd be able to squeeze out through the space that was left. And after that . . . She closed her mind to what came after that. What she had to concentrate on at the moment was what she was doing now. She had already cut through half the ropes holding the beam in place, working her way slowly from right to left. The great wooden beam was beginning to sag.

"Just a few more," Arkan said. He was crouched beside her, eyes agleam. "And then we'll spike some bogans."

Kate shook her head. Half the time Arkan seemed ready to crawl into a hole and the other half he was ready to take on the world. He was certainly no slouch when it came to a fight—she hadn't forgotten the way he'd handled himself at the ambush—but she had to wonder at the seesaw aspect of his character.

"Here it goes," she said as her little penknife cut through the last bit of the rope she was working on.

She moved away as the beam tilted, trembled, then its unbalanced weight dropped it to the stone floor with a loud thunk. In their cell, the five prisoners held their breath. When no one came, Kate quickly began to saw through the last couple of ropes so that they could roll the log away from the front of their cell. Thankfully, the floor sloped downward, away from them.

When she got to the last rope, the other four joined her at the front of the cell. As soon as the rope gave away, Arkan and Eilian kicked the beam. It hit the ground with a louder thunk and began to roll away from them.

"Let's go!" Kate cried.

She grabbed Moddy Gill and pushed her towards the opening, squeezing through after her. Arkan, Eilian and Finn were quick to follow. The beam rolled down the corridor, setting up a huge racket now. The sound, echoing from the walls and ceiling, rebounded, growing in volume. Bogans appeared down the hall, scrambling for cover as they saw the huge log rolling towards them. One wasn't quick enough and his shriek as the beam crushed him pierced their ears. On their feet now, the five of them ran after the beam.

"Where do they keep Lorana?" Eilian asked Moddy Gill, running at her side.

A bogan jumped out at them and Kate stabbed him with her little knife. She wasn't sure what she was expecting, but she certainly wasn't prepared for the bogan's reaction. It was though she'd run him through with a sword. He howled, tearing himself free, almost tugging the penknife from her hands. But then, instead of attacking her again, he merely clutched at his stomach and fell to the floor, moaning.

"She won't be in her cell just yet," Moddy Gill said. "They'll be bringing her in about now."

"Bringing her in from where?"

"Oh, they hang her out on the cliffs by day—curing her, you know?"

Eilian blanched. They reached Kate where she stood over the bogan. Collecting himself, Eilian tugged at Kate's arm.

"Well done," he said. "Now let's keep moving."

But they were too late. The corridor in front of them was suddenly filled with swarming creatures. Before anyone else could react, Kate ran forward, brandishing her little Swiss penknife, feeling like a fool. But the creatures directly threatened by its steel blade, tiny though it was, fell back in frantic haste to get away from

181

it. Unfortunately, not all of the Host was so affected by iron. There were bogans and other creatures who had become as much acclimatized to it as the Seelie faerie.

These pushed forward and when Kate stabbed at one of them, he smashed the penknife from her grip with a curse and then used the flat of his big hand to club her to the ground. Gullywudes and spriggans, and a bogan or two, leapt away from where the penknife skittered across the stone floor, throwing up sparks. Then the whole crowd rushed forward to attack.

In moments they were subdued once more and hauled back to face Gyre the Elder. Their captors were none too gentle in their treatment of the prisoners. They were bruised and battered, with Kate almost too dizzy to stand on her own, as they were brought before the giant. His ugly face snarled down at them, a special hatred in his eyes when he saw his own daughter with her pig's head on her shoulders standing there with them.

"WHERE'S YOUR JACK?" Gyre the Elder demanded of them. "TELL ME, AND MAYBE I WON'T MAKE YOU SUFFER LIKE SOME."

As he said that, the prisoners caught their first glimpse of the Laird of Kinrowan's daughter. She was being brought back from the cliff and taken to her cell for the night. Two bogans supported her, dragging her roughly between them by her wings. Her head lolled against her chest.

"GIVE ME YOUR JACK AND YOU'LL BE SPARED THIS."

Kate could hardly focus her vision. All she saw hanging between the two bogans was a fuzzy shape. But Eilian cried out in anguish, while Finn hid his eyes. Arkan stared, then looked away. Any hope he'd had was burned away at the sight of Lorana's torment.

"THE JACK, YOU TURD-SUCKING BUGS!" Gyre the Elder roared. "GIVE HER TO ME!"

Kate tried to face him, but everything just kept spinning around her. The blow on her head had almost made her forget where she was. This was just a nightmare and it didn't make sense that anything could have a face as big as this thunder-voiced monster did. She tried to speak, but the words stumbled in her throat and wouldn't come out.

"I'LL PULL YOUR LIMBS OFF, ONE BY ONE," the giant swore, "UNTIL ONE OF YOU TELLS ME. I'LL POP YOUR HEADS! I'LL CHEW YOU TO PIECES!"

He reached for Kate.

When Jacky reached the larger opening, she collapsed in it and lay weakly there, unable to move. She had cramps in her fingers and cramps in her calves and her neck muscles were so knotted from tension that she didn't think they'd ever loosen up again. It was long minutes later before she could even roll over and peer down once again.

She was very close to Gyre the Elder and his throne now. The floor of the cavern was a good forty foot drop from her hiding place, but the head of the giant on his throne was no more than ten feet or so down, and about five over. The Horn, hanging there from its thong on the wall, was another fifteen feet over.

I'll never reach it, she thought. And she had no tricks.

She slumped back against the wall of this new tunnel, too tired to be curious about where it went. She tried to massage her neck, but it didn't help. She noticed her gift from Bhruic then and pulled the brooch free from her jacket, turning it over in her hands. A tiny silver rowan staff, crossed by a sprig of berries. Why couldn't it have been magic? A special kind of magic something or other that would even work in a place fouled by the Unseelie Court. But that, of course, would make everything too easy, and things were never easy. Jacky had discovered that a long time ago.

She heard a rumbling sound, above the cacophony of the crowd below her. It sounded like something rolling down a stone corridor. She looked out across the cavern as a quiet fell across the giants and their Court. Now what was that? And could she use it to some advantage? She was ready for any sort of help. At this point she'd even welcome Bill Murray and his Ghostbusters. At least they'd make her laugh and she needed a laugh right about now. It was that, or cry from frustration.

But then she saw what the disturbance had been caused by as a number of prisoners were dragged in front of Gyre the Elder's throne. Her heart gave a surprised little jump at the sight of Eilian, but that died quickly.

Oh, Kate, she thought. I never meant to get you into this. Why couldn't you just have stayed home?

She listened to Gyre the Elder rant, saw the bruises on Kate's face, saw the pitiable figure of the Laird of Kinrowan's daughter dragged into the cavern as well, saw that Eilian and the others were all going to die. When Gyre the Elder reached for Kate, something just snapped in Jacky.

She scrambled to her feet. Backing up a few paces, she ran forward and launched herself at the broad, ugly head of Gyre the Elder. The GoJackyGoJackyGo chant was roaring in her ears again, but this time it was fed by adrenaline, not panic. She landed with a jarring thump against the monster's skull and started to slide down the side of his head, gripping at his greasy hair with one hand to stop her descent while she stabbed at him with the heavy pin of her brooch.

"You want a Jack?" she screamed in his ears as she slid by it to his shoulder. "I'll give you a Jack!"

Gyre the Elder turned his face around and down towards her and she stabbed him in the eye. He roared and started to stand. One meaty hand flew to his wounded eye. Jacky tumbled from his shoulder. Her hand closed on the thong of the pendant the giant wore around his neck, but it snapped under her weight and she fell with it to his lap. But before she could regain her balance and get away, he was standing and she tumbled from his lap right into the crowd of bogans holding Kate and the others captive.

Gyre the Elder swung his head back, roaring from the pain in his eye, and cracked his head against the stone wall behind him. Stunned, he rose and staggered to one side, away from his throne. One huge leg kicked out, scattering bogans and the like in all directions. His younger brother rushed to help him, but he was too late. Gyre the Elder dropped like a felled oak, arms pinwheeling uselessly for balance.

When he landed, the cavern floor shook and rumbled. Directly above his head was the entrance of the airhole through which Jacky had entered. The largest of the boulders there tottered, then dropped from the ledge to crack the giant's head wide open. Blood fountained from the wound. His huge limbs kicked and jumped like a fish floundering in the bottom of a fisherman's boat. And then he lay still.

While all gazes were locked on the dying giant, Jacky rose to her feet only to stare at the Horn that hung uselessly out of reach. Any moment now, she knew, the creatures of the Host were going to come to their senses and grab her. Could she get to the Horn in time? Could she throw something at it and hope to knock the Horn down and catch it before it shattered on the stone floor? Right. Why not ask if a bogan could sit down and have a cup of tea with Kate's Auntie?

But adrenaline still rushed through her, firing her courage. She picked up the nearest thing at hand—a twist of gold that had once been a candlestick—and meant to give a try at knocking the Horn down.

"SMASH THEM!" Gyre the Younger roared, rising up from beside his brother's corpse. "CRUSH THEM! SPIKE THEM!"

A bogan rushed for Jacky, but Moddy Gill jumped in his way and tangled up his feet so that he fell down, taking the next few charging creatures down with him. Jacky drew back her arm to throw the twisted candlestick, but then she saw the box sitting at the foot of the dead giant's throne. The rubble was thick there, broken bottles and trash, mixed with more precious things like real jewels and gold and silver goblets. And sitting in amongst it all was a delicate wooden box with a berried tree carved onto its lid.

Oh, you sly bastard, Jacky thought.

A gullywude jumped onto her shoulder. More grabbed her legs, trying to pull her down, but she dragged them with her as she moved forward. She brought the candlestick down on top of the box with a jarring blow and the wood shattered. Oh, a horn hung there on the wall by the throne, in plain sight for all to see, complete with its speckle of red for berries, and who'd think to look further? And who could get it down but a giant? Anyone else trying would be caught so fast it would make their head spin.

Well, my head's spinning now, Jacky thought, but it was from success. Out of the ruin of the box she pulled a strange twisting shape of a horn. The gullywudes were a swarm on her, trying to drag her down. Gyre the Younger was looming over her. The other four giants were wading through the Court, knocking their folk everywhichway in their hurry to get at her. But neither the gullywudes, nor the threat of the giants and their Court, nor the fear of what using that Horn might mean could stop her now. She dragged her arms up, gullywudes hanging from them, brought the mouthpiece of the Horn to her lips, and she blew it.

The sound of it was loud and fierce. At that first blast, the Court drew back from her—even the giants. She blew it again and again until its sound was all that filled the cavern—a wild, exulting sound that thrilled the blood in her veins, making it roar in her ears. She could feel its power fill her. The Hunt was coming. The Wild Hunt. And she was its mistress now.

She stepped away from the throne and Gyre the Younger moved to take it, sitting down to glare at her. The Court had cleared a great space around her. Her friends stood or lay around her. Kate and Eilian. Finn and Arkan. Lorana lay sprawled where her bogan guards had dropped her. There was a pig-headed woman there too—the one that had stopped the bogans from taking her as she'd lunged for the Horn.

Jacky brought the primitive instrument down from her lips and surveyed the Court. They could all hear it now—a distant sound like the rushing of wind, like the echoes of the Horn's blasts, like answering horns, winding out from dark cold places beyond the stars.

Of her friends, Eilian was the first to move. He tugged Kate and Moddy Gill, each by an arm, to stand behind Jacky. Finn and Arkan followed, Arkan carrying the frail limp shape of the Laird of Kinrowan's daughter. There were tears in his eyes as he pulled loose the nettle tunic and freed her from the Unseelie spell that had held her.

But Gyre the Younger, sitting on his dead brother's throne, he never moved. Nor did his Court. They knew enough to know that it was not who held the Horn but who blew it, and thereby summoned the riders, that ruled the Hunt. The blasting sound of that Horn had frozen them, sapping their strength, forbidding them to lift a hand against the Jack that the Seelie Court had sent against them.

And Jacky . . . the power of command boiled in her. What couldn't she do now, with this Horn in her possession? Then there was no more time to think.

The Hunt was come.

They didn't ride their Harleys here. They came on great horned steeds, horses with flanks that glittered like metal, but were scaled like fishscales. Stags' antlers lifted from the brows of the proud mounts. While the riders . . . They were cloaked in black, each one of them, all nine of them, come to the summoning. The leader stepped his mount closer, its hooves clipping sparks from the stone as it moved. The face that looked down at Jacky was grim, but not unhandsome. It was the eyes that made it alien—for there was no end to their depths. They studied her with disinterest, remotely. Obeying, but not caring who or what it was that summoned them.

"We have come," the leader said.

At his words, the cavern seemed to shiver. Jacky's friends and the Unseelie Court alike trembled, wishing they were anywhere but here. Only Jacky stood firm. With the Horn in her hand, nothing could stop her, no one could hurt her. That was what it promised her. But as she opened her mouth to speak, to command the Hunt, to send out the doom that would take down this Unseelie Court, once and forever, Kerevan's words came back to her, as though from a great distance, warning her.

From one puck to another . . .

I'm not a puck, she told that whispering memory, but she knew the words to be a lie. The Jacks were always pucks. They were the fools and the tricksters of Faerie, and knowing that, she knew that Kerevan's true name was Jack as well.

The Horn is too great a power. . . .

But that's just what we need to undo the evil of the Unseelie Court, she replied. Don't you see?

It corrupts any being that wields it. . . .

I'm not going to wield it. I'm only going to use it once—that's all. Just once.

But she knew that to be a lie as well. Why should she give up the power that the Horn offered her? Why let it fall into another's hands? It was better that she used it. Better that she chose who the Hunt chased, and who it didn't.

What would you command? the voice of memory forced her to ask herself. *That any who disagree with you be slain?*

I won't be like that. I'm fighting evil—I'm not evil myself.

It corrupts any being that wields it. . . .

Then what should I do? she demanded of that memory, but to that question it remained strangely silent.

The steeds of the Hunt began to shift as though sensing her indecision. Gyre the Younger stirred on his brother's throne, his hatred for her, for the death she'd brought his brother, for the pain and defeat she'd brought them all, was beginning to overpower his fear of the Hunt. Hadn't his own brother commanded the Hunt before? Wouldn't it sooner listen to him, who *knew* what he needed done, than to this trembling Jack who stood there, overawed by it all?

Jacky could feel the change in the room. The Horn whispered, telling her of the power that could be hers. The Wild Hunt demanded to know why it was summoned. Kerevan's voice, in her memory, told her she was doomed. Gyre the Younger made ready to take the Horn, as he'd already taken his brother's throne, and crush this Jack under his foot with a pleasure that would never be equalled again.

I don't know what to do, Jacky admitted to herself.

Use us, the eyes of the Wild Hunt demanded.

I am power, the Horn told her. *Yours to wield.*

She could use it and doom herself, or not use it and the power would go to Gyre the Younger and doom her anyway. There was no middle road, no road at all. But then she laughed. No road? Wrong! That was a lie! There was only one road she could take and she knew it now. She straightened, stooped shoulders losing their uncertainty. She met the gaze of the Wild Hunt's leader without flinching from its alien depths.

"Dismount," she said. "Come here to me."

On the throne, Gyre the Younger froze, uncertain once more. From a small creature, weighted down with fear and ignorance, she had gained stature once more.

Inside her, the Horn's voice exulted. *You will not regret the power I can give you*, it told her.

But Jacky only smiled. She watched the Huntsman dismount stiffly and approach her. When he was only a couple of paces away, Jacky reached out with the Horn.

"Take it," she said.

The alien depths changed. Confusion swam in the Huntsman's eyes. "Take it?" he asked slowly, not lifting a hand.

Jacky nodded. "Take it. It's used to command you, isn't it? Well, take it and command yourself."

Now the gaze measured her carefully. "And what is the bargain you offer?"

"No bargain. Please. Just take it."

The Huntsman nodded slowly. "Do you understand what you are doing?"

Jacky wet her lips. "Yes."

"Hill and Moon," the Huntsman whispered. "To think such a day could come." He took the Horn reverently from her.

"NO!" Gyre the Younger roared. "YOU MUSTN'T!"

"Oh, Jacky!" Kate cried. "What've you done?"

Consternation lay across all their faces, except for Eilian's. He smiled as understanding came to him.

"For years beyond count we have answered this Horn's call," the Huntsman said. "Men and faerie both have commanded us. They have had us slay and slay and slay again. They have had us spy for them. They have had us capture their foes, then made us watch them be tortured. But never was there one being that saw beyond the power the Horn offered to *our* need." The Huntsman bent his knee to Jacky. "Lady, I thank you for our freedom." Then he rose and, dropping the Horn to the stone floor of the cavern, he ground it to pieces underfoot.

A great wind stirred in the cavern. When they saw the Horn destroyed, the stasis that had bound the Unseelie Court finally fell away. But there was no place for them to flee now. At each entranceway stood one of the horned steeds of the Hunt, and on its back, a grim-faced Huntsman.

"Go from here," the leader of the Hunt said to Jacky. "Take your friends and go. There is a reckoning to be made between my brothers and those who rule this Keep—a reckoning that you should not be witness to."

Jacky nodded. "But . . . but you're really free now, aren't you?"

The Huntsman smiled. In his eyes, the alien depths wavered and for one moment Jacky saw a being of kindness look out from those eyes. Then the moment was past.

"We are truly free," the Huntsman said, "once this final task is done. And this task we do for ourselves. Go now, Jacky Rowan. You have our undying thanks. We will never forget this gift you have given us."

He touched her shoulder gently and steered her towards the entranceway. One by one her companions fell in step beside her. Kate took her hand.

"I'm so proud of you," she whispered, for she understood now what Jacky had done.

Arkan carried the frail body of the Laird's daughter. Eilian and Finn walked with Moddy Gill between them. When they reached the cavernous doors of the Keep's main entrance, the doors swung open to let them out. They went through, and the huge doors thundered closed behind them.

It was night outside, dark and mysterious, and air had never tasted so clean and fresh before.

"Now what do we do?" Kate said, thinking of the long way home and how they had only their legs to take them.

"Now," said a voice from the shadows, "I'll take you all home."

Jacky turned to see Kerevan leaning against a tree. "Did you know what was going to happen in there?" she demanded.

He shook his head. "Not a bit of it. You did what none of us had even considered, Jacky Rowan. Now I found this car in a ditch, and with a wally-stane—well, two or three really—I've got it working again. The ride will be more cramped than comfortable, but better than walking, I think."

"Judith!" Kate cried. "You rescued Judith!"

"The very vehicle," Kerevan replied.

"I thought you said your magics were all tricks and illusions," Jacky said as they all made their way down the mountain slope to where the car was waiting for them.

Kerevan glanced at her, then winked. "I lied," he said.

Twenty-two

They gathered in the room of the Gruagagh's Tower that overlooked Windsor Park—what faerie called Learg Green. The
room had settled from its shifting shadows and ghostly furnishings
into a warm kitchen with chairs for all. Bhruic had removed the last
of the spell from Moddy Gill, who proved to be a plain-featured,
friendly woman who now sat in a corner of the room with Arkan,
telling him how she thought he was rather brave. Arkan appeared
entranced. Finn perched on a stool, while Jacky and Eilian sat with
Kate in the window-seat. Kerevan leaned with studied ease against
the door near the hall.

The Gruagagh looked different. He was no longer dressed in
his black robes, but wore trousers and tunic of various shades of
brown and green. And he was smiling. The only one missing of those
who had escaped the Giants' Keep was the Laird's daughter, and she
was safe at her father's Court once more, with her father's faerie
healers to look after her.

"I have something for you, Jacky," Bhruic said.

He handed her some official looking papers which proved to
be the deed to a house. This house—the Gruagagh's Tower. There in

black and white was her name, Jacqueline Elizabeth Rowan. The owner of a new home.

"I told you I didn't want anything," Jacky said.

"Someone must live in the Gruagagh's Tower and who better than the Court's own Jack?"

"Where are you going?" she asked.

"I have a bargain with Kerevan to fulfill," he replied.

Kerevan grinned at Jacky when she turned to him and gave her a mocking, but friendly tug of the forelock. "And yes," he said, "I'm a Jack, too, though my Jack days are gone now. Jack Gooseberry was the name then, and wasn't I the wild one?"

"Too wild," Bhruic said wryly.

"I'd rather know why," Jacky said.

Bhruic sighed. "Why what?"

"Why couldn't you just have told us everything? Why were you so unfriendly? Why didn't you help more?"

Bhruic looked uncomfortable. He glanced at Kerevan, but there was no help there. The others in that room, except for Moddy Gill, were all giving him their full attention, for they too wanted the answer to those questions. Bhruic sighed again and pulled a chair closer to the windowseat.

"I didn't trust you," he said. "It was too convenient—a Jack out of nowhere, willing to help, Kate Crackernuts at her side. I thought you were one more attempt by the Host to pry me from my Tower. They knew my weakness better than my own Laird's folk ever did."

"Always sticking your nose in where it didn't have to go," Kerevan said.

"Always wanting to help those in trouble," Bhruic corrected him.

Kerevan shrugged. "Different ways of saying the same thing—that's all."

"I wanted to believe in you, Jacky Rowan," Bhruic went on. "Truly I did. But there was too much at stake. If it had been just myself, I would have taken the chance. But there was all of Kinrowan to think of as well."

"So now you're going and leaving me with"—she held up the deed to the Tower—"with this."

Bhruic nodded.

"But Samhaine night's still coming—and Kinrowan needs its Gruagagh."

"The Laird's daughter will be recovered enough by then, and we don't have the Unseelie Court to worry about—at least not this year. They'll grow strong again, they always do, but it will take time."

"But there's still got to be a gruagagh . . . "

"I thought a Jack such as you would be more than enough to take my place," Bhruic said.

"But *I* don't have any magics."

"Well, now," Kerevan said. "You've at least nine wally-stanes, and if you're sparing with them, and use your noggin a bit, you should do fine."

"But . . ."

"Oh, just think," Kate said. "Your own house. I think that's wonderful."

"But it's so big," Jacky protested half-heartedly.

She caught a smile pass between Bhruic and Kerevan and knew what they were thinking: She wanted to live here. She wanted to be Kinrowan's Jack. She didn't ever want to not know the magic of Faerie. They were right.

"If it's too big for you," Kate said, "then I'll move in with you. I'm not too proud to invite myself."

"So's it going to be a commune already?" Jacky asked. Her gaze flitted from Finn to Arkan.

"Not me," Finn said. "I've already got a snug little place just down the way from here, but I'll be dropping by for a hot cuppa from time to time. And there's always that comfortable perch in your tree between the Tower's garden and Learg Green—a fine place for a hob. You'll see me there often enough."

"I'm thinking of getting myself a wagon and pony," Arkan said, "and travelling some again. It's been years since I've seen the old haunts and Moddy here could use a new view or two."

It wasn't hard to see that they were already an item, Jacky thought. And speaking of items . . . shyer now, her gaze moved to Eilian. She was still attracted to the Lairdling, but wasn't sure how much of that was just her rebounding from Will and latching onto the first available—and gorgeous, she added to herself, let's admit it—fellow that came along.

Eilian smiled and lifted the hair at the back of his neck where the braids his Billy Blind had plaited hung. "I've one left," he said. "I wouldn't want to bring more trouble to you—I don't doubt you've seen enough to last a lifetime. But if there's room, I'd like to stay, at least till you're settled in."

"You see?" Bhruic said. "It's all settled."

"How come everybody settles things for me, but me?" Jacky wanted to know.

Bhruic smiled, but it was a serious smile. "I think that you settled everything yourself, Jacky Rowan, in a way that no other could, or perhaps even would have. You're the best Jack Faerie's known since, oh—"

"Me," Kerevan said without any pretense at modesty.

Jacky rolled her eyes. "Does this mean I have to learn to play the fiddle now?"

Kerevan shrugged. "There's worse fates."

"But not many," Bhruic added. "It's when you're learning the fiddle that you find out who your real friends are. It's no wonder they call it the devil's own instrument."

It was almost morning before those who were leaving actually took their leave. Arkan and Moddy Gill had slipped away rather quickly and Finn was asleep in one corner, with Kate nodding in another, when the Gruagagh, Kerevan, Eilian and Jacky went out into the park.

"I'm sorry it was so hard for you, Jacky," Bhruic said. "I'm sorry there was too much to risk that I couldn't trust your freely offered help. And as for that silence the last time you stayed in my Tower—you've Kerevan here to blame for that. It was part of my bargain for your safety that I not see you, or speak to you of our bargain."

"I know," Jacky said. "I just wish you weren't going away without my ever getting to know you. Why *do* you have to go now anyway? There's no more danger."

"But that's just it. I never wanted the mantle of a gruagagh. I was a poet first and a harper, Jacky." He nudged Kerevan. "This lug here was my master in those trades. Now that I know Kinrowan's safe, I can go back to being what I want to be."

"But what about me? What if I don't want to be Kinrowan's protector?"

"Don't you?"

That smile was back on the Gruagagh's lips again. Jacky thought about it, about Faerie and how her life had been before she fell into it. She shook her head. "If that's what it takes to live in Faerie, then I'll do it."

"You could live in Faerie without it."

"Yes . . . but then I'd just be wasting my time again. Now at least I'll have something meaningful to do."

"Just so."

"Except I don't know what it is that I *am* supposed to do."

"There's a hidden room on the third floor that will never be hidden from you, now that you are the Tower's mistress. The answer to your questions lie in it—it's not so hard. Not for a clever Jack like you."

"Yes, but . . . "

Bhruic smiled. "Farewell, Jacky Rowan, and to you, Eilian. Take good care of each other."

"The devil's own instrument!" Kerevan muttered, and then there was a rush of wind in the air, a taste of magic, and two swans, one white and one black, were rising on their wings into the wind. They circled once, twice, three times, dipping their wings, then they were gone, down the long grey October skies.

Jacky sighed and turned to Eilian. "Did you want to go with them?" she asked.

He shook his head.

"I did. Just a little. Just to be able to fly . . . " Her voice trailed off dreamily.

"I like it here just fine," Eilian said.

"Better than Dunlogan?"

"Much better than Dunlogan."

"Even though there aren't any swangirls here?"

"I never cared for swangirls. I always had my heart set on a Jack—if I could ever find myself one."

"Even one with corn stubble hair?"

"Especially one with corn stubble hair."

"I can't make promises," Jacky said. "You're getting me on the rebound."

"I know."

They looked at each other for a long moment, then Jacky reached for his hand, captured it, and led him back to the Gruagagh's Tower. No, she amended. It's the Jack's Tower now.

"The trouble with Jacks," she said, "is once you've got one, they're often more trouble than they're worth."

Eilian stopped her on the back steps of the Tower and tilted her head up so that she was looking into his eyes. "So long as it's the right sort of trouble," he said.

He kissed her before she could think of a suitably puckish sort of reply.

Drink Down the Moon

Sun & fire & candlelight
To all the world belong
But the moon pale & the midnight
Let these delight the strong.

—Robin Williamson,
from "By Weary Well"

Where the wave of moonlight glosses . . .
We foot it all the night,
Weaving olden dances,
Mingling hands and mingling glances
Till the moon has taken flight . . .

—W. B. Yeats,
from "The Stolen Child"

One

The King of the Faeries was abroad that night—in a fiddle tune, if not literally.

He slipped through the darkness in the 4/4 tempo of a slow reel, startled an owl in its perch, and crept through the trees to join the quiet murmur of the Rideau River as it quickened by Carleton University. At length, he came to the ears of a young woman who was sitting on the flat stones on the south bank of the river.

The fiddle playing that tune had a mute on its bridge, substantially reducing the volume of the music, but it was still loud enough for the woman to lift her head and smile when she heard it. She knew that tune, if not the fiddler, and yet she had a sense of the fiddler as well. There was something—an echo of familiarity—that let her guess who it was, because she knew from whom he'd learned to play.

Every good fiddler has a distinctive sound. No matter how many play the same tune, each can't help but play it differently. Some might use an up stroke where another would a down. One might bow a series of quick single notes where another would play them all with one long draw of the bow. Some might play a double stop where others would a single string. If the listener's ear was good enough, she could tell the difference. But you had to know the tunes, and the players, for the differences were minute.

"There's still a bit of you plays on, Old Tom," she whispered to the night as she stood up to follow the music to its source.

She was a small woman with brown hair cropped short to her scalp and a heart-shaped face. Her build was more wiry than slender; her features striking rather than handsome. She wore faded jeans, frayed at the back of the hems, sneakers, and a dark blue sweatshirt that was a size or so too big for her. Slipping through the trees, she moved so quietly that she found the fiddler and stood watching him for some time before he was aware of her presence.

She knew him by sight as soon as she saw him—confirming her earlier guess. It was Old Tom's grandson, Johnny Faw. He was a head taller than her own four foot eleven, the fiddle tucked under his clean-shaven chin, his head bent down over it as he drew the music from its strings. His hair was a darker brown than her own, an unruly thatch that hung over his shirt collar in back and covered his ears to just above his lobes. He wore brown corduroys and black Chinese rubber-soled slippers and a light blue shirt. The multi-coloured scarf around his neck and the gold loops glinting in each earlobe gave him the air of a Gypsy. His beat-up black fiddle case lay beside him with a brown quilted-cotton jacket lying next to it.

She waited until the tune was done—"The King of the Fairies" having made way for a Scots reel called "Miss Shepherd's"—and then stepped out into the little clearing where he sat playing. He looked up, startled at her soft hello and sudden appearance. As she sat down facing him, he took the fiddle from under his chin and held it and the bow on his lap.

With the tunes stilled, a natural hush held the wooded acres of Vincent Massey Park. The quiet was broken only by the sound of distant traffic on Riverside Drive and, closer to where they were sitting, Heron Road, both thoroughfares hidden from their sight by the treed hills of the park. What they could see from their point of vantage, through a screen of other trees, were the lights of Carleton University across the river.

They sat regarding each other for a long while, each one trying to read the other's expression in the poor light.

He was as handsome as Old Tom, she thought, studying the strong features that were so familiar because, like the fiddling, they reminded her of his grandfather. Some might say he was a bit too thin, but who was she to talk?

"I didn't think anyone would come," he said suddenly.

"I didn't know I was invited."

"No. I mean . . . "

She took pity as he grew flustered.

"I know," she said. "The tune was supposed to call me."

He nodded.

"And it did—for here I am. I'm sorry about Old Tom, Johnny. We all loved him. I know he stopped coming to see us, but some of us didn't forget him. We went and saw him, once in a while, but it was hard to do."

"I hated that place, too," Johnny said, "but it got to the point where I couldn't take care of him anymore. I wanted to, but he needed more than I could give. A nurse on twenty-four-hour call. Somebody to always sit with him. I couldn't afford to hire anyone. I have trouble just paying the rent as it is."

"We asked him to stay with us," she said, "but he wouldn't come."

"He could be pretty stubborn."

She smiled. "I'm not stubborn," she said in an excellent mimicry of Old Tom's voice. "I just know what's *right*."

"He used that argument on me, too," Johnny said with a grin.

They were both quiet for a long moment, then the woman stood. Johnny quickly put his fiddle and bow in their case and stood with her.

"Wait," he said.

"I have to go. I only came because . . . " Her voice trailed off and she shrugged. "For old times' sake."

"You can't go yet."

"But I can't stay."

"Why not? I mean, it's just . . . Who are you? How did you know Tom? How do you know *me*?"

She smiled. "I've seen you with Old Tom—and he talked to me about you."

"Before he died, he told me to come here and play that tune—

'The King of the Fairies'—but he wouldn't say why. 'They'll come,' he said, and that's all he'd say. So I played the tune and now here we are, but I don't know why."

"You miss him, don't you?"

Johnny nodded. "I went to see him just about every day."

"We'll miss him, too."

As she turned to go, Johnny caught her arm, surprised at the hardness of her muscles.

"Please," he said. "Just tell me: Why would you come here when that tune's played? Who are you?"

"We knew each other a long time ago," she said. "Old Tom and I. That's what I always called him—even back then—because he never seemed young. But he and I didn't wear our years the same and it bothered him. We didn't see him much for a while and then, when he married your grandmother, we didn't see him at all—not for years. Not until she died. Then he came back, looking for what he'd lost, I suppose, and we were still here. But it wasn't the same. It's never the same."

"You're not making any sense," Johnny said. "How could you know him before he met Gran? You don't look any older than I am."

A strange uneasiness was settling in the pit of his stomach. The feeling of being lost that had come over him since his grandfather had died intensified, leaving him with the sensation of being cut off from the rest of the world, from history, from everything that was, except for this moment.

"I know," she said. "It bothered Old Tom, too."

"You're confusing me. How can . . . ?"

But his voice trailed off. He wasn't sure what he wanted to ask anymore.

"I'm sorry," she said. "I don't mean to confuse you." She loosened his fingers from her arm. "You can call me Fiaina."

His hand fell limply to his side when she let it go. She reached up and brushed his cheek with the backs of her fingers.

"It's hard for me to ignore the music," she explained, "but I can't go through it all again, Johnny. Be well. Be good at everything you do. And especially keep the strings of your fiddle ringing—that keeps Old Tom alive, you know. He's in your music, because it's from him that you learned it."

She dropped her hand and stepped back.

"Now I do have to go."

Johnny took a half-step towards her, but kept his distance, not wanting to scare her off.

"What . . . what sort of a person are you, Fiaina?" he asked.

A look came to her face that was both merry and sad. She reached into her pocket and took out a small object that gleamed white in the starlight before she pressed it into his hand.

"We call ourselves sidhe," she said. "But you know us better as faerie."

And then she was gone.

She didn't step away into the trees. She never moved. One moment her fingers were light on his palm; the next she had disappeared.

Johnny stared at the spot where she had vanished, not sure what had happened. He took a step or two forward, moving his hands through the air, half-expecting to come into contact with her, but the little glade was empty except for him. The feeling in the pit of his stomach grew stronger. The sense of dislocation intensified. He looked down at what he held in his hand.

It was a small piece of flat bone, no longer than an inch and a half, carved into the shape of a fat fiddle. He turned it over in his fingers, feeling its smoothness. There was a tiny hole where the fiddle's scroll would have been if it was a real instrument— to hang it from a thong, he supposed.

He closed his fingers around it and slowly sat down. She couldn't have just vanished. It had to be this weird feeling he had— like he had the flu or something. Because people didn't just vanish.

We call ourselves sidhe . . . but you know us better as faerie. . . .

Faerie. Right.

It had to be a joke, only how had she pulled off that vanishing trick? For a moment he thought of picking up his fiddle and playing the tune again, but he knew without trying that it wouldn't work a second time.

Not tonight.

It might never work again.

He swallowed dryly and gave the bone fiddle another look. The sense of dislocation was beginning to fade, finally, but he didn't feel any better. Something had happened here, something strange, and it left him uneasy. If it had been a trick, then what was the point of it? And if it hadn't . . . what did it mean?

Faerie. We call ourselves . . .

But that was even more preposterous.

His hand started to tremble. He thrust the little carving into his pocket. She'd been touching his hand, and then she'd just vanished. How could she have done that? Nobody could move that fast.

Nobody human, he thought, but firmly pushed that thought away.

He studied his surroundings, the dark trees, the empty glade, waiting for someone to jump out and cry, "April fool!" Except it wasn't April. Though maybe he was a fool.

A shiver went through him and he put on his jacket. Picking up his fiddle case, he gave the spot where his mysterious visitor had vanished a last quick glance, then hurried off down the paved bike path that would take him by Billings Bridge Plaza to Bank Street.

They stood in Faerie—a half-step sideways from the world as Johnny Faw saw it—and watched him go. The woman who had named herself Fiaina had been joined by two others.

One was a small old man, shorter than her by a few inches, be-whiskered and thatch-haired, with a dried apple of a face. He wore a blue jacket over brown trousers and shirt, small leather boots that laced up, and a large, wide-brimmed hat with a three-cornered crown. His name was Dohinney Tuir.

The other was taller than either of them—a stocky, muscular woman with a blue-black mane of hair. There was a certain equine set to her features, accentuated by her broad flat nose, the wide set of her dark eyes, and the squareness of her jaw. Her name was Loireag and there was nothing but the wind between the night air and her ebony skin.

"You answer to 'Fiaina'?" Loireag asked the first woman. There was a bite of gentle humour in her voice as she spoke. "There's a new one."

"You're not the only one can claim that name, Jenna," Dohinney Tuir added.

Jenna shrugged. "It wasn't a lie. I've been called wild before, and worse. I wasn't about to give him a true name—not even a speaking one."

"And if he goes out some night calling for Fiaina?" Tuir asked. "Arn knows what'll come in answer."

Jenna looked up to where Arn hung in the sky—a round full moon, deep with mystery.

"I gave him a charm," she said.

"Oh, yes!" Loireag broke in with a whinnying laugh. "And Arn knows what *that'll* call to him."

"Nothing unsaintly—that much I can guarantee."

"Nothing evil, perhaps," Tuir agreed, "but maybe the Pook of Puxill?"

Jenna sighed and looked away from her companions.

"I've had too many tadpoles in my pond," she said. "I've neither the time nor the heart for yet another."

Tuir nodded knowingly. "It's no comfort watching them wither away and die in the blink of an eye—I'll give you that."

"I still can't understand why you bother with them in the first place," Loireag added. "They've no stamina."

"They shine so brightly," Jenna said. "It's that light in them that always draws me. They're here and gone so quick that they have to burn brightly, or not be seen at all."

"How can you miss them?" Loireag asked. "Set a pair of them down any place and quicker than you can blink, you'll be up to your ears in them. They breed like rabbits."

"They *are* a lusty race," Jenna said with a smile.

Loireag snorted. "Give me a hob any day. At least they last the whole night."

She grinned at Tuir, who was puffing up his chest at her words.

"When they're not too old, that is," she added.

The little man lost his breath, chest sagging, and scowled at her.

"If he comes again," he said, turning to Jenna, "will you answer his call?"

She shook her head. "I won't be here to answer any calls. I gave him the charm, the same one Old Tom had before him, only Tom returned it to me. Johnny Faw can either follow where it will lead him, or not—it's his to choose."

"You're still going, then?" Loireag asked.

"Someone has to—if there's to be a rade at all this year."

All three of them were quiet then, thinking of how long it had been since the fiaina had gathered for the luck rade.

The fiaina sidhe were solitary faerie, not aligned with either the Seelie or Unseelie Courts, and got their luck in ways different from those of their gentrified cousins. They gathered, once a moon, to ride a long and winding way through the land, following old straight tracks and other moonroads in single file. This was how they got their luck. There was something in the long winding file of faerie, following those roads with the full moon shining above them. . . . Some combination of it all made the luck grow strong in them, recharging them like batteries.

Without it, they diminished. Their magics weakened. They faded.

Last autumn there had been a struggle between the two Courts, a struggle that the Seelie faerie won. The Wild Hunt had been freed from centuries of bondage, the Gruagagh of Kinrowan had given his Tower to a Jack, and the Unseelie Court was cast to the winds—many of them slain. The weeks following that time, from Samhaine into Midwinter, had been a period of change. The Seelie Court settled back into its old familiar ways, the Wild Hunt was gone—Arn knew where—and the Unseelie Court slowly began to regroup and gather into new alliances.

The fiaina sidhe, never ones to join either Court, had stood back and watched it all.

The closest they came to a communal effort was their rade, for solitary or not, all faerie followed the Moon-mother Arn and she had imbued even the fiaina with a certain sociability—even if it was only realized once every four weeks when Arn turned a new face to the world below. So they had gone about their own ways until they realized that something was taking advantage of the upset in the balance between the two faerie Courts to make inroads into the Borderlands that the fiaina claimed for their own.

Old haunts were found deserted of their inhabitants. Here a hob was found slain, stripped of his blue coat and stitcheries. There a derrie-down was taken from her river holt, lying stretched out and dead on the shore. And the rade was disrupted, time and again.

When they gathered for their rade, a foul wind with the smell of old graves would rise to hang about them. Clouds would cloak the moon's face. Whisperings and ugly mutterings could be heard all around them, but nothing was seen. And Jenna Pook, the Pook of Puxill who led the rade, who alone knew the twists and turns of the old tracks and moonroads, would find her mind fogged and clouded until she was too confused to take a step.

As their luck faded, many of the fiaina sidhe fell back from their old haunts in the Borderlands, faring deeper into their secret territories to come no more to the gatherings. Where the Courts would band together in a time of crisis, the fiaina withdrew as though it was a disease that beset them and they might catch it if they came too close to each other.

Too proud to go to their cousins for help, and unwilling to pay what that help would cost them, there were still a few fiaina who were determined to stand up to whatever it was that threatened them. Foremost of them was the Pook who led the rade.

As though sensing that she was its greatest danger, the enemy concentrated on her. More nights than one she'd spent fleeing . . . something. She had no clear picture of what it was that chased her. Sometimes she thought it was a black dog, other times a black horse. Sometimes it came upon her so quickly that she barely escaped. Other times it merely crept up on her like a mist, or a tainted smell. It was only constant vigilance that kept her free of its clutches.

So it was that she made her decision to look for help—not from the Courts, for like all the fiaina, she wouldn't pay their price. The Laird of the Seelie Court would demand allegiance in return for his help, and the fiaina would never give up their independence. As for the Unseelie Court, no one knew if they had a new chief to approach in the first place, and if the Laird's folk would demand allegiance, the Host of the Unseelie Court would take their souls.

So it was to their own that the fiaina must turn—a skillyman or wisewife of the sidhe. The first that had come to Jenna's mind was the Bucca who'd taught her the way that the rade must follow, who'd untangled the skein of old tracks and moonroads and given her their proper pattern.

"A Fiddle Wit would help us," Dohinney Tuir said after a while.

"If we had one," Jenna said. "But Johnny Faw's a tadpole, not a Fiddle Wit."

"He could learn."

"He could," she agreed. "If he wanted to. He has the music—I won't deny that. But wit takes more than music, more than luck and a few tricks as well. From what little I've seen of him, I don't know if he has what's needed."

"It's hard to learn something," Tuir said, "when you don't know it's there to learn."

"But if we led him every step of the way, it would mean nothing. He'd be no closer. The wit needs to be earned, not handed to any tadpole who looks likely—*if* it even was the sort of thing that could be handed out."

"Still. You gave him the charm."

"I did. I owed him that much—for Old Tom's sake."

"So you'll go off, looking for the Bucca," Tuir said, "while—"

"It's not my fault the luck's gone!"

"No. But only a Pook can lead the rade, and the closest we have after you is your sister, who—"

"Half-sister."

"It doesn't make that much difference. She had fiaina blood and—"

"Not to hear her tell it."

"—she's the closest to a Pook we'll have if you don't come back."

"I'll be back."

"Yes, but—"

"Don't forget," Jenna said a little sharply. "We have no rade as it is—whether I go or I stay."

"I think it's the Gruagagh that's to blame," Loireag said firmly. "It's always a gruagagh that's to blame when there's trouble in Faerie. A wizard never knows to leave well enough alone. They're as bad as humans—always taking a thing apart to see how it works."

"The only gruagagh we've had near here was Kinrowan's," Jenna said. "And he's gone now."

Loireag frowned. "It's a new one then—one who hasn't made himself known yet."

"What I want to know," Tuir said, "is this: Gruagagh or whatever, it has your scent. When you go, will it follow you, or will it chase down your sister, or some innocent like your tadpole whose only crime is that you gave him a charm with your scent upon it?"

"You're too soft-hearted," Loireag told the little man before

Jenna could reply. "It's just a human we're talking about. Better the enemy goes sniffing after him than follows our Pook. At least *she's* doing something to help us."

"Johnny Faw will be in no danger," Jenna said. "The charm will sain him from evil influences. And as for my half-sister, she goes her own way—as we all do."

Tuir nodded and kicked at the turf with the pointed toe of his boot.

"I just wish you didn't have to go," he said.

"Or that you'd at least not go alone," Loireag said.

"The Bucca will be hard enough to track down as it is," Jenna said. "I'll never find him with you in tow. He's never been one for company—two's a crowd, so far as he's concerned. I don't doubt he's hiding away in an Otherworld of the manitous and I'll have a stag's own time chasing him down."

There was nothing the other two could say. They'd been through this argument before—too many times since Jenna had announced her intentions to leave a few days ago.

"When do you go?" Tuir asked.

"Tonight. Now. Johnny Faw's calling-on tune strikes me as a sign of sorts. Giving him the charm was like completing the last piece of unfinished business I had. So I'll go now with my own calling-on tune . . . for the Bucca."

Loireag nodded and stepped close to her, enfolding Jenna in a quick embrace.

"Luck," she said gruffly, and stepped back.

Jenna found a smile, but Loireag had already turned and was making for her home in the river. Halfway between the water and where Jenna and Tuir still stood, the running figure of the ebony-skinned woman became a black-flanked horse. She reared at the edge of the river, hooves clattering on the flat stones, then the water closed over the kelpie's head and she was lost from sight.

"Don't worry so much," Jenna said to her remaining companion. "I'll be back before you know it, and then I'll lead us all on such a rade as we've never seen before—high and low, we'll follow more roads than a spider has threads in its web."

Tuir nodded, blinking back tears. In his eyes, Jenna could see the same foreboding that had been in the kelpie's. She watched him swallow uncomfortably, his Adam's apple bobbing, as he obviously tried to think of something cheerful to say. Finally, he gave her a quick kiss and a tight hug, then hurried away, following the bicycle path that Johnny Faw had taken when he'd left earlier.

Alone now, Jenna stood for long moments, breathing the night air. Everything had a clarity about it in the moonlight, a sharpness of focus that kept her standing there, drinking in the sight of it, the smells, all the sparkle of the moment. Then she shook herself, like a person who'd caught herself dozing. Fetching a small journeysack from where she'd left it by Loireag's river, she shouldered it and set off, crossing the river and heading north.

It was the quest itself that was as much to blame for what happened, as anything else.

After long weeks and months of fretting and danger, of losing the rade and its luck, of being hunted but not being able to strike back . . . to finally be *doing* something . . . Jenna let her guard down as she ran at a pace-eating lope that she could keep up for hours.

She was thinking of the road before her and the Bucca at its end, not about what had driven her to set off on this quest. Her heart felt lighter than it had for a very long time, for she'd always been a doer, not a thinker. She even hummed a tune to herself, a fiddle tune—not one of Johnny Faw's, but one that Old Tom used to play in the old days.

A mile or so north of where she'd left her friends, after speeding through city streets to the landscaped lawns that the National Capital Commission kept neat and trim along the Parkway that followed the Ottawa River, the enemy found and caught her.

It came like a pack of dogs, spindly creatures, with triangular goblin faces, that ran on all fours, but could clutch and grab and tear with fore and hind legs. They made no sound as they came up from behind her, rapidly closing up the distance between them. When they struck, she never knew what hit her. She never had a chance.

Attacking, they were no longer silent. Snarls and high-pitched growls cut across the night as they circled her still body to slash, dance away, then slash again. By the time the brown-cloaked figure arrived to drive the pack from its prey, there was only a heartbeat of life left in her. The figure bent over Jenna, pushed back its hood to look into her eyes as her life drained from her. When the moment passed, the figure rose, its pale eyes gleaming as though it had stolen the Pook's life force and taken it into itself.

Tugging its hood back into place, the figure stood and walked away, leaving the broken body where it lay. Of the pack that had taken Jenna down, there was now no trace, but the sharp sting of magic stayed thick in the air.

Two

Henk Van Roon was sitting on the stairs of Johnny's porch
when Johnny arrived home, the octagonal shape of his lac-
quered wood concertina case on a step by his knee. He was a few
years older than Johnny, having just turned thirty the previous
week—a tall, ruddy-cheeked Dutchman who seemed, at first glance,
to be all lanky arms and legs. His long blonde hair was tied back at
the nape of his neck with a leather thong and he was dressed in jeans
and a Battlefield Band T-shirt, with a worn and elbow-patched
tweed jacket overtop.

"How're you holding out, Johnny?" he asked.

Johnny sighed and sat down beside him, laying his fiddle case
on a lower step. "Like I've got a hole inside me—you know?"

"You want some company?"

Johnny didn't answer. He looked across the street, thinking of
how many times he'd sat on these steps with Tom, playing tunes
sometimes, or talking, or sometimes just not doing anything, just
being together. He turned slowly as Henk touched his shoulder and
found a weak smile.

"Yeah," he said. "I could use some company. C'mon in."

Grabbing his fiddle, he led the way inside. The house was an old three-story brick building on Third Avenue of which he rented the bottom floor. He unlocked the door to his apartment and stood aside to let Henk go in first, closing the door behind them.

"You want something—coffee, tea?" he asked.

"You got a beer?"

"I think so."

Johnny left his case by the door and went into the kitchen. Henk stood for a moment, then lowered his long frame into the beat-up old sofa that stood under the western window. There was a fake mantelpiece on the north wall, snugly set between built-in bookcases that took up the rest of the wall. The bookcases were filled with an uneven mixture of tune books and folklore collections, the remainder made up of paperbacks of every genre, from mysteries to historicals and best-sellers.

The mantel was covered with knickknacks, most having something to do with fiddlers or fiddling. There were wooden gnome fiddlers and ceramic ones; a Christmas rabbit complete with a red and green scarf and a pig standing on its hind legs, both with instruments in hand; pewter fiddles lying on their sides; even a grasshopper, playing its instrument like a cello.

Two old Canadiana hutches stood against the south wall, holding Johnny's stereo and record collection. The west wall didn't exist, except as a hall that led from the front door to the rest of the apartment—a kitchen at the end of the hall, two bedrooms and a washroom. A door at the back led from the kitchen to a storage shed that was set snug against the rear of the house. The walls of the living room and throughout the apartment were covered with posters and pictures of folk festivals, Irish crofters' cottages, Scottish landscapes and the like.

"All I've got is a couple of domestics," Johnny said as he returned with a can of Labatt's Blue in each hand.

"No problem," Henk said.

Johnny gave him one of the cans and took the other to one of the two chairs that stood opposite the sofa. There was a low coffee table between sofa and chairs, covered with magazines and a coffee mug that was half full of cold tea.

"You going to pick up Tom's stuff tomorrow?" Henk asked.

Johnny nodded.

"You want a hand with it?"

"There's not that much—but thanks."

"I was thinking more of some moral support."

"Well, I could use that. Thanks, Henk."

"Hey, no problem."

They sipped at their beer, neither speaking for a while. Just when Henk thought he'd better come up with something to pull his friend out of his funk, Johnny looked up.

"I had something weird happen to me tonight," he said.

"Weird curious, or weird spooky?"

"A little of both, I guess."

He related what had happened to him.

"She was touching my hand," Johnny said as he finished up, "giving me the bone carving, and then she was gone. Poof. Just like that. Now, I know I've been a little out of it lately, what with Tom and everything, but there's no way she could have just slipped away from me. She vanished, and I can't figure out how she pulled it off. Or what it was all about in the first place. Does it make any sense to you?"

Henk shook his head. He picked up the bone fiddle from where it lay on the coffee table between them and turned it over in his hands as he had when Johnny first showed it to him.

"Do you believe in ghosts . . . or fairies?" Johnny asked.

Henk smiled. "Only when I'm stoned."

"Know anybody who does?"

"I'd've figured you—with all those books."

"Those are—were mostly Tom's," Johnny said. "And besides, they're not the same thing. They all talk about old farmers seeing things—country stuff. Old country stuff at that. I mean, some old guy living in the Shetland Islands, maybe, or the Black Forest—who knows what they'd see. But this is the city—or at least a park in the city."

He sighed, staring at the carving in Henk's hand.

"And I don't believe in them either," he added. "I'd like to, I guess. But . . . you know."

Henk nodded. "It doesn't make sense." He laid the bone fiddle back down on the coffee table. "Did she really seem to know Tom?"

"We didn't talk that much, but she seemed to. Except she acted like she knew him when he was young, and she didn't seem any older than you or me."

"And she really just vanished?"

Johnny nodded.

"Somebody's playing games with you, Johnny. I don't know how, or why, but that's what it's got to be."

"I guess."

Talking it over with Henk made it all seem different. When Fiaina had stood there talking to him, when she'd just vanished . . . it had seemed very real. Or very unreal, but actually happening.

He picked up the bone fiddle and rubbed his thumb against it. "This thing's old."

"Seems to be."

"What if she really was what she said she was?"

"Uh-uh. You're setting yourself up for a bad fall there. Somebody's playing a scam on you and if you start taking it seriously, you'll be playing right into their hands. Don't go with it, Johnny. The best thing you could do is put that carving up on the mantel, with the rest of your fiddle collection, and forget about it."

"But I've got a feeling. . . . "

"Yeah. Me, too. And it's a bad one."

Johnny gave him a curious look. "What makes you say that?"

"I don't know. I wasn't there, so I didn't see what happened. But I know you, Johnny. You're a pretty straightforward kind of a guy. You've never chased phantoms. We both know there's no such thing as elves and goblins and all that kind of thing, so why start believing in them now?"

"That's a pretty lame reason," Johnny said. "But I know what you mean."

He glanced at the wall of books, not at the paperbacks so much as the hardcovers that Tom had collected over the years. Douglas's *Scottish Lore and Folklore.* Alan Garner's *The Guizer. The Folklore of the Cotswolds,* by Katharine Briggs. Evans's *Irish Folk Ways.* There were over a hundred of them, all collections of old stories and anecdotes, country customs, and the like. Johnny had read through some of them, liking the connection they made with his music—just liking them for what they were, really. Even those that were a little heavier going, like Graves's *The White Goddess* or Baughman's index of folktale types and motifs.

"But I like the idea of hobgoblins and little people still being around," Johnny said, looking back at his friend. "I never liked the idea that we'd chased them away to some Tir na nOg, you know?"

"If," Henk said, "and remember I'm saying *if* they ever existed, I don't see any reason why they couldn't adjust to the way the world's changed."

Johnny smiled, his first real smile since he'd got the phone call late one night last week, telling him that his grandfather had died.

"See?" he said. "It's beginning to intrigue *you* now."

His smile widened at the big "Why not?" grin that came to Henk's features.

"Can you see punk elves?" Henk asked.

"Disco dwarves!"

They both laughed.

"We've got to have a plan," Henk went on. "Whoever that woman was, we've got to track her down."

"How are we going to do that?"

"Go back to the park tomorrow night."

Johnny shrugged. "I suppose."

"You've got a better idea?"

"No. It's just that she gave me the feeling that she wouldn't be showing up there again."

He glanced at the books again.

"It's too bad," he added, "that there's no one collecting contemporary folktales. Citylore. There's got to be stories."

"You hear about that kind of thing in a place like New York," Henk said, "but Ottawa? What've we got? Anyway, what good would that do?"

"It'd give us a place to start looking, for one thing. Maybe there's a certain part of the city that's got more weird stories about it than another. We could go check it out . . . ask around."

"If we asked most people about fairies, they'd think we were looking for gays."

"Cute."

"No, really. We can't just go around and do what? Talk to winos and bag ladies?"

Johnny nodded. "Now, there's an idea."

"Oh, come *on*. You can't seriously expect we'll find your mysterious fairy queen by chatting up bums?"

"No. I'm not really thinking about her, to tell you the truth. It's the idea that intrigues me now—of elves and the like living in an urban environment. Not that they *really* are—just what sort of perception people have of them in the city."

"What?"

"You know. What kind of odd little stories or unexplained incidents people talk about."

"Oh. Like the lunatic fringe. UFOs and stuff like that. We'll have to have certain criteria to go by. Everybody we interview will have to have pink hair, say, and—" He paused and snapped his fingers. "Wait a minute."

Johnny rolled his eyes. "Come on, Henk. You're getting out of control—and on just one beer. Think of your rep."

"No. This is something different. I just thought of somebody who fits your bill perfectly. Have you gone to see Greg's new band yet?"

"No, I've just heard of them. What're they called—AKT? I hear they've got a dynamic lead singer."

Henk nodded. "I was thinking of their sax player."

"I don't listen to a lot of R&B."

"You don't have to. You just have to talk to this girl. She's always making up stories about gremlins living in the sewers and stuff like that."

"Oh, yeah? What's her name?"

"Jemi Pook."

It was one of the Laird of Kinrowan's own foresters who found Jenna's body just before dawn. He was a young hob named Dunrobin Mull, somewhat taller than most hobs and beardless, with a dark red stocking cap, and trousers and jerkin of mottled green. He rode a brown and grey speckled pony that was shaggy and short-legged. The pony came to an abrupt halt as it and its rider spied the Pook's torn and battered body.

For a long moment the hob sat astride his mount, staring down, his stomach turning knots as he looked on the gruesome sight. His pony sidestepped nervously under him, nostrils widening.

Mull leaned over and patted its neck, then slowly slid from its back and stepped closer towards the body.

Being neither gruagagh nor skillyman, he knew little of magic and so sensed nothing of the traces of it that were left in the air, nothing except a weird tingle at the nape of his neck that lifted the hair from his skin. He put that down to the eeriness of the moment. But he was a tracker, and it surprised him to find only a single set of man-sized tracks leading up to the corpse, and then away again. There was no sign of what had done such damage to the Pook, only the marks of her flailing about as she had tried to fight off her attacker.

"Hempen, hampen," Mull muttered as he sketched a quick saining in the air. "What sort of a beast can do this damage and leave no sign?"

It hadn't been the man, for it was plain by the tracks that he'd done no more than bend down over the Pook before turning away again. Mull looked about in all directions, through both Faerie and the world of men, but saw nothing. There were only the tracks of the man who'd come and gone.

It was a poor neighbor who left a body lying like this after discovery, Mull thought. He'd not treat the dead so poorly himself — none he knew would.

He took a blanket from where it was tied in a tight roll at the back of his saddle and gingerly placed Jenna's body upon it. He folded the blanket around her, tied it shut, then struggled with it to his pony, staggering under its weight. The pony shied at the burden until Mull spoke a few comforting words, but it was still long moments before the beast was calm enough to let him tie the bundle to his saddle. Giving a last look around, Mull spotted the Pook's journeysack where it lay a few feet away. He fetched it and tied it to the saddle as well.

"Come on, Goudie," he murmured to his pony. "It's not so far to the Laird's Court."

The pony whickered, thrusting its nostrils against the hob's shoulders. Mull gave the broad nose a quick comforting pat, then led the pony away, heading eastward to where the Laird's Court stood overlooking the Ottawa River from the heights that men named Parliament Hill.

Three

All Kindly Toes, better known to friends and fans as AKT, were playing a street dance the next night. According to the posters stapled to telephone posts, the dance was being billed as "The Last Days of Summer Tour." It didn't seem to bother anyone that just one gig was being advertised as a tour—it was all in good fun.

The band was already on stage and halfway through their first set by the time Johnny and Henk arrived. The easternmost block of Chesley Street in Ottawa South had been closed off and the stage squatted where the street made a "T" as it met Wendover, speakers racked up on either side. The sound board was set up on the northeast corner and there was a crowd of over a hundred people dancing in front of the stage or standing and watching from the sidewalks. The band was just finishing up a funky version of "Love Potion No. 9" and immediately launched into "River Deep, Mountain High."

"They're good," Johnny said, speaking into Henk's ear to make himself be heard over the music.

Henk grinned and nodded. He kept his gaze on the stage as he led them closer.

On the right side of the stage, Greg Parker, the founder and old man of the band, was playing guitar. He had short dirty-blond hair and was wearing a Hawaiian shirt with a clashing burgundy and white striped tie, blue jeans, and an off-white cotton sports jacket with the sleeves rolled up to the elbows. The bass player, Tommy Moyer, was dressed similarly, if a touch more tastefully, as his shirt and tie matched. He was a big bearish man, the Fender bass he played looking like a toy in his hands. David Blair, a thin black man wearing a UB40 T-shirt, was playing drums. Both he and Tommy, like the rest of the band except for Greg, looked to be in their early twenties. Greg was thirty-eight.

On the far left, Trudy MacDonald was playing the organ. She had short brown hair and a round face, and grinned as she played. Center stage was the lead vocalist, an old girlfriend of Henk's, Johnny remembered as he looked at her. Her name was Beth Kerwin. She swayed as she sang, holding the microphone in one hand, head tilting back as she hit the chorus. Her brown hair was cut short on top, the sides and back long and gathered into a French braid that fell halfway down her back. She wore a short black fifties-style dress that was covered with a design of multi-coloured jelly beans.

As the band went into the bridge between verses and the sax cut in, Johnny turned his attention to the girl they'd come to meet. Jemi Pook was tiny, her tenor sax seeming as huge in her hands as Tommy's bass was diminutive in his. She was wearing a grey and pink minidress, the rectangular-shaped colours arranged in an Art Deco pattern. Her hair was pink, too, a brighter shade than her dress, and stood up in punky spikes—a look that was already passé, but on her it still worked.

Looking at her, Johnny's chest went tight. He knew her, knew that face. With only a late-night memory of it, he still knew her.

There were three more songs before the band took a break, but Johnny hardly heard them. He watched the sax player, trying to understand her. She was relaxed and loose on stage, strutting in time with Greg and Tommy like Gladys Knight's Pips, sharing Greg's mike on choruses, leaning back, the bell of her sax rising up to her own mike when she had a riff to play. There was nothing in what he saw of her on stage during those songs that explained last night.

"Come on," Henk said as the band finished "Baby Love" and left the stage.

He made his way behind the stage to where the band was relaxing with friends on the broad lawn of the tall three-storied house that towered over the proceedings. Johnny followed, the tight feeling in his chest still there. He wasn't sure if he was nervous, or afraid. Maybe a little of both.

We call ourselves sidhe....

There was something weird going on and he was beginning to have second thoughts about getting involved in it. The last thing he needed was to get mixed up with a bunch of ... what? She'd said nothing last night to make him afraid. All she'd done was talk about Tom. She'd been nice about it all. Only why had she come when he'd played that tune? Why had she given him the carving. *How* had she pulled off that vanishing trick?"

He thought of just leaving, then and there, but then it was too late for second thoughts.

"Hey, Jemi!" Henk was calling. "I've got a friend I'd like you to meet."

She turned at the sound of her name, a beer in hand. She appeared taller than last night, her hair was a little longer. But, then, she was wearing black pumps now, and her hair had been gelled to stand up in spikes.

"Hi, Henk." She glanced at Johnny. "What've you got in there?" she asked, looking at his fiddle case. "A clarinet?"

"No. It's a—"

"I know. A fiddle. I was just teasing."

Johnny tried to think of something to say, but she was already looking back at Henk.

"What brings an old hippie like you out of the woodwork?" she asked, a quick smile taking any possible sting from the question.

"Thought I'd take Johnny slumming," Henk replied. "You know—show him what it sounds like when white folk play black music."

David Blair, the drummer, was standing near.

"This isn't exactly a deep tan," he said, holding out a dark-skinned arm.

"Well, that's all the band's got going for it, isn't it? Solid rhythm."

David grinned. "Yeah. And I play great basketball, too."

Greg appeared at David's elbow. "Hey, you guys want a drink? We've got pop and beer."

"Sounds great," Henk said.

As everyone started to drift off, Johnny touched Jemi's shoulder.

"Fiaina," he said.

She turned towards him, a strange look in her eyes. "What did you say?"

Her eyes didn't seem as big now as they had last night. Eye shadow was dark around them. She wore rhinestone earrings, each with three gleaming strands, and a necklace of fake pearls, tight like a choker around her neck. The thin spaghetti straps of her dress were pale against the brown tan of her shoulders.

"How did you do that last night?" Johnny asked. "How'd you just vanish?"

"Wait a sec—let's back up a minute. Right now's the first time I've met you."

Johnny shook his head. "I played the tune, like Tom said I should, and you came. I'm not about to forget it. And you gave me this."

Jemi had tossed her friends a quick glance and was backing away when Johnny brought the bone carving from his pocket and held it out to her on an open palm.

"I never . . ." Jemi started to say.

Her voice trailed off as she looked at the bone fiddle. She reached out with one finger and touched it.

"Where did you get this?" she asked, her gaze lifting to meet his.

"Last night. You gave it to me."

She shook her head. "It wasn't me—but I think I'm beginning to get an idea of just who it was you did meet."

"It was you," Johnny said.

"Wasn't. We had a rehearsal last night that went on till around two. Ask around if you don't believe me."

"But—"

"You met my sister. Jenna."

"She said—_you_ said your name was Fiaina."

"Fiaina's just a generic term," Jemi told him. "It's not a name.

It's like saying a Scotty dog. Or a Clydesdale horse." She took pity on his confusion. "Look, I know what Jenna can be like. Are you planning to stick around for the rest of the show?"

"I guess so. Sure."

"Okay. Let's go get you a beer and relax a bit. I really don't feel up to getting into anything too heavy on a break—I've got to get up and play again in a few minutes, you know? But afterwards, we'll talk."

"This Jenna—"

"Afterwards," Jemi said firmly.

She grabbed him by the arm and steered him to where Henk and some of the others were talking around a cooler.

"Here," she said as she got him a beer. "Your name's Johnny—right?"

"Johnny Faw."

She pointed at his fiddle case. "Are you any good with that?"

"I'm all right."

"Great. Maybe we'll play a couple of tunes together later. Do you know 'Jackson's'? Ever heard it played on a sax?"

Johnny shook his head. "But I've heard Moving Hearts."

"Great band. I jammed with their piper once. Boy. Pipes and sax trading off on trad tunes—you wouldn't think they'd sound so sweet together. Course, they're both reed instruments, so—"

"Okay, kids!"

They looked over to see Greg waving his arms around as though he were leading a cavalry charge.

"Time to go wow 'em again," he said.

The Eurythmics tape that had been playing during the break faded out as the band began to get back on stage.

"Stick around—okay?" Jemi said.

Johnny nodded. "Break a leg," he said.

Jemi shook her head. "In this band," she told him, "it's stub a toe." She grinned when he smiled. "Get out there and dance, Johnny. I'll be watching for you."

And then she was gone, bounding onto the stage and strapping on her sax. Johnny drifted around to the front of the stage as the band kicked into "I Heard It Through the Grapevine."

"She's okay, isn't she?" Henk said as he joined Johnny. "Did she give you any hot leads?"

"Things've gotten a little more complicated," Johnny said.

"How so?"

"She looks just like the woman I met last night, only she says that woman's her sister."

"Go on."

"No, really. She's going to talk to me later."

"So you're going to stick around?"

Johnny nodded.

"Well, I'm taking off. Mountain Ash are playing up at Patty's Place and I haven't seen either of those guys for a long time. Maybe we can meet there later."

"I don't know. It all depends on what Jemi's got to say."

"Okay. Then maybe I'll just call you tomorrow."

"Sure."

As Henk left, Johnny turned back to the stage and met Jemi's gaze.

"Dance !" she mouthed at him.

The Jack of Kinrowan's Tower, formerly the residence of Kinrowan's Gruagagh, Bhruic Dearg, was an old three-storied house. It faced Belmont Avenue in Ottawa South, while its backyard looked out on Windsor Park. When the Gruagagh had lived there, the building had always had a deserted look about it. The new owners soon changed that.

Outside, the lawns were mown, the hedges and shrubberies trimmed, the flowerbeds weeded. The backyard held a small vegetable plot now, and if the rear hedge was a little unruly, that was only to ensure privacy from the park beyond. Three tall oak trees, two by the hedge and one closer to the house, stood watch over the yard, throwing their shade over most of it except for where the vegetable garden was laid out, close to the house.

Inside, things had changed as well. Bhruic Dearg had lived frugally. The downstairs rooms had ranged in decor from spartan to bare, for the Gruagagh had only used two rooms on the second floor. Now the downstairs had a homey, if somewhat cluttered, air to it. There were Oriental and rag carpets on the floor, bookcases overloaded with books, two sofas, three fat easy chairs, cabinets for the stereo and records, side tables, funky old standing lamps, and every kind of personal knickknack and treasure.

The kitchen had a nook with a small table and four chairs in it. There were pots, pans and utensils hanging from its beamed ceiling and the walls. Pictures of wild animals, English cottages—at least five of Anne Hathaway's, showing the famous garden—and barnyard scenes hung wherever there was room.

Upstairs, there were two bedrooms in constant use, with a pair of guest rooms and a large bathroom. It was on the third floor that the building retained the strangeness of a wizard's tower.

There were bookcases all along one wall here as well, but its books held the lore and histories of Faerie as fact, unlike the books that Johnny Faw's grandfather had collected, which contained only mankind's view of Faerie. Another wall held a long worktable, with a window above it. On either side of the window were hundreds of tiny drawers, each filled with herbs, medicines and remedies. The table itself was a clutter of jars and bottles, notebooks, quill pens now long dried, various knives, pestles and mortars, and tools. Against a third wall were a pair of comfortable reading chairs with a low table and a reading lamp between them. The fourth wall held a large window. Leaning on its sill and looking out was the Jack of Kinrowan.

Jacky Rowan was a young woman in her early twenties with short-cropped blonde hair and a quick smile. She was dressed casually in faded jeans, moccasins, and an old patched sweater. Her eyes were a dark blue-grey, her gaze intent on what she studied through the window.

The curious property of that particular window was that the entire city could be seen from it, every part of it, in close enough detail that individual figures could be made out and recognized. It was a gruagagh's window; an enchantment born of Faerie.

The Tower itself stood on a criss-crossing of leys, the moon-roads that the fiaina sidhe followed in their rade to replenish their luck. In this Seelie Court, it was the Gruagagh who had been the heart of the realm, gathering luck from the leys and spreading it through the Laird's land of Kinrowan. As Jacky had taken his place, she was now Kinrowan's heart as well as its Court Jack. The realm that the window looked out upon was all under her care.

Her attention was focused on a house in the Glebe, an area just north of Ottawa South that the faerie called Cockle Tom's Garve. Earlier in the evening she had noticed a greyish discolouration about the house—a vague aura of fogging that emanated from every part of the building. As that house also stood on a crossing of a number of leys—though not so many as the Jack's Tower—it was a matter of some concern.

Jacky looked down at the book she had propped up on the windowsill beside her, running her finger down half a page as she read, then returned her gaze to the house.

"Basically," she said, "it just says it's some kind of depression."

"How so?"

"Oh, I don't know," Jacky said, feeling frustrated.

She turned and sat on the sill to look at her friend.

Kate Hazel was sitting on a tall stool by the worktable, a number of other books and one of the Gruagagh's journals spread out in front of her. She was Jacky's age, a slim woman with dark brown curly hair that was tied back in a short ponytail. Jacky envied Kate's natural curls. Jacky's own hair, if she let it grow out, tended to just hang there.

"Well, according to this," Kate said, tapping one of her books, "a grey hue on a building or place—especially one situated on one or more lines of power—means something's interrupting the flow."

"And that means?"

"That it needs to be fixed, or we'll have a problem. If the flow of the leys gets too disrupted, or if it spreads out through their networking lines . . . Dum da dum dum."

Jacky sighed. "How can a house be depressed?"

"I think your book's referring to the flow rate of the current being depressed," Kate said. "Not that the house is bumming out."

"Does *your* book say how to fix it?"

Kate shook her head, then grinned and waved at the wall of books. "But I'm sure it's in there somewhere."

"Oh, lovely. One day we really should take the time and index them."

"I'll bet one of the wally-stanes would do the trick."

"We've only got six left," Jacky replied. "I think we should save them for something important."

Jacky had won the wally-stanes in a bargain with another

Jack—nine of them, all told. They were spellstones, the proverbial wishes of fairy tales, though unfortunately, they weren't quite as all-encompassing as in the stories.

They'd wasted their first one trying to wish Jacky into being a gruagagh. All that had happened was that she'd walked around for a few weeks in Bhruic Dearg's shape until they found a hob skillyman who could take the charm off. The next two had been used for them each to gain a working knowledge of the languages of Faerie so that they could read the books that the Gruagagh had left them. After that, Jacky had hoarded the remaining six stones like a miser might her gold.

"I think an index is of prime importance," Kate said, looking at the wall of books.

She stood up from her stool, stuffed a loose tail from the white shirt she was wearing back into the waist of her skirt, and walked over to where Jacky stood.

"Show me the house again," she said.

Jacky started to point it out when the doorbell sounded downstairs.

"Who's that?" Jacky muttered.

"That was the back door," Kate said.

She had a better ear for that sort of thing than Jacky did. Only faerie came visiting at the back door.

"Maybe it's Finn," Jacky said as she led the way downstairs. "Do you think he knows anything about ley depressions?"

Kate laughed. "You sound like a pop psychiatrist."

"Ho ho."

They had reached the kitchen by then. Jacky flung the door open—a "Hello, Finn," on her lips—but though it was a hob standing there, it wasn't their usual visitor. Instead it was a younger cousin of Finn's—one of the Laird's foresters.

"Dunrobin Mull, if you please, Missus Jack," the hob said. "At your service."

He was nervously turning his red cap in his hand and the two women knew immediately that whatever his reason for coming was, it wasn't to bring good news.

"You'd better come in," Jacky said.

Four

The dance ended at eleven—in accordance with city noise ordinances. Johnny pitched in, helping the band and their friends dismantle the stage and load all the equipment into the van and pickup truck that it had come in. By a quarter past twelve, he and Jemi were saying their farewells and started to walk slowly down Chesley towards Bank Street.

"Wow," Jemi said. "I'm still buzzing."

Johnny nodded. He felt that way himself when a gig went well—all wound up with excess energy.

"What happens now?" he asked.

"Let's walk a bit and take it as it comes—okay?"

"Sure."

Jemi was wearing a silver-buttoned piper's jacket over her dress now, carrying her sax in its case. She refused his offer to carry it for her. Looking at her, Johnny had to shake his head. She certainly knew how to catch the eye. Her whole look—from pink hair to what she was wearing—made him smile, though not in any superior sense. He found himself liking the look, liking her. He'd never known anyone quite the same before.

"Are you hungry?" she asked as they reached Bank Street.

"Some."

She nodded to a Chinese restaurant on their left. "Want to grab a few egg rolls?"

"Sure."

Fifteen minutes later they were sitting inside the South Garden, munching egg rolls that they washed down with Chinese tea. Jemi ate with great gusto, dipping her egg roll first in the little pool of soya sauce on her plate, then in the plum sauce, before each bite. Johnny followed her example at a slower pace. At last he had to ask her as she finished her sixth egg roll.

"How do you stay so small—"

"When I eat so much?" she finished for him. She shook a finger in his face. "That's not very polite, Johnny Faw."

"I guess not," he said with a smile.

She grinned back. "I've just got a quick metabolism—I burn it all off before it has a chance to settle."

They had the restaurant to themselves. Chinese pop songs, sung by a woman with an incredibly high-pitched voice, issued softly from the ceiling speakers in each corner of the room.

"So where do we start?" Jemi asked as she finished her seventh and final egg roll.

She replenished both their teacups from the pot on the center of the table.

The enjoyment in Johnny's eyes clouded as he remembered why he'd looked her up in the first place. He'd been having such a good time, listening to her band, and she was so full of lighthearted energy, that he'd just let the reason fade away.

"Maybe you should tell me just what happened last night," Jemi said softly, seeing the look in his eyes.

She put the teapot down and patted his hand, before picking up her cup and taking a sip.

So Johnny went through the story again. Jemi was a good listener and didn't interrupt. She waited until he was done to ask a few questions.

"That was Jenna," she said when Johnny again described the woman he'd met.

"So what's going on?" Johnny asked.

"I knew Old Tom—he used to bring me sweets, but that was a

long time ago." There was a far-off look in her eyes. "I've always had a sweet tooth."

"But," Johnny began, then he paused, deciding on a different tack. "Are you twins—you and Jenna?"

"Oh, no. She's much older than I am."

"Well, how old are you?"

"How old do I look?"

"About twenty-one, twenty-two."

"That's close enough."

Johnny sighed. "Look. She said she knew Tom before he met my grandmother. That's a long time ago. And now I'm getting the feeling that you knew him back then as well. But that's impossible. You'd have to be in your forties at least."

"Oh, I don't know about that," Jemi said.

"I'm really not trying to pry," Johnny said. "It's just that I'd like to know what's going on. Why would Tom tell me to play that tune in Vincent Massey Park? Why would your sister come when I played it?" He took out the bone fiddle and laid it on the table beside the teapot. "What's this thing mean? What did she mean by saying she was a fairy?"

"You've got so many questions," Jemi said, "and it's most unfair not to answer them."

She shook her head.

"C'mon," she said, and stood up.

"Why? Where are we going?"

"To Puxill."

Johnny remained seated. "I'm not going anywhere. I don't know what you and your sister are playing at, but I don't like it. I think I'll bow out now."

"I'm not playing at anything," Jemi said.

"Well, I don't believe in fairies. I suppose you're going to tell me that you're one, too?"

Jemi laughed. "Of course not!"

"Well, then, where are you planning to take me? Where's Puxill? *What's* Puxill?"

"It's what the—it's what Jenna calls Vincent Massey Park."

"And what are we going to do there? Play 'The King of the Fairies' again?"

Jemi shook her head. "No. We're going to talk to Jenna. Now, c'mon."

Johnny stared at her for a long moment, then slowly got to his feet.

"You're not much of a one for whimsy and wonder, are you?" Jemi said.

"It's not been a good week."

Jemi touched his cheek with the backs of her fingers. The gesture reminded him of her sister.

"I know," she said. "I'm sorry about your grandfather. Everybody liked him."

"How come I've never heard of all these everyones before?"

"Maybe your grandfather just liked to keep a secret or two."

"He's not alone in that," Johnny said.

"That's true. Poor Johnny Faw. Did you never have a secret to keep?"

"It's not that. It's just . . . "

He shook his head. He didn't seem able to frame what he wanted to say.

"It all came at a bad time, didn't it?" Jemi said.

Johnny nodded. "And I don't even know what 'it' is."

"Let's find out what Jenna has to say."

They paid their bill and left the restaurant. Outside, the traffic was sparse on Bank Street. They followed the street down to Billings Bridge, weaving their way through the construction on the bridge as they crossed the river, then turned right to follow the water west. Here there was even less traffic on Riverside Drive, just the occasional car. They kept to the bicycle path, with the river and its reeds and its slow-moving water on one side, neatly-kept lawns on the other. Overhead, the sky was thick with stars.

"Does she do this kind of thing often?" Johnny asked.

Jemi shook her head. "But she likes tricks. I don't think she meant you any harm. It's hard to know sometimes—don't you think? I mean the way things can go. You might mean one thing, but somebody might take it otherwise. She probably did just want to see you for old times' sake, to see you and leave it at that. Instead, she just filled you up with questions. I don't think she planned that. You were supposed to just forget about her."

"It's hard to forget someone who comes at the call of a tune and then vanishes into thin air."

"It depends on what sort of a person you are." Jemi glanced at him, a smile touching her lips. "And just how used to that sort of thing you are."

Johnny sighed, but didn't rise to the bait. He was tired of questions, tired of puzzles, tired of not really knowing what was going on.

"Don't be glum," Jemi said. She took his free hand. "Enjoy the night for itself, if nothing else."

With that small hand warm in his, Johnny didn't reply. He kept hold of her hand, almost afraid that if he didn't, she would disappear on him just as her sister had. He tried not to think of what the familiarity meant. There was no denying to himself that he was attracted to her; he got the feeling that she liked him as well. What he wasn't sure of was how he felt about it all.

There was something going on, some undercurrent that lifted goosebumps on his arms when he considered it. He tried to follow her advice and not think about it. He tried to just enjoy the night and her company.

Just when he was beginning to have some success, Jemi began to hum a fiddle tune, very quietly. At least it wasn't "The King of the Fairies," Johnny thought. Then he recognized the tune. It was "The Fairies' Hornpipe." He shot her a quick glance. In the vague lighting, she looked back at him, a guileless look on her face.

"Whatever you're thinking, Johnny Faw," she said, breaking off the tune, "remember this: I don't mean you any harm."

As she spoke, Johnny got the impression that he was walking through some fairyland, hand in hand with a diminutive princess. He blinked, and the moment was gone. The bicycle path was back, Ottawa's night around them. Jemi Pook was still holding his hand, walking at his side, in her pink and grey dress with the piper's jacket overtop and her hair all spiked.

A warmth and closeness grew up between them as they walked, and the empty feeling inside that Johnny had known since Tom's death lost some of its grip. Right then he was happy that he'd gone out with his fiddle last night and called up the sister of the woman who walked at his side.

He wondered, looking at Jemi, if there was such a thing as

punk elves. If he ever did put together a collection of city folklore, he didn't doubt that they'd have a place in it.

They listened to the hob's story over herb tea, sitting around the table in the kitchen nook, Dunrobin Mull perched in his seat, sitting arrow-straight, not touching its back, Jacky slouched in hers, only Kate using her chair in the way it was designed to be used.

"What I don't understand," Jacky said when Mull was done with his tale, "is why you've come to us. Shouldn't you go to the Court with this?"

"I've been to the Court," Mull said, "but the Laird wasn't there to see. No one was. Hay of Kelldee sent me to put the matter in your hands."

Jacky remembered then. The Laird and most of his Court had left yesterday afternoon for the Harvest Fair in Ballymoresk. Hay of Kelldee, a Brown Man who was the Court's seneschal, was looking after things in the Laird's absence.

"But still," she said, "isn't this something you foresters should handle? Who's the Chief for that area?"

"What area's that?" Kate asked. "Avon Learg?"

Jacky nodded. That was the faerie name for the whole strip of land along the Ottawa River that ran from the headland of Kinrowan where the Court was kept, all the way west to Britannia Beach.

"Then Shon Buie's the Chief," Kate said.

"And he's gone, too," Mull said. "They're all gone. It's been so peaceful of late since you killed all those giants—"

"Two giants," Jacky corrected, though she couldn't help feeling a little pride still.

"There's been no trouble," Mull continued, "not for all the year. This is the first time in a long while that the Court could go to the Fair, so most of them went."

The Harvest Fair was one of the two big yearly gatherings of the Seelie Courts—one for the harvest, one for the sowing and winter's end. The closest Fair to Kinrowan was in Toronto, what faerie called Ballymoresk, Big Town by the Water.

"Howsoever," Mull said, being how things are, this is the sort of problem that the Laird would have brought to the Gruagagh anyway."

But I'm not a gruagagh, Jacky wanted to say.

And it was true, even if she *had* accepted a gruagagh's responsibilities and done well enough so far. But that might only be, she admitted in moments of honesty, because a real challenge hadn't come up yet.

She caught Kate's gaze, but Kate only shrugged as if to say, We're stuck with it, kiddo.

"The victim," Jacky asked. "She wasn't a Seelie fey?"

Mull shook his head. "She was the Pook of Puxill. One of the fiaina sidhe. Her name was Jenna."

"Do they fight amongst themselves?"

Jacky didn't know as much about the solitary faerie as she'd like to. She didn't know enough about a lot of things, really. Every day something came up to remind her of how much there was still to learn.

"Oh, they'd quarrel—the same as we," Mull replied. "But not like this. She was butchered, Missus Jack. I'd say it was a bogan or some other Unseelie creature did the deed, only the tracks are all wrong. Whatever she fought, whatever butchered her, it left no sign."

"But you saw footprints . . . "

"Walking up, bending down for a look, walking away again. I didn't know that track, but I do know this: Whoever made it didn't kill the Pook."

"This doesn't make sense," Kate said. "There had to be tracks."

"I saw what I saw," Mull replied somewhat huffily.

"Oh, we believe you—don't we, Kate?" Jacky said. "It's just . . . strange, that's all."

Kate nodded and the hob looked mollified.

"That's why the Hay of Kelldee sent me to you," he said.

The two women regarded him blankly.

"Don't you see?" he said. "It was a magic that killed her. So this isn't a matter for foresters—it's for gruagaghs and skillyfolk."

"But . . . " Jacky shook her head as the hob turned to her. "Never mind," she said.

She wasn't about to tell him that she couldn't help him. She might not be a gruagagh, but she *was* the Jack of Kinrowan. She'd taken on the Unseelie Court and won.

"Will you be wanting to see the body?" Mull asked.

"Uh, no. No, that won't be necessary."

She felt a queasiness in her stomach just at the thought of it. Glancing at Kate's blanched features, she knew she wasn't alone.

"You did a real good job describing it," she added.

"Hay of Kelldee was keeping it in case you did. We should see about finding someone from the fiaina to claim it." A bleak look came into his eyes and both Jacky and Kate knew he was seeing the body again. "She'll need a proper cairn, to be laid to rest by her own people . . . "

None of them spoke for a long time. Faerie aged at a different rate from humans. Their birthrate was much, much lower as well. Deaths diminished their ranks far more quickly than they could be replenished.

"I'll have to look at the spot where you found her," Jacky said after a while. "To see if there are any . . . "

She looked at Kate for help.

"Residual emanations," Kate filled in. "Of a magical nature."

Jacky shot her a quick smile of thanks.

"Can you take us there?" she asked Mull.

When the hob nodded, the two women left him to change and fetch jackets.

"Are we getting in over our heads?" Jacky asked.

She stood in the doorway to Kate's bedroom, putting on her jacket while Kate changed into a pair of jeans.

"We pulled out okay the last time," Kate said. She paused, one leg in, the other out, to look at Jacky. "We accepted the responsibility from Bhruic. We can't just back out the first time things start to get a little rough."

"I know. I wasn't saying that."

Kate got her other leg into her jeans and tugged them up. "You just don't want to blow it, right?"

"Something like that. I don't want to make a muddle. I guess I'm scared of making things worse, instead of fixing them."

"We've done fine so far."

"Little things. But—"

Kate joined her in the doorway and laid a finger across Jacky's lips.

"Listen up, kiddo," she said. "If it wasn't for you, there wouldn't be any Seelie Court left in Kinrowan. Remember that. And since then you've kept the luck replenished, just the way you're supposed to."

"Right. So now we're supposed to play detective and figure out who murdered some poor little fiaina sidhe? And what do we do if and when we *do* find out? What are we going to do about something that can cause that kind of damage without leaving any trace of itself behind?"

"Run like hell?" Kate tried. She gave Jacky's shoulder a light punch. "Just kidding. Don't worry, Jacky. Things'll work out."

"Easy for you to say. You've got a valiant tailor complex."

"While you're a giant-killer—remember? So let's not keep our hob waiting."

She led the way downstairs.

"I only brought the one pony," Mull said when they rejoined him. "I never thought—"

"That's okay," Kate said. "We'll follow on our bikes."

Five

The night was quiet in Puxill.

The only real sound was that of the Rideau River washing across the flat stones by which Johnny and Jemi Pook were sitting. There was a mist on the river, making a blur of the university's lights on the other bank. It muffled the already vague sound of distant traffic until it seemed that he and his diminutive companion were the only ones about at this hour.

At first the time passed pleasantly enough. While they didn't talk much, Johnny was content to wait until Jemi's sister came before asking any more questions. But as they continued to sit there waiting, the earlier sense of warmth and closeness slowly drained from him and he grew impatient again.

Why were they just sitting here? For that matter, how did he even know that Jemi had a sister? The whole affair was beginning to feel like another prank—or a part of the same one that he'd fallen for last night.

He stood up suddenly and walked to the edge of the river. Picking up flat stones, he skimmed them across the water, growing more angry with each throw.

"She's not coming, is she?" he asked.

He turned to face Jemi. She seemed tinier than ever—a small bundle of shadow, perched on a rock.

"It doesn't seem so."

"Of course, how could she even know that we're waiting for her? We didn't phone ahead or anything."

"It doesn't work like that."

Johnny nodded. "I know. It needs a fiddle tune. What should I play?"

"That won't work," Jemi said. "She should have known we were here by now. I guess she's just not around tonight."

"*If* she even exists in the first place."

The shadow that was Jemi moved as she looked up from the stones at her feet to frown at him.

"Are you saying I lied to you?" she asked.

Remembering the warmth, the feeling of closeness, even if he couldn't regain it at the moment, Johnny shook his head. But it was too hard to simply set aside his frustrations and forget.

"I just don't know what I'm doing here," he said. "I mean, last night was strange enough. You'd think I'd have learned my lesson. But no. Here I am, back again."

He skimmed another stone across the water, using far more force than was necessary. It skipped all the way across to the other shore.

"What *are* we doing here, Jemi?" he asked as he turned back to look at her once more.

"Waiting for Jenna."

He shook his head. "C'mon. What would she be doing here?"

Now even the memory of the warmth he'd felt with her was fading.

"She lives here," Jemi said.

Johnny looked around.

"Here?" he asked. "Under these stones, maybe? In the base of the train bridge? In a tree?"

"I'm worried," Jemi said, ignoring his questions. "It's not like Jenna to leave like this."

"Leave what?"

"Puxill," Jemi said impatiently.

"Your sister's a baglady?" Johnny asked. "She lives in this park?"

240

Quicker than he might have thought possible, Jemi was on her feet, closing the distance between them and poking a finger in his chest.

"Don't talk like that about her!" she said. "I said I was worried. I don't need your stupid jokes on top of it."

"Oh, excuse me. How rude of me to not take this all more seriously."

He took a step back as she lifted her finger to poke him again. A wet stone slid under his foot and he would have fallen, except Jemi reached out and grabbed his arm, hauling him erect. As soon as he regained his balance, Johnny moved gingerly around her and onto safer ground. He rubbed his arm where she'd grabbed him. Like last night, the grip had been very strong.

"It *was* you last night, wasn't it?" he said. "Why are you going through with this charade of looking for a sister who doesn't even exist?"

Jemi looked at him for a long moment, then shook her head.

"Screw you," she said, and vanished.

Johnny stared at the spot where she'd disappeared. This time there couldn't be any other explanation. Last night she might conceivably have slipped into the trees somehow—she *could* move fast, he remembered—but there was no place for her to have done the same here.

The stones were bare, pale as bones in the starlight. She couldn't have gone into the mist on the river because he would have heard her in the water. They'd been standing on a slight promontory jutting out into the river. To get to the forest behind him, she would have had to pass by him, and she hadn't.

She'd just disappeared.

"Jemi?" he called quietly. "Jemi! Look, I'm sorry. Please don't take off like you—uh, like your sister did last night. I thought you were just having me on again—pulling my leg."

There was no reply.

He turned slowly, head cocked slightly as he strained to hear her move. He caught sight of their instrument cases and hurried over to them, staking claim to them with either hand. She wouldn't just take off and leave her sax behind, would she?

"Okay," he said. "I'm going. I'll leave your sax with Greg, or you can come and get it now."

He looked around some more. Maybe she'd fallen into the river, he thought suddenly. The water could have taken her under before she had a chance to call out. He just hadn't heard her fall — that was all. The water wasn't running fast, but all it needed was a slip on a mossy stone — he'd slipped himself a moment ago — maybe crack your head on a rock as you fell . . .

He started for the river, alarmed now, then stopped dead in his tracks. Like a magician's rabbit, pulled from an empty hat, Jemi was suddenly standing in front of him. They studied each other, neither speaking. Johnny swallowed, his throat unaccountably dry.

"Look," he began. He cleared his throat, started again. "I don't know how you're doing that, but — how *are* you doing that? Wait. Don't tell me. I know you don't like questions. So how about if I just leave your sax here" — he set the case down on the stones between them — "and I'll just go, okay? No hard feelings, right?"

He began to back slowly towards the bicycle path, trying not to think about what she might do next. If she could just pop in and out of existence the way she did, who the hell knew what else she could do? Best not to find out. Best just to get out while he could.

"Don't go," she said.

He stopped moving immediately. She'd asked him, not told him, but he wasn't taking any chances.

"You've got nothing to worry about from me," Johnny told her. "I won't tell anybody about you. Well, I told Henk, but I won't tell anybody else, okay? And even Henk doesn't know that you . . . that you're . . . what you can do . . . " He looked helplessly as her. "Christ, I don't even know what I'm talking about."

"I'm sorry," Jemi said. "I really am worried about my sister, but I never stopped to think about what this must all seem like to you. Since she got you into it, I was going to let her explain it, but now I don't know where she is and . . . "

She sighed.

"Hey," Johnny said. "It's no problem. Really. I'll just go and you won't have to worry about — "

Jemi stamped her foot. "Would you *stop* acting like I've got three heads and I'm about to take a bite out of you with one?"

"Well, it's just . . . "

"I know. You thought I'd just disappeared on you like Jenna did last night."

"Well, you did."

"But it's not disappearing—not really. It's just sort of . . . stepping sideways. I'm still here, but you can't see me."

"That might not seem unusual to you," Johnny said, "but it doesn't make a whole lot of sense from where I stand."

"I want to show you something," Jemi said. "And after I've shown it to you, I'll answer your questions. Okay?"

"Ah . . . sure."

She picked up her saxophone case with one hand and took his with the other.

"It's up the hill a bit," she said.

"Puxill?"

She smiled briefly and nodded. They crossed the bicycle path and plunged into the woods on the other side of it, angling in a southwesterly direction, which took them to the park's steeper slopes. In a small clearing, Jemi paused.

"Now, don't get all weird on me again," Jemi said as she let go of his hand.

"Me go all weird on *you*? Hey, I'm not the one that—"

"Whisht!"

Obediently, Johnny fell silent. He closed his mouth and concentrated on what Jemi was doing. She bent over a granite outcrop and tapped it with her finger. Once, twice, quickly. After a pause, a third tap. Giving him another quick smile, she stepped over to him and took his hand again. Her grip was very tight.

"That's starting to hurt—"

But then he knew why she was holding him so firmly. Given his druthers, he'd have preferred to simply bolt.

A large piece of sod was slowly lifting from beside the outcrop. As it moved to one side, Johnny could see a short tunnel that led into something wider which was dimly lit.

"What . . . what is it?" he managed.

"This is my home—where Jenna and I live," Jemi said. "Though I spend more time in the city itself lately, this is my real home, Johnny."

Johnny stared down the tunnel. "So you . . . you're a fairy, too?"

"A halfling, actually. And we're not exactly faerie—not Court fey, at any rate. We call ourselves fiaina sidhe."

"A halfling?" Johnny asked. "Like a hobbit?"

"No. I'm just half fiaina—the other half's as human as you."

"And Jenna's really your sister?"

"Half-sister. She's pure fiaina."

"Right. And you live in this hill."

"Well, not so much lately. But Jenna does."

"And you can step sideways, which is like disappearing, but isn't."

"It's stepping into Faerie, actually. The Middle Kingdom. Not everyone can see into it."

"You need special glasses, right?" Johnny tried.

Jemi smiled. "Do you want to come inside?"

Johnny looked down at the short tunnel, then back at her.

"Why are you showing me this?" he asked. "Why are you telling me your secrets?"

"I'm not sure. Partly because of Old Tom, I suppose, and partly because Jenna's been a little unfair to you. But mostly because I have a feeling . . . " A look Johnny couldn't read came into her eyes. "I've a feeling that I'm going to need a friend and I'd like you to be it."

Jemi's explanation put Johnny through another mood shift. The puzzled anger he'd been feeling earlier was gone as though it had never existed. He felt like he had to be dreaming, but he couldn't deny the tangible evidence that lay before his eyes. The hill was hollow and Faerie existed. If he accepted that—he had to accept it, it was lying right there in front of him—then by the same token he should be willing to believe that Jemi meant him no harm.

He wasn't sure how the logic of that worked; it was just the way it came to him.

"I'd like to be a friend," he said, "but I've got to admit that my head's still spinning."

"Duck that head," Jemi said, and she led him into the tunnel.

Without looking into Faerie, there didn't seem to be anything out of the ordinary in the place where Dunrobin Mull had found the Pook's body, but in the Middle Kingdom, it was plain to see the scene of the butchery for what it was. The sod was torn up where the Pook had struggled, the grass still stained red with her dried blood. Jacky and Kate laid their bikes on the ground nearby and walked gingerly forward to look around. Behind them, Mull slipped from Goudie's back and followed.

"It wasn't bogans?" Jacky asked after having taken a slow turn around the disturbed ground.

"No bogan tracks," Mull said. "Just what the Pook made in her struggling."

Jacky nodded, deciding that a forester would know. She couldn't even see any tracks made by whoever had looked at the Pook after she'd been murdered.

"What about the sluagh?" she asked, unable to suppress a shudder just thinking of the restless dead.

"They would have left a bog scent," Mull said.

"And there was none of that," Jacky said thoughtfully.

"But there is something," Kate said.

Both Jacky and the hob looked at her.

"What do you mean?" Jacky asked.

Kate shrugged. "There's just a feeling in the air—like when Finn works his stitcheries. It's not strong, but I can feel it. Just a tingle."

"Magic," Mull said.

"You can really feel that?" Jacky asked.

"You can't?"

Jacky shook her head.

"Can you tell what sort of magic it was?" Mull asked. "A gruagagh's or a skillyman's or what?"

"No," Kate said. "I'm sorry. But it reminds me of something. Sort of like . . ."

Her voice trailed off and the other two waited for her to finish. Finally Jacky spoke up.

"Like what?"

"Look," Kate said, instead of replying. "Over there."

She pointed towards the downtown skyline behind them. Standing on a rise, watching them, was a huge black dog. Because of the distance and poor lighting it was difficult to see it properly, but they all got the impression that it was very large—at least the size of a Great Dane, but bulkier, more powerfully muscled, with shaggy hair.

It studied them for a long moment after Kate had spotted it, then abruptly turned and sprinted away. The shadows below the rise upon which it had been standing immediately swallowed it.

"What was that?" Jacky asked in a small voice.

She was suddenly very aware of the fact that they were standing in the open, unprotected. Mists clouding the surface of the Ottawa River nearby did nothing to lessen the sudden attack of the creeps that came over her.

"An unsainly beast," Mull said, and he quickly shaped a saining in the direction it had vanished.

He looked to Jacky, to Kate, then mounted his pony and rode to where the dog had stood watching them. The women fetched their bicycles and walked them to the top of the rise where Mull was poring over the ground.

"You see?" he asked when they joined him. "There's nothing. No track, no sign it was ever there. There's something new haunting Kinrowan."

"You think it was that dog that killed the Pook?" Jacky asked. Mull nodded.

"Then why didn't it attack us?" Kate asked.

Mull shrugged. "I don't know. Perhaps its bloodlust is sated for the moment. Perhaps it has a master and it was only spying out the lay of the land for now. Oh, I don't like it."

He stood slowly, a frown wrinkling his brow.

"I think it's time we talked to Hay of Kelldee," Jacky said.

Mull nodded and mounted his little hob pony. He followed his companions as they walked their bikes to the parkway. When they reached the pavement, Jacky and Kate pedaled downtown, going slowly so that Mull could keep up, Goudie bearing him at a brisk trot.

Six

J emi kicked off her shoes as soon as they were inside and
turned to Johnny.

"So what do you think?" she asked.

All Johnny could do was stare out the big window that was set
in the wall. Through it he could see the trees and slopes of Vincent
Massey Park. The window, reason told him, could not exist. It was
impossible. He *knew* there was just a hillside out there.

"This . . . this window," he said slowly. "It's . . . when we were
outside . . ."

"We're in Faerie now."

"Just a step sideways. Right. Only . . ."

He shook his head and turned to look at the rest of the
room.

At first glance it reminded him of his own apartment. There
was a wall of books—old leather-bound volumes and paperbacks
evenly mixed. A sofa and two easy chairs stood near a large stone
hearth—the chairs were wooden frames filled with fat comfortable
pillows. A pair of battered wooden cupboards on either side of the
room held a clutter of knickknacks and the like. The floors were pol-

ished oak, islanded with thick carpets. Tapestries hung from the walls. A door at the far end of the room led off into darkness.

The room was well lit with the light coming through the window. Johnny got the impression that there was something about the window that heightened the light. He wondered if it dimmed it accordingly during the day. A pair of oil lamps stood on the mantel above the cold hearth, neither of them lit.

Jemi leaned her sax case up against a wall and settled down on the sofa.

"There's more rooms through there," she said, pointing to the door.

Johnny nodded and slowly crossed the room to where she sat. He lowered himself into one of the easy chairs across from her and held his fiddle case between his knees.

"It's . . . not quite what I expected," he said, looking around the room.

"What did you expect?"

"I don't know. Piles of gold and jewels lying around?"

"We're not rich faerie."

"There's rich faerie?"

She shrugged. "Some. You should see the Court of Kinrowan sometime. There's treasure there. Do you want something to drink?"

"Ah . . . "

"Oh, don't worry. It's just some beer that Jenna brews. It won't keep you here for a hundred years or anything—that's just in the stories."

"Sure. A beer'd be great."

She got up and went through the door that led deeper into the hill, the darkness obviously not bothering her. When she returned, Johnny was standing in front of one of the three tapestries that hung in the room. It showed an old-fashioned schooner anchored off a rocky shore. Pines grew near the beach and a longboat was being lowered onto the water. All around the men lowering the boat and standing at the ship's rail, faerie were depicted, perched on barrels, riding the longboat as it was lowered, swinging from ropes—a whole crowd of little folk.

"My father wove that," Jemi said as she handed him a mug of beer.

"Thanks," Johnny said. He took a swig, foam mustaching his upper lip. "Hey, this is good."

Jemi nodded. "Jenna brews the best beer this side of Avon Dhu—the St. Lawrence."

She went back to the sofa. After a few moments of studying the tapestry, Johnny returned to his own chair. Jemi leaned forward.

"You're probably wondering why I've gathered you all here tonight," she began with a smile.

Johnny laughed. "That's how faerie came here, right?" he asked, pointing his mug at the tapestry. "You hitched a ride with the early settlers."

"Not all at once," Jemi replied, "but that's about it."

She told of the migrations then, of the two Courts, the Seelie and Unseelie, and of the fiaina sidhe, who were aligned to neither.

"Were you around back then?" Johnny asked.

What the hell, he thought. If he was going to accept part of it, he might as well go the whole route.

"Oh, no. I'm just a babe compared to most faerie. I'm probably not much older than you are."

"Thirty-one."

Jemi shrugged. "Okay. So I'm a little older."

"How'd you end up playing sax for AKT? I mean, it's not exactly what I'd picture a faerie to be doing. And neither's, well, the way you look."

"You don't like my look?" Jemi asked, running her fingers through her short pink hair.

"I didn't say that. It's just . . . "

"I know. We're all supposed to be little withered dwarves, or these impossibly beautiful creatures. Sorry." She shot him a dazzling smile. "But as for AKT, I just love that sound. I like our music, too—faerie music, which is more like what you play—but there's something about the excitement of an electric sound. . . . Everything seems more alive these days—music, fashion, everything. I like being a part of it, that's all.

"Jenna says it's my human blood coming out in me, but I don't know. I'm a Pook, and we just like to have fun. Jenna does, too, but she finds hers in other ways."

"Are you the only one that . . . I guess you'd say, mixes with us mortals?"

"Oh, no. But you wouldn't know a faerie to look at one—we're good at wearing shapes that don't set us apart if we don't already have an appropriate one."

"And you . . . ?"

"This is all there is to me, Johnny." She touched her hair. "I don't even have to dye this brown or blonde anymore to fit in."

Johnny smiled. "Natural pink hair?"

"What can I say?"

Her gaze drifted to the tapestry that he'd been looking at.

"It's a funny thing," she said, more seriously. "The old folk say that we depend on you, on your belief, to sustain us. I don't know if that's true or not, but with the current upsurge of interest in fantasy and make-believe, our luck *is* getting stronger. I've always wondered about that dependence faerie are supposed to have on mortals, myself."

"You don't think it's true?"

"I don't know. But if it is, then it doesn't affect me so much as a pureblood—only that confuses me more. It's like, we don't exist unless some of you believe in us, but at the same time we can crossbreed. How can that be possible if we're just born from your imagination? Imagoes brought to life."

"Are you?"

She shrugged, troubled. "I don't know. It's mostly the older sidhe like Jenna who feel that way. The younger ones figure the world turns around them—but I guess that's what everybody thinks when they're young. What I do know is that we keep our luck by our rade—that's a night the fiaina sidhe get together and follow the moonroads to wherever they'll take us.

"There hasn't been a rade for a while, though. I guess I've ignored it, living mostly with mortals, but I know it was worrying Jenna. Even in the city I've heard rumours, of hobs leaving their holdings, derrie-downs dying. . . . "

"Hobs? Derrie-downs?"

"Hobs are like gnomes, I guess you could say. Little men. Brownies. And derrie-downs are like . . . selchies. Only they live in fresh water—rivers and lakes and the like—and they're otters in the water, instead of seals. This far from the ocean, only those with Laird's blood can take a seal or a swan's shape."

She fell quiet then and they sat for a while, neither speaking. Johnny regarded her and felt very odd. Rationally, he knew that none of this could exist. Everything she was talking about—this house inside a hill, for God's sake—but at the same time, it all wound together inside him to form a sensible pattern. One that fit within the boundaries of its own rules—not the ones he wanted to impose upon them. That left him feeling that he was either going right off the deep end, or it was all real.

He preferred to think it was real.

Looking at Jemi ensconced in her sofa, he sensed her spunkiness falling from her. She looked tiny still, but frail now, too. He could almost see the tears sitting there behind her eyes, just waiting to be released.

"What's the matter?" he asked softly.

She looked at him, eyes shiny. "Oh, I'm so worried, Johnny. I think something terrible's happened. I wasn't sure before—it was just a vague kind of a feeling—but now I know something is wrong. Something's happened to Jenna and I don't know what to do."

"Isn't there someone we could go ask? One of her friends?"

She bit at her lower lip and shrugged. "I suppose."

"Where does the closest one live?"

In a tree? he thought. Under a mushroom?

"Down there," Jemi said, pointing to the window. "In the river."

Johnny followed her finger with his gaze. Right. In the river.

He sat there and stared out the window, wondering just how deep into this he wanted to get. But then he looked at Jemi, remembered her saying she was going to need a friend, and what he'd said to her then.

"Come on," he said, standing up. "Let's go talk to him."

"Her," Jemi said. "It's a her. Her name's Loireag and she's a kelpie."

The Parliament Buildings—housing the Senate, the House of Commons, and numerous members' offices and committee rooms—stood on a headland in the Nation's Capital, overlooking the Ottawa River. They were originally built in the 1860s, partially destroyed by fire in 1916, then rebuilt thereafter in their original Gothic Revival style, the final work being completed on the Peace Tower in 1933.

While the federal government went about its business above,

underground in the limestone cliffs that made up the headland, the faerie of Kinrowan kept their Court and Laird's Manor. The hollowed cliff contained a bewildering complex of chambers, halls and personal residences, all the while remaining hidden from the eyes of various groundkeepers and RCMP patrols.

Jacky and Kate chained their bicycles to a street sign on Wellington when they arrived, then followed Mull on his pony around the wall fronting the Hill to the bottom of the cliffs in back of the buildings. The mists gathering on the river were thicker here, drifting to land and making visibility difficult. But Mull knew the way. Jacky and Kate walked with a hand on either flank of his little hob pony until they reached the entrance to the Court. Hay of Kelldee was waiting for them at its stone doors.

The Brown Man was a dwarf, brown-skinned with red frizzled hair and beard, and dark glowing eyes. As befit his name, he was dressed in various shades of brown, from the dark of forest loam to the mottled brown of a mushroom. He took one look at their faces, then ushered them away from the curious eyes of those faerie who hadn't accompanied the Court to Ballymoresk. Not until they were in his private rooms would he let them speak.

"Oh, that's bad," he said when they told him about the dog.

He paced back and forth across the room, stopping to stare out a broad window overlooking the river, before turning back to them.

"What's to be done?" he asked Jacky.

"Ah. Well . . ."

"We'll have to study this in the Tower," Kate said. "It's not a simple thing."

"No," Hay agreed, nodding his head slowly. "It's not simple at all."

He studied them sharply from under thick red brows.

"I've heard rumours," he said finally, "that there was trouble amongst the fiaina—but nothing like this."

"What sort of trouble?" Jacky asked.

"Oh, the usual sort with such solitary folk—or so it seemed. This hob's not been heard from for some time, the rade was not so good this moon. . . . Even some talk of mysterious deaths. Nothing that any of us saw personally, but even the rumour of such is disturbing. We should have looked into it sooner, I suppose, only things being as they were—with no word of the Host abroad, save for the odd troll or bogan—we've grown lazy. It's a bad time for the flower of the Court to be away."

Jacky didn't say anything, but she found it hard to stay quiet. The last time there'd been trouble in Kinrowan, the "flower" of the Court had been noticeably absent as well—at least from taking a part. They'd hidden in their halls and in the Court, while Jacky and her friends had taken on a host of giants, bogans and other Unseelie folk.

"We should go," Kate said.

Jacky nodded. "We'll be in touch. If you hear from Finn, could you ask him to come to the Tower?"

Hay nodded. "If you need any help . . ."

"We'll let you know," Kate said before Jacky could speak.

Jacky waited until they were outside again and making their way back to their bikes before saying anything.

"Why didn't you want to take him up on his offer of help?" she asked.

"Oh, think for a moment," Kate replied. "The Laird's gone and while Hay means well, what's he going to do on his own? The only ones left behind are those too weak to make the trip to Toronto—and of course a few foresters to patrol the borderlands. If and when we know something, then we can ask them for help—or we can ask the foresters, at least. But until then, they'll just get in our way."

"Lovely. And in the meantime, we're going to take this thing on by ourselves?"

"Don't be silly. We're going to go through the Gruagagh's books and find out just what it is that we're up against. Then we'll call in the cavalry."

"I suppose. I'd like to talk to some of these fiaina—see what they know. Do you think Finn could introduce us to any?"

"It won't hurt to ask." Kate shot her a quick look. "This time we've got to use another of the stones—you do know that."

"To do what?"

"Index all those books!"

"We'll need to think that through carefully. I don't feel like walking around looking like a mobile file card system, or changing the Tower into a computer or something. Anything's liable to happen."

"We did okay learning the language."

"Yes, but—shit."

They'd reached their bikes and were unlocking them when Jacky froze. Kate didn't say anything. Taking her cue from her companion, she followed Kate's gaze. The black dog was back, sitting on its haunches not a half-block from where they stood.

"Jacky?" Kate began.

Jacky shook her head. "I'm not even wearing my stitched shoes."

They each had a jacket and a pair of shoes into which Dunrobin Finn had stitched a skillyman hob's enchantments. The jackets made the wearer invisible to mortals—and to faerie as well, if you stayed very still. The shoes gave you quickness. They were both wearing their jackets, but not the shoes.

"If it comes towards us I'm going to scream," Kate muttered.

The black dog chose that moment to rise to its feet and move in their direction.

"Jacky!"

"I'm thinking, I'm thinking."

Fingers fumbling, Jacky continued to work on her bike lock. When the lock sprang open, she stuffed it into her pocket and tugged the chain free. She felt like a bad actor in some biker B-movie, but the weight of the chain in her hands was far more comforting than facing the dog empty-handed.

The beast continued its approach, a low rumble of a growl starting up deep in its chest. The hackles around its neck rose thickly. It drew back its lips, showing sharp rows of teeth that made Jacky's knees knock against each other. Her throat was dry and felt like sandpaper when she tried to swallow.

About three yards from them, the dog crouched down. By now its growl was like the constant revving of an engine without a muffler. Still feeling weak-kneed, Jacky took a step towards the beast, the chain held awkwardly in her hands. The chain was cold iron—not much good against urban faerie who had grown so accustomed to its sting that it no longer hurt them, but still a powerful enough weapon against those creatures that hadn't yet acquired an immunity to it. If she was lucky, the dog was one of the latter.

She could see it tense, getting ready to lunge. She stared into its eyes, then remembered someone had once told her something about not trying to stare down a dog, it just made them madder. She didn't need monstrous Fido here any madder, but she couldn't look away.

"Get on your bike, Kate," she said over her shoulder.

"Jacky, what are you—"

"Kate, just get on your bike! I'll try to scare it off."

"No way. I'm not going to—"

The dog leapt.

Jacky screamed and flung the chain at it, only just remembering to hang onto one end of it. Before the chain could hit it, however, before the dog was upon her, a tall shape moved out of the shadows from beside the wall separating the Hill from Wellington Street. Jacky caught a glimpse of a pale face inside a dark hood before the newcomer turned on the dog. Grabbing it by the scruff of the neck, the figure started to haul back on its massive weight. But at his touch, the dog simply dissolved.

The hooded figure took a step back, obviously surprised. Jacky, her own mouth gaping, started to pull the chain back to her in case the beast appeared again.

"What in the Moon was that creature?" the cloaked figure asked.

The voice was a man's, deep and resonating. He turned towards the two women, pushing back the hood of his brown cloak.

"One moment I had Laird knows how many pounds of some black monstrosity in my hands," he said, "and the next nothing but smoke."

"I . . . we're not sure," Jacky said.

She was happy to see that she'd kept most of the tremble from her voice.

The man's features, revealed by the streetlight now that he was fully out of the shadows, proved to be strong and not altogether unhandsome. The brow was smooth, eyes somewhat wide-set, cheekbones high, chin firm. Under the brown cloak, he wore a simple shirt and brown trousers.

"Thanks," Jacky said.

She left it at that. Rescuer or not, she wasn't about to give him their names. Finn had taught her that much caution long ago.

The man nodded. "My name's Cumin," he said. "Of Lochbuie. That creature . . . " He frowned. "Have you ever heard of such a thing before?"

"It killed a Pook last night," Jacky said.

"Did it now."

Kate stepped to Jacky's side. Her nostrils flared as she caught a scent, sensed a tingle of magic in the air.

"Are you a gruagagh?" she asked the stranger.

"The Gruagagh of Lochbuie," he said. "At your service."

"Boy," Jacky said with relief. "Could we use a gruagagh right about now."

Cumin's brows rose quizzically. "Surely Kinrowan still has its gruagagh? He's an old friend of mine that I haven't seen for a very long time. Bhruic Dearg. Do you know him?"

Jacky nodded. "But he's not around anymore. I live in his Tower now. I'm the Jack of Kinrowan," she added, feeling it was safe to give their names to a friend of Bhruic's, "and this is my friend Kate."

"I'm pleased to meet you both. But Bhruic—he's left Kinrowan?"

"Maybe you should come back to the Tower with us," Jacky said. "It's a long story. Do you have a place to stay?"

"I'd thought to stay with Bhruic."

"We'll give you the hospitality that he would have—it's the least we can do after you chased off that dog for us. Right, Kate?"

"Sure," Kate said with a nod.

But she wondered at the scent of magic that she could still sense in the air. Jacky was wrapping her chain around the seat post of her bicycle now, locking it in place, chatting to Cumin the whole time. Kate looked at the place where the gruagagh had stepped from the shadows. How could they have missed seeing him there? And why would the dog disappear when he grabbed it? It had killed a Pook. . . .

"Coming, Kate?"

She started guiltily and hurried over to her own bike.

"Sure," she said again, and fell in behind them, walking her bike as Jacky was.

What she wanted to do was jump on hers and leave this gruagagh far behind, but she didn't know why she felt that way. There was no real reason for her nervousness, except that once it had turned into an unpleasant night, why should it necessarily change at this point?

She listened to Jacky talk about the Pook and how she would-n't like to be the Hay of Kelldee, who was taking the body to Puxill right now in hopes of finding a fiaina to claim it, and wasn't it a shame . . .

Oh, don't tell him too much, Kate wished at her friend.

She stepped up her pace so that she was walking abreast of them.

"So where's Lochbuie?" she asked in a pause of the conversation, speaking quickly before Jacky could launch into something else.

Cumin's eyes appeared to narrow for a moment, but then he smiled and Kate wasn't sure if he'd actually looked angry just then, or if she'd projected that on him because of the way she was feeling.

"Far east of Kinrowan," he said. "Though not so far as the sea itself. I'm on a trip to Gormeilan, you see. . . . "

The rest of the way back to the Tower, Kate kept the Gruagagh talking about himself. Jacky didn't interrupt, but whether that was because she understood what Kate was doing, or because she was simply interested in what Cumin had to say, Kate didn't know.

Seven

Leaving their instruments in the hollow hill, Johnny and Jemi returned to the riverbank. The mists were thicker now. The night had grown still quieter. The flat stones shifted underfoot as they walked, the rattling sound loud in the stillness. When they paused by the water's edge, the sound continued. Johnny wasn't aware of it immediately, but Jemi turned her head quickly to look behind them.

"Faerie," she murmured.

Johnny turned then as well to see three small ponies soft-stepping across the stones. Two had riders, the third a long bundle tied across its back. Jemi's hand crept to Johnny's arm, her fingers tightening painfully as she clung to him.

A half-dozen yards from where they stood, the ponies stopped and their riders dismounted. The foremost was a fat dwarf with a dark beard and darker hair. The other was taller and smooth-shaven. The dwarf cleared his throat.

"Are you friends to Puxill's Pook?" he asked.

"I am," a voice said from behind them before Jemi could reply. The tall, ebony-skinned figure of a naked woman stepped around them to face the dwarf. Water glistened on her skin. This'll be Loireag, Johnny thought. Before the woman could speak, Jemi let go of his arm and pushed her way in front of the woman.

"I'm Jenna's sister," she said.

She shot the kelpie a quick glance. Loireag briefly touched Jemi's shoulder with the long dark fingers of one hand—a feathery touch that was gone almost before it was made—then returned her attention to the two Seelie faerie.

"My name's Hay of Kelldee," the dwarf said. He frowned, then cleared his throat again. "Oh, it's bad news I have for you tonight."

While he spoke, the other faerie was loosening the bundle from the third pony. Tenderly he laid it on the ground and Johnny had a sudden premonition. He started to move towards Jemi, meaning to comfort her, then froze, abruptly aware that there were more than just the five of them abroad tonight.

They came from all sides, slipping from the forest and through the field, sidling from the river behind them, dozens of strange beings, not one quite the same as the other. There were little men no taller than his knee, with twigs and leaves in their hair, their arms and legs like spindly roots. Pale-skinned women with wet-green hair, dark eyes, and sinuous bodies. Rounded little men with grey beards and wrinkled faces. A woman with the face of a fox and a long bushy tail.

Some were tiny, others taller than Johnny. Some he could see clearly and wished he couldn't; others were hidden in shadow allowing him only brief glimpses of narrow pretty faces, all those he wished he could see better. Towering over them all was a nine-foot-tall troll, his hands hanging below his knees, his back stooped, his eyes glittering.

Johnny found it hard to breathe. His chest was a tight knot and there was a sour taste in the pit of his stomach. The crowd of creatures pressed closer, encircling them. They filled the night with strange smells and a hushed whispering. Johnny could feel himself trembling, but couldn't stop it.

He felt like he had the one time he'd tried acid—years ago, and never again. That same sense of dislocation from reality pressed on him now. The sensory overload made it difficult for him to maintain any semblance of balance. He flinched when a small twiggish creature touched his leg, tugging at his trousers. Moving back, he bumped into a tall man, so thin he seemed skeletal, just bones and skin, without flesh. The man grinned at him, flashing rows of sharp teeth, and Johnny stumbled away from him.

He lost Jemi in the crowd. He was aware that the dwarf was still speaking, but couldn't hear what was being said. He tried to push through the press of bodies, to get away. When he came upon a sudden opening, he slipped into it only to find himself standing by the third pony. Jemi was bending over the bundle, opening it.

A dead Jemi stared up from the blanket—skin alabaster, bloodied and torn, eyes bulging, but the features still all too recognizable. Jemi's sister. Jenna.

Jemi lifted her face to the sky and howled her grief. The sound was a wailing shriek that froze the blood in Johnny's veins. This was what a banshee's scream would sound like, he thought. This despair. This grief. This anger underlying both.

His vision spun and he staggered back into the crowd, flailing his arms, trying to get away from that sound. Hands—little hands, big hands—shoved and pushed him out of the way. Jemi's wail burned through his mind. He fell to his hands and knees on the stones, scrabbling for purchase, trying to stand, to flee.

His limbs gave out from under him and he went face down on the ground. He cut his lip, tasted blood. His vision still spun, but the sound was finally gone—not faded, just abruptly cut off. Slowly he raised his head and looked around.

He was alone on that beach of flat stones. The river mist was ghostly and writhing on one side of him, the forest dark on the other, while he was crouched on the pale strip between them.

A nightmare, he thought. I've freaked out. Somebody slipped me something in a drink. A Mickey.

Jemi. Jemi Pook. She . . .

It all became a blur. He fell forward on the stones once more, only this time he didn't rise.

It was late when they finally got back to the Tower. While Jacky sat the gruagagh down in the kitchen nook and fussed about getting tea ready, Kate excused herself and went upstairs. Ostensibly, she was going to bed, but instead she made her way up to the third floor where she took down a familiar book from its shelf and sat in a chair to leaf through it. The fat leather-bound volume bore the title *The Gruagaghs, Skillyfolk and Billy Blinds of Liomauch Og* and, like everything else pertaining to Faerie and Kinrowan in that room, had belonged to the original Gruagagh of Kinrowan.

Bhruic Dearg's books had a peculiar property Kate and Jacky had discovered very early on in their residence. Their content tended to change so the various reference volumes remained up-to-date all the time. It was Kate who had first discovered this one day, looking through the very book she was holding now. She'd come to a heading for Kinrowan and discovered that under the Court, rather than Bhruic's name being listed as its principal magic-worker, it now had Jacky's name, with her own underneath, listed as an assistant.

The book called her Kate Crackernuts, but that didn't stop her from getting a little smile of pleasure every time she turned to that page. She knew that in Faerie the hazel tree was often called the crackernut.

She went straight to the index tonight, looking up Lochbuie. Surprisingly, for all her suspicions, there was such a place listed in the book. From the map she was directed to, she realized it was a part of Gaspé. But there was no Cumin listed as its gruagagh, in fact no gruagagh listed at all. There were two hob skillymen in the area—one named Scattery Rob, the other Dabben Gar—a wisewife named Agnes Lowther, and a longer list of Billy Blinds for the various faerie holdings in and about the immediate vicinity.

There was a Court mentioned as well, but it appeared to be a small one. Not big enough for a gruagagh, it seemed, though there had been one at the turn of the century. According to the book, his name was Balmer Glas, which, even by a long stretch of the imagination, didn't sound a bit like Cumin.

Kate frowned. She turned to the index again, this time looking under the C's for Cumin's name. When she found the listing, it referred her to "Comyn." That listing sent her to a brief paragraph that told her that the Comyns were an old family of Billy Blinds and gave her various other references to turn to, none of which helped her with her present search.

Sighing, she laid the book aside and went to stand in front of the wall of bookshelves. There were just too many titles. What they needed—as she kept telling Jacky—was a proper index. A file system like in a library, or even a general index book that could send them looking in the right direction. Kate knew that it wasn't important how much you knew, so much as that you knew where to look for what you wanted to know. Anyone could keep a clutter of information in their head—after all, people were supposed to remember, somewhere inside them, everything that they had ever experienced. The trick was accessing that information.

She replaced *The Gruagaghs, Skillyfolk and Billy Blinds of Liomauch Og* on the shelf and went to stand by the window. Kinrowan lay spread out before her. She checked on the house with its grey aura and found that while the aura was still present, its greyness didn't seem as pronounced at the moment.

A thought came to her, and she looked at where the Pook's body had been discovered. She shivered at the small smudge of grey she saw there as well. It wasn't near a moonroad, so she probably wouldn't have noticed it if she hadn't been looking for it. The spot where the black dog had attacked them had a grey smudge about it as well.

She turned her back on the window and leaned against the sill. They were connected. Whatever had sent the dog after them and killed the Pook was connected to that house on the criss-cross of leys. Had something terrible happened there as well—something really bad, she realized, for the aura to be so dark—or could that even be where the black dog and its master were? It was worth looking into.

She sighed again. This was their first real crisis in the year or so since they'd taken over the Gruagagh's responsibilities in Kinrowan.

Normally, they did a daily check on the various leys, making sure that the luck flowed properly. There really wasn't much to the task. Since the Gruagagh hadn't been all that well liked or trusted, and the faerie had gotten out of the habit of coming to him for advice, they hadn't had to deal with very many requests for help beyond that duty. The few times they had, long hours of going through the Gruagagh's books—with the help of Finn—had pointed them to a solution. But now . . .

It wasn't just the house's aura, or the Pook's death, or even the dog's attack, Kate realized. It was that man downstairs. She didn't trust him one bit.

Jacky had the unfortunate habit of being impressed with important people. She liked hobnobbing with the Chiefs of the Laird's Court when she could. Liked to spend time with the Laird and his daughter. She had an on-again, off-again relationship with Eilian, the Laird of Dunlogan's son.

There was no real harm in any of that so far as Kate could see, because Jacky didn't lord it over anybody just because she knew some highborn folk. But it was just like her to latch onto a strange gruagagh without so much as a thought to the possible consequences. There was something about Cumin, supposedly of Lochbuie, that told Kate he was far more dangerous than anything they could deal with. He was a gruagagh, after all. He had magics that they couldn't hope to match. If he should turn on them . . .

Her gaze went to the door, then to the secret hollow in the worktable's leg where the six remaining wally-stanes were hidden. The wally-stanes could be a problem. After Jacky and her first failure . . . It had been disconcerting to see Jacky walking around looking like Bhruic Dearg, and a little funny to hear her woman's voice coming from the tall shape of a man.

After that, they'd waited to use any more of them until they'd found some working instructions in one of the Gruagagh's books—a long process with Dunrobin Finn translating for them. The next two spells had worked out fine. The stones just took a lot of concentration. You had to fill all your thoughts with what you wanted, keeping them crystal clear in your mind as you broke the wally-stane.

Kate knew what she wanted right now. She knew it very clearly.

She argued it out with herself for a few moments longer— weighing her need against the unfairness of using one of Jacky's stones without asking her—then made her decision. She crossed the room quickly, locked the door and fetched the wally-stanes from their hiding place. She took out one of the crystalline spheres and replaced the others. Taking it in hand, she pulled a blank book from the bottom shelf—these were the books that Bhruic had been using to keep his notes and journals in—and brought them both over to the worktable.

She needed a general index and this was going to be it. The blank book, when she opened it after using the wally-stane's magic on it, would answer all her questions. It would tell her where to look for what she needed so there wouldn't be any more of these marathon expeditions through the hundreds of books that made up the Gruagagh's library. She just hoped that Jacky wouldn't be too mad at her. But there was no way she was going downstairs to ask her—not with that gruagagh sitting there, listening.

She held the wally-stane between her hands. It was hard and smooth against her palms. It was odd how the stones worked. They were virtually unbreakable. But when you held it between your hands and worked the spell, pressing your hands together, the stone just dissolved, like candyfloss did in your mouth.

Keeping the book in front of her, she held the stone over it and concentrated for all she was worth. A fierce scowl wrinkled her features. She breathed slowly. Not until she was absolutely sure she had it perfect in her mind—that the book would answer her questions, that it would tell her where the information she needed lay—did she press her palms together.

The feeling of the wally-stane breaking sent a pleasant tingle up her arms. She grinned as she opened her hands and looked at the sparkle of crystal dust that filled her palms. She counted to ten slowly. When all the crystals had dissolved, she picked up the book and opened it to the first page.

Blank.

Quickly she flipped through the book.

All the pages were blank.

Now she'd done it.

She went through the book carefully a second and third time, holding the pages up to a lamp in case the words were written very, very lightly in it.

Still nothing.

She went over her thoughts. Had she kept them absolutely focused? The book was supposed to answer her—

I've got marshmallows for brains, she thought.

Oh, she'd been so clever. She'd concentrated on what she

expected the index to do for her, but faerie magic, like the denizens of Faerie itself, were a capricious lot. They were fair. A bargain made was a bargain kept. But you had to spell it out so bloody carefully. . . .

She looked at the book. Clearing her throat and feeling somewhat foolish, she spoke aloud.

"Will you answer my questions?"

Nothing.

She rifled through some more pages, but they were all the same. Blank.

"Oh, come *on*!"

The leather-bound cover of the book looked back at her. She flipped through the pages some more, shook the book. She was so sure that she'd figured it out. But the book wasn't obliging her. Jacky was going to kill her for wasting a wally-stane on an empty book. . . .

A grin touched her lips again. Quickly she found a pen and opened the book to the first page. What was a book? Pages bound together with words on them. If a book was going to answer her questions, how would it speak? With words. On a page. And how would it hear her questions?

Will you answer my questions? she wrote at the top of the blank page.

As she lifted the pen, words began to form under her question. They were in a neat script, the letters rounded. In fact, she thought, it looked a lot like Bhruic's handwriting, which she knew from the journals he'd left behind.

What would you like to know? the words said.

Kate gave a sharp sigh of relief. Picking up the book and pen, she went to her chair and sat down, the book open on her lap.

Do you know a gruagagh named Cumin? she wrote. *He claims to be from Lochbuie, but he's not in the book of wizardfolk listings.*

Did you look under his name?

Of course. She underlined "course."

There was a moment's pause.

Touchy, the words finally said. After another moment, they continued with, *If this Cumin is not listed in the Annals, he will be a rogue gruagagh and should be considered dangerous.*

But what should I do about him?

Avoid him.

Lovely. She could have figured that out by herself. She reread what was on the page so far, then wrote again.

Who are you?

I am your answer book.

I meant do you have a name?

Only if you give me one.

There was something that Kate had read in one of the Gruagagh's books about the indiscriminate giving of names — a warning. Once named, a thing began to have power of its own. Like all things dealing with faerie magic, that too could be dangerous. But it didn't seem right to Kate that the book should be without one.

How about Caraidankate? she wrote, which meant "friend of Kate" in faerie. *Caraid for short?*

Now that is a gynkie choice, the book replied, meaning a well-thought-out trick.

Kate smiled and looked at the spine of the book. Embossed in the leather now was the word "Caraidankate."

How can I find out more about this gruagagh? she wrote.

Catch his reflection in a mirror and show it to me, the book replied. *Perhaps I will recognize him.*

How will I show it to you?

Catch his reflection, then hide it quickly before that of another is reflected in the glass. Place the mirror face down on one of my pages and I will see him.

Are you Bhruic Dearg? Kate wrote next.

I am his wisdom. I am the friend of Kate Crackernuts.

Kate smiled. *Goodbye for now, Caraid,* she wrote.

Goodbye, Kate.

She closed the book and held it on her lap. She sat thoughtfully for a long moment, then went to the worktable. Amongst the litter of paraphernalia, she found a tiny mirror, which she put in her pocket. With the book in hand, she went to her own room and dug about in her closet until she came up with a small shoulder bag that just fit the book properly. She didn't mean to go anywhere without it from now on.

With the book safe and bouncing against her side, she tiptoed down the front stairs and slipped out the front door. Once outside, she made her way to the back of the house.

She hugged the wall when she got near the windows of the kitchen nook. Underneath the closest one, she took the mirror from her pocket and held it over the ledge of the window, hoping that the gruagagh was sitting in the same place as he had been when she'd gone upstairs. She held it there for a few moments, then quickly covered it with her free hand and shoved it back into her pocket. Ten minutes later she was back on the third floor, carefully taking the mirror from her pocket and laying it face down on the page under where the book had written, *Goodbye, Kate.*

With her usual method of measuring time, she counted from one to ten, then just to be sure, did it again before she took the mirror away. On the page, like an ink drawing, an image of the kitchen nook began to appear.

Kate stared at it in fascination. The picture formed like a developing photograph. When the image was clear, she could clearly make out the gruagagh, the nook around him, and even the back of Jacky's head. She studied the gruagagh's face. There was a bit of a haze around his head. As she turned the book this way and that, she realized that it was a vague image superimposed over his—that of a dog's head.

She shivered and quickly put the book down. It was a few moments before she could pick up her pen again to write.

Do you know him now, Caraid?

The book's reply was slow in coming.

No, it wrote finally. *But I know what manner of gruagagh he is. He steals the luck of faerie for his magics, rather than using the luck that the Moon would give him. Beware of this creature, Kate.*

Does he mean us harm?

He means every living thing harm.

How can we stop him?

You must find where he has hidden his heart—when you find it, you must destroy it.

Kate stared at the words. The gruagagh had hidden his heart? That was something that just happened in fairy tales. She no sooner thought that than she realized how ludicrous a thought it was. As if she hadn't been living in the middle of a fairy tale for the past year or so.

Where can I find his heart? she wrote.

I don't know, the book replied. But it will be in a place that he considers very safe. To find his heart, you must understand him. But be careful that he doesn't steal your own luck first.

Kate swallowed nervously. Oh, Jacky, she thought. What have we gotten ourselves into this time?

Eight

By about one-thirty, Patty's Place was empty except for Henk and the restaurant's employees. He sat at a small table by the stage, which consisted of a space in the corner of the room where the tables had been slightly pushed aside for the two musicians who had been playing there that night. The members of the duo Mountain Ash had finished packing up their gear and joined Henk for a last pint before heading home.

Mick Cully, the guitarist and bouzouki player, was a short, dark-haired man, more burly than fat, with a quick easy smile. His partner, Toby Finnegan, had a thick mane of light brown hair and a full beard that hung below his collarbone, giving him the look of a leprechaun. He played the fiddle mostly, with a little tin whistle on the side.

"Looks like Johnny's not coming," he said to Henk. "Too bad. I was in the mood for a bit of a session with another fiddle."

Henk nodded. "Johnny's going through some hard times right now, what with his grandfather dying and all."

"We'll miss Tom," Toby said. "He was a grand fiddler."

"Hope Johnny remembers his tunes," Mick added. "It'd be a shame for them to be lost."

"Oh, Johnny's got the tunes," Henk said. "A head full of them—don't doubt it. But he's acting a little strange lately."

"That'll happen," Toby said. "Your man Tom—he was Johnny's only family, wasn't he?"

"Yeah. And Johnny's taking it hard. I wish he'd just, oh, I don't know . . . "

Henk realized that he'd been about to talk about Johnny's strange ideas of the previous night. Not a good idea.

"Pull out of his slump?" Mick asked.

"Something like that."

"Not everyone wants to sit around here all night," a voice said from behind them.

They turned to find the waitress Ginette giving them a hard stare. It wasn't very successful. Blue-eyed and blonde-haired, with features that looked as though they'd been filmed through a soft focus, it was difficult for Ginette to look firm, little say cross.

Toby grinned at her and finished off his pint. "Give you a lift?" he asked Henk.

Henk shook his head and finished his own drink. They left chorusing farewells, Mick and Toby heading for Toby's car while Henk stood outside on Bank Street and thought for a moment. He knew that Johnny probably hadn't been in the mood to come up to the pub after All Kindly Toes finished playing and he'd talked to Jemi, but Henk didn't like the idea of leaving him on his own to brood. Johnny's apartment on Third Avenue was on the way home to Henk's own downtown apartment, so he decided to walk up and see how Johnny was doing. When he got there, however, the ground floor of Johnny's building was dark.

Johnny could be asleep, Henk thought. It was almost two-thirty now—but going to bed before three or so just wasn't like Johnny.

He went around to the back and fetched the front door key from under the brick by the rhubarb and went inside. A quick walk through the place told him that Johnny wasn't home. Was he still with Jemi? Maybe getting interested in something more than little hobgoblins living in the sewers? That'd be nice. Johnny hadn't had a regular girlfriend for at least a couple of years. Though, with what Henk knew of Jemi, he wasn't all that sure that she'd be the right one for

Johnny. She was a little wild—loved to party—where Johnny was a bit of a homebody, staying in except for when he had a gig.

Henk returned outside, replaced the key, and was about to go on home when another thought struck him. Johnny could also have had his talk with Jemi, and then gone back to Vincent Massey Park, waiting for his mysterious visitor to show up again. Now, *that* sounded more like something Johnny would do.

He opened Johnny's apartment again, stashed his concertina inside, then wheeled Johnny's five-speed out onto the street. He sure hoped Johnny didn't come home in the meantime and think somebody'd walked off with his bike. But Henk doubted that would happen. The more he thought of it, the more sure he was that Johnny had gone to the park.

It took him fifteen minutes to pedal to where the bike path started to incline up into the park. He got off and walked the bike, listening for fiddle music, footsteps, looking for some sign of his friend. It was a nice night to be out. The mist on the river was pleasantly eerie and the park was so quiet. Almost magical. He could see now how Johnny had got the impression that there was something otherworldly about the woman he'd met here last night.

He went the full length of the bike path, taking his time. When he reached Hog's Back Falls, he turned back again. It was getting on to four o'clock now and he was having second thoughts about Johnny being here. And even if Johnny *had* come . . . For all Henk knew, they could have passed each other while he was cycling down from the apartment.

He almost missed the figure sitting on the beach of flat stones on his way back. He was riding the bike, coasting down the hills, using the brakes a lot because of the darkness. When he saw the figure, he stopped and called out.

"Johnny?"

There was no answer. Putting the bike on its kickstand, Henk left it on the path and walked towards the figure. Stones crunched underfoot and there was a dampness in the air, a wet smell that came from the mist.

"Johnny?" he tried again.

The figure finally turned. "Is that you, Henk?"

"Yeah." He made his way to Johnny's side and sat down on the stones. "What're you doing, Johnny?"

"I think she drugged me."

"What? Who drugged you?"

"Jemi. She took me inside a hill, Henk." Johnny turned to look at his friend. "Right under the ground. She tapped on a stone and this sod door opened and down we went. And then we came here and there were more of them—all kinds of them. Little stick-men and trolls and you name them, they were here. Jemi's sister was dead, you see, so all these creatures from Faerie were gathered around. It was Jemi's sister I met last night. But she's dead now. And Jemi wailed . . . I never heard a sound like that before, Henk. Christ, I hope I never hear it again . . ."

Henk touched his shoulder. "Why don't you let me take you home, Johnny?"

"She had to have drugged me, right? When she gave me the beer inside the hill? Because those things couldn't have been real. They sure weren't human. And then when she cried—it was like a banshee, Henk. When that happened, everything got muddy. I think maybe I blacked out, just for a second, and then they were all gone. So it had to be drugs, right?"

"Jeez. I don't know, Johnny. Why don't you get up and I'll get you home?"

"But it couldn't have been the beer," Johnny said, looking out into the mist again. "Because she gave me that inside the hill, and the hill couldn't be real either, right?"

"If you say so. Look, Johnny—"

"So I guess it was in the restaurant. Or maybe it was all real. Christ, I just don't know."

He let Henk help him to his feet. When they reached the bike, he drew back.

"My fiddle," he said. "I left my fiddle inside the hill."

Henk looked back to where he'd found Johnny. He couldn't see the instrument down there. The black case would have showed up easily against the pale stones.

"You sure you brought it?"

"Sure, I'm sure. I bring it everywhere."

That was true. Henk couldn't remember ever seeing Johnny go somewhere without it. He'd had it when they went to see AKT earlier this evening.

"Tom gave me that fiddle," Johnny said. "It was really old. It was a great fiddle. And Tom gave it to me. I'm not going to let her keep it."

He started off up the hill, shrugging off Henk's hand when Henk tried to stop him. Henk put the kickstand up and quickly walked the bike up behind Johnny.

"It's okay," Johnny said. "I remember the place."

They entered a small glade and Johnny paused. Henk laid the bike on the grass. Turning, he could see the lights of Carleton U vaguely through the mist on the river.

"I've just got to remember which stone it was that she knocked on," Johnny was saying. He crawled around on his hands and knees in the damp grass. "Two quick raps, then you pause, then another rap. But I can't remember which stone it was."

There were a number of outcrops in the glade and Johnny went to each, rapping his knuckles sharply on each one. Henk followed him, really worried now. He wondered if someone *had* given Johnny some kind of drug, because he sure was acting weird.

"That hurts," Johnny said as he rapped on another stone. "I guess that means I'm not dreaming," he added, and sucked on his knuckles.

Henk checked the glade out quickly, but he couldn't spot the fiddle case.

"Look," he said. "If Jemi's got your fiddle, I'm sure she'll hang onto it for you. Tomorrow we can give Greg a call, find out where she lives, and go pick it up. Okay?"

"She lives here," Johnny said. He hit the sod with his fist. "Inside this hill."

Right, Henk thought. In the hill.

"We'll try the other place that she lives. She does have an apartment in the city, doesn't she?"

"Yeah. At least she said she did."

"C'mon, Johnny," Henk said gently. He got an arm around Johnny and hauled him to his feet. "Let's go home."

Johnny let Henk lead him away without further protest.

"I know I sound crazy," he said, "but it's been a really weird night."

"We all have 'em." Henk shot him a sharp look. "*Did* you take any drugs tonight?"

Johnny shook his head. "Not unless she slipped them to me in the tea."

"Where'd you have tea?"

"In the South Garden."

"And then you came here?"

"Yeah." Johnny rubbed at his temples. "I know it had to have been a dream," he added, "but it sure did seem real."

"Maybe things'll make more sense in the morning."

"Christ," Johnny said. "I sure hope so."

"You let them go?" Dunrobin Finn said, his voice almost a shout. "With trouble abroad, you let them go and gave them no escort?"

The hob was taller than Hay, though a half-head shorter than his cousin Mull. He stood over the seated Hay, his craggy face pressed close to the Brown Man's, a knobby finger poking Hay in the chest. His quick feral eyes glared at the dwarf over the top of a nose that had a curve in it like a hawk's beak.

He'd woken earlier this evening with a bad feeling about Jacky and Kate and made his way to the Jack's Tower, only to find them gone. A passing hob he met in Cockle Tom's Garve mentioned that he'd seen them in the company of his cousin, Dunrobin Mull. The night was alive with odd rumours and an uncomfortable sense of foreboding, sharpening his fears. When he'd learned of the Pook's death, and the black dog that had been spying on his friends, those fears spilled out in anger.

"Oh, damn," he muttered, turning away. "Weren't you all so clever."

"She is the Jack," Hay said.

"And what is that supposed to mean?" Finn demanded.

"Well . . . she's killed giants. She fought the Host and won."

"With no help from you."

"You shouldn't talk like that, cousin," Mull said. "Hay is the Laird's seneschal and—"

"More like the Laird's senseless arse," Finn said.

Hay rose angrily from his seat, but Finn stepped closer again and pushed him back onto its seat.

"Understand," he said. "She's not faerie—neither she nor Kate. She's done a grand job, keeping the luck of Kinrowan—being our heart and all—but there's far more that she doesn't know than what she does."

"There's not much we know either about how the Pook died," Mull said. "Or about that black dog either."

Hay nodded. "She took on Bhruic's responsibilities. That's what we feed and clothe a gruagagh for—for times like these."

"And besides," Mull added, "we had to bring the Pook to her kin. With the Court in Ballymoresk, we're stretched very thin."

Only between the ears, Finn thought. But he supposed he wasn't being altogether fair. No one in the Court knew Jacky and Kate the way he did. They all thought the pair were skillyfolk at least, if not gruagaghs. They had never seen the pair of them fumbling about, trying to work something as simple as Kerevan's wallystanes. They didn't know that for each decision or bit of advice the Jack gave to the Court, Kate and she spent hours poring through Bhruic's library to find the right thing to do or say.

Better the Court didn't know, he supposed. Better things stayed as they were or perhaps the Laird would have second thoughts about leaving a pair of mortals in the Gruagagh's Tower. He only hoped that they had managed to get back to the Tower in one piece.

"There are no new gruagaghs in and about Kinrowan?" he asked finally.

Hay shook his head. "None the Court knows of."

"But you did see a black dog?" This question he directed at Mull.

His cousin nodded. "And it left no sign—the same as around the Pook's body."

Oh, damn, Finn thought. And that hound would have their scent. Now he was really worried.

He pulled his red cap from his pocket and stuck it over his thatch of brown hair. With a quick nod to his cousin and the seneschal, he left the Court through a passage that let him out near the Rideau Canal. He looked around, sniffing the air. The dark bulk of the National Arts Centre loomed over him. He crept out, still cautious, and slipped by the open-air restaurant that overlooked the canal. The chairs were all stacked and chained together in a corner of the patio.

A minute or so of brisk walking brought him under the MacKenzie King Bridge, where he paused again. When he was sure he was alone, he gave a sharp rap on the stone supports.

"Hey, Gump!" he called, and rapped again.

On the third rap a bulky trow stepped out of the stone wall, blinking at the little hob. He stood a good seven feet tall, with long black hair that fell to his waist like a Rastaman's dreadlocks. There were bits of twigs and shells wound up in the locks. His features looked as though they'd been chiseled by an apprentice stoneworker, just learning his trade. Two uneven gouges for eyes, a fat thick nose, square chin, huge ears.

Most trows were aligned with the Unseelie Court, but there were some, like Gump, who didn't have the heart for the Host's evil ways. Such trows lived in the middle of Seelie realms, not quite a part of them, but not quite fiaina sidhe either.

"I was sleeping," Gump grumbled in a deep voice. He squatted down so that his head was more level with the little hob's.

"It's not so late," Finn said.

"It's not so early either, skillyman. Why did you wake me?"

"Well," Finn said. "You know what they say. There's those that look, but don't see; and then there's those that no one pays any attention to, who see everything. Like you."

Gump grumbled a bit more, but he was obviously pleased.

"And what I'm wondering," Finn continued, "is whether you've seen a new gruagagh in Kinrowan—one who might have a black dog for his familiar, or perhaps one who wears the shape of a black dog himself."

Gump thought about that for a moment.

"There's been a thing," he said at last, "that has taken on the task of disrupting the fiaina's rade—you know of that?"

Finn shook his head. Like most Seelie faerie, he had little commerce with the fiaina sidhe.

"Don't know what it is," Gump said, "but I've heard them talk of it. A black dog was mentioned."

"Then that's what killed the Pook earlier this night."

"Jenna's dead?" Gump asked. "Oh, that makes me want to hit something, Finn. She was a good Pook."

"Why would anyone want to disrupt the fiaina's rade?" Finn wondered aloud.

"It's their luck," Gump said.

Now Finn understood. If the Pook's killer was the same one

who was disrupting the fiaina's rade, it didn't take a great deal of cleverness to know that it would soon be turning its attention to the heart of Kinrowan—the Jack's Tower, where Kinrowan's luck was stored. The evening's premonitions grew stronger.

"Oh, damn! I'm off, Gump, to the Jack's Tower. Keep an eye out for me, would you, and pass on anything you learn?"

"Which eye?" The trow's face split with a great gap-toothed grin, then he looked serious again. "I'll watch for you, Finn. Spike him once for me when you catch him. I liked Jenna."

"I'll do that," Finn said.

It was best to talk brave around a trow—they understood things like bravery and jokes. It wouldn't do to have Gump know that he was shaking in his hob-stitched shoes.

Gump faded back into the stone wall, for the dawn was coming and while he might hide in stone, he didn't particularly care to become stone, which is what would happen if the dawn's light caught him. When he was gone, Finn set off for the Tower at a run.

This was the problem, he thought, with knowing important people like gruagaghs and Jacks. Trouble was drawn to them like a magnet and it didn't stop to differentiate between the important folk and the odd hob who might just be standing around them.

But I don't stand around anymore, do I? Finn thought.

Not since he'd gone up against the Unseelie Court with Jacky and the others and lived to tell the tale. No, he'd become a doer now as well. But why was it that being a doer only felt good afterwards, when you could sit around and chat about it, maybe boast a little? Why couldn't you feel all brave and sure of what you were doing *while* you were doing it?

He wondered if the answer to that was in one of Bhruic's books.

Kate spent the remainder of the night poring over books.

She made a quick foray into her own room, gathering up all the fairy tale books she'd kept since she was a child, and then went into Jacky's room. Jacky had never been one for fairy tale collections when she was young, but ever since the events of last autumn, she'd taken to collecting them with a vengeance.

With her arms full, Kate returned to the third floor, wincing at every creak of the wooden stairs going up. Once there, she dropped her tottering load beside her reading chair. The area was already filled with piles of books she'd taken down from Bhruic's shelves. Slumping in the chair, she picked up a book.

The first reference she'd run across in one of Bhruic's books when she had started to read had a footnote directing her to human literature. In the thematic indexes of folklore, what she was looking for was listed under Tale Type 302 — "The Ogre or Devil's Heart in an Egg." There were over two hundred and sixty versions of the story, collected from around the world — Irish, Indian, African, Native American. That was what had sent her down to the second floor for the fairy tale collections. Now she went through the books, searching for the stories in question. She was looking for hints — for the "understanding" of her foe that Caraid had told her she'd need to deal with the gruagagh Cumin.

Most of the versions she found were similar to the Scandinavian story. "The Giant Who Had No Heart in His Body." In that one, the giant's heart was hidden far away from the giant's castle. In a lake there was an island, on the island a church, in the church a well, in the well swam a duck, in the duck was an egg, and in that egg was his heart.

Lovely, she thought as she put it aside. In other words, Cumin's heart could be just about anywhere.

After a thorough search, she found only two more versions of the story in the books she had on hand. One was Russian — called "Kostchi the Deathless" — the other was Italo Calvino's Italian version, "Body Without Soul." She read them both through, then turned to the faerie books she'd pulled from Bhruic's shelves.

She put her feet up on a stack of books, the spines facing towards her. Gwyn Jones's *Scandinavian Legends and Folktales*. Books by Stith Thompson, Jane Yolen and William Mayne. *The Giant Book*, by de Regniers. Asbjornsen and Jorgen's *East of the Sun and West of the Moon and Other Tales*. Even classic nontraditional books that collected stories by Oscar Wilde and William Dunthorn and contemporary titles like Christy Riddle's *How to Make the Wind Blow*.

I could be at this forever, she wrote in Caraid.

Understanding is like wisdom, the book replied. *Not easily acquired, but the endeavor is nevertheless worthwhile.*

"Easy for you to say," Kate said aloud, and picked up another of Bhruic's books.

The faerie versions of the same stories tended to be either much plainer or wildly exaggerated. In one, an evil gruagagh carried his heart in a pouch at his belt. In another, it had been reduced to the size of a pea and hidden in a gem that the ogre wore dangling from his ear. Then there were complicated ones that echoed "The Giant Who Had No Heart" story that she'd read a little earlier. But there were few facts that were prevalent in the histories of Faerie that the human books hadn't touched on.

The branch of faerie magic that beings such as Cumin followed was far different from that usually followed by Seelie gruagaghs or skillyfolk.

Whereas the luck gathered from the moonroads that a gruagagh tended in a Seelie Court, or called up by the rade of the fiaina sidhe, was more a borrowing of the Moon's luck, the droichan—as such beings were called—stole their luck. Borrowed luck returned to Arn, where she rode the night sky in her moon house; stolen luck was gone forever. Borrowed luck returned the gift of its giving, twice and threefold, making a circular pattern so that both giver and gifted were strengthened and sustained; stolen luck pierced the fabric of Faerie like a disease and left only sickness and death in its wake.

It was because droichan were more often human that the various tales of the diminishing of Faerie came to be. The less luck there was—it took a very long time for Arn to make new luck to replace that which had been stolen—the fewer faerie could exist. So it wasn't so much a lack of belief in faerie by humans that diminished them, as the amount stolen by droichan.

Droichan were next to impossible to kill—naturally enough, Kate thought with a heavy sigh. You had to find their heart first, and the mystery of their hiding places would tax the greatest of riddlemasters. The only hope that the books could offer was that a droichan had to repeat a spell over his heart once every three months, in the same phase of the moon that he had worked the spell to set his heart free from his body in the first place. This was invariably on the darkest night of the new moon.

Kate sighed again and set aside the last book. It was almost dawn and her eyes were bleary from too much reading and a lack of sleep. As she leaned back in her chair, she was suddenly aware of how quiet the Tower was.

Had Jacky and the gruagagh gone to sleep? Did she dare tiptoe to whatever room the gruagagh was sleeping in and try to find his heart before he woke up?

She shivered and hugged herself. She wasn't feeling that brave right now—not by a long shot.

She'd better not do anything, she decided—not until she'd had a chance to talk to Jacky. And if not her, then perhaps someone like Finn. They'd left a message at the Court for him to come to the Tower. How long would it take him? Oh, why couldn't things have stayed the way they were—just a day or so ago?

I'm finished for tonight, she wrote in her book *Goodnight, Caraid.*

Wear a sprig of rowan, the book replied.

What for?

To protect you against the gruagagh's spells. Wear it under your jacket—close to your heart.

Does it matter how big a piece it is? Kate asked.

She glanced at the top shelf above Bhruic's worktable where a number of cylindrical containers held bunches of twigs. Rowan. Birch. Yew. Oak. Ash. There were dozens of them.

Rowan, lamer, and red threid, Pits witches to their speed, the book replied.

What's lamer? Kate wrote.

An old word for amber. They are all reddish, you see—like a hob's cap. The size doesn't matter. Goodnight, Kate.

Kate went over to the worktable. She had to get right up onto it to reach the containers. Once she'd chosen her piece of rowan wood, she searched about for a safety pin to fasten it to her jacket, then realized that the iron in the pin might negate the rowan's protection. Many faerie had acquired an immunity to iron, living in cities as they did, but iron still undid many faerie enchantments and glamours. She found a needle and a piece of red thread instead, and sewed the little twig to the inside of her jacket.

She stowed Caraid away in its pouch. We should have got ourselves a book like this ages ago, she thought.

Leaving the mess behind, she headed downstairs, being as quiet as possible so as not to wake sleepers. But when she got downstairs to the kitchen, all set to make herself a cup of tea before going to bed herself, she found Jacky still sitting at the table in the nook.

"Morning, Jacky," she said.

She went on to get the kettle, pausing only to turn back when there was no reply from her friend.

"Jacky?"

She walked back to the table. Jacky's gaze had a glassy look about it. When Kate moved her hand up and down in front of her friend's eyes, there was still no response. She shook Jacky's shoulder. Nothing.

She's been enchanted, Kate realized. The gruagagh's gone and enchanted her.

She started to pull her rowan twig from her jacket, hoping that it could undo the spell Jacky was under with its touch, when she felt another presence in the kitchen. Turning, she saw Cumin standing in the doorway.

"I need her to show me a thing or two of Bhruic's ways," he said conversationally. "Unfortunately, the same doesn't apply to you."

It hurt Kate to do it, but she knew she had no choice. She had to leave Jacky behind.

Before the gruagagh could step into the kitchen, she grabbed the half-full teapot from the table and hurled it into his face. He lifted his arms to ward it off, stepping back into the hall. That was all the time that Kate needed to get to the back door. She heard the gruagagh shout something in a language she didn't understand, and felt a tingle run all through her body, but whatever spell he'd tried didn't take hold.

Kate didn't look back. She just hauled the door open and bolted outside.

The sun was peeping over the horizon and everything was in a haze of early morning light and tendrils of mist that had drifted up from the river. Kate didn't spare a moment to take in the eerie beauty of the sight. She ran headlong for the gate at the back of the yard that would let her out into the park beyond—glad that she was wearing her hob-stitched shoes that lent her their extra speed.

She reached the gate, jumped over, and ran smack into somebody. They fell in a tangle of limbs.

"Kate?" Finn asked, recovering first. "What's the—"

But Kate's attention was on the backyard where the gruagagh was coming after her.

"We've got to run!" she cried, and jumped to her feet.

She dragged Finn to his feet beside her and set off, pulling him along. It wasn't until they'd crossed the park and were standing by the river, partly hidden by the trees there, that she dared to pause and look back. The gruagagh stood at the gate of the Tower's backyard, staring at them across the trimmed lawn.

"Stag's heart!" Finn complained. "What's possessed you, Kate?"

Kate just pointed back across the park.

"He's a droichan, Finn," she said. "He's got no heart. He's captured Jacky and the Tower and we can't kill him unless we find his heart."

Finn stared numbly in the direction she was pointing. With a skillyman's sight he could see the ghostly shape of a black dog that hung about the gruagagh like an aura.

"Oh, damn," he said.

He'd come too late.

9 Nine

"I can't get her out of my mind," Johnny said.

He picked at the mushroom and zucchini omelette that Henk had set before him. Disjointed images from the previous night were still floating through his mind, leaving him with the disconcerting feeling of coming down from the effects of a hallucinogenic drug.

Everything, from his familiar kitchen to Henk's face across the table, had edges that were too sharp, then wavered when he moved his head. There was a curious metallic taste in his throat and his eyes stung. When he closed his eyes he saw, in amidst the swirl of strange creatures that his memory called up, Jemi Pook. Sometimes she was as she'd been in the South Garden, sitting across from him, putting away egg rolls like they were her first meal in a week. But mostly she was lifting her head from her dead sister's body, screaming into the sky, neck muscles stretched taut, eyes closed to slits, her pain like a raw file rasping against his nerves.

That wailing. . . .

He shoved the plate away. Henk pushed it back.

"Eat," he said. "If you were fed some drug last night, you're going to want something in your stomach. It'll flush your system quicker."

Henk had stayed over last night. He'd put Johnny to bed, wondering as he did if he shouldn't have taken him to the hospital instead. But he didn't think Johnny had been drugged. There was a bump on Johnny's head and his lip was split, but Henk didn't think he had a concussion either.

What Johnny was suffering from was a trauma of some sort. Henk couldn't quite sort out exactly what had happened to his friend last night—the things Johnny babbled about were just too unreal—but something had happened to him. He was sure of that much.

"We'll go see Greg," he said as Johnny finally took a few more bites.

He noted that this time, Johnny, after mechanically taking the first few mouthfuls, was now finishing the omelette. Henk poured them both another cup of coffee.

Johnny pushed the plate away again, but this time it was empty. He rubbed his temples, his hand drifting to the back of his head where it gingerly felt the bump there. He could remember falling face down on the stones, but he couldn't remember getting a knock on the back of his head. All he could remember . . .

The crowd of alien creatures swirled through his head again.

He drank his coffee, then stood up from the table, waiting for a moment to see if he felt woozy.

"Let's go," he said when everything stayed put. "I want my fiddle back."

Henk nodded. He took the dishes to the sink, then followed Johnny outside.

Greg Parker lived in the Glebe as well, on Fifth Avenue, just a few blocks over from Johnny's apartment. His eight-year-old daughter, Brenda, opened the door when they pushed the buzzer and studied them for a few moments before allowing that, yes, her daddy was in, and yes, she'd go get him. They waited outside on the porch, listening to Brenda shouting for her father. Greg appeared a minute or so later, wiping his hands on an apron.

"Making cookies," he explained. "Larry's helping me."

There were smudges all over the apron, the most recent of

which looked like chocolate chip batter. Some of the handprints were very small. Larry was Greg's four-year-old son. His head, topped by tousled blond hair, peeked around Greg's leg.

"Henk!" he squealed when he recognized who was there, and threw himself forward.

Henk caught him up and swung him around in the air.

"How's it going, tiger?"

"We're making cookies!"

"Sounds great."

"You guys want a coffee or something?" Greg asked.

Henk shook his head. "No. We just wanted to get Jemi's address from you. Johnny left his fiddle with her last night, but he forgot to find out where she lived so that he could pick it up today."

Greg gave them the address.

"We've got a rehearsal today," he added, "so if you don't catch her at home, I'll let her know that you're looking for her."

"What's her phone number?" Henk asked. "Maybe we should give her a call before we drop by."

"She doesn't have a phone."

"So how do you get in touch with her?"

"Oh, you know Jemi. She's always around. Are you coming to see us this weekend? We're playing the Saucy Noodle—three nights."

"We'll definitely make it." Henk put Larry down and gave him a pat on the rump. "Better get back to those cookies, tiger."

Larry looked fiercely at him and growled. Henk laughed and pretended to back off from him.

"Listen, thanks, Greg. If we don't see you sooner, we'll catch you at the Noodle."

Greg nodded. "I'll tell Jemi you're looking for her if I see her first."

"That'd be great," Henk said. "Stub a toe—okay?"

Greg laughed and waved them off.

They took a #1 bus downtown and walked over to the Sandy Hill address that Greg had given them. It proved to be a three-story wood-frame rooming house on Sweetland, near the corner of Laurier. The building stood at the top of a hill, the street dropping sharply down the remainder of its three-block length. They tried the front door and it was open, so they walked in. Jemi's name was on the mailboxes in the foyer—room 11.

"Anybody here?" Henk called.

They waited a moment or so, then, just before Henk called out again, a large woman came from the back of the building. She wore a tent-like pinafore over a T-shirt and faded overalls. Her face was like a full moon—big and friendly—and she wore her hair in a long braid that hung over one enormous breast.

"Can I help you?" she asked.

"We're looking for Jemi," Henk said.

"I don't think she's up yet—at least I haven't seen her. Come to think of it, I don't remember her coming in last night. My room's just beside hers and I was up late last night reading the new Caitlin Midhir book—*To Drive Away the Northern Cold*. Have you read it yet?"

"Uh . . ." Henk began.

"Well, it's not like her other stuff at all," she informed them. "She's having fun here, with the way we see things in the here and now, you know? But it's still got that magicky feel that—"

"Excuse me," Johnny broke in, "but would you mind knocking on her door to see if she's in?"

The woman blinked, then frowned.

"Room eleven," she said. "Go knock yourself."

The she turned and went back down the hall.

"What floor?" Johnny called after her.

"Second. Turn right at the top of the stairs."

"Thanks."

There was no reply.

Johnny and Henk looked at each other, then shrugged. Johnny took the lead up the stairs. Room 11 was at the far end of the hall. The door had an All Kindly Toes poster on it, dating back to a gig at the Rainbow earlier in the summer. Johnny knocked briskly, knocked again after a few moments when there was no answer.

"Well, that's that," he said, turning away from the door after a third knock and the same lack of success.

Henk bent over the lock. "I can get us in."

"We can't do that, Henk. It's not right."

"Maybe your fiddle's just sitting in there, Johnny. Besides, she gave you a runaround last night, didn't she?"

"Yeah, but—"

"It'll just take me a couple of secs."

"That woman downstairs knows we're up here," Johnny said as Henk took his wallet out. "She's probably listening for us right now."

"Let her listen."

Henk took out a credit card and wedged it behind the door's casing trim. The trim was loose—obviously somebody had used this way of getting in before.

"What are you doing with a credit card?" Johnny asked.

"I just use it for ID when I'm writing a cheque. Hang on now."

He slipped the card down behind the angled latch bolt, turned the door handle, and pushed. The door swung open.

"See?" he said. "Nothing to it."

Johnny looked nervously back to the head of the stairs.

"Come on," Henk said, and pulled him inside, shutting the door behind them.

Now that they were inside, Johnny looked curiously around. At first glance there was no sign of either his fiddle or Jemi's tenor saxophone case. Instead there was a double bed that took up about a quarter of the room, a closet, a dresser, a bay window with an easy chair and a reading lamp beside it, and a small bookcase near the bed, the top of which was obviously being used as a night table.

The two men moved quickly through the room.

Under the bed were dozens of pairs of shoes and boots. The closet was full of clothes, mostly brightly-coloured and dating from the forties and fifties, though there were some T-shirts and jeans. A sopranino sax sat in its case on the windowsill with a handful of tin whistles, all in different keys. The bookcase held mysteries and best-sellers. The dresser was a clutter of makeup and costume jewelry. Necklaces hung from a small knob on the side of the dresser's mirror—rhinestones and fake pearls, beads and coloured glass.

"Look at this," Henk said.

Johnny came over to the dresser and saw what Henk was pulling free from the other necklaces. It was a carving of a little bone flute that was hanging from a leather thong. Johnny took his own bone carving from his pocket.

"They're like a matched set," he said.

Henk nodded. "Well, they *were* sisters, you said."

Johnny frowned, remembering Jemi's anguished features.

"Let's get out of here," he said.

"You should take this," Henk said, holding out the bone flute. "Trade it to her for your fiddle."

"It's just a pendant."

"Yeah. But I don't know. I've got a feeling it means something important."

Johnny did too, more so than Henk perhaps. He'd felt a tingle touching it, and for some reason envisioned the two carvings pulling at each other like the opposite ends of a pair of magnets.

He took the pendant from Henk's hand and rehung it with the other necklaces.

"I'm not taking anything," he said. "Now, let's go."

He opened the door and peered nervously out, but the hallway was empty. Motioning to Henk, he stepped out into the hall. Henk joined him, shutting the door, and they made for the stairs.

Johnny felt terrible. He was missing his fiddle and last night was still a weird collage of disjointed images in his head, but it wasn't right to go poking through somebody else's personal things. It was too much an invasion of their privacy.

They made it downstairs and outside without meeting anyone. It wasn't until they were a few blocks away that Johnny began to breathe easier.

"Listen," Henk said. "I've got to get to work. Are you going to be okay?"

Henk worked afternoons in a record store called Record Runner on Rideau Street.

"Yeah," Johnny said. "I'll be fine."

"What're you going to do about your fiddle?"

"Drop in on the AKT rehearsal, I guess."

"Okay. Talk to you tonight—and watch it around those pink-haired ladies."

A faint smile touched Johnny's lips—gone almost before it was there.

"Sure," he said. "Thanks again, Henk."

Henk lifted a hand in farewell and set off, leaving Johnny at the corner of Laurier and King Edward. Johnny decided to walk home by way of the bike path along the canal, taking his time. When he finally got back to his apartment, he was feeling a little more clear-headed, if no closer to understanding anything. He had some lunch, then phoned Greg's place. Greg's wife, Janet, gave him Trudy MacDonald's number where the band was rehearsing. When he called there and got Greg on the line, Greg told him that Jemi hadn't shown up yet.

"Don't know what happened to her, man. She's usually pretty good about rehearsals—she just likes to play, you know?"

"Sure. If she shows up, will you have her call me?"

He gave Greg his number.

"No problem," Greg said. "And if you see her, tell her to shake her ass down here, okay?"

"Sure."

Johnny hung up and stared at the phone. When he thought of Jemi, the way she'd looked the last time he'd seen her, head tilted back, screaming at the sky . . .

If that was a true memory, he supposed he wasn't all that surprised that she hadn't shown up for the AKT rehearsal. But where did that leave him? He had a gig himself on the weekend—two nights at the Earl of Sussex—and while he had a spare fiddle, there was no way he was going to give up the one he'd lost. Tom had given it to him. Just one day, out of the blue. He'd handed Johnny the fiddle, saying, "I think you're ready for this one now."

Johnny had never played a fiddle that sounded so sweet. The bass strings woke a low grumble, the high strings just sang. Everything sounded good on it—though by the time he first played that instrument, he'd been studying with Tom for twelve years. If Tom hadn't taught him everything that Tom himself knew, Johnny couldn't imagine what it could be.

He got up and stared out the front window, hands in his pockets. He felt the bone carving, remembered the bone flute in Jemi's apartment, remembered a hollowed hill. . . .

He stood there for a few moments longer, just staring, then got his bike and pedaled down to Vincent Massey Park.

Puxill, he thought. I'm going to look for the Pook of Puxill.

He said the words aloud, then smiled, seeing the play of words on the title of the Kipling book.

He wondered which had come first.

Dunrobin Finn had a small underground home under the grassy verge between Rideau River Drive and the river itself. Fifteen years or so ago, the spot was a public beach. Now all that remained of its former use was a low stone wall near the river. The sandy beach had been taken over by reeds and rushes. Swans and ducks floated nearby in summer. In winter, the north winds blew down the frozen expanse of the river. But Finn's home was cool in summer, and snug in winter.

Physically it stood in Faerie, so that its grassy door, or the smoke from his hearth, could only be seen by those few mortals who could see into the Middle Kingdom.

Inside, the hollow was one large, low-ceilinged room, with a small sleeping area curtained off on one side. The hearth was used for both warmth in winter and cooking. At the moment a pot of tea sat steeping on the warm stones in front of it, the fire already burning low. Woven reed carpets covered the floor, except for near the old sofa and reading chair where a worn Oriental carpet that Jacky and Kate had given the hob lay. Like most faerie not directly connected to the Court; Finn preferred comfortable furnishings—old-fashioned stuffed sofas and Morris chairs with fat pillows.

Near the hearth was a tall pine kitchen hutch with an enamel counter where Finn did his preparations for cooking. A stool stood nearby that he used to reach the top shelves of the hutch, where he kept the herb simples and poultices that he used as a skillyman. The walls of the big room were covered with antique portraits. Finn collected sepia-toned photographs from bygone years—mostly portraits—and loved to hand-tint them on long winter nights. Each photo had its own wooden frame, ornately carved by the hob. Kate and Jacky each had a few of his portraits hanging in their bedrooms.

Kate and Finn were sitting by the hearth now, Finn in his chair, Kate stretched out on the sofa with Caraid on a cushion beside her. They sipped hot honeyed tea and were quiet now that Kate had finished telling the hob all of what she'd learned the previous night. She'd been nodding off when they first arrived, but the conversation and tea had quickly revived her.

"These droichan," Finn said finally. "They're quite rare now. So few mortals are prepared to accept that Faerie even exists, they don't much seek out its secret knowledge anymore."

"They don't sound much different from the Unseelie Court," Kate said.

"Oh, they're quite different. For all their enmity to us, the Host gets its luck the same as us—as a gift from the Moonmother Arn."

"But they're evil. . . . "

"Oh, they're bad all right, but not much different from our own Court, really. We're like two of your countries in a constant war, Kate. The folk of both countries need to eat the same food, need to sleep at night and relieve themselves. It's the same with faerie— only our ideologies are different. But droichan . . .

"They turn widdershins to Faerie. In the old days, they started out mostly as shargies—changelings that one or another of the Courts took in. Sometimes they'd just go bad, and no one knows why."

"Caraid says they could be giants or ogres, too, but that they're mostly gruagaghs."

Finn shrugged. "Don't know enough about it myself. But a droichan usually becomes a gruagagh in the end—there's no argument there." He looked at Caraid then. "Now, that book of yours— isn't it a skilly thing!"

Kate smiled. "I feel like I've had it all my life."

"That's a true gruagagh's use of magic, making that thing. I couldn't stitch a spell like that if my life depended on it."

"I just used a wally-stane."

"But there's a good and a bad way to use a wally-stane," Finn said. "As you well know from the first time you tried yourself."

He grinned suddenly. Mostly his eyes had a cunning, almost sly look to them, but when he was in a good humour, they sparkled with a light all their own and left others wondering how they could ever have seen him as other than a cheerful hob.

"And see," he added, "what you spelled just goes on. It's not a one-time thing—useful as that can be. This wee book of yours will give you knowledge, Kate. Maybe even turn you into a wisewife or gruagagh yourself. You've already got the name—the only Cracker-nuts in Kinrowan, that's for sure, though once the name was a bit more common. You're clever enough, by far. All you need to do is learn a few tricks and a bit of magic, and away you'll go. I didn't know you were looking to learn, or I would've taught you some stitcheries myself. It's not too late to start now."

"There's the droichan to be dealt with first," Kate said.

"Oh, yes," Finn said grimly. "There's not a light in the sky that a cloud can't cover. Spike the damn hound for breathing."

"Finn. What are we going to do?"

"I don't know. Rescue Jacky. Look for help." He sighed, staring at the last embers of the fire. "What does your book say?"

"Just that we have to find the droichan's heart."

"And that won't be easy. Let's see that book a moment, Kate."

She passed Caraid over. Finn took the stub of a pencil from his pocket and opened the book to a blank page. He sucked on the end of the pencil, thinking, then wrote:

Where do we start?

Kate leaned forward to see what Caraid would answer, but the book made no reply. She had the sudden fear then that it would only work in the Tower, in the Gruagagh's study.

"Oh, Finn. Does this mean—"

"Only that you spelled it to listen to you," the hob said. "To you and no one else." He handed the book back to her. "You ask it."

"I wish I could just talk to it and it could talk back to me," Kate said. "Could that be done?"

"Well, now . . . I can't make it speak to you, but maybe I can let it hear you."

He got up and fetched a silver needle and a spool of red thread from the hutch. The spool for the thread was a thick chunk of a rowan branch. He took the book back from her and with quick deft movements, stitched an embroidered ear onto the front of the book.

"Ask it something," he said.

Kate started to reach for the book, but Finn shook his head.

"Just speak the question," he told her.

Kate cleared her throat. "I feel silly—talking to a book."

"There's sillier things. Try chasing a spunkie into a marsh like some mortals do. The sluagh just grab them and that's not nice at all—at least not for the one that's caught."

"I suppose." She cleared her throat again, then gave it a try. "Uh . . . hello, Caraid. Can you hear me?"

Under the four words that Finn had written earlier, her question appeared, in her own handwriting.

Hello, Kate, the book replied.

"Can you just hear me, or can you hear everything that goes on around you?"

Everything. But I'll only answer to you. You're my only friend.

"That's the thing with names," Finn remarked.

"What should we do?" Kate asked the book. "Where do we start? The droichan's caught Jacky and I can't just leave her to him while I go off looking for his heart. I might never find it."

Her words appeared on the page as quickly as she spoke them. Kate watched them take form, fascinated.

"We need help, Caraid," she added.

Rowan will break the droichan's spell on the Jack—unless he has blooded her. But you must be careful. The white wood or the red berry are only effective against his spells. If he was to catch you, neither will help you then.

"What does 'blooding her' mean?" Kate asked.

It made her stomach feel a little queasy as her imagination brought up images of what she thought the phrase meant.

"Luck flows like blood," Finn answered. "To free the luck from a body, the droichan will have to cut it open."

"Oh, God!" Kate stood up quickly. "We've *got* to get back to the Tower."

"First we need a plan."

"A plan? Finn, this is Jacky we're talking about!"

"Yes. But if he catches us as well, then what hope does she have? And there's this to think about as well: A creature like a droichan will gather the mean-spirited and evil about, simply by his presence. Bogans and other Unseelie folk."

"But wouldn't he just feed on their luck as well?"

"Not if he has all of Kinrowan's luck at hand—and that's what the Tower gives him."

"But—"

"The Host *will* gather to him, Kate. They have no leader at the moment."

"Caraid," Kate said to the book. "Jacky's my best friend ever. I can't let her die!"

I will still be your friend, the book replied.

Finn caught Kate's arm before she could respond.

"Don't make it jealous," he mouthed silently.

Kate looked at him, bewildered.

"That's the danger of names," the hob added, still just moving his lips but uttering no sound. "A skilly-born thing like your book here can take what it hears too literally."

Then Kate understood. It wasn't as if she hadn't had forewarning about this kind of thing.

"My best friend next to you, of course," she told the book. " —Won't you help me rescue her?"

I've told you all I know, Caraid replied.

"But there must be something else."

Find allies, the book told her after a few moments. *Others that the droichan has harmed. Perhaps, with their help, you can find his heart and free your next-best friend.*

"The fiaina sidhe," Finn said.

Kate looked at him. "Are they related to the Pook?"

"They are all kin of a sort. Perhaps they could help us."

"Perhaps! But that doesn't do anything for Jacky now."

"Kate, there's nothing else we can do."

"Oh, yes, there is. We can go back to the Tower with as much rowan as we can carry and get Jacky out of there."

Finn regarded her mournfully. His eyes plainly said, Why won't you listen?

"Kate," he began.

"If I can get to the wally-stanes, couldn't I just use one of them on him and turn him into a toad or something?"

Unlikely, Caraid replied. *Wally-stanes are a Jack magic. They wouldn't be strong enough for such a task. Especially not with the droichan fighting the spell.*

"Jack magics work subtly," Finn explained. "And remember how much you had to concentrate to make them work properly. Just imagine the droichan's will opposing you at the same time. You'd never have a chance to collect your thoughts."

Kate nodded. "Okay. But I'm still going. I have to, Finn."

"I know," he said. "But at least let us find what help we can close at hand. Crowdie Wort left Gwi Kayleigh in charge of his bally before he left. Why don't we at least find her first?"

Ottawa South was known as Crowdie Wort's Bally to the faerie of Kinrowan, Crowdie Wort being its Chief. Like most of the Court, he was in Ballymoresk for the Fair, and like the other Chiefs, he'd left a few foresters behind to keep watch over the acres under his care.

It's unlikely that a forester could stand up to the droichan, Caraid offered.

Kate ignored the book.

"Where can we find her?" she asked.

"She'll have left word at the bridge as to her whereabouts."

Kate closed Caraid and stuffed it in her pouch.

"Then let's go," she said.

Finn gave his comfortable home a longing look, then hurried after Kate, who was already outside and striding west to Billings Bridge.

Her predicament was the most terrifying thing that Jacky could imagine. She could hear and see and smell and feel and think, perfectly well. But she had no control over her body. Her lungs still worked, drawing in air, letting it out. The blood kept moving through her veins and arteries. All the automatic functions of the various systems that kept her alive still worked. But she couldn't get up out of the chair. She couldn't turn her head. She couldn't even blink.

The gruagagh had paralyzed her and she was as helpless as a newborn babe.

She heard footsteps. As she listened, she remembered Kate appearing in her range of vision earlier, moving a hand in front of her eyes. She hadn't been able to warn Kate. Hadn't been able to do a thing. But these footsteps weren't Kate's. They belonged to the gruagagh, who sat down across the table from her and regarded her with a smirking expression on his handsome face.

How could she have been so stupid as to have let him capture her? Kinrowan was her responsibility and she'd as good as handed it over to him. She thought of what Bhruic would say if he could see her now, what the Laird's Court would say when they returned from Ballymoresk, and hated Cumin of Lochbuie with a vengeance.

"There's a thing or two about this Tower," Cumin said, "that I don't understand. The smell of Bhruic Dearg's enchantments are very strong. I know the luck of Kinrowan is bound up in this place.

But he's hidden the workings of the how of it from me. I think it's time we took a walk upstairs and you showed me the lay of things."

Dream on, Jacky thought.

Cumin smiled. "I know you're raging, locked in there behind those glazed eyes, but it makes no difference, Jacky Rowan. You're mine now. And you'll show me what I want—don't doubt it for an instant."

To Jacky's dismay, her body lurched to its feet and, whether she wanted to or not, the gruagagh set her to walking across the floor and up the stairs. She moved like a marionette in an amateur puppeteer's jerky hands, but she moved. And there was nothing she could do about it.

As they reached the top of the stairs, her gaze touched briefly on her room, before the gruagagh moved her on. There were a pair of bogans in there now, rooting through her belongings. Bogans in the Tower! There was a boggy smell in the air, too. The whispery sound of sluagh voices.

The gruagagh moved her up the next flight of stairs before she could see more, up to Bhruic's study, up to his books of lore and the window that looked out on Kinrowan and showed the criss-crossing network of the moonroads that gave the realm its luck.

Kinrowan was doomed, she knew. And it was all her fault.

"There's nothing so satisfying," the gruagagh said from behind her, "as learning new lessons, discovering how things work. Perhaps when you've shown me Bhruic Dearg's secrets, little Jacky, I'll take you apart and see how you work." He laughed. "Would you like that?"

I'll see you dead in hell first, Jacky thought, but how she was going to manage that, she didn't know. The way things were going, she'd be lucky to make it through the next half hour, little say take her vengeance on her captor.

The door to the third floor loomed before them. Her hand—directed by the gruagagh's will—moved to the knob, twisted it, and then she was leading the gruagagh into the heart of Kinrowan.

Ten

Johnny couldn't find Puxill.

What he did find was Vincent Massey Park on a Wednesday afternoon, late in the summer. There were no sidhe, pink-haired or otherwise. No crowds of strange faerie creatures. Just the odd jogger—perfectly human—in jogging suit and running shoes. Once another cyclist passed him by, seriously bent over the handlebars of his ten-speed, stretchy black thigh-length shorts half-covering muscular legs, gaze fixed on the path ahead. Black squirrels were busy burying nuts. Sparrows and crows watched him from the trees.

But there were no magical beings.

No faerie.

He chained his bike to a tree by the railway bridge, and hiked up to the spot where Jemi had led him into her hollowed hill. The glade lay still in the afternoon sun. He walked slowly up and down its length, trying to remember just how they had approached it, until he was sure he had the right stone. Kneeling beside it, he studied it carefully. After a few moments, he lifted his hand hesitantly, then knocked on it the way he remembered Jemi had done.

Two quick knocks, pause, another knock.

Nothing.

He lifted his hand to try again, then turned away. What was the use? He sat down on the grass beside the stone and stared out through the trees to what he could see of the university.

He had to be crazy to have taken any of last night seriously. Something had happened to him—he didn't doubt that—but it hadn't been real. Whatever her reasons, Jemi had slipped him something and then his own imagination had taken over, peopling the park with the weird beasties and beings from his grandfather's library.

They had appeared to be real—*very* real, oh, yes—but then hallucinations usually were.

Illusions. Delusions.

Why was she—Jemi, Jenna, whatever her name was—doing this to him?

He pulled the bone carving from his pocket and fingered its smooth surface. The bone gleamed in the sunlight. He remembered the bone flute carving in Jemi's room on Sweetland, the attraction he'd felt between the two artifacts. . . . He kept rubbing the little fiddle with his thumb, only now his thoughts turned to Tom.

It was hard to believe the old fellow was gone. That didn't seem real either—never mind his being so sick this past while. The world didn't seem the same anymore, knowing Tom wasn't in it.

Sitting there in the sunlight, this was the first time Johnny had thought of his grandfather without wanting to cry. The sadness was still there—the empty place inside him hadn't been filled, or gone away—but it was different now. He found himself remembering good times—long nights spent talking. Times when they played tunes, the two fiddles singing in unison until Tom suddenly went into the perfect harmony, underlying the original tune with a resonating depth that made it sound like far more than a simple two- or three-part fiddle tune. There were times when the music bridged something between them and some mystery that lay just beyond their reach.

Tom had talked about it a few times. Johnny wondered now if what his grandfather had been talking about was Faerie. Was that where he'd gone? Was Tom some ghostly fiddler in a fairy hill now? Johnny's fingers yearned for the instrument that wasn't in his hands. If he played a tune now, would it reach to Tom in that other-world?

Johnny turned once more and, using the bone fiddle, rapped on the stone again.

Twice, pause, another rap.

Nothing.

"Goddamn you!" he cried. "Just give me back my fiddle! Give it back, or I swear I'll come back with a shovel and dig you out. . . . "

His voice trailed off as he sensed someone behind him. He looked up from the stone. In the meadow between the bike path and where he sat stood a skinny man in shorts, T-shirt and running shoes, watching him. The curiosity in his eyes turned to guilt when he realized that Johnny had caught him staring. He began to back away, then simply vanished.

"Oh, Christ," Johnny muttered. "Let's not start this disappearing shit again."

"It's not him," a familiar voice said from higher up the slope. "It's you that's been moved into Faerie."

She was crouched above him, something feral in her stance and in the look in her eyes, her pink hair standing up at all angles from her head. She was wearing calf-length trousers and a tunic-like shirt, both tattered and of an old-fashioned cut. Their greens and browns gave a first impression that she was wearing clothes made from twigs and leaves. Her face was washed out and pale without its makeup.

Beside her, its head on a level with hers as she crouched, was what Johnny first took to be a dog. Then he realized it was a small wolf.

"Listen," he began.

He wanted to just grab her and shake her, but he found his anger had just drained away again. Instead, he felt close to something rare, something wondrous, and he didn't want to lose it. He wanted to comfort the hurt he saw lying behind the fierce look in her eyes. He wanted to run away from her and never see her again.

"I know you mean well," Jemi said. "And we've given you nothing but grief."

"It's just . . . I don't . . . I'm not sure what's real."

Jemi moved suddenly, scuttling down the slope towards him. The dog, or wolf, turned and loped off into the trees. Johnny watched it go, then looked at Jemi. Her face was very close to his.

"Oh, we're very real," she said.

She lifted her hand to touch his cheek in that curious gesture that both she and her sister had.

"Your sister," Johnny said.

Her eyes went bleak.

"I just wanted to say I'm sorry about what happened to her. I know how you're feeling. . . . "

Jemi looked away, past his shoulder, into unseen distances.

"I won't let them get away with it," she said. "Whoever killed her—they'll pay." Her gaze went to him, the feral light fierce in her eyes. "Will you help me, Johnny Faw? I want to call the sidhe. I want to ride on Kinrowan. Something in Kinrowan killed my sister, and not just her alone. The Seelie Court *has* to pay for what they've done."

"What can I do?"

Here I go again, Johnny thought as he spoke. Believing it all again. But it was impossible not to—not with her sitting so close to him, radiating her otherworldiness.

"Be my strength," she said. "I've never called a rade—never led the fiaina. But I'm all that's left with Jenna gone. I'm the Pook now."

"But what would I do?"

"There's power in music, Johnny. We both know that. We've both made people smile, made them dance. Now we must gather my people from all their hidden places. Summon them with skilly tunes. Lead them against our foe."

She was using words that made no sense to Johnny. Rade and Kinrowan and skilly.

"How will you find this—foe?" he asked.

"We'll ride on Kinrowan, and if the Court doesn't deliver up the murderers, we'll take up our quarrel with them. Will you help me?"

"I . . . "

Johnny looked away from her. It was hard to think with her sitting so close. She smelled like apples and nuts, freshly harvested. She radiated heat, presence.

He didn't want to promise what he might not be able to deliver. He wanted to help her, wasn't sure he could, wanted her. . . .

And that was another part of the problem. He was drawn to

her, as surely as the two bone carvings were drawn to each other, and he was afraid of that. He was also afraid of it all turning around on him again. Of accepting that this was real, then finding himself alone once more. In a glade. Or on a riverbank. Without her. Thinking he'd imagined it all again. Thinking he was crazy.

He caught hold of her hand.

"They say that faerie can enchant mortals," he said. "Is this . . . have you laid a"—he searched for the right word—"a glamour on me?"

Jemi shook her head. Her fingers tightened around his.

"I've felt it too," she said. "With you. I might ask you the same question. But I didn't spell you, Johnny. All I know is that together we can make a skilly music that'll set our world a-right again. Heal its hurts. That can't be wrong, can it?"

"No."

He turned to her, lost himself in her eyes again, and had to look away. He remembered her anguish last night. The dead face of her sister, so like her own. The dislocation from reality that he'd been feeling ever since he'd escaped the crowd of faerie creatures that had been pressing around him. . . .

"I'll help you," he said. "Or at least I'll try. Just don't disappear on me again."

For a long moment neither of them spoke. Then Jemi put a hand on either side of his face and turned his head until he was facing her once more. She rose slightly off her heels and kissed him once on each eye, her tongue licking the lids.

"Now I *have* enchanted you," she said. "But only so you can see into Faerie on your own."

She smiled. The sadness, the fierceness in her eyes, eased slightly. She kissed him on the lips, a brief, brushing contact, then rocked back onto her heels, hands on her knees.

"Just . . . just like that?" Johnny asked.

A simple nod was her only reply.

Johnny sighed. He wanted to reach for her.

Instead, he said, "I was in your room on Sweetland. I was looking for my fiddle."

"It was a bad night," Jemi said softly. "I'm sorry you were pushed from Faerie the way you were."

"That's okay. I just wanted to tell you. I wasn't snooping, you see, but . . . " He opened his hand. The bone fiddle lay in his palm. "I saw a flute pendant that looked—no, that's not right. It *felt* like a twin to this."

Jemi looked down at the carving.

"I'd forgotten about the flute," she said. "It was Jenna's, but she gave it to me a long time ago. The Bucca gave them both to her. I think he got them from my mother, but he might well have given them to her in the first place."

"Do they mean something?"

"I'm not sure. Maybe there is some glamour involved here after all, though it's neither mine nor yours."

"What do you mean?"

"We fiaina aren't like the Courts, Johnny. We don't get our luck in the same way they do. We need our rade. The Bucca led the rade until Jenna learned it well enough to take his place, and then he left. It's always been a Pook or a Bucca or someone like that who leads the rade, but old tales say that a mortal leads it best. Man or woman, it doesn't matter. It depends on the Pook at the time, I suppose."

"What's a Bucca?"

Jemi smiled. "An old and very wise being, Johnny. He's been gone for a long time now. We're a restless folk, we fiaina sidhe. Me, not so much—I think it's my human blood—but the others, oh, how they like to wander. . . . "

"And the two carvings?" Johnny asked. "Where do they fit in?"

"They shape a bond between mortal and sidhe."

"Is that why your sister gave it to me? So that I'd meet you? Not that I'm complaining or anything, but how could she know that we'd like each other?"

The sadness washed over Jemi again.

"I don't suppose we'll ever know," she said.

Johnny reached for her and held her head against his shoulder, but she didn't cry. She pressed against him, then slowly sat back.

"Evening will be coming on—sooner than we'd like," she said. "Let's go inside and see what skilly tune we both know that we can use to summon the sidhe."

She slipped past him, into the hollow hill. Johnny stood at its sod entrance. He looked around the glade once more, trying to figure out why this was all happening to him. Then he shrugged and followed her inside.

"I see bogans," Gwi said.

"And I smell sluagh," Finn added.

Kate nodded glumly, her gaze fixed on the Tower.

It was late afternoon now, the past hours spent in tracking down Gwi Kayleigh. The forester was a tall faerie, lean with angular features. There was troll blood in her, from a few generations back, Finn had explained to Kate before they found her, but before Kate asked how they had come about, they'd spied Gwi and the chance was gone. Gwi wore the mottled greens and browns preferred by most foresters, and carried a bow and quiver. Instead of a pony, she trusted her long legs to carry her through her patrol.

She had listened to Kate's tale, added a curse or two to Finn's, then returned with them to Learg Green, where they now spied on the Tower.

"A few bogans we can deal with," she said, after studying the lay of the land, "and the sluagh won't be a danger until nightfall."

"That leaves the droichan," Kate said,

Gwi looked at the small bundle of rowan twigs that Finn was carrying.

"Those won't be enough," she said. "Not if he's all that the old tales make droichan to be."

"I'm *not* leaving Jacky in there with him," Kate said firmly.

"No one's asking you to," Gwi replied. "We just need more of a plan than catch-as-catch-can."

Kate sighed. She didn't like to admit it, but the forester was right. What Kate wanted to do was just rush in and get Jacky out of the gruagagh's clutches. Never mind waiting and thinking and planning. Just get in and out with Jacky, and worry about the gruagagh later. But the gruagagh was the whole problem, as Finn had rightfully pointed out earlier, and if they just charged ahead, they'd all end up as his captives with no one left free to rescue any of them.

"What're we going to do?" she asked.

Gwi plucked a stem of grass and put it between her lips.

"What we need," she said, chewing thoughtfully, "is a skin-walker."

"A shapechanger," Finn explained at Kate's puzzled look. "Like those with Lairdsblood who can take swan or seal shape."

"But the Laird and the whole Court's gone," Kate said.

The only other person with Lairdsblood that she knew was Jacky's sometimes beau, Eilian, the Laird of Dunlogan's son, but he was too far away to reach quickly, having gone back north to his father's Court at midsummer.

"There's others that know a trick or two about changing their skins," Gwi said.

"What good would a skinwalker even be?" Kate asked. "Just saying we could find one?"

"We need to get inside," the forester explained. "Without raising an alarm. And what better way to do so than disguised as one of their own? Then, with a bit of luck and surprise on our side, I'd hope we could snatch the Jack and win free with our hides all still in one piece. Now's not the time to confront the droichan. I'd rather wait until I have his hidden heart in my hand before I go face to face with him."

"And with Jacky free," Finn said, "we'll be able to concentrate on finding that heart."

"So where do we find a skinwalker?" Kate asked.

"In the borderlands," Gwi said. "I know a sidhe or two that have the knack and might be persuaded to help."

Finn shook his head. "No need to go that far." Before either of the women could ask him what he meant, he took out a needle and a spool of thread. "I can stitch us the illusion of being a bogan or whatever you wish."

"Oh, I don't know," Gwi said. She pulled the grass stem from her mouth and pointed it at the hob. "How well would it hold?"

"Well enough for what you want. If we're subjected to close scrutiny . . . " He shrugged. "But for something like this, it'll do."

"All right," Gwi said. "I'm game. Kate?"

Kate blinked. She looked from the forester to the Tower, then back again. She wished she felt a little braver, or at least more competent. But there was Jacky to think of.

"I guess so," she said.

Finn rubbed his palms together.

"Fine," he said. "I'll use buttons to start the spell. Strips of cloth for headbands to keep it firm. . . . "

He began to pull pieces of cloth from the small bag that held his bundle of rowan twigs and set to work.

"There's nothing like stitcheries to enthuse a hob," Gwi remarked dryly.

Finn didn't look up, but he grinned.

Kate nodded and went back to studying the Tower. From time to time she'd see a bogan move across a window, or in the backyard.

We're on our way, Jacky, she thought, wishing she could feel as enthused about bearding the gruagagh in the Tower as Finn was about stitching his spells.

What if Jacky wasn't even alive anymore?

She remembered what Caraid had said earlier. That Jacky would be fine—

Unless he had blooded her. . . .

"Don't worry," Gwi said. "We'll get the Jack free."

Oh, I hope so, Kate thought.

She gave the forester a quick smile, but returned to her worrying all the same.

Both Kate and Gwi eyed the result of Finn's handiwork with a certain dubious concern. Lying on the grass between them were three headbands. Each was made of strips of cloth, woven and stitched together, from which hung a number of long loose pieces like the ribbons of a May tree. To each of their jackets he had sewn a small wooden button.

"I know what you're thinking," the hob said with a grin, "but watch first before you decide."

He put on one of the headbands, adjusting it so that the ribbon-like streamers hung at his sides and back. It gave him a curiously festive air. Before either of the women could comment on the silliness of it, he attached the foremost ribbon on his left side to the button on his jacket. Kate blinked as he wavered for a moment, then blinked again and edged away from the hob as the bulk of a small bogan appeared where he'd been sitting. The bogan had a foolish look on his face.

"Not bad," Gwi said, reaching for one of the headbands. "Not bad at all. A little fuzzy about the edges, and it wouldn't stand up to a scrutiny by the beastie's mother—just saying such creatures are born and not hatched from refuse—but it'll do."

A moment later, Kate was sitting with two bogans.

"We'll have to growl a bit when we talk," Finn said. "I've disguised our looks and our scents, but I can't touch voices."

Kate nodded and grabbed the last of the headbands. She put it on, slipped the button on her jacket through the buttonhole that Finn had provided in the appropriate ribbon, and then there were three of the Unseelie creatures sitting on the riverbank in Windsor Park. The Finn bogan studied each of his companions critically, then nodded to himself and undid the button from his own ribbon.

"We'll wait a bit," he said as Kate and Gwi followed suit. "The day'll be gone soon and the twilight's the best time for this sort of work."

"What about the rowan twigs?" Kate asked.

"I'll stitch one in Gwi's jacket and one in my own," Finn said. "The rest we can each carry in our pockets. But don't forget, Kate. They might work well enough to shield us from the droichan's spells, but a bogan can still spike us, quicker than you'd like, and the rowan won't work if the droichan should lay his hands physically upon us."

"I don't like waiting," Gwi said. "We'll have the sluagh to deal with then, as well as the droichan and his bogans."

Not to mention, Kate thought, that the longer they waited, the less chance there was of Jacky still being all in one piece.

"Twilight's best for this sort of work," Finn insisted.

"Oh, I know that," Gwi said. "I just don't like it."

The forester found herself a new long stem of grass to chew on and settled down against the bole of a fat oak to wait, her gaze fixed on the Tower across the park. She had a hunter's patience—an attribute that neither of her companions seemed to share, for they fidgeted and were continually adjusting this and that, shifting their weight from one side to another, and generally feeling uncomfortable. It seemed to take forever before Gwi sat up, head cocked and nostrils widening.

"It's time," she said. "I can smell the nightfall on the wind."

"A bare room," the gruagagh said, "yet it stinks of magic." He stepped past Jacky and walked into the center of the room. "Having spent the better part of the day attempting to discover the secrets of Bhruic's Tower, I think it's time now for you to show me what has been hidden so well from me."

Jacky looked at him as though he were crazy. A bare room? The third-floor study looked no different than ever, except that there was an unruly pile of books around Kate's reading chair. Was Cumin blind?

He walked out of her range of sight once more and she heard the door close.

"I'm guarding the door," he said, "and the window lets out on a three-story drop. I trust you'll agree that escape is futile. Turn and look at me."

Her body obediently turned her around so that she was facing the gruagagh. He lifted his left hand and made a brief pass in the air between them, fingers moving in a quick, controlled pattern. As his hand dropped to his side, she regained control of her body, only to have it crumple to the floor.

Every limb was numb. Pin pricklings went through her as circulation was restored. She remembered what he'd said about having spent the better part of the day searching the Tower. A quick glance at the window showed that it was indeed late in the afternoon. Almost night. No wonder she had this numb, swollen feeling in every part of her body. She'd spent the same better part of the day, and some of the night too, sitting on a hard kitchen chair.

The gruagagh watched her patiently as she got the lumps that were her legs under her and pushed herself up, first to a crouching position, then finally to her feet. She swayed there, lifting and putting down her feet, shaking her arms, trying to get the numbness out of them.

"Show me the key," Cumin said.

"Can't you see it?" Jacky asked.

A frown moved fox-quick across the gruagagh's face.

"Would you like me to have your body throw itself out that window?" he asked.

"But then you'd never find out, would you?" Jacky replied sweetly.

She was acting far bolder than she felt, but she knew she had to put up a good front.

"You are trying my patience, you little fraud of a Jack."

"Why don't you just read my mind?" Jacky asked. "Why don't you have my hand write it all out for you? Or are those tricks beyond *your* capabilities?"

Something flickered in the gruagagh's eyes. Before he could do anything, Jacky shrugged.

"But I'll show you what you want," she said. "Why should I care? I'm tired of this Tower, tired of its responsibilities. Everyone wants me to be a gruagagh—to replace Bhruic—but I'm sick to death of being compared to him. Let them see how much they like having a gruagagh back in charge when it's you."

Jacky knew that there was enough of her real frustration in what she said to make her words ring true to the gruagagh. She looked around the room, still surprised at how it seemed empty to him, while its clutter and furnishing were very physically present to her—from a pair of teacups that hadn't been taken downstairs last night, to the books around Kate's chair, to the mess Kate must have made last night on the worktable where a scatter of twigs lay on top of a mess made up of a sheaf of papers, one of Bhruic's journals, a rolled-up map, an empty porcelain jar, a knife. . . .

Jacky wandered over to the table and stood near the weapon.

"I guess Bhruic was paranoid about what someone like you would do with this place," she said, "so he put some spell on it to keep it invisible from you." She turned, her back to the worktable. "The trouble is, I don't know how to make you see what's here. What if it's keyed to one's purpose? What if when someone comes in with all kinds of bad intentions, everything just shuts down? What can we do about that? Do you know a spell to hide your intent?"

Cumin regarded her through narrowed eyes and Jacky knew just what he must be thinking. He had to be reconsidering his earlier impression of her. Last night she'd been childishly easy to put under his control—but then he'd taken her by surprise. But if Bhruic had left her in charge of his Tower, if Kinrowan's Laird had agreed and not replaced her with someone else for as long as the year since Bhruic was gone, then there must be more to her than what he could see. Right now her assessment of why the key to the Tower remained locked away from him had to be making sense because, as anyone who knew, or had even heard about Bhruic knew, it was just the sort of thing that Kinrowan's Gruagagh—with his old-fashioned desire "to do things right"—would lay upon the place.

"I know such a spell," he conceded, "but it is based upon hiding one's intent from a living creature . . . not a wizard's Tower."

Jacky shrugged and leaned back against the worktable.

"That's too bad," she said. "This is a table I'm leaning against right now. A worktable. Should I try to hand things that are on it to you? Maybe one of Bhruic's journals? Tell me what you want me to do. I'm not a gruagagh. I can't wave my hand and make everything visible to you."

"His journals are there?" Cumin asked.

"One is," Jacky replied.

She lifted it from the table, noted that Cumin could see it while it was in her hand, then set it down again.

"There's more of them over there," she added, waving to the bookshelves on another wall.

"Give me that one," Cumin said, pointing to the invisible spot where she'd set the journal down.

"Sure."

Jacky swallowed dryly as the gruagagh moved towards her to take the book. The knife was lying there, waiting for her hand, but she didn't know if she could use it. It was for the good of Kinrowan—which was under her protection. It was to save her own skin. But it was one thing to knock a giant down a flight of stairs and kill him in the heat of the moment, and quite another to deliberately stab a human being—even one so evil as this gruagagh.

"The book," Cumin demanded, looming over her.

"What . . . what do you think these are good for?" she mumbled, trying to buy time.

In her left hand she held up a handful of rowan twigs, plucked from the table.

The gruagagh bared his teeth, like a dog snarling, and swung a fist at her, but she ducked. And grabbed the knife. She saw him step into the same space that the table occupied, still unaware of its presence, except intellectually because she had told him it was there. On a physical level, it didn't exist for him.

He stopped when he saw the knife in her hand.

"You pitiful thing," he said. "What do you mean to do with that?"

Jacky's anger returned in a rush. She stepped in close, stabbing him in the chest. He staggered slightly under the blow, but remained standing, a faint smile touching his lips. Jacky stumbled back. Before her horrified gaze, he reached up and plucked the knife from his breast, tossing it to the floor.

"You can't kill what has no heart," the gruagagh said.

It was too much for Jacky. Seeing him standing there in the middle of a table which didn't exist for him . . . plucking the knife from his chest . . . and there was no wound, no blood, nothing. . . .

She backed steadily away from him until she bumped against the sill of the window and could go no further. She lifted her hands to ward off the approaching gruagagh, and didn't know why she bothered. There was a shadow around him now, a black aura that clung to him, and it seemed that he wore the head of a black hound superimposed over his own features.

Desperately, she flung the handful of rowan at him. The gruagagh threw back his head and laughed.

"Was that your best?" he asked. "A knife and a handful of rowan twigs? You're mine, child, and I will have the secrets of this Tower from you. I will tear them from you as my bogans chew your flesh. You'll die—eventually—but in such pain . . ."

Jacky glanced behind her. The gruagagh saw a three-story drop through a window, but she saw all of Kinrowan spread out before her.

"Oh, no, you don't!" the gruagagh cried.

He lunged for her, but he was too late.

Jacky's gaze, drawn by the flash of a hob's red cap and a familiar head of tousled curls, latched onto Kate, Finn, and a tall woman who were crouching together by the riverbanks on the other side of the park. Before the gruagagh could reach her, she threw herself out the window, screaming Kate's name.

Behind her, she heard the gruagagh howl in rage. He grabbed for her leg, but caught only a handful of air. He was either not brave enough or not foolish enough to follow her when she vanished from his sight.

Henk stopped off at Johnny's apartment after work, but there was no answer to his knock. He went around back, fetched the key from under its brick, and let himself in. A quick prowl-through told him that while Johnny had been back since they'd gone up to Sandy Hill earlier this morning, he was gone now. His bike was missing as well. It didn't take Henk long to work out where his friend had gone.

"Christ, Johnny," he muttered as he returned the key to its hiding place. "You've got to give it up."

But he knew Johnny too well, knew that Johnny wasn't one to give up. Whatever Jemi Pook had done to him, Johnny would push through it until he'd worked it all out. Henk had seen it too often before.

So where did that leave Henk himself? There was really no question about it, he realized. He wasn't exactly happy to have to be doing it, but he wasn't going to leave Johnny on his own to wander around Vincent Massey Park, knocking on rocks until God knew what kind of trouble he might get into.

Giving the empty apartment a last look, Henk set off for Bank Street, where he could catch a #1 to take him down as far as Billings Bridge. It was a relatively short walk from there to the park.

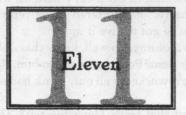

Eleven

Jenna's cairn was smaller than Johnny had imagined it would be. He'd been thinking in terms of the stone works in the British Isles and Brittany, in larger-than-life terms, but the cairn was just a small mound of rocks at the top of the hollowed hill above the entrance, not even visible from outside of Faerie.

With his fiddle case in one hand, Johnny took Jemi's hand in his other and gave it a squeeze. She turned to him, grateful, then looked back at the cairn, eyes brimming with unshed tears. The small wolfish dog had been waiting for them by the mound of stones. It gave Johnny the impression that it had been guarding the cairn.

"Is that your pet?" Johnny asked.

Jemi shook her head. "No. That's Mactire."

At the sound of its name, the animal wavered in Johnny's sight. It stretched, lost hair, gained stature, took on recognizably human-like figures. . . . In the next moment, a small feral boy crouched by the stones. He appeared to be about twelve years old—but only until Johnny looked into his eyes. He was naked, except for a soft covering of light downy hair that was the same grey colour that his wolfish fur had been, only not so thick. A mane of longer, coarser hair tumbled down his shoulders, matted with twigs, leaves and dried mud.

"Ah . . . " Johnny mumbled.

He really wasn't ready for this kind of thing yet. Maybe he never would be. Jemi he could take, Faerie in small doses, but the rest of the denizens of the Middle Kingdom still left him with the feeling that he was tripping out.

"Mactire's a skinwalker," Jemi explained.

"Right."

"He's a friend, Johnny."

Johnny nodded. "How do you do?" he said lamely to the small wild boy.

"Not good," Mactire replied gruffly.

His voice was deeper than Johnny had expected it to be, coming as it did from that slender frame. The wild boy met Johnny's gaze steadily for a long heartbeat, then turned to Jemi.

"Are you calling up a rade?" he asked.

Jemi shook her head. "It's the wrong time of the Moon, Mac. I'm calling up an army."

The wild boy grinned, baring two rows of sharp, pointed wolf's teeth.

"Oh, that's good," he said. "It's time we showed the night that we can bite back."

Looking at those teeth. Johnny didn't have any doubt about that. The wolf boy looked at his fiddle case.

"Can you play that thing?" he asked.

Johnny nodded. That, at least, was something of which he was sure.

Mactire grinned again. "That's good," he said, looking at Jemi once more. "He's not a Fiddle Wit, but they'll follow him all the same."

"I know they will," Jemi replied. "Pipe and fiddle and Arn's own luck—they'll have to follow. And he might make a Wit yet."

"What are you talking about?" Johnny asked.

"Remember what I told you before?" Jemi asked. "That a mortal leads us best? Don't ask me why, but that's the way it is."

"A brief flicker in the night," Mactire said. "Gone quick, but oh, they burn so bright."

That was almost poetry, Johnny thought, giving Mactire a considering look.

"And what's this about a Fiddle Wit?" he asked.

"It's just a name," Mactire explained. "See, the thing that binds us is music—music and the rade when we catch our luck. We can't have one without the other, and the luck's never so strong as when a tune calls it down. A Fiddle Wit is like a Jack—do you understand? Clever. A skilly sort of a person. Like our own Pook here, but all the way mortal. Not tied to any Court. No allegiances but to the Moonmother Arn, whatever shape she takes. It's a good name, Johnny Faw."

Johnny didn't even bother to ask how the wolf boy knew his name.

"It's time now," Jemi said, and then that unspoken question faded from Johnny's mind as well.

He cracked open his fiddle case and took his grandfather's gift from it. Plucking the strings, he found them still in tune. He put the fiddle under his chin, then reached into the case for his bow. Tightening the frog, he gave the bow a quick shake to loosen the hairs. When he was ready, he gave Jemi a nod.

She had taken a wooden flute-like instrument from her pocket and she was sitting by the stones, watching him. Her instrument had reeds at one end, finger holes along its length, and a bell shape at the other end. Resembling a bombard, it played more softly with a sweet tone that was like a cross between an oboe and a Northumbrian pipe chanter. When he nodded, she brought the reed end to her mouth and blew softly.

Watching her play, Johnny felt a closeness to her once more. She made such an incongruous picture with the mottled greens and browns of her shirt and tunic, her black piper's jacket with its tarnished brass buttons, and the pink hair standing straight up in a wild thatch. For a long moment he forgot to play, then he remembered why they were here and set his bow to the fiddle's strings.

The tune they played was "Brian Boru's March"—an old harp tune, supposedly composed in commemoration of the Battle of Clontarf, when the Irish under Brian Boru repelled an invasion of Vikings in 1014. But the tune was only a borrowed one, Jemi had told him that afternoon, and dated far earlier than that.

"It's the 'Bri' in Brian that's as close to the original title as your people can remember now," she had explained, "and that's an old word that the Gaels borrowed from the people of the hills. It means the female force, you see—the earth, the moon, growth and growing things. Like the luck we need to keep us hale. They found Brigit's name in that word, and many another word besides, but the old bri was more than just the Bride—it was every face that she ever wore. 'Briall Ort' is what we call this tune, and the closest I can tell you to what that means is 'cheer up.' Be happy. Persevere. Rise from your sorrow."

And it was that kind of tune, Johnny thought. It had always been one of his favorites. A tune that dripped age, was solemn as a saraband, yet sprightly too. Sadness and happiness mingled in its bittersweet turns, just as they did in one's life.

That evening, with the grey twilight creeping over the hills, Jemi's piping joining his fiddling as though they were meant only for each other, "Brian Boru's March" made a music that lifted his heart the way a hymn cheered a devout Christian, but it kept his foot tapping at the same time. There was mystery in it, and a magic, and a calling on, too. For he could see now, as the twilight deepened, that they were no longer alone by Jenna's cairn.

Like the previous night, the fiaina sidhe came by ones and twos. One moment there were just the three of them on the hilltop—piper, fiddler and listening wolf boy—and in the next, a crowd of faerie had gathered. But tonight they were different.

Last night they had come as the moment had found them—drawn from whatever task they were about when they first heard the call.

Tonight they came riding for war.

Hobs on their shaggy ponies and a big troll with a shield the size of a small car and a club like a sawed-off lightpost. Skinwalkers in their beast shapes: foxes and wolves, bears and snarling bobcats. Three kelpies in horse shape, their black flanks shining in the dying light. Tiny creatures armed with little bows and arrows, spiked armour on their backs and arms, making them look like oversized hedgehogs riding small spotted brown dogs. Narrow faces, broad faces, painted for war, like ancient Celts or Native Americans. Stout dwarves with knobby walking sticks spiked with sharp silver tips, and wearing leather helmets.

By the time the twilight gave way to night, there were over two hundred of them gathered on the hill. A bearded hob on a small pony rode forwards as Jemi and he finally set their instruments aside. He nodded briefly to Johnny, then turned his attention to the new Pook.

"Jenna was wrong," Dohinney Tuir said, "and I was right, but I take no pleasure from it. She should have listened. She should never have gone. For now she's dead, and we still have war on our hands—a war we cannot hope to win. Kinrowan is not our enemy, Jemi."

"Jenna died in Kinrowan," Jemi replied.

"And curse the creature that slew her—but it was not a member of the Seelie Court."

A murmur rose from the gathered sidhe, but Johnny wasn't sure if it meant that they were agreeing with the hob or not.

"Our enemy is in Kinrowan," Jemi said. "They must deliver him to us."

A black horse stepped forwards, shifting its shape, and then a kelpie stood at Tuir's side.

"I want revenge as much as you do," Loireag said, "but Tuir has the right of that much of it. Do you have the name of our enemy for us, Jemi?"

The new Pook shook her head.

"We can't ride to war without a name," Loireag said.

This time the murmur of the sidhe was in agreement—even Johnny could hear that much.

"This murderer—" Jemi began.

"Must be punished!" Loireag broke in fiercely. "But our quarrel isn't with the Court in Kinrowan."

"So we're supposed to wait?" Jemi demanded. "Wait while more of us are slain or chased away? Wait without our rade until we're so diminished that we're not strong enough to even flee, little say fight? Look at us. We've lost a third of our number as it is. Kinrowan owes us the name of our enemy."

"And if they don't know it?" Tuir asked.

"They have troubles of their own," a new voice said.

Deep and grumbling, it issued from the troll who stepped closer, towering over them all.

"There are bogans loose in Kinrowan again," he went on, once he had their attention. "Bogans and sluagh and all the Host. The better part of the Court is gone south to the Harvest Fair and what's left is just beginning to discover the troubles that they have. They can't give us what they don't have, Jemi Pook."

"If we ride on Kinrowan with your demands," Tuir added, "we might well make an enemy of the Seelie Court as well. We're borderfolk, Jemi. We live at the sufferance of both Courts. Either of them could easily rise and finish us off—the Seelie Court, if we bring trouble to them, or the Host, if it can gather itself, for the sake of mischief alone. We can't fight them both and this new enemy besides."

Johnny could feel Jemi wilting at his side.

"Then what are we supposed to do?" he asked.

The weight of hundreds of sidhe gazes settled on him and he wished that he'd never spoken. There were feral lights in those eyes, and no love for humanity.

"Find the enemy's name," Tuir said wearily. "We will help. Each one of us will peep and pry, but until we know what we face, there must be no battle rade." He shook his head slowly. "That such a thing should *ever* be. I don't doubt that we could lose the Moon's luck for all time, whether we win or lose."

"But—" Johnny began.

"Watch where you step, tadpole," Loireag said. "Some might have use for your kind, but there's few of them among our number."

Jemi drew herself up at that.

"Do you forget it all so soon?" she asked. "Who can lead a rade better than a mortal?"

"It needs a mortal with some wit," Loireag replied immediately. "And that tadpole has none. He might find it, given time, but time we do not have."

Jemi laid her pipe down by Johnny's knee and stood up to face them, arms akimbo.

"Fine," she told them. "Go! we'll seek out the enemy. And maybe we'll find him and be able to deal with him, and maybe we won't, but I'll tell you this—you, Loireag, and you, Tuir, and you, Garth." She held their gazes with her own, that of kelpie, hob, and troll, and other in that number. "When all's said and done, you'll not have a rade led by this Pook, nor by any mortal that I can put a name to. I'll do what needs doing for Jenna's sake, but after that you can lead your own rades."

"You know we can't," Tuir said. "We need—"

"Don't tell me what you need," Jemi said. "I've given you my need, and you've thrown it back at me. Don't you ever tell me what *you* need."

Loireag took a step towards her, but backed down from the fierce glare in the Pook's eyes.

"Jemi," she tried softly. "Listen to reason—"

"Go!"

The word hung in the still night air, for one long moment, for another, and then slowly they began to disperse. Once moving, they were quickly gone. Johnny watched them, but they faded too fast for him to make them all out in the dark.

The last to go were the kelpie and hob. Tuir looked as if he might speak again, but then he shook his head, turned his pony, and walked it slowly away into the trees. Loireag followed him a moment later. When Johnny turned to Jemi, they were all gone, even the wolf boy, Mactire.

"If the Bucca was here, they'd follow him," Jemi said. "If it was Jenna asking them, they'd follow her. But not me." Her gaze met Johnny's. "This is what I get for straying, Johnny. I've walked among men for so long that their blood must run stronger in me now than my Pook blood does."

Johnny shook his head.

"You chased them away," he said.

"Please. Don't you start."

"No. Listen to me. I don't know everything—about the Courts and where you people stand with them—but what your friends were saying made sense."

"They're not my friends."

"Whatever. But think about what they said. Why take it out on Kinrowan? You don't think that the Seelie Court is behind this, do you?"

Jemi didn't answer for a long time. She stared off into the distance, looking for something. When she returned her gaze to Johnny, he could see that, whatever she'd sought, she hadn't found it.

"No," she said softly. "I guess I don't really think they are. But surely they must know our enemy's name? How can such an evil thing live in their realm and they not know?"

"Maybe we should just go talk to them."

"I suppose."

Johnny put away his fiddle and bow, then picked up Jemi's pipe.

"Come on," he said. "Let's see what they have to say."

Jemi let herself be led along.

"It's just that they know it all," she said. "Do you know what I mean? Loireag and Tuir and the rest. Even when they don't know, they still act like they know it all. A show of force wouldn't hurt. It'd prove that we mean business. I wasn't trying to start a war."

"You came off sounding like you did."

"I just want Jenna's killer to pay for what he's done."

"We'll find him," Johnny said.

He just hoped that they'd be able to deal with him when they *did* find him. The sidhe had seemed like as tough a bunch as he'd ever want to run up against, but he'd sensed a genuine fear in them. And if *they* were scared . . .

He tried to put that out of his mind for the moment, concentrating instead on getting them both back to the entrance of Jemi's hollowed hill without either of them breaking their necks in the darkness. Jemi might be able to see like a cat in the dark, but she wasn't being much help right now, and whether he could see into Faerie or not, once they left the relative brightness of the hilltop, he was lost in the shadows.

"I shouldn't have gotten so mad," Jemi said. "That always happens to me with them. I always get mad. That's the real reason I don't live with them."

"Why do you get mad?" Johnny asked.

Jemi's shoulder moved up and down under his arm in an invisible shrug. "I don't know. I wish I could tell you, just so I'd know."

It was because she tried to be too hard around them, Johnny thought. Too tough. He'd seen her doing it when she was arguing with them, seen it while she was getting ready to call them up this afternoon, but he didn't think this was the time or place to bring it up.

"Let's get some tea," he said, "and then see what we can do about finding someone in Kinrowan who'll talk with us."

"I don't really know anyone there," Jemi said.

Which made two of them, Johnny thought. But he just gave her another hug.

"That's okay," he said. "We'll find someone. We'll just ask around. We can look in the phone book under 'Kinrowan faerie, information.' "

"If only it could be so easy," Jemi said.

They reached the entrance to the hill then. As they went inside, Johnny wondered, not for the first time that day, just exactly what he'd gotten himself into. The only thing he really knew, when he thought it all through, was that so long as Jemi was here, he'd stick it out. Maybe they were enchanted by two little bone carvings, or maybe they weren't, but he couldn't deny that he wanted to be with her, no matter how weird it got.

Jacky pinwheeled through the air.

Arms outspread, she spun and whirled like a winged sycamore seed. She expected to hit the front lawn of the Tower, for all that the whole of Kinrowan was spread out from the study's window, but instead found herself in a sort of free-fall where time had stepped out for a moment, leaving her in an endless spiral, eyes shut tight and her own scream for Kate still ringing in her ears.

Kate.

She opened her eyes, blinked back a blur of tearing, and looked for the threesome she'd spotted by the riverbank.

Kinrowan was still spread out below her, the Tower now a part of that panorama. She was turning slowly, falling but getting nowhere, above it all, stalled like a bird riding an updraft. She found the Tower, Windsor Park, and then—her eyesight sharp as an eagle's—focused on Kate and Finn and the tall woman with them. She tried to angle herself towards them, gasped at the sudden rush as she dropped like a stone.

This, she realized belatedly, was probably the wrong way to go about it.

She tried to pull up from the fall, but the long moments of timeless floating had been swallowed by the inevitable march of microseconds into seconds, seconds into minutes. Time sped on again; accelerated. There was no stopping the momentum of her fall now that it had begun again. All she could do was angle herself towards the river beside her friends, but for all the panicked flapping of her arms, she fell straight and sure in the wrong direction.

She was going to miss the river. She was going to land directly on top of Kate and the others.

She cried Kate's name again, this time in warning, saw her friend look around herself puzzledly, and then it was too late for Jacky to do anything but close her eyes and tense herself against the coming impact.

She knew it was the wrong thing to do. She should be concentrating on relaxing her muscles, but they were bunched so tight she couldn't even breathe, little say let up the knots of her tension.

It was dark by the time Henk reached the beach of flat stones where he'd found Johnny the previous night.

It was still early in the evening and he could hear the traffic on the nearby thoroughfares, but here in the park he felt entirely cut off from the city that surrounded him. He started at little noises, and had the feeling that he was being watched from all sides. It was patently ridiculous, of course, but Johnny had filled his head with those stories about goblins in the park, and all grown up and matured as he was, Henk found himself returning to a childhood fear.

He'd always been terrified of the dark.

It was something he'd had to work hard at to get rid of—this uncontrollable fear that there were bogeymen out in the shadows, just waiting to tear him apart. He'd grown up outside the city, in a rural area where, when night fell, it came like a black curtain. He used to have fights with his father about it back then. One night in particular he could call up with disturbing clarity. He'd forgotten to put the garbage out by the road that afternoon and, because the garbage collectors came at dawn, he'd had to go put it out in the dark.

It had been his own fault. He should have remembered. But he hadn't, and he couldn't face the walk down the lane to the road. Even with the light on by the garage, it was too much. Its light only went so far. Shadows pooled beyond its reach, thick on the route he had to take, and he just couldn't do it.

He was twelve years old. At that age he knew how stupid it was to feel like that. But the unreasoning fear wouldn't go away and he'd wept as his father made him go out and do it. By the time he got to the road, loaded down with the unwieldly pair of aluminum cans, he was sobbing uncontrollably.

The bogeyman hadn't gotten him that night, but the darkness had lodged itself inside him even deeper than before, so that years later he might be walking down a street at night and suddenly be hit by that same blind panicking fear.

Last night he'd been fine. He'd been worried about Johnny, looking for him, finding him. No problem. He hadn't even thought about it. But tonight. It was just too quiet. Too dark. And Johnny had been too serious about the things he said he'd seen.

All bullshit, of course.

But what if? Just *what if?*

People did disappear—*snap!* Just like that. Going out for some milk to the corner store and never coming back. Ordinary people, with no problems, no reason to drop everything in their lives and just take off. Vanished. Into the night.

So maybe a supernatural answer was unfounded. Sure, it was all bullshit anyway—right? But what about your plain, everyday psycho? Some serial killer, hiding in the bushes. In the shadows.

Christ, why did the darkness seem to be watching him?

Henk knew he was cursed with an overactive imagination. He just wished he could figure out how it got turned on, what kicked it in. That way he might be able to shut it off.

He stared across the river to the lights of the university. Mist was rising from the water again tonight—another too-cool night following a warm day. That was all it was. Nothing mysterious about it. Just the natural order of things. Like the darkness. The sun was on the other side of the planet, that was all. Nothing creepy about that. Nothing hiding in the shadows, waiting for him. . . .

He froze, staring at a clump of trees by the bicycle path.

He'd heard something. He was sure he'd heard something. He took a step forwards, determined to walk right up to the trees and get rid of this bad case of the nerves that was giving him the heebie-jeebies.

"Johnny," he called softly. "Is that you, man? Jemi?"

He took another step forwards and that was when a tall shadow detached itself from the darker bulk of trees and moved towards him. Henk stared at the figure, not willing to accept what he was seeing. It was a tall black woman with a horsey face, entirely nude, nightmares burning in her eyes.

Henk wanted to bolt, but he just couldn't move. He remembered Johnny describing this woman to him. She'd been with the crowd of faerie that had encircled Johnny last night. Right here. On this beach.

He shot terrified glances from the corners of his eyes, looking for more of the creatures, but he and the woman were alone.

"I am weary to death of your kind," the woman said.

And then she changed.

There was a moment when her features seemed to melt into each other, when she became a swirl of shadow. The spin of the air made Henk dizzy and he stumbled back, slipped on a stone, and tumbled to the ground. When he looked up again, the woman was gone and a huge black horse was in her place.

It snorted, breath wreathing from its nostrils in the cooling air. Prancing in place, its hooves made a clatter against the stones. And then it reared up above him, forelegs cutting the air.

Henk scuttled out of the way of the dropping hooves, too panicked to even try to get to his feet. He just churned his arms and legs and moved like a crab across the stones.

The horse reared again.

All Henk could see was its eyes. That's what scared him the most. The horse's eyes were the same as the woman's had been. They were *her* eyes.

He didn't want to think about what that meant. But the part of him that had always succumbed to his childhood fears was chanting, *It's real, it's real, it's real. . . .*

The bogeyman had turned out to be a woman and she'd finally come to get him.

With the coming of twilight, Kate and the others buttoned the appropriate ribbons to their jackets and made ready to cross Windsor Park. She felt weird looking at her companions, knowing that she looked the same as they did.

Bogans were an unpleasant sort, and all of a kind. They had dark oily skin, wrinkled like old leather, and greasy yellow hair. Broad and squat, their wide heads sat on their shoulders without the benefit of necks. Their eyes were narrow, noses flat, and for clothing all they wore were animal skins tied around their waists. And they stank.

Kate wrinkled her nose at the smell that was a part of Finn's enchantment.

"Are we all ready?" Gwi asked.

Kate started to nod, but then she heard it.

At first it didn't register. When she realized it was her own name being called, she looked around, trying to find out where the sound was coming from—for it was Jacky's voice that she heard. And it wasn't coming from very far away.

"That's—" she began.

Before she could finish, there came a loud *fwbuft* of displaced air and a small familiar figure appeared in the middle of where they stood, tottered for a moment, then collapsed in a heap on the ground.

"It's Jacky!" Kate cried.

Jacky looked up at the sound of her name, but then she frantically began to sidle away from the trio.

"Gagh!" she mumbled. "Bogans."

Kate ran over to her, which only made Jacky increase her attempts to get away.

"It's okay, Jacky," Kate said. "It's us. We're just disguised."

Jacky studied her nervously, obviously puzzled by the sound of Kate's voice coming from the ugly mouth of a bogan. Then another sound came, this time from the direction of the Tower, and they all froze. It was an outraged roar—a howl that sent a shiver up their spines. Looking towards the Tower, they could see bogans and sluagh streaming out into the park.

"Quick!" Gwi cried. "Finn, get a button on the Jack's coat and give her your headband."

The forester had a voice that was obviously used to commanding—and to being obeyed. Before Finn could even question her orders, he found himself doing as she'd asked. He tore the button off his jacket and immediately began stitching it to Jacky's shirt. Gwi took off Finn's headband and fitted it to Jacky's head.

"No one speaks but me," she said.

"This won't work," Kate protested. "Finn won't be disguised."

"All Finn has to do is pretend he's frightened. We're three bogans and we've caught him for our supper."

"I won't have to pretend," Finn muttered as he tied off his thread. "It's good to see you, Jacky," he added as he attached the ribbon from her headband to the newly attached button.

Her form wavered and a bogan's shape took its place. They were not a moment too soon. The nearest bogans had almost reached the lip of the riverbank where they were hiding.

"Oh, no, you don't!" Gwi cried.

Her voice was deep and very bogan-like—so much so that when she grabbed Finn, he struggled against her in earnest.

"You'll not get away from us so quick," Gwi went on. "Hot damn!"

Kate and Jacky exchanged glances, remembering the times they'd been in the clutches of bogans and it hadn't been "let's pretend."

Before either of them could speak, real bogans appeared at the top of the riverbank.

"Whatcha got there?" the foremost one demanded.

"Supper, arse-breath," Gwi replied. "Are you blind?"

"Give us a leg."

"Get spiked."

The bogan growled and was about to start down towards them when his companion grabbed his arm.

"The Jack's escaped," he told Gwi.

He glanced at Kate and Jacky. Kate put a fierce look on her face and almost grinned when the bogan took a half-step back. Now that Jacky was safe, so to speak, she thought, this could almost be fun.

"The boss won't like you snacking when there's work to be done," the second bogan added. "Put you in his bad books, he will."

"I can't read, so what do I care?" Gwi replied.

"Haw! That's rich. Can't read."

The bogan nudged his companion, but the first of the pair was still scowling and looking hungrily at Finn.

Gwi dragged Finn protectively closer. Pushing him to the ground, she put her foot on the hob's neck and glared at the bogans.

"Whatcha staring at, shithead?" she demanded.

Kate made a snorting sound and stepped nearer to Gwi.

The two bogans retreated. Among their kind, bravado ruled.

"Save us a bite," the first bogan said, trying to save some face.

"I'll save you his arse," Gwi told him.

"Haw!" The second bogan was having a good time. "That's richer. They'll save his arse for you, Groot."

Groot snarled. "Get your own arse in gear, Lunt.

There's work to do—the boss is waiting and you don't want that, hot damn."

The retreated from the lip of the rise and fared on. Kate was ready to collapse with laughter.

"We did it!" she cried. "Did you see their faces? I thought—"

"Whisht," Gwi said. "We must be gone and quick. Those bogans won't be gone long. They'll search awhile, but their stomachs will soon send them back here to see if they can't beg a piece of the hob from us. We've got to be gone by then."

"Where will we go?" Kate asked.

"My hollow's close," Finn offered.

Gwi considered that. "Too close."

"The Court?" Kate tried.

"That's no good either. We'll want to be free to move and they'll be watching the Court now. We might get in, but we'd never get out again unseen."

"*What* is going on?" Jacky asked. "Has everyone gone mad?"

"It's too long to tell you it all," Kate said. "But your gruagagh's not what you think he—"

"I know just the place!" Finn broke in.

"Where?" Gwi asked.

"Never you mind. What isn't spoken can't be overheard. Just follow me."

Gwi regarded him for a moment, then shrugged. "All right. But you two," she added to Kate and Jacky. "You keep those bogan shapes on until we're somewhere safe. That droichan will have your scents and it won't be more than a moment's work to track you down if you take off your disguises."

"Droichan?" Jacky asked.

"I'll explain it all to you later," Kate said.

"I feel like I've come in at the middle of a movie."

"You're not far off."

Finn had already set off and they all hurried along behind him—three bogans chasing a hob.

"I'm glad you're safe," Kate told Jacky between breaths. "We were just about to storm the Tower, looking for you. That's why we're wearing these disguises."

Jacky wrinkled her nose. "I hope Finn can stitch us something not so smelly when he's got a chance."

"There's gratitude."

"Thank you, thank you," Jacky replied. "Don't mind me—I'm just a little stunned from it all."

Kate glanced at her. "How *did* you pop in out of nowhere like that?"

"That's *my* long story that I'll tell you later."

They conserved their breath then to keep up with Finn and the forester. As she trotted along, Jacky went back over the last few moments after she'd jumped out of the window. It seemed that the gruagagh had inadvertently showed her yet another of the Tower's magics—one that made sense, too. If all of Kinrowan was in one's responsibility, one would want to be able to reach any part of it as quickly as possible in case of an emergency. By that reckoning, she wondered, there should also be a quick way back. So how did that work?

"Beam me up, Scotty," she muttered.

"What?" Kate asked.

Jacky shook her head. "I'm just thinking about teleportation," she said.

"Oh, is that all? I thought it was something more humdrum, like reliving old episodes of *Star Trek* in a moment of danger."

Jacky grinned. "It's good to see you again, too, Kate."

They slowed down once they were out of the park and a few blocks north of the Tower, but Gwi would let no one remove their disguise. She kept her own on as well.

"He'll be looking for you, too," Gwi said when Kate complained. "And besides, we don't have it so bad as Finn. He's got to both smell and look at us."

It was an hour or so later that Finn brought their roundabout journey to a halt in the shadows under the MacKenzie King Bridge. He knocked on the stone wall, a sharp *rap, rap, rap.*

"Who lives here?" Jacky asked.

"My friend Gump," Finn said.

As he spoke, Gump's bulk stepped out of the stones and peered down at them. Jacky and Kate took quick steps back until they were up against the railing by the canal.

"He's a trow," Finn added unnecessarily.

"Now, here's a strange sight," Gump boomed. "Dunrobin Finn in the company of three bogans."

"They're not what they seem," Finn said.

The trow nodded. "Nothing ever is." He waved to the stones. "Come along inside. I know there's a tale behind what I see here, and I'd rather hear it in comfort than stand out here with the mist curling up at my toes."

Jacky and Kate regarded the stone wall with misgivings, but Finn waved them through. To their surprise, they didn't run smack up against the stones, but passed right through them. Finn and Gwi followed—Gwi removing her disguise—and Gump brought up the rear.

"I hope I can get the bogan smell out again," the trow muttered to himself.

Then he remembered that he was playing host. He put a smile on his face and led the way down the tunnel to the big hollowed-out room that was his home. Everything was oversized—the chairs around the big table, the hearth with its cookware hanging from its stone mantel, the worktable along one wall where Gump pursued his hobby of making mechanical birds, the bookcases which held hundreds of his creations as well as a small library of bird books, and his big four-poster bed.

"Who'd like tea?" he asked.

A chorus of yesses sent him to the water barrel. He lifted its lid, dipped in a kettle, and set it hanging above the coals in the hearth. Drops of water hissed and spat as they fell from the kettle. Kate and Jacky seated themselves on the edge of his bed. Gwi climbed onto a chair. Finn remained standing, looking up at his friend.

"This is very kind of you," Kate said.

"Mmmmm," Gump replied.

He studied the pair of them on his bed and wrinkled his nose.

"If you're wearing those shapes as a means of disguising your essence as well as your looks," he said, "there's no need in here. A trow's home is always shielded against magic."

Kate undid her button and showed Jacky how to undo hers. Then she hopped off the bed and studied her face in the bottom of one of the trow's shiny pots.

"Thank God for that," she said. "I was beginning to feel the way I smelled."

"A marked improvement now," Gwi said with a smile.

"So what's the to-do?" Gump asked.

He looked at Finn, but the hob shrugged.

"There's more than one tale to tell before it's all untangled," Finn said. "I think Kate should start off, since she knows the most."

Oh, no, Kate thought.

She shot Jacky a quick glance. Now she'd have to tell Jacky about using the wally-stane. She touched Caraid in its bag at her side, gave Finn a withering look which he ignored, then started to tell what she knew.

Three times Henk managed to evade the kelpie's flashing hooves. He scuttled backwards over the stones, scraping his fingers, not caring, just trying to get out of the way. But now the river was at his back and there was no place left to go.

The mist wreathed around his legs as he slowly rose into a kneeling position. The kelpie moved towards him, hooves clacking on the stones. Henk could smell the sweat of his own fear, clinging to him. He'd gone all the way through and past his terror into a place where only resignation was left.

The kelpie rose on her hind legs.

This was it, Henk realized. There was no escape, not with the river at his back, the kelpie in front of him. He was too tired to even stand—adrenaline having stolen all his strength in his earlier moments of panic.

But before the hooves could strike, a voice called out.

The kelpie hesitated, forelegs slashing the air close enough to Henk's face that he could feel the air of their passing. She backed away, came down on all fours, then turned her head in the direction of the interruption, regaining human form as she did.

Henk stared numbly at the little man on his shaggy pony and couldn't feel a thing.

I don't want to be here, he thought, but he still couldn't move to take advantage of the distraction and escape.

"Why do you deny me his life?" the kelpie asked Henk's saviour.

Dohinney Tuir sighed. "Because it's not yours to take, Loireag. He's an innocent."

"He's a man," Loireag replied. "That used to be reason enough. And he's no innocent. He called the Pook's name—and that of her consort as well."

"You turned Jemi away from Kinrowan. If you killed this man, you would do as great an injustice as the Pook would have done had she led us against the Court."

Loireag grimaced.

"I have to do something," she said finally. "Jenna's dead, Tuir. I can't just leave it at that."

"Now you know how Jemi feels—why she called the rade to go against the Court. Neither of you has the right of it."

"The man is on my shore," Loireag said. "He's prying about my haunts. It's my right to take him if I so choose."

"When your anger is directed against another—not him?"

"Don't, Tuir. Don't confuse me."

Henk listened and watched, still not moving. The woman was silent for a while now and the little man on the pony turned to him.

"This is a bad place for such as you," Tuir told him. "On a night like this—and for many a night to come, I'll warrant. Go. Now."

As though the hob's words were the catalyst to free him, Henk stumbled to his feet. He stared at the two figures, then, from his new vantage point, caught a metallic gleam by a tree nearby and knew it to be Johnny's bike. As he thought of his friend, his mind began to work once more.

"Johnny," he said. "Give me back my friend."

I don't believe I'm doing this, he thought. I'm talking to fairies in Vincent Massey Park, for Christ's sake. I'm going as bonkers as Johnny.

Except it was all real.

"We don't have him," the hob said.

"And we don't want him," Loireag added.

"But—"

"Go!" Tuir cried. "This is not your place, man. Tonight it belongs to us."

Henk fought down the impulse to argue any further. He edged his way around them to where Johnny's bike was chained to the tree. With fumbling fingers, he worked over the combination lock, loosened the chain, and wound it around the bike's seat post. The two faerie watched him, eyes not blinking, silent as statues.

Shivering, Henk got on the bike and turned it away from them. Fear cat-pawed up his spine as he turned his back on them. He aimed the bike in the direction of Billings Bridge and set off down the bike path. When he dared a quick glance back, the stony beach was empty.

He tried to fight down his fear, but it built up in him again and he pedaled for all he was worth until he reached the shopping mall near the bridge. Gasping with relief and lack of breath, he steered the bike into its lit parking lot. He was shaking as he chained the bike up to a lightpost and stuck his hands in his pockets as he entered the twenty-four-hour donut shop standing by itself across the parking lot from the plaza.

He ordered coffee and managed to take it to a stool by the window without spilling it. As he sipped, his nerves slowly grew less jangled. He stared out the window then, into the almost empty parking lot.

It was a Wednesday night. Sensible people were at home, watching TV, maybe reading a book, doing normal things—not tripping through a park looking for a friend who'd gotten himself kidnaped by goblins.

Faerie.

We don't have him, the little man had said.

Then who did?

And we don't want him, his nightmare had added.

But I still want him, Henk thought. Only I don't know how to get to him.

The kelpie had called Johnny the Pook's consort and what the hell did that mean? He took another sip of his coffee and continued to study the parking lot. He wanted to do something, but didn't know what. In the end, he just sat there, trying to convince himself that none of it had really happened, knowing all the while that it had.

After a while, he got a second cup of coffee, then a third, but by the time he'd finished them as well as some donuts, he was still no closer to an answer. At length he returned to the bike and started to pedal back to Johnny's apartment.

Twelve

H is true name was Colorc Angadal and though he'd passed through Lochbuie once, it was not a place that he could call home.

There was no place he called home. A droichan could have no home. They stole their sustenance from the Moon and, sooner or later, if they remained in one place too long, the Moon would see that a price was paid. So the droichan took what they wanted, from here, from there, moving on before the local faerie grew aware of what it was that threatened them and banded against the enemy, or the Moon found some other method of payment.

It was heroes, usually, that the Moon called up. Sometimes skillyfolk, like a Pook. Sometimes it was a combination of the two and Colorc hated them the most: the Jacks. Too clever. Too brave. The Moon sained them too well, and filled them with luck in the bargain.

When Kinrowan's Jack disappeared through the third floor window of her Tower, his anger at her kind burst forth in a long shrieking wail of rage. Then he regained control of himself, went downstairs, and sent them out—those of the Host who'd come under his banner in their twos and threes, eager to feed on the luck he gave them and always eager to bring chaos to Seelie folk. He sent them out to hunt that Jack—bogans and sluagh, little twig-thin gully-wudes and toothy hags, trolls, and other Unseelie creatures. He sent as well the shadow from his own back that could take the dark shape of a kelpie and the winged shape of a crow, but mostly ran free as a black hound.

They would find her and bring her back. If not the Host, then surely his shadow, for his shadow had her scent.

He watched them go, then returned to that room on the third floor that stank of Bhruic Dearg's magic. The Jack had played him for a fool, but she'd had it right. The Gruagagh of Kinrowan had left a strong spell to protect his Tower and especially its heart—this room. He'd tied it to intent, no doubt of that, and there was no way that Colorc could hide his intent from its spell.

He frowned, walking about the room. He stood where the Jack had lifted a book from a worktable, but there was nothing for him to feel there. He looked out the window and saw only the street outside, not what the Jack had seen. Not what she had escaped to.

"Too clever by far," he muttered.

Both the Jack and he himself had been too clever, but she'd won out, while he was left with only the ashes of her trick tasting dry in his mouth.

He had heard of Kinrowan, of its troubles and how this Jack had put an end to them. By luck, the tale went as it journeyed through the Middle Kingdom. Shining with luck was Kinrowan's Jack. And then he heard the rumour that Bhruic was gone, leaving this new Jack—lucky, yes, but largely untried—in his stead.

Colorc hated Bhruic. Colorc had known the Gruagagh before becoming a droichan; more than once in those early years Bhruic had stood against him. It was Bhruic who convinced Yaarn not to take him on as an apprentice. Bhruic who had kept him from the sea wisdoms that the merfolk had been willing to teach him. Bhruic who spoke against him in the owl's parliament.

"He has no compassion," was the Gruagagh's explanation for his persecution. "He has no heart."

No heart? If that was what they thought, then let it be true. And he turned to the forbidden knowledges of the droichan.

He kept a wide berth of Kinrowan, for he was unwilling to confront Bhruic Dearg until he was sure of his victory. But he'd kept an eye on the realm. And when he learned of Bhruic's departure . . . It seemed befitting that he choose the faerie of Kinrowan as his next prey.

The risk to himself appeared minimal. Kinrowan no longer had a gruagagh. Its Court was small. Its Unseelie neighbors were recently defeated and in need of a leader. Its fiaina sidhe few in number. It had seemed perfect.

And at first, it had been so.

Colorc had begun—as he always did—by stealing the luck of the sidhe. The solitary faerie rarely banded together for anything but their rade, so it was unlikely that they would rise against him in a group. All went well until their Pook went in search of help. That he couldn't allow. He'd meant to play her out for as long as he could— the taste of her luck, even diminished from lack of a rade, was so tenderly sweet—but he had no wish for a Bucca in Kinrowan. A Bucca was worse than a Jack. And almost as bad as a gruagagh.

With the Pook dead, he'd meant to continue his slow assimilation of Kinrowan, but that was before luck—ill luck, he saw now, the Moon's sainly curse on him—had delivered the Jack and her friend into his hands. It had seemed so clever to threaten them with his shadow, and then "rescue" them. Oh, yes. The Moon had made that seem so simple. And then the Jack's own naive simplicity had let her invite him into her Tower.

But he'd been—

"Too clever by far," he repeated bitterly.

And too greedy.

It was greed that made it all go wrong. For first the Jack's companion escaped. Then the Jack herself. All because he'd reached for too much, all at once.

He tasted the ash of his defeat again. He had to be careful. The Moon's influence was strong in Kinrowan. With the widdershinning of his plans, he could well lose it all. His heart. Safely hidden, yes, but with the Jack loose . . .

He turned away from the window, shaking his head. No, that must never be. Better he cut his losses than risk that. If they found his heart . . . A droichan who died, died forever. There were no further turns on the wheel of life for them. No final rest in the Region of the Summer Stars.

He would give it a day, he decided. No more than two. If the

Jack wasn't in his power again by then, he would move on. There were other realms. Not so sweet as Kinrowan, perhaps. Without such a perfect mix of the Courts and sainly borderfolk. But they would do.

Power was sweet, but life was sweeter.

Closing the door to the third-floor study, he made his way back downstairs to wait for word. From the Host, perhaps, though it was more likely that his shadow would bring her back.

Without fire, there was no light, the old saying went. But the fire could leave ashes, too—a good thing to keep in mind, for a Jack's luck burned like fire. It was good to remember the ashes.

Dark-eyed, Colorc stared out into the night beyond the kitchen windows and waited for his shadow to return. But when it finally did return, it was to bring him word that the Pook was abroad in Kinrowan once more.

Colorc ran his fingers through his hair and frowned.

That could not be. He had stood over her body himself, drunk the final flicker of her fire from her death. But the image that his shadow gave him was of the Pook's face, dark with sorrow and anger, walking the streets of Kinrowan.

For a long moment the droichan stared out into the night beyond the kitchen's windows. Then he arose and, drawing his shadow close to him like a cloak, he went out into the night himself.

Thirteen

Jemi Pook, Johnny discovered, was very easy to argue with. She insisted on going alone into Kinrowan, arguing that what she was looking for would be easier to find by herself. She had sidhe blood, after all; he didn't. She knew Kinrowan and its faerie, by sight at least, if not to speak to; he didn't. It was her sister who had died; not his. It was her responsibility; not his.

"I just want to help," Johnny said.

"I know. And you can help right now by letting me do this on my own. I'm not helpless, Johnny." Her expression softened. "It's better this way," she added. "I can go places that you can't. The faerie will at least talk to me. If they see you with me, they'll only hide. You see that, don't you?"

"All I can see is that something out there killed your sister and if you go chasing after it, it'll probably get you as well."

"I'll be careful."

Like Jenna was careful? Johnny wanted to say, but it was unnecessary. The question hung between them, unspoken.

"I'll go as far as your apartment with you," Jemi said. "Will you wait for me there?"

"It'll be hard—just waiting."

"I know. But I will need your help later, Johnny. Once I have a name. I'm not trying to shut you out of my life. We've only just met and I want to know you better. I want to see if the Bucca's bone carvings know what they're doing."

The look she gave him was pure warmth. It melted away Johnny's reservations. The thought of enchantment, of being ensnared in a glamour, crossed his mind, then dissolved and was gone. He didn't care if it was magic that had brought them together. This Bucca, whoever he was, could work all the magics he wanted. What Johnny wanted to do was follow through on the promise he saw in Jemi's eyes, because he'd never before experienced anything like what he was feeling now.

"I'll wait for you," he said.

"I wasn't sure you would," Jemi said, "but I'm glad you will. Things have got to get better."

But the warmth was fading from her eyes and the pain was back again. She touched his cheek with the back of her hand, then stood. Johnny fetched his fiddle case and they went out into the night.

They didn't speak much on the walk up to Johnny's apartment. At the corner of Bank and Third Avenue, they paused.

"Wish me luck," Jemi said.

Her voice was small, almost plaintive, but Johnny didn't start the argument up again.

"Luck," he said.

A quick fierce grin came and went across her features. Johnny could see the strain of her sorrow, the dark feral light of her anger in her eyes.

It had to be her sidhe blood, he thought. That was what made her so mercurial.

She leaned close for a moment and tilted her head. When Johnny kissed her, she nipped his lower lip, then stepped quickly back. Without another word, she turned and headed up Bank Street.

Johnny rubbed his lip and watched her go until she reached Second Avenue. Sighing then, he turned down his own street. He didn't see the light on in his apartment until he was right on the porch.

As Jemi walked on alone, it all came back to her. She saw the Bucca's face—broad and dirt-brown, lined like the patterning luck of moonroads; the dark curly hair; the small eyes, darker still, but golden like honey as well.

Salamon Brien.

He was a fat-cheeked, stout old man no taller than her own shoulder, always dressed in a motley array of Gypsy colours, with a rattling necklace of bone ornaments around his neck, and in each earlobe a gold ring—the gold so pure it looked brassy. He'd left the borderlands near Kinrowan years ago. And Jenna had gone looking for him. To renew the rade.

She thought of the rade, of all those times—late afternoons crisp with autumn, nights dark with summer's mystery—listening to the Bucca talk of the moonroads and the rade, of the patterns in both and the luck they gave to the fiaina sidhe. He was teaching Jenna, but Jemi had listened to it all, feigning indifference, far more interested in the speckles on this mushroom than in what he said. Pretending to watch that bat flit, but her head was cocked near to hear it all.

The pattern of the rade rose in her mind's eye. She saw Salamon walking it, a crow with white-speckled wings perched on his shoulder, Jenna pacing at his side silently mouthing what the Bucca told her so that she'd remember, and then there was her own younger self, straggling along behind them, hair as pink then as it was today. What Jenna studiously repeated to remember, Jemi could repeat word for word without needing to think about it. But Jenna was the elder and she had no mortal blood, and Jemi wasn't interested in any of it anyway. But now . . .

Now it was all in her lap.

The memories washed through her, impossible to avoid. Her eyes misted with tears. The Bucca long gone. Jenna dead.

She steered her steps away from the Court of Kinrowan where she had been going and turned instead towards her own apartment in Sandy Hill.

Click, clack.

She could recall the rattle of the Bucca's necklace so well.

Click, clack.

Little bone ornaments carved into the shapes of instruments and animals and trees, buildings and faerie and even mortals. He told stories about them. A gnarled brown hand would reach up to stroke a tiny badger and he would tell a tale of mischief and tricks that made everyone laugh until their stomachs ached.

Click, clack.

"A tale in each one," he'd said once. "And more tales when one touches another. And more again. And still more."

He stroked one perfectly carved ornament after the other, the creamy bone gleaming under the touch of his fingers. He would never say who made them or where he'd gotten them, only that there were tales in them. Tales of times past. Tales of days to come. Every kind of story.

Jemi wished he was here now. She wished that he would touch a carving and turn back the Moon until Jenna arose from under her cairn and was back in the world to argue with her again.

How often had they argued? A dozen times a day? A hundred? They couldn't agree about one thing, except they never fought. They weren't that sort of arguments.

"You're too much the same," Salamon told them once. "You argue with yourself."

But they weren't the same. Not anymore.

Jenna was dead.

Jemi had reached the front walk of her building. She wiped her eyes on the sleeve of her piper's jacket, wished for a Kleenex, but didn't have one. Sniffling, she dug about in her pocket for her key and went inside, up the stairs. She opened the door to her room and the air seemed stale inside. Dry. Like a crypt. A room where no one had been for decades.

But Johnny had been here.

She crossed to her dresser and lifted her little bone flute from where it hung.

Click, clack.

It had rattled against the Bucca's other ornaments once. She slipped it around her neck and tucked it under her shirt, then she stared at her reflection in the mirror.

They'd been too much the same, the Bucca said.

Jenna had talked to Jemi about her worries, about how the rade was disturbed time and again. But she hadn't spoken of any danger. She hadn't said she was going to look for Salamon. Where would she even begin to look? Had she known all along where he'd wandered off to?

Too much the same, and not the same at all.

She heard the floor creak in the hallway and turned quickly, adrenaline pumping through her, but it was only her next-door neighbour, Annie Hamilton. She tried to still the frenzied beating of her heart.

"Hi," Annie said. "There were a couple of guys here looking for you today. I think maybe they broke into your room. Is there anything missing?"

"No."

Jenna's features flashed through her mind and she bit at her lip.

"It's ... it's okay," she told her neighbour. "They were friends."

Annie shifted her bulk and the floorboards creaked again.

"You don't look so good," she said. "Are you sure you're okay?"

Jemi nodded.

"Greg was by as well—around suppertime. He wants you to call him."

Greg. AKT.

Jemi remembered that there had been a rehearsal this afternoon. The memory came to her as though it belonged to someone else. It came from an entirely different world.

"I have to go," she said suddenly.

She flicked off the light in her room and shut the door. Annie looked at her with a worried expression, but there was nothing Jemi could say to her. They weren't really friends. A talk or two on the porch, or late at night in the kitchen after a gig. That was about it.

"Jemi ..."

Before Annie could finish, Jemi bolted for the stairs. She ignored Annie's voice, calling her name after her, just took the stairs three at a time and ran outside, up the street, ran until she reached the brighter lights on Rideau Street, then leaned against a building to catch her breath. Her hand went to touch her flute pendant through the fabric of her shirt.

What's wrong with me? she asked herself.

But all it took was Jenna's face to rise up in her mind, and she knew. It was the pattern of the rade, incomplete. It was the luck lying broken on a moonroad, looking like a scatter of bone ornaments, a broken necklace, or like a stout, brown-skinned Bucca sprawled there in the dirt—

No!

She looked around herself, really frightened now.

All this time, she thought, and I never offered to help. Jenna's problems, the rade . . . Why didn't I do something? Why wasn't I there? Jenna wouldn't have had to go looking for Salamon. She wouldn't have had to die.

The bright lights hurt her eyes, which were misty with tears again. She turned away from Rideau, back to the darker streets of Sandy Hill, trying to keep to the shadows, but the streetlights, though not so numerous as those she'd left behind, were still bright. Her eyes stung now, the tears fell freely. Her head was awash with memories that were all tied together with a moon-bright ribbon that was the pattern of the rade.

And something else. A presence that spoke to her from the shadows. A whispering sound. Beckoning, calling to her. . . .

She'd always preferred the loud sounds, music in bars, the bright lights, friends laughing, dancing, blowing her sax, and now she wanted only darkness and quiet. But it wasn't to be found. The city surrounded her. The lit windows of the houses were like eyes peering into her soul. The whole night seemed to be watching her. She sensed a malevolence loose in the darkness, and once again she started to run.

When she finally stopped, she was in amongst the buildings of Ottawa University. It wasn't so bright here, though her sidhe sight pierced the darkness as though it were merely twilight. It was quieter as well, but her head rang with an odd warning buzz. And then she realized what it was that she felt, what it was that was out in the night, loose and haunting—hunting—her.

It was the very thing she'd sought.

She turned slowly, pin prickles starting at the nape of her neck and scraping down her spine. The black dog regarded her from across an empty expanse of lawn. It was half-hidden in the shadows of a building, but she could see its gleaming eyes and black shiny fur, smell its strong odour, hear the rasp of its breathing. Behind it stood a silent figure in a brown cloak, its features hidden in the fall of its hood.

Now she knew why she'd really gone on alone. She couldn't

have been brave enough for both Johnny and herself. She wasn't even brave enough for herself.

"The same," the figure in brown said softly, echoing her own earlier thoughts, "yet not. Who would have thought that there would be two of you?"

She wanted to throw herself at him, claw at his eyes, tear out the throat that voiced those words so calmly, but for once common sense got the better of her temper. As the dog rose from its haunches, she turned and, with fiaina skill, began to scale the side of the building, her small hands finding fingerholds in the stonework where a mortal would never even look. She could sense the dog coming for her—as it had come for her sister—but she didn't look down, not until she reached the roof.

The man in his brown cloak stood below, looking up. His dog—which seemed to be more ape-like now than canine—was climbing after her.

Now she knew what she faced.

The man was a gruagagh and the thing he had sent after her was his shadow. She couldn't match that kind of magic. She was just a Pook, a halfling at that.

She stared down at the creature, searching through the wash of her memories for something that the Bucca might have said about dealing with this kind of a creature, but her mind just went blank.

"You're not mad, are you?" Kate asked.

Jacky tried to put what she called her "Squint Eastwood tough gal" look on her face, but all it did was squinch up her features and make her look silly, so she gave it up. And looking at Kate sitting beside her on Gump's bed, the leather-bound Caraid on her lap and the worried look in her eyes, Jacky didn't have the heart to tease her.

"No," she said. "It's something we should have done a long time ago. But you know me—I'm such a pack rat. I always want to hoard everything for that someday when it's going to be needed, but in the end, nothing ever gets used at all." She put out a hand to touch the book. "It really makes you stop and think, doesn't it? All this magic. I wonder what makes it work."

"There's a piece of Bhruic in those pages," Finn remarked from beside the hearth.

He and Gwi were sharing cushions there, while the big trow sat in his chair. He was the only one who fit the furniture.

"The books replies as Bhruic spoke," Finn added.

A wistful look came into Jacky's eyes. "I wonder where he is now."

"With the Summer Stars," Finn said. "Or maybe not. He's traveling with Kerevan, after all. They could be anywhere—walking on the Moon, or deep in an Otherworld of the manitou."

"I'd like to go to one of them someday," Jacky said. "I'd like to meet the native spirits—the ones that were here before any of us came."

"They're skinwalkers, most of them," the hob said. "And Arn's luck touches them in other ways than it does us. She takes shapes for them and walks the world in different guises to teach and talk with them."

"Totems," Kate said. "That's what you're talking about. But I don't see Bhruic needing a totem."

Finn smiled. "I suppose not. But I don't doubt he'd like to talk to them all the same."

"I'd like to see *him* again," Jacky said.

Gump cleared his throat. "Better you were worrying about the gruagagh that's here—not the one that's gone. Time enough for Bhruic after. If there is an after."

Jacky's warm, thoughtful mood slipped away at the trow's words.

"How can we do *anything* about him?" she asked. "He could have hidden his heart anywhere. There's no way we can find it."

Gwi stirred beside Finn. "We don't even know his name," she added. "We can't kill him with weapons, and we can't kill him with spells."

Jacky nodded, remembering her knife sticking from the droichan's chest and the way he had just plucked it out again. There was nothing inside him, she decided. Just shadows, like the bit of himself that he let loose to do his killing for him.

"Maybe we're going about it all wrong," Kate said. "Caraid told us that we have to know him before we'll find the heart. What we should be doing is backtracking him—find out where he came from, that sort of thing."

"A good point," Gump said, "but we don't have his name, so how could we do that?"

"I don't know."

Kate frowned, idly flipping Caraid's pages. She looked up suddenly.

"He can't have come from nowhere," she said. "And wherever he's been before—he'd have done the same thing there, wouldn't he? Can't we contact other Courts and find out if they've had this kind of trouble?"

"There would be nothing left of a Court for us to contact," Gwi said. "Not if he'd been there first."

"But what about their neighbours? Wouldn't they know something?"

"The idea has merit," Gump said. "We could put out the word, through all of Faerie. Someone will have to remember hearing of a similar situation in the past year or so. A Court suddenly barren of its folk, perhaps. A cairn emptied of its luck. A crossing of moonroads no longer so hale . . . "

"It will take time," Gwi said. "Time that we don't have."

"But most of the Courts are in Ballymoresk," Finn said. "For the Fair."

Gump grinned. "Then what better place to ask? Who will go?"

"Wait a minute," Kate said. "You said something about a place where moonroads cross each other not being so healthy anymore?" When Gump nodded, Kate turned to Jacky. "Remember the night Mull came to the Tower to get us?"

"We were looking at that house!" Jacky cried.

"That's where he was," Kate said.

At their companions' blank looks, Kate explained what they'd seen.

"That also bears looking into," Gump said.

"But we can't ignore asking the other Courts," Gwi said. "I'll go to the Fair and get Deegan to ask the other Lairds and Ladies, but I'll need a swift mount for the ride."

Deegan was the Laird of Kinrowan.

"Hay will lend you one of the Laird's own mounts," Finn said.

"I'll speak to him myself. You'll ride down in style, Gwi, and have the sons of Lairds falling over themselves to get to know you."

The forester harumphed. "Not with my blood," she said, but she smiled.

"And I'll go spy out this house," Gump said.

"You'll need someone to guide you," Jacky said.

Gump nodded. "That's true—but it can't be you. I can still hear the cries of Cumin's folk hunting you beyond the safety of these walls."

"I'll show you where it is," Kate said.

"That will be good. It's always better to have a skilly-woman at your side when you go to spy on a gruagagh."

Kate laughed uneasily.

"I wouldn't put too much stock in any magics you think I've got," she said. "About as magic as I get is making tea without burning the water."

The trow hooted—a big, booming sound. "Oh, that's rich! Well, I'll take the chance. If you can't spell him, Kate, perhaps you can quip the information from him. Now, come on. We don't have much time. My sort of folk don't take to the sun, and the dawn's far closer than I'd like."

Jacky looked uncertainly about herself as there was a sudden rush of everyone getting ready to go.

"I won't be long," Finn told her. "Just up to the Court to get a mount for Gwi, then I'll be back."

Kate gave her a big hug.

"Don't do anything silly like stepping outside for some fresh air," she said. "I couldn't bear for the droichan to get his claws on you again."

"Not to mention that he might find some way to force you to break Bhruic's enchantment on the Tower," Gwi added.

"I'll be fine," Jacky said. "You're the guys who are going out there, not me."

There was some more bustling about, then a few moments later they were all gone. Jacky closed the door to the trow's home and walked slowly back to the bed. She poked at the side of it a few times, then wandered over to the hearth, where she slumped down on a pillow.

"Great," she muttered. "This is just great. Some Jack I've turned out to be. The first time something goes wrong and the most I can do about it is to hole up in some trow's place and let everyone else do my job for me. Lovely. Wouldn't Bhruic be proud of me now?"

The worst thing was that it was all her fault. She'd invited Cumin into the Tower in the first place. A real Jack would have sniffed him out for what he was right away. Bhruic would have sent him packing, quick as a blink. But *she'd* asked him home for tea.

She caught her own reflection in the shiny bottom of one of Gump's pots hanging from the hearth above her and frowned at it. Getting up, she trailed about the big room, not really looking at anything, just berating herself.

She should have sent Cumin packing. But he'd seemed important and she'd been flattered that he paid attention to her. And that was the problem—part of a bigger problem that kept screwing up her life. After years of being a relative nobody, becoming a Jack had finally put her in a position where she was somebody, never mind that it was all irrelevant, that in her heart she truly believed that people were important for who they were, how they acted, not for their position in life. Wasn't that what kept getting in the way of her relationship with Eilian? Did she care about him because of who he was, or because he was a Laird's son who happened to love her?

It was all so confusing. Things had to change. It was high time she got it all straightened out in her mind. She was going to have to do something better with her life. Buckle down with Kate and learn everything there was to learn in Bhruic's study, make her own Caraid, find an honest gruagagh to teach her more, or maybe go to a Billy Blind like the one in Eilian's Court.

Eilian.

She had to work out what they were going to do with their relationship.

Oh, yes. Things were going to be different. She was going to become responsible if it killed her.

She paused by the bed—having paced by it at least twenty times already—and picked up the curiously ribboned headgear that Finn had given her. She'd get Finn to teach her his skilly stitcheries as well, to learn how to make disguises like this where no one could recognize you. . . .

Her train of thought trailed off as she lifted the headband from the bed. Of course. With this, Cumin wouldn't be able to spot her. And neither would any of the Unseelie Court that had rallied around the droichan. She could just waltz into the Tower wearing it, grab the wally-stanes, and be useful for a change. Maybe she could wish up a magic mirror or something that would show them where the droichan's heart was hidden.

She put the headgear on, buttoned the appropriate ribbon to her shirt, then studied herself in another of Gump's pans. She didn't make a very fierce-looking bogan, but that didn't matter. She still looked like a bogan and *that* was what mattered.

Don't do this.

A voice of reason spoke up in the back of her head.

Be sensible for once.

She shook her head. I'm being *responsible* for once, she told it. I'm cleaning up my own mess.

But the voice inside her continued to argue. It told her that she was safe here. That she'd promised the others she'd stay. That even with her disguise, she wouldn't necessarily be hidden from the droichan. Not when he had her scent.

Except he's looking for Kate, too, she argued back, and Kate's disguise isn't any different from mine. If it's safe for her, then it'll be safe for me.

The voice seemed to have run out of arguments, because it stayed silent now.

I *won't* screw up this time, Jacky promised.

Finding some paper and a stub of a pencil, she left a quick note for Kate and the others. She didn't say anything in it about trying to regain some pride in herself, about wanting to fulfill responsibilities that were hers and alleviating the feeling that she was a half-wit for fouling everything up in the first place. It simply said:

Dear Kate,

I can't sit around doing nothing, so I'm going back to the Tower to get the wally-stanes. Don't worry. I'm being smart this time and wearing the bogan disguise that Finn gave me. No one'll even know

me. I'll be a walking, talking "purloined letter" and very, very careful.
Love, J.

She put it on the table where it was sure to be noticed and left the room through the trow's tunnel.

Getting into the Tower was going to be the only problem, she decided as she followed the canal south to where it stood. Once she was in the study, it would just be a moment's work to grab the wally-stanes and jump through the window, landing right on Gump's front porch, as it were. But the getting in . . .

Worry about that when you get there, she told herself.

It just never stops, Johnny thought. As he sat listening to what had happened to Henk earlier tonight, he wasn't sure if he was glad that somebody else—somebody normal—was experiencing the same strangeness that he was, or if it just made things worse.

"I was never so scared in all my life," Henk finished. "Johnny, just what the hell's going on?"

Johnny didn't know what to say.

"I was sitting there in the donut shop," Henk went on, "and I just couldn't leave. I must've been there for over an hour, Johnny, just staring out at the parking lot, waiting to see more of them. To see if they were still out there. Waiting for me."

"But you made it back," Johnny said.

Henk nodded. "Yeah. I was on my third coffee, I guess, when it all just went away. Like someone had turned off a switch in my head. I got on your bike—"

"My bike. I'd forgotten about it."

"Well, it's back here, safe and sound. Just like us. Except I got the shakes again, waiting for you . . . "

Henk took a sip from his coffee. His hand shook and the cup rattled on the table, slopping coffee over the side.

"Christ," he said. "Look at me. I'm a wreck. You know what's doing this to me—what's *really* doing it to me?"

Johnny shook his head.

"Knowing that all that stuff I was scared of when I was a kid—all those bogeymen—they're all real. I don't want to sound like a pussie, Johnny, but I had a rough time with that kind of thing when

I was a kid. It took me a long time to convince myself that that kind of thing just couldn't be real. And now look what happens."

Neither spoke for a while. Johnny got up and poured them both another coffee and then told Henk about his own night. He spoke in a quiet voice and, for all that what he was saying was only more fuel for Henk's fears, by the time Johnny got to the end of his story, Henk was more like his old self again.

"I just can't figure out why Loireag attacked you," Johnny said.

"She was pissed, Johnny. And with what you've told me, now I know why."

"I suppose."

"You'd better watch out with Jemi," Henk warned. "That's all I can say. She may look human—a lot of them do, if you believe all the stories—but they're still not like us. They're volatile. Christ, they're just plain dangerous."

"I don't know," Johnny said. "There's something special about her—not because she's what she is, either. I mean, not because it's like she stepped out of some storybook. There's just something that sparks inside me every time I'm with her—that kind of special. Like we were meant for each other. Something binds us together."

"Right. Two bone carvings from some other weirdo's necklace. Come on, Johnny. It's not right."

"You don't know—"

"You're right. I don't. But just tell me this: What does Jemi turn into? Can you tell me that? What kind of thing does she become? Another horse? A wolf, maybe? Some kind of slime monster out of a B-movie?" Henk shook his head. "Jesus. Maybe it's better that we don't know. . . ."

Johnny stared at him. There was nothing he could say. He didn't know either. He just knew the bond was there and, enchantment or not, he wanted it to be there.

"Do you mind if I crash here again?" Henk asked. "I don't think I can get it together to, you know . . . get myself home."

"No problem," Johnny said. "You can take . . . " He swallowed hard. "You can take Tom's old room."

He waited until Henk had left the room, then slowly got up and walked out onto his porch.

Tom. That's where it had all started. With Tom's bone carving and that talk about "The King of the Faeries" and where to play it. But with all that had happened, his grandfather had been pushed out of his mind, only returning now on the heels of that simple phrase. And with it, the sorrow returned as well.

Johnny sat down on the steps. His eyes were dry, but tears welled up behind them. His chest was tight.

Why did you leave me, Tom? he asked the night.

The street was still. Above the haze cast by the street-lights, he could see a speckle of stars, not nearly so bright and close as they were in Puxill. He wondered where his grandfather was—if faerie were real, then what about God and angels, heaven and hell? Or maybe, because of his music, he was hanging out in some Celtic afterworld, putting back a pint with Yeats and the lads, playing his fiddle.

And what part had Tom played in all of this? Had Jenna wanted Tom to lead the rade, so long ago, and Tom had turned her down? Had the needed spark between them just not been here, or was it really enchantment and Tom had just been stronger than Johnny knew himself to be? Because whatever Tom had done, Johnny knew he couldn't resist the spell himself.

He wished Tom was here to talk to him now. They'd always talked things out, problems either of them had, problems they saw around them, just talking sometimes, sometimes not saying anything at all and communicating more in those silences than in all the words that had ever existed.

It wasn't that Tom had left him that was so important, as why he'd left him. Why did he have to be taken away? Why did he have to die?

The tears welled up in earnest now and filled his eyes. Then he looked out at the street and saw it all through a shiny sheen. He should never have let Tom talk him into letting him go into the old folks' place. He should just have kept Tom here, at home, where he belonged. Not in the hands of strangers, no matter how better qualified they were. Maybe if Tom had stayed here he wouldn't have died. Maybe. . . .

Johnny pressed his face against his knees and his tears wet his jeans. He never heard the scuffle of bare feet on the pavement, not the sound of breathing close by his ear. He started violently when a small hand touched his arm and a raspy voice broke the stillness.

"Why are you so sad?"

He was half off the porch and stumbling onto the lawn before he realized that it was Jemi's little wolfish friend who was crouched furry and naked on his porch. Mactire regarded him worriedly, Jemi's name forming on his lips, but no sound issuing forth.

Johnny took a deep steadying breath.

"No," he said. "She's all right. At least I think she is. She went off to talk to Kinrowan's faerie, but I don't know where she'd be looking for them."

Mactire frowned. "It's a bad night for faerie—Court folk and sidhe alike. There's a darkness riding the wind that has nothing to do with a lack of light."

"Yeah," Johnny said. "I know."

He returned to sit on the steps, wiping at his eyes with the sleeve of his shirt.

"Why are you here?" he asked Mactire.

The wild boy shrugged. "I felt . . . bad. Running away with the others, instead of staying with you and Jemi. I was going to where she lives in the city, but remembered that this place was closer. I thought she might be here with you. I suppose I'll go look for her at her own home now."

"She won't be there," Johnny said. "She's gone off to do what everybody wanted her to do: find the name of whatever it was that killed her sister."

"It's not just her sister," Mactire said. "It's the rade, too. The luck's all gone."

"I know," Johnny said. "But it's because of her sister that Jemi's gone. It . . . it's not easy losing someone you love."

Mactire nodded. "He was a good man, Tom. We all knew him, you know."

"What did he do with you people? How did he get involved?"

"He played tunes for us. Not rade tunes, not luck music, but skilly tunes all the same. We'd dance to his fiddling, Johnny Faw."

"And Jenna?"

"There wasn't the light in her eyes when she looked at him as there is in Jemi's when she looks at you. But Tom—a long time ago, he led the rade. It was only once or twice, and as good a Fiddle Wit you'd be hard put to find, but it wasn't for him. He went away for a while, and when he came back, he'd only play for fun, not for the luck."

Johnny sighed. "I still miss him."

"He's not gone until you forget him," Mactire said. "So long as you remember him and love those memories, a part of him will still be alive."

"Words," Johnny muttered. "That's just words. Something you say to make someone feel better. But it doesn't fill the emptiness inside."

"Maybe you just need to catch hold of some more memories until you do fill that empty place."

"I suppose." Johnny glanced at the wolf boy. "Do you want a drink or something to eat?"

Mactire shook his head. "But a tune would be good. One of Tom's. Do you know the one he called 'The Month of May'?"

"Sure."

They went inside and after some hesitating stops and starts, Johnny played a few tunes for his sidhe guest. It did help to ease the emptiness a bit, but then he just found himself worrying about Jemi instead. It was getting so late. Where could she be, was she all right, would she come back?

It never stops, he thought for the second time that night. Tom was gone, his own life all changed, and Jemi . . .

Looking into Mactire's eyes, he saw the same question there that worried at his own mind.

Jemi.

Out there in the night.

Alone.

As her sister had been.

He set fiddle and bow aside and the two of them sat in the ensuing quiet, wondering where she could be.

Fourteen

Jemi Pook was in the Ottawa University campus, on the roof of Tabaret Hall, standing near its domed skylight. She watched the black dog shape of the gruagagh's shadow approach her. The university was quiet all around her

North stood Academic Hall, dark and still. Behind her, to the west, were red-bricked buildings, and then Nicholas Street, not one car moving on any of its lanes. South were the two grey-bricked buildings that housed the Linguistics Department. East was the broad lawn of the Hall, dotted with red-leafed maples. The gruagagh was down there, out of sight now as he'd moved from the lawn to stand by the fat round pillars at the front of the Hall. She couldn't see him, but he watched her through the dark eyes of his shadow.

The dog, now that it had her trapped, didn't appear too eager to attack her. Maybe the gruagagh was just being cautious, maybe he thought she was just like Jenna. How could he know that with her half-blood, she had only half her sister's strengths? She was fast, but not quicksilver as Jenna had been. Strong, but not as strong either. She knew a few spells, but nothing like those Jenna had known. The beast would have had to take her unawares, or Jenna would have escaped it.

Or maybe the gruagagh wanted to know where Jemi fit in. Knowledge was a powerful weapon. He'd been surprised by her existence. Perhaps he hoped to ransack her mind and spare himself more surprises.

The initial numbness clouding her mind had worn away, but she still couldn't think of what to do. She had nothing with her that she could use for a spell—only the Bucca's flute carving, and that was a different sort of charm. The small bag holding her pipe hung from one shoulder, but this wasn't a moment for skilly music. If she played the right tune, she might be able to call up some luck, or sidhe, but she doubted that she'd get the chance to free the pipe from its bag, little say play the first few notes she'd need. All her purse had was her makeup, some money and ID, her compact. . . .

Gaze fixed on the beast, she reached into her purse. The dog growled and took a step forward, then paused when it saw that all she took out was her compact. Without seeing him, she knew that the gruagagh was only moments from reaching the roof himself. That was why his creature kept her at bay—it was waiting for him. So she only had moments in which to work.

She didn't think for a moment that she could deal with the gruagagh himself—that needed a level of magery that she couldn't hope to match. But a trick, played on a gruagagh's shadow, that wasn't beyond the capabilities of a halfling Pook like herself.

She flipped open the compact and thrust the mirror towards the dog. Whether it looked with its own gaze as well as that of the gruagagh, or if it was only the gruagagh's gaze that was upon her, wouldn't matter. She whispered a brief phrase in an old tongue.

"Gaoth an iar liom a comhnadh." Wind from the west, protect me.

She moved the mirror sun-wise in a quick circle, then spat at it and threw it at the dog.

It was only the smallest of spells. A charm, really. A call to the west wind who opened the doors between flesh and spirit. A deasil turn of the mirror to wake it and make it ready. Her saliva, a gift from her body.

The west wind touched her briefly. The mirror took her saliva and made of itself an image so that the dog saw Jemi attacking. It snarled, lunging up from the ground to confront the image, while Jemi bolted in the other direction. She counted the seconds as she ran.

One thousand and one, one thousand and two.

She reached the far side of the roof and swung herself over.

One thousand and three, one thousand and four.

Fingers and toes found the tiniest of perches as she went down the wall, moving like a spider, limbs outstretched.

One thousand and five, one thousand and six.

The black dog howled. It had seen through the mirror-charm. She tried to go faster, but even sidhe had their limits in such a situation. Especially halflings.

One thousand and seven, one thousand and eight.

She was past the halfway mark now, but there came a sound from the roof. Daring a glance up, she saw the gruagagh leaning over the side, looking down at her. The black dog hung like an aura about his head and shoulders. She continued her descent.

One thousand and nine, one thousand and ten.

As the gruagagh loosed the dog and tossed it down towards her, Jemi let herself drop.

It was some fifteen feet to the ground. Turf absorbed some of the impact, her bent knees some more, but it still jarred her enough to rattle her bones. Cat-like the sidhe could be, but she was out of shape.

She dared another glance up, saw the gruagagh's shadow dropping towards her, riding the air with wide bat wings, then she took off, running for all she was worth. She zigged and zagged her way across Nicholas Street, heading across it to where the land dipped towards the Rideau Canal, every sense strained to gauge the position of the creature. When she sensed it dropping towards her—a shift in the air currents warned her, an almost inaudible whisper of its shadowy wings—she threw herself to one side.

The creature swooped down to where she'd been, then angled back up once more. By then Jemi was on the grass verge at the far side of the street, coming out of a roll to slip and slide down the sharp incline towards the canal. The creature dove at her again, but she moved too quickly and it missed, rising up on its vast wings for a second time. Without hesitating, Jemi threw herself into the chilly waters of the canal and began to swim across.

Above her the creature seemed to come apart in the night air. It became one, three, a dozen airborne creatures, all swooping down at her. Jemi dove deep, still stroking strongly for the other side. When she came up for air, she half-expected to find that the gruagagh had given his shadow aquatic shapes, but the bat creatures were still in the air above her. They hovered in place with great sweeps of their wings, their attention no longer upon her as they gazed south.

Reaching the far side of the canal, Jemi hauled herself out of the water, teeth chattering. She wrinkled her nose at the smell of her wet clothes. The water of the canal wasn't exactly known for its purity. She reeked of algae and stagnant water. Getting to her feet, she looked up once more. The flock of bat creatures had become one again, its attention upon her, its voice ringing in her mind.

It seems that Bhruic's pet has returned to her lair, the creature said. *But don't fret, my ghostly Pook. There will be time for you later.*

Without another word, it bent its wings against the air and flew silently south.

Jemi leaned weakly against the metal rail that ran along the length of the canal and watched the creature go. She was safe. For now. But what had the gruagagh meant? Bhruic's pet. . . . And then she knew.

It was the new Jack. Her sister's murderer was after the new Jack, and why not? It made perfect sense. The Jack's responsibility was for the luck of Kinrowan. The gruagagh had been disturbing the fiaina rades, which was what the sidhe used to gather their luck. Of course he'd go after the Jack. Kinrowan's luck would be like a treasure feast compared to what he could steal from a sidhe rade.

She shivered from the chill of her wet clothes and ran a hand through her hair, pushing it back from her brow. Water puddled all around where she was standing.

It wasn't a name, she thought as she looked south, but it would have to be enough.

She took her pipe from its soggy bag and shook it free of water. Pulling out the reed, she blew through the hollow body of the instrument until it was dry as she could get it. She held the reed up, studied it for a moment, then fit it back into the pipe's mouthpiece.

The first notes she blew had a ragged sound to them, but soon she was playing a calling-up tune faultlessly. The belling cry of her pipe was loud in the quiet air. She saw a light go on in one of the upper stories of the houses near the canal, then another. But if the tune was loud in the world that men knew, in Faerie it rang from one end of Kinrowan to the other and out into the borderlands, a piercing insistent music that no sidhe could ignore. For it was a calling-on tune, a skilly music. It was the sound of a Pook calling up her rade to lead her folk to war.

She played the tune through once again, and then a third time. Before the echo of the last notes died away, she'd thrust the pipe back into its wet bag and was running silently along the canal, south to where the Jack's Tower stood in Crowdie Wort's Bally.

The first bogan was the worst.

Jacky came upon him where the Rideau Canal made a sharp westward turn near the corner of the Queen Elizabeth Driveway and Waverley Street. He was a great hulking squat lump of a creature, reeking of stale sweat and old swamps. She stopped dead in her tracks at the sight of him, her knees knocking against each other. The little voice of reason in the back of her head came back, but now it was only crying getawaygetaway in an ascending panicked wail.

She was all set to do just that, but the creature merely nodded in greeting to her.

"I'd rather be eating than creeping, hot damn," he muttered to her.

Jacky remembered Finn's warning about how his stitcheries couldn't disguise their voices, and managed a rough assenting grunt.

"Spike 'em all," she added.

Her voice didn't have the right sort of deep grumble to her ears, but the bogan didn't appear to notice. She stilled the tiny voice wailing in the back of her head and stood a little straighter.

"Ho!" the bogan said. "I'd like to see you spike the droichan — a little toadsucker like you."

"Spike you, too," Jacky told him, growing braver.

It was the right thing to say. The bogan laughed and gave her a rough clap on the back before going on. She watched him go, breathing through her mouth until the air wasn't quite so filled with his reek, then headed on herself.

That wasn't so hard, she thought, her confidence boosted by the encounter. Though, she had to admit, she didn't smell much better than he did.

She ran into more and more Unseelie creatures, the closer she got to the Tower, and no one seemed to pay her any more mind than they did to each other. Only the little creatures called gullywudes— that appeared to be nothing more than little stick and twig bundles held together by who knew what—eyed her strangely, plucking at her arms and legs. She got quite nervous until she saw that they did much the same with the other bogans, who merely clubbed them with their big fists when they got too near. She hit a few of the ones closest to her and they soon left her alone as well.

"Damn little shitheads," a bogan remarked to her as a new crowd came upon both of them on the street in front of the Tower. They both battered them away. "I'd eat the crowd of them, hot damn, if they didn't taste like toothpicks," he added.

Jacky nodded in agreement and followed him up onto the porch of the Tower and inside.

"Find anything?" a black-bearded duergar asked the first bogan when they stepped into the hallway.

The dwarf was two-thirds the bogan's height, but the bogan took a half-step back from him. Jacky wondered if he was an Unseelie skillyman by the way the bogan acted, then spotted the elder wand thrust in the dwarf's belt. By that she knew he was a gruagagh of sorts—what Finn called a widdyman. He had skilly abilities, but used them widdershins to work bad luck rather than good.

"Not a damn hair," the bogan replied.

"What about you?" the duergar demanded of Jacky.

She simply shook her head.

"Then what are you doing back here, you toadsuckers?" the widdyman demanded. "The boss said find her!"

"I look better with a full belly," the bogan told him.

"Nothing could make you look better, arsebreath."

"No, Greim. I mean—"

"I know what you meant," Greim replied, and shook his head wearily. He jerked a hand over his shoulder towards the kitchen. "See what you can find," he added, "but then get your arses back out there. You wouldn't like to see the boss get mad at you, now would you?"

Taking her cue from the bogan, Jacky shook her head as he did and followed him into the kitchen, where a great crowd of creatures were milling about. The door to the fridge stood ajar and there was little left in it. Every bit of foodstuff had been pulled from the cupboards and the crowd was picking through the remains.

Gullywudes tugged and plucked indiscriminately at empty cereal boxes and the clothing of other creatures. A troll sat hunched in the kitchen nook, all nine feet of his length folded up so that his knees almost touched his brows as he popped chunks of bread into the maw of his mouth. He held the remainder of the loaf protectively under his arm and swung out at any creature that came near him. A hag stood by the sink and was pulling down cups and saucers. She dropped them one by one on the floor, where they shattered to the applause of a pair of goblins and some gullywudes that were standing around her. Two bogans were hacking at a frozen roast with their knives, cursing picturesquely as only bogans can.

Seeing that crowd of creatures, the mess that they were making of the kitchen and with their reek in the air, Jacky had to lean against the doorjamb for a moment. The mess almost broke her heart. When Kate saw this . . . Her collection of English cottage pictures smashed to the floor, her teacups and saucers all broken, her pride-and-joy teapot—a cow sitting on its haunches that poured tea from its mouth—lying in a dozen pieces right by Jacky's feet. . . .

Jacky blinked hard. She cast a quick look down the hall to where the widdyman Greim was berating a new set of arrivals, another look into the kitchen where everyone was too busy to notice anything she might do, then she slipped up the stairs.

Any moment she expected to hear the alarm go off, but she soon discovered that the upper floors of the Tower weren't off-limits. Through the open doors she passed, she saw more Unseelie creatures lounging about in the ruins of what had been Kate's and her own bedrooms. The reek was stronger up here as well, for there were sluagh drifting restlessly about. A pair passed her going down-stairs and she almost cried out at the cold clammy touch of their misty bodies, the drowned faces that they turned towards her. The restless dead of the Unseelie Court probably scared Jacky more than all the others combined, giants included.

Shivering, she hurried up to the third floor. There, perhaps be-cause of Bhruic's spell that made the room seem empty, she finally found herself alone. She'd half-expected the droichan to be in here, but she realized now that he must be out searching with the rest of them.

She moved quickly to the hollowed leg of the worktable and removed the wally-stanes, tying their bag to the belt that held up her jeans. This was going to be easier than she'd thought. Congratu-lating herself on her wisdom for going through with it, she went to the window.

There she hesitated, looking out on the broad nightscape of Kinrowan spread out before her. She was still a little nervous about this mode of transportation. Sure, it had worked once. She just wished she knew more about it. Maybe it would be smarter than to go back downstairs and brave her way through the Unseelie crea-tures once more.

She started to turn, then shook her head. No, that was being a chickenshit. This was going to work.

She put her foot up on the sill and started to draw herself up, when the view disappeared. The window went black. She stumbled back, almost losing her balance. Catching hold of the sill, she drew closer, trying to look out through the sudden darkness. It was as though someone had dropped a curtain down in front of the win-dow. She put out her hand and touched something cold and ghostly damp. Before she could withdraw, two red eyes blinked open and stared at her with a mocking expression in their depths.

Leaving so soon? a voice said in her mind.

Jacky recognized the droichan's voice. She stepped back from the window, her knees going all watery on her again. She thought of making a break for the door, but the droichan had foreseen that. A long, tentacle-like shadow arm lunged out from the deeper darkness beyond the window and slammed the door shut.

I thought you might be back, the droichan went on conversation-

ally. That's why I left a little safeguard on the door to warn me if you returned. The amused gaze studied her again. *Not a bad disguise. Did you make it yourself, or did one of your little hob friends put it together for you?*

Jacky's fear was like a nail screeching on a chalkboard. Whatever courage she might have had shivered up and down her spine, then huddled cowering in some deep corner of her mind.

"What . . . what are you going to . . . to do with me?" she asked in a small voice.

Oh, we'll talk some, the droichan replied. *I have some distance to travel before I can be here with you in person, but then I'm sure we'll find some way to amuse ourselves. You might consider how you'll transfer Bhruic's power to me.*

"But I don't know . . . how. . . . "

The red eyes seemed to pin her soul. The droichan's voice when it echoed in her mind again, went through her like shivers of ice.

We'll find a way, little Jack. Even if I have to take you apart, piece by piece. We'll find a way.

All the strength went out of Jacky's body and she sank to her knees on the hardwood floor. She slumped there, hardly hearing what the droichan was saying anymore as he rambled on. All she could do was wait for him to return to the Tower in person, numb with the realization that she'd blown it again.

How did you spell Jacky Rowan?

That was easy. S-T-U-P-I-D.

She didn't doubt that the droichan would find a way to get the information out of her—even if she didn't consciously know it herself. And then her friends—no, not just them, but all of Kinrowan—would be in the droichan's power.

Distantly, she heard a sound then, a faerie pipe playing a calling-on tune. The eyes of her captor closed, returning the window to a wall of blackness, and she knew that the droichan's shadow was looking outward, seeking the source of that sound. She thought of trying to escape while his attention was turned away but before she could move, the red gaze was fixed on her once again.

The ghost of the Pook is calling up her rade, he informed her.

The *ghost* of the Pook? Well, why not?

I will have to see that a suitable welcome is waiting for her if she plans to ride on this Tower.

Jacky closed her eyes. Strangely enough, she didn't feel so frightened anymore. Something in that calling-on tune had heartened her. But when the droichan's gaze fixed on her once more, a bleakness settled over her and she just felt dead inside.

Finn and Gwi said their farewells on Wellington Street. The forester was mounted on a tall, golden steed—one of the Laird's own mounts that could claim a direct lineage from the huge White Horses of the old country who left their chalk outlines on the sides of hills when they died. Gwi, even with the stature that her troll blood gave her, looked like a doll perched on its back.

"At times like these," she said, "I wish we'd acquired the use of some human tools like a telephone."

"I'd use one," Finn said, "only who in Faerie could I call?"

A brief smile touched Gwi's lips. "Exactly. I'll be back in two days—with what word I can gather and a company of foresters. Don't do anything foolish until then, Finn."

"I'm not brave," Finn assured her.

"I'm not so sure—the line between the two's a thin one at the best of times."

"Take care," Finn said.

Gwi nodded and the hob slapped the horse's flank. Such was the animal's speed that before he could count to three, Gwi and her mount were long gone from sight. He hoped Gwi *would* take care. The Harvest Fair was at Ballymoresk and faerie from all over gathered to it. But near Ballymoresk was also the largest Unseelie Court in eastern Canada.

He sighed and started back for Gump's home, hoping that the trow and Kate would be back when he arrived. When he returned, all he found was Jacky's note.

"Oh, damn!" he muttered. "That foolish, well-meaning Jack."

He crumpled the note in his hand, was about to throw it away, then thought better of it and thrust it into his pocket. He'd have to gather up Gump and Kate and go back to the Tower with them. He only hoped they'd still find Jacky in one piece.

When he stepped outside, he smelled the darkness in the air—the darkness of Unseelie creatures loose and abroad. Oh, they were brave now with a droichan to boss them and most of the Court away to the Fair. And why shouldn't they be?

He shut the entrance to Gump's home with a softly spoken word. Before he could take a step, though, he heard the faltering sound of a sidhe pipe finding its tune, then the ringing notes of a calling-up music. The sound came from close by and he started to jog in its direction, reaching its source just in time to see a bedraggled and wet Pook thrust her pipe into a bag hanging from her shoulder before she set off at a quick pace.

Oh, this was a bad night, no doubt of it. The Court away, a droichan loose, the Unseelie Court abroad and hunting, and now the sidhe gathering for a war rade.

As he ran after the Pook—the direction she'd taken was the same he needed to follow to find Gump and Kate—he hoped that there would be something left of Faerie when the sun finally turned its dawn face their way.

With her hob-stitched shoes, Kate was just able to keep up with Gump's pace-eating stride. After a few blocks, the trow took her on his shoulders to go more quickly and they reached the street they were looking for in record time.

"This has to be it," Kate said.

Gump crouched so that she could clamber down from her perch and then the two of them stared across the street, studying the building. The house stood in the middle of the block, empty windows staring darkly out onto the street. On the lawn of the two-storied structure was a sign that read:

ANOTHER RENOVATION BY
J. COURS AND SONS LTD.

A red maple, its leaves beginning to turn, and a clutch of cedars appeared to lean away from the house as though avoiding even its shadow. The lawn was somewhat unkempt, riddled with clumps of spike-leafed weeds.

Kate didn't like the look of the place, and now that they were here, she wasn't all that sure exactly what they were going to do.

The house looked deserted, but there was a sense of something sentient about the way its windows looked out at the street, the drop of its roofline hanging over them like the low hairline of a browless troll. She glanced at Gump.

"What should we do?" she asked.

"We go in."

"That's what I was afraid you were going to say."

The trow patted her shoulder. "Don't be afraid, Kate. The droichan's not here—I'd sense him if he was. Now, come on."

He rose up like a small mountain standing at her side and started across the street. Kate sighed and followed in his wake.

"I was worrying more about what the droichan might have left behind," she muttered to Gump's back.

"Only one way to find out," Gump replied.

The porch creaked under his weight. The question of how they were going to get in died on Kate's lips as Gump struck the door with the flat side of his elbow. He hit it near the lock and tore the lock right out of the wood.

"They took more care in building doors in the old days," he remarked to Kate as he stepped into the darkened hallway. "I can remember a time when it took myself and a brother a good minute to break one down. Of course, every hall had its own skillyman in those days."

Kate kept close behind him, not really listening to what he was saying. She felt an all too real sensation of being watched as they moved slowly down the hall and stepped into the first room. To her surprise, the room was furnished. True, the sofa and chairs were old, the coffee table's surface scarred with deep scratches, the carpet threadbare and faded, the two pictures on the wall hanging askew with their glass broken on the floor below them, but it was still more than she'd expected.

"Can you sense someone in here with us?" she whispered to Gump.

The trow turned away from the fake mantelpiece and cocked his head, considering.

"Something," he admitted finally. "But it's more an echo than a presence, as though it's only a memory of something that was here and is now gone."

"The droichan?"

"Something with his kind of power—if not the droichan himself."

"Wonderful," Kate said. "The last thing we need now is two of him."

"It seems to be stronger upstairs," the trow said.

He moved back into the hallway, floorboards creaking ominously underfoot. Kate clutched at the bag that held Caraid, quite happy to let Gump take the lead again. The stairs sagged under the trow's weight, but that didn't seem to particularly concern him. Kate followed uneasily, sure that if some creature of the droichan's didn't get them, then the house would simply collapse about them and bury them in its basement.

She passed a light switch at the top of the stairs and gave it a try, but nothing happened. That made sense. Why would the electricity be on in a place like this? J. Cours and his sons had quite the job lined up for themselves in renovating it.

Her eyes were beginning to adjust to the dimness now, enough so that she thought she'd be able to read. Tugging Caraid free from its bag, she began to tell the book about the house and its condition.

"Any ideas where the droichan might have hidden his heart?" she asked when she was done.

She held the book up to a nearby window for better light.

Dear Kate, the book replied in Bhruic Dearg's clear script. *I told you before. You must know the droichan's mind before you can riddle the location of his heart.*

"Can't you even guess?" Kate asked.

I need something to base my guess on.

"Oh, come on," Kate said. "Guessing's just luck—that's all."

"Then perhaps we *should* have had Jacky accompany us," Gump said. "We could use a Jack's luck in this."

"This house had a grey aura when we saw it from the special window in the Tower," Kate said. "Doesn't that mean the droichan was here?"

It means something disrupted the flow of the Moon's luck in this place, Caraid replied. *It need not necessarily have been the droichan.*

"But it was the same grey as was in the places where he *did* work his magics," Kate said. "Doesn't that mean something? Or are we on a wild-goose chase?"

"I could use a goose," Gump said. "I'm feeling peckish."

Kate glanced at him, hoping his appetite didn't run to human women.

What you have postulated could be true, her book admitted. *The droichan could well have worked magics here. But that doesn't necessarily mean that his heart is hidden here. Or that it was ever hidden here.*

"Well, what magics could he have worked here? What did he need this place for?"

Magics are always stronger when worked in a place where moonroads meet.

Kate looked at the trow. "Oh, what are we going to do?"

"For one thing," Gump said, "we should finish looking through the house before we give up."

He set off again, making his way down the second-story hall to the first open door. Kate glanced at Caraid, but the book had nothing to add. She put it away in its bag, then left the window where she'd been standing to follow the trow. Gump was waiting for her in the second doorway down the hall.

"Here," he said. "Can you feel it?"

Kate squeezed in beside him and stood just inside the room.

"I . . . " she began.

The feeling of being watched returned to her, stronger than ever. On top of that sensation lay the taste of old magics, used and discarded, only their echoes remaining.

"Yes," she said. "This is where he worked his magics. And he's left something behind"—she glanced at the trow—"hasn't he?"

The room was longer than it was wide. It had been someone's study once, but the bookshelves were all empty now. A table, that had once served as a desk, she guessed, stood by the window, a stained and tattered ink blotter and a scatter of pencil stubs and paper on its surface. A chair stood by the table. In the middle of the room were a few cardboard boxes.

"Just trash," Gump said as he looked through a box.

"Gump," Kate said. "You didn't answer me. He left something in here, didn't he?"

"I'm not sure," the trow replied. "When mages and gruagaghs settle down to work their spells . . . things tend to gather, to watch them. That's what we're sensing, I think."

"Things? What kind of things?"

"I'm not really sure. I'm not a gruagagh, Kate. I've just heard the same stories that everyone knows. There were spirits in this land long before we reached its shores. They like to spy on our skillyfolk—some say to make sure that they work within allowed boundaries, but mostly it's thought that they do it simply out of curiosity."

"And that's what's here now?" Kate asked.

The trow nodded. "I think so. I hope so."

"And there's no droichan's heart?"

"I can't say yes or no, Kate. Someone worked powerful spells here. Maybe one such spell was the droichan hiding his heart."

Kate sighed. She went over to the table and pried about, moving to the boxes when she was sure there was nothing of interest on either it or its adjacent windowsill. She emptied the first box unceremoniously on the floor and pawed through its contents. Most of the papers had something to do with governmental statistics.

How boring, she thought.

As she started on another box, Gump left the room and went into the next one down the hall. Kate followed his progress by listening to his weight creaking the floorboards. She was bitterly disappointed at coming up with nothing in this house. The idea had seemed so perfect when it first came to her at Gump's home.

But that would have made things too easy, she realized now. And nothing was ever easy when it came to Faerie, and especially when it came to Faerie's skillyfolk like the gruagaghs.

When she was finished going through the boxes, she stood in the center of the room and made a slow turn, trying to *feel* where the magic echoes were the strongest, or where the hidden watchers were concealed. She felt a tug near the table and returned to it, wishing she'd had the foresight to bring a flashlight with her. Holding up papers to the window was all well and good, but it didn't do much for looking into crannies or finding hidey-holes.

She ran her fingers over the table, wishing she knew something about dowsing. That'd do the trick—just wave some stick over the table until it bent down at the required hiding place. But she didn't have a magical dowsing stick—didn't even know all that much about dowsing in the first place—and the table had no secrets to give up, or at least none that it was willing to give up. She turned away, defeated, to find Gump standing in the doorway.

"This is the only room with such strong echoes," he said.

Kate nodded glumly. She toyed with the buttons of her jacket, started across the room to join him, then remembered the rowan twigs sewn to the inside of her jacket.

"Wait a sec," she said.

Gump watched with interest as she unfastened the twigs from the inside of her jacket and tied them into a rough Y-shape.

"You know how to do that?" he asked as she stood with her makeshift divining rod in hand.

"Not really. But Finn seemed to think I could work magics if I studied hard. And this isn't really magic anyway, is it? Even humans can do it."

"If they have the skill."

"Oh, don't be such a poop," Kate told him. "Have a little faith."

The trow shrugged in agreement and sat by the door to watch, leaving Kate wondering if she'd bitten off more than she could chew. She'd read a book once on the Cambridge don Tom Lethbridge and his experience with dowsing. Having fully planned to immediately try it herself, she'd ended up getting distracted by something else and never really coming back to it. But she tended to remember everything she read, so she settled down now to concentrating on the task.

Keeping her mind empty of everything but the vague "something" that both she and the trow had sensed in the room, she made a slow circuit, her divining rod loosely gripped in her hands and held out before her. To her delight, the rowan twigs gave a definite tug in the direction of the table.

Without looking at Gump—though she was feeling very pleased with herself and dying to tell him, I told you so—she walked slowly over to the table, the makeshift rod increasing its tug against her fingers, the closer she came. Behind her, Gump lumbered to his feet and creaked his way across the floor after her. He towered over and watched as she made a circuit of the tabletop with the rod.

In the center of the table, closest to where she was standing, the rod jumped sharply downwards. The movement was so quick that Kate involuntarily held on tighter to the rod. Threads snapped and her divining rod fell to pieces.

Kate jumped back, startled, bumped into Gump, and almost screeched before she caught hold of her nerves and steadied herself. She took a deep breath and let it out again before turning to face the trow.

"It's right here," she said, pointing to where the twigs had fallen. "There's something right here, Gump."

She gathered up her twigs and stuck them in her pocket, moving aside so that Gump could have a look. The trow bent down until one big eye was level with the spot and he could study it.

"Something . . . " he agreed in a bemused voice.

He reached out a hand and moved it around the spot.

"Oh, look!" Kate cried unnecessarily since Gump's eye was still inches from the spot.

A vague outline was taking shape on the wooden tabletop, slightly luminous like the failing display on a digital watch. Kate stared with rounded eyes as it became clearer. It was a round, slightly domed shape, with a flourish of intertwined ribbonwork encircling the central design, which appeared to be a pair of cow's horns.

"What is it?" she breathed.

"An echo of magic," Gump replied.

They both stared at it, trying to make sense of what it was. Before trying to touch it, Kate took out Caraid and held the book open overtop of it so that a copy of the design could be made on a blank page. Then she tried to touch it, but whatever it was, at the contact of her fingers, it simply dissolved away.

"Was that his heart?" Kate asked.

Gump shrugged. He looked from the table to where the design was now taking shape on Caraid's page.

"I don't know what it was," he said. "Perhaps his heart—more likely some magical object that he was imbuing with power."

I agree, Caraid wrote under the image on its page. *This is a droichan's work—there is no doubt of that. Notice the symbol of the broken crescent moon.*

And she'd thought they were cow's horns, Kate thought, glad that she hadn't said anything.

"We should show this to Finn," Gump said. "He might recog—"

The trow broke off as a distant music rang through Faerie.

Only slightly aligned to the Seelie Court through his friendship with Finn, Gump felt the strong pull of the sidhe calling-up tune. He wanted to run out into the night and find the piper, to follow her anywhere.

A rade called up.

The thought of it filled him with an inexplicable joy.

"What's that sound?" Kate asked.

For a long moment, Gump said nothing, then he slowly shook his head. The hold of the tune on him lessened. He blinked and concentrated on ignoring the music as it continued to sound.

"The fiaina sidhe are being called up for a rade," he said.

"And you want to go?" Kate asked.

Gump nodded, surprised at her insight. "I don't need its luck, but I've been there, a time or two, following the winding pattern of a fiaina rade. It's not something you forget."

"I sort of feel like gathering with them myself," Kate said. "What does that make me?"

"A skilly mortal who's spent too much time in Faerie."

"You make it sound dangerous."

"Not dangerous," Gump said. "But it changes you. Faerie don't steal mortals—not so much anymore, at any rate—but the Middle Kingdom is still a chancy realm for mortals, Kate. Too long in it and you'll never want to leave."

"Then I've already been in it too long." She gave him a quick grin. "We should go back to your place and show Finn and Jacky what we've found."

The music had died away now, but there was a new sound in the air of Faerie. Gump paused, staring at the window, listening. Then Kate heard it, too. Part of the sound was the wind, rising at the call of the sidhe to mask the sound of their movement. But part of that sound was something else, a sound like dark wings cutting the night skies, of Unseelie creatures called to their own gathering.

"War," Gump said. "The Pook's calling up the sidhe to ride to war and the droichan's gathering his own army to meet her. Oh, this is a bad night for Faerie, Kate." He sat down in a slump and leaned against an empty bookcase. "I don't like fighting. I don't like it, Kate. I'll stand up and do what needs doing, but I don't like it. It makes us all small—winners and losers alike."

Kate had a moment of thinking it was odd that such a big, gruff creature like the trow would feel this way, but then she remembered the beautiful mechanical birds she'd seen in his home and realized that she was being very small-minded. Just because Gump was a trow didn't mean he had to like hurting people. She sat down beside him and leaned her head against his arm.

"No one likes it," she said. "Not if they're at all decent."

Gump nodded unhappily. "I don't take sides, because I don't like being a part of what comes from taking sides. Unpleasantness. Fighting. But this . . . We'll all lose our luck if we allow the droichan to win."

Kate tried to think of something she could say to make it easier, but there was nothing. Just because something had to be done didn't make it any easier to do it. She stroked Gump's arm.

"I'll be fierce for both of us," she said. "You can—"

She broke off as she heard a sound downstairs. Someone had entered the house. She shot Gump a quick glance, then stood quickly and moved towards the door.

"Now it begins," the trow muttered.

He rose as well and took up a stance on the other side of the door. The floor creaked as he moved and Kate hoped that maybe the sound would drive the intruder away, but while the noise downstairs ceased when Gump moved, after he'd been still for a few moments, it began again. A stealthy movement up the stairs.

Gump lifted an arm so that it was raised above the doorway. He looked at Kate and gave her a smile, but it didn't reach his eyes. Kate tried to smile bravely back, but all she could think of was, What if it was the droichan? What could they possibly do against him?

The intruder paused at the top of the stairs, then moved to the first doorway, stopping abruptly when a floorboard creaked underfoot. Long moments of deathly silence followed. Kate thought she was going to collapse from holding her breath, but she didn't dare breathe. Then the intruder moved again, coming towards the doorway that they were guarding.

I should have grabbed a chair, Kate thought. Maybe a double-whammy—chair and trow-fist—would at least knock the droichan out long enough for them to make good their escape. Instead she was just standing here, hands closed into small fists, staring wide-eyed at the door and still holding her breath.

A figure moved into the doorway, Gump's big fist started to come down, then Kate lunged forward.

"No, Gump, don't!" she cried. "It's Finn."

The little hob froze at the sound of his name, then stepped hastily back as Gump's fist narrowly missed him. The trow lost his balance, but Kate managed to steer him against a wall where he caught hold of a bookcase and saved himself from falling. Finn stood shaking, looking as though he was ready to bolt at any moment. Slowly he regained his composure and glared at the pair of them.

"You should have called out," Kate said sweetly.

"There was a stink of magic about the place," Finn replied. "I should have realized that it was no more than that of a trow and his sweetheart playing hide-and-go-seek in the dark."

"We thought you were the droichan," Kate said.

"And I thought—oh, never mind. Listen closely now, for I—"

"Look," Kate broke in.

She thrust Caraid towards Finn, open to the page with the circular image on it.

"We dowsed and pried," she said, "until we got a magical echo to give up this much. What do you think it is, Finn?"

"Kate. You're not listening to me."

"Oh, don't be mad," she said. "We didn't know it was you, and you didn't know it was us. It was an honest mistake."

"I'm not talking about that," Finn said. He caught hold of her arm. "Jacky left Gump's home and has gone to the Tower by herself. I'm afraid the droichan's captured her again."

All the blood drained from Kate's face.

"Oh, no," she said in a small voice. "What are we going to do?"

Gump straightened up at her side.

"Rescue her," he said.

Johnny woke with a start to find that he'd dozed off on the couch. Mactire was standing over him, shaking him awake.

"Huwzzat?" he mumbled, sitting up and rubbing his eyes.

"Listen," the wild boy said.

"But I don't hear anything . . ." Johnny began, then his voice trailed off.

There was no mistaking that sound, nor its urgency. It was Jemi's pipe, its music ringing through all of Faerie. The tune went coursing through him until it seemed that his every cell vibrated to its call. He sat dumbfounded by the intensity it awoke in him, sat there long after its last notes died away.

"What . . . that tune . . . ?"

"It's the calling-up music of the fiaina sidhe," Mactire told him. He caught hold of Johnny's arm and hauled him to his feet.

"But—"

"We mustn't delay. She calls the sidhe to war. That means she knows the name of our enemy."

Johnny looked down the hall to where Henk was sleeping.

"But," he started again.

Mactire shook his head. "There's no time. Are you coming, or do I leave you behind?"

"No. I . . ."

Still fuzzy with sleep, and dazed from what the music had woken in him, Johnny finally started to move. He grabbed his jacket and started for the door.

"Your fiddle," Mactire said.

Johnny went back for it.

"Jemi's going to be okay, isn't she?" he asked as he started for the door again, fiddle case in hand this time.

"Not if we don't hurry," the wolf boy said.

Outside he set off at a lope that Johnny was hard put to keep up with, but keep up he did. Down Bank Street they went and over Lansdowne Bridge into Ottawa South. In the Middle Kingdom they had another name for this place, Johnny remembered from talking to Jemi. They called it Crowdie Wort's Bally. It was there that the Tower of the Jack of Kinrowan stood, and on the grassy park south of that Tower, the sidhe were hosting tonight.

Behind, in Johnny's apartment, Henk awoke in time to hear them leave. He'd fallen asleep on the bed fully dressed, so that when he reached the door and saw Johnny and the wild boy hurrying off down the street, he had time to snatch his own jacket from where it lay on a chair, and set off into the night, following them.

His night fears scurried up and down his spine, but this time he was determined to ignore them. Unsure of where they were going, he still knew he had to follow. Just before he'd woken, he'd been dreaming. Nothing remained of that dream, not one image; only a haunting music that had called him up from sleep to find Johnny and his strange companion leaving the apartment.

As he ran in their wake, he wondered what was so important that it had sent them hurrying out into the night as they had.

Fifteen

The droichan's shadow had congealed on the floor between Jacky and the window, crouching there in the shape of a large black dog. It stared at her with its hot-coal eyes, silent now.

Jacky wouldn't look at it. She couldn't. She sat on her haunches, chin against her chest, and stared at the floor. The noise of a large commotion downstairs rose up through the floorboards, but it didn't really register. It wasn't until she heard a certain footfall coming up the stairs, until the door opened, that she lifted her head and slowly turned.

The droichan had returned.

He filled the doorway, his brown cloak hanging in loose folds to the floor, its hood thrown back to show his handsome features. The fire from his shadow-creature's eyes flickered in his own gaze as he regarded her.

"Sweet Jack," he said. "The time for kindness is past."

Jacky couldn't suppress an involuntary shiver at the sound of his voice. The strength to get up just wasn't in her, so she sat where she was, staring back at him.

"What . . . what do you *want* from me?" she asked.

"Everything."

"But I never hurt you. Why would you want to—"

The droichan made a sudden gesture with one hand and she was jerked roughly to her feet by an invisible force.

"Nothing?" he asked softly. "You stuck a knife in my heart, sweet Jack."

"But you—"

"Enough."

He made another gesture. Jacky heard a roaring of storm winds in her ears. The unseen force took her and slammed her against a wall, spread-eagled. She hung there, a foot or so from the floor. Helpless. Unable to move.

The droichan stepped slowly across the room until he was a foot or so away from her.

"It's time to end this," he said. "I want the luck of this Tower, sweet Jack. I want what Bhruic left you. It's as simple as that. A sidhe army is hosting behind the Tower. Perhaps my bullyboys— unruly rabble that they are—can defeat them, perhaps not, but why should I bide the outcome? I want what Kinrowan has to offer me—every drop of its luck, sweet Jack. Nothing less will do."

"But . . . they . . . can't . . . hurt you . . ." Jacky mumbled through taut jaws.

"Not forever, no. But they could conceivably best the Unseelie army that I can field at this moment. They could catch me and cut me to pieces. I wouldn't die, no. But think how long it would take me to become whole once more. I won't have that. I will *not* allow it. This Tower is the key to Kinrowan, and you are my key to the Tower, sweet Jack. You will unlock Bhruic's secrets for me. I will brook no more argument."

"But I don't *know* how to unlock—"

Invisible hands drew her back from the wall and slammed her into it again.

"No argument," the droichan repeated softly.

Fires glimmered wickedly in his eyes. He made a gesture with his hand in front of her face, fingers moving in an odd pattern, and cobwebs covered her features. They clung thickly to her skin, letting her only see the world through their grey gauze. She moved her head back and forth, trying to dislodge them, but they stuck to her like a second skin.

"When my kind dies," the droichan said, "*truly* dies, this is where we go."

One by one, Jacky's senses deserted her. Sight went first—from a gauzy veil to nothingness. Her other senses compensated, becoming more acute.

She heard her own raspy breathing, the droichan's light breaths. In the Tower itself, the cries of the bogans and other creatures readying for war. The sound of them issuing forth from the Tower to the park behind, gathering under an Unseelie banner—a flag with the image of a crucified swan-man encircled by briars upon it.

Then her hearing went.

Now she could smell the sharpness of her own fear, the earthy smell of the droichan. The open window of the Tower brought in the scents of autumn, mingled with a bog-reek of sluagh and bogans.

Smell went.

She could taste her fear now—a raw vomit sour in her throat. The salty sweat that beaded her lips.

Taste went.

There was nothing left but touch. The hard wall at her back. The vague kiss of a breeze on her skin. Then her nerve ends began to tingle and go numb. Limb by limb, feeling withdrew until she was devoid of all sensation.

No outside stimuli entered her. She might as well have been immersed in a sensory-deprivation tank. But there was no peace to be found in this. No rest. No solace. She hadn't chosen to withdraw from the world to capture some inner harmony. She'd had her senses stolen from her by a monster and been cast adrift in a bleak void of his making.

There was no way to measure time.

A moment could have passed and it could have been forever. An eternity slipped by in a scurry of seconds. Blank, utter panic came gibbering up from the back of her mind and flooded her brain.

Had he left her here?

Could anything exist in such emptiness?

She tried to call up comforting images in her mind's eye, but they were slow to come. She managed a small candle, its flame spluttering.

The flame went out.

A residue of its light remained as a faint nimbus. She built that into a spark of light—just one tiny star that she could focus on.

The star went out.

The void encircled it. Choked it. Swallowed it.

Her panic worsened.

She was here forever.

She might already have been here forever.

Escape was impossible. Without the droichan's help, she couldn't return to the world.

Give him what he wants, her panic told her.

But I don't know, she wailed. I can't give him what I don't know how to give.

Give it to him. Giveittohim. Give. It. To. Him.

No, she told that voice. Even if she could, she wouldn't.

She clung to that thought, repeated it, used it to force the panic away. The Tower had been her responsibility. It was already half-fallen to the enemy, and for that she had to pay. But she wouldn't give the droichan any more. He could leave her here forever, if that was what it took, but she wouldn't give in to him.

Her terror receded fractionally.

The spark she'd tried to call up suddenly burst into the image of a full moon, hanging swollen in the bleak night skies of her mind.

It flickered and was gone.

A woman stood in its place, regarding her. She was silver-haired and round-faced, full-lipped and dark-eyed, generous body wrapped in a tattered cloak of moss and leaves and twigs. Mushrooms grew from her shoulders. Fungus glimmered palely in amidst the dark debris that made up her cloak. She smiled at Jacky—a warm smile, the kind a mother would give to a child who had pleased her. Then the image was gone and the void returned.

But the fear didn't return with it.

That must have been the Moon, Jacky thought. The Moonmother Arn, herself. She came to me. She came and looked at me, with her luck in her eyes.

It wasn't much, she realized, floating there in the void. She hadn't been offered freedom, or revenge. Merely a look of pride. But it would have to be enough. She'd have to hold that memory forever, because she wasn't going to have anything else. She'd—

Her senses returned to her in a choking flood.

Sight and sound. The droichan's face, eyes mocking her; the heaving rasp of her own breathing.

Smell. The stink of her fear and the bog-reek of the Unseelie Court.

Taste and touch. The sour bile in her throat; the ache of her back and shoulder muscles pulled tight against the wall.

She drank in their return, ignoring the droichan. Her resolve to stand firm faltered as she savoured sensation. Even fear and bile and pain were something. Anything was better than the void, wasn't it?

The droichan let loose his invisible bonds and she slumped to a boneless heap on the floor.

"That is where we go when we die," he said. "I can send you there, if you don't give me what I want. Into that bleak eternity. Or you can give me the key to the Tower and when you die you'll walk the green fields of the Region of the Summer Stars, perhaps even to be born again.

"There is no escape from that void. No rescue is possible."

Jacky slowly lifted her head to look up at him. She wanted, she so desperately wanted to be able to say, Just you go to hell, you bastard, but she couldn't imagine returning to that emptiness. Just thinking of it made her hard-won resolve drain away.

"Which is it to be?" the droichan asked.

"I . . ."

Her voice came out like a frog's croak. Slowly she pushed herself up along the wall until she was half-sitting, half-leaning against it. She wanted to be standing when she answered him. Maybe that would lend her bravery. Lying at his feet, she could only give in. She clawed at the wall, struggling to find purchase, but her fingers kept slipping. She tried to find the Moon's face inside her again—that strange woman in her foresty cloak, with the luck in her eyes.

I want to be strong, she told that memory. But I can't be strong, just lying here.

She tried again.

The droichan stood back, watching her efforts with a half-smile on his lips.

Damn him. He could be so patient. He was just drinking in her pain, stealing her luck. That was why she was so weak. He had to be sucking the life right out of her.

But she wouldn't give in. She'd get to her feet and spit in his face and damn the consequences. But not if she lay here. Lying here, she just wanted to give up. She just wanted to say, I don't know what the key is, but you're welcome to it, only don't send me back to that place.

The droichan made a gesture with his hand, and invisible fingers plucked at her shirt, lifting her a few inches, before letting her fall again.

"Do you want a hand up?" he asked.

Jacky didn't bother to answer. She concentrated on forcing her limp body to do what it was told. She brought Bhruic's face to her mind's eyes and was surprised at how easily it came. She called up Kate then, and Finn. Eilian, the son of Dunlogan's Laird. The big trow, Gump. Sly Kerevan, the trickster with his fiddle in a bag, hanging from his shoulder.

Calling them all up, feeling the weight of their gazes upon her, she found the strength she needed. They were faerie—and faerie, Kinrowan's faerie, depended on her.

She made a slow, faltering progress, but she clawed herself to a standing position, supported herself against the wall, and looked at the droichan.

"Well done, sweet Jack," he said. "You've more strength than I gave you credit for. But are you wise as well? Which have you chosen? The void, or to aid me?"

"I . . . I'll give you the key," she croaked.

The droichan smiled as she reached into the pouch hanging at her belt, but the smile faltered as she drew out a wally-stane. The fires, just glimmering in his eyes, woke into a raging blaze.

"You—" he began, a hand rising to shape a gesture in the air between them, but Jacky moved more quickly.

"No, you!" she cried as she broke the wally-stane against her own chest.

A sparkle of crystal dust exploded from between Jacky's fingers like a puffball's spores floating free from a kick. The droichan stepped back from her and continued to make a spell with the twisting gesture of his hands. When he loosened the magic, Jacky stood in front of him, unaffected.

"You can't touch me," she said.

She moved towards him. From the droichan's feet, his shadow reared up in dog shape and lunged for her throat. Before it could reach her, it slid sideways as though it had run up against an invisible wall. It tried again, and again, to get at her, but it too couldn't reach her.

"I've made myself safe from widdy spells," she said. "Do you know any kindly magics? You might try one of them."

The droichan's hands fell to his sides.

"Clever Jack," he said. "You knew not even a magic could kill me, so you turned your spell on yourself."

"A mouse could kill you," Jacky replied. "All it needs to do is take a bite from your heart."

"But first it must find that heart."

"You can't stop me from looking for it—and I'll tell you now, I'll never give up."

The droichan shook his head in admiration. "What a droichan you would make, sweet Jack. But you forgot something."

He moved towards her, edging her into a corner away from both the window and the door. Nervously, Jacky eyed him, unsure of what he was up to. She racked her brain, trying to think of what she'd forgotten when she spelled the wally-stane. It wasn't until he lunged at her that the truth dawned.

She was safe from widdyshin magics—his or another's, oh, yes. But not from physical harm.

She tried to knee him in the groin, but he moved too quickly. He twisted to one side, grabbed her by the shoulder, and spun her around. Before she could recover her balance, the flat of his shoe hit her in the small of her back and she went pinwheeling against the wall. She hit hard, slumping to the floor. He was upon her immediately, knees on her back, grinding her against the hardwood floor, hands at her throat.

"You've played your last trick, sweet Jack," he said. "Now give me what I want, or I'll snap your neck."

She was safe from his spells, but the trick had backfired. As usual, she'd blown it. A smart person would have been out that window so fast it would have made the droichan's head spin, but not Jacky Rowan. Oh, no. She was the Jack of Kinrowan, wasn't she just, and oh so clever. Rather than do the smart thing, she'd stuck around to rub the droichan's face into his failure, never bothering to think things through.

But at least he couldn't send her back into the void. And she might die, but that was all the satisfaction he was going to get from her. The Tower's secret was safe because she couldn't give it to him even if she wanted to.

Somehow, none of that brought her any consolation.

Because now, helpless under his weight, with his hands at her throat, she was still going to pay.

"I've been all around," Finn said when he rejoined Kate and Gump, "and there's no sign of her."

He'd left the pair of them hidden in the back yard of the house across the street from the Tower while he made a circuit of its grounds in his bogan disguise. He'd found sluagh and real bogans and all manner of Unseelie creatures in great numbers, but not even a rumour of Jacky.

"She's gone inside, then," Gump said.

Kate looked at the Tower and shivered. After just a day, it already looked different. There was a veil of corruption about the Tower, just like there had been at the house in the Glebe that she and Gump had investigated. The trees were beginning to lean away from its walls, the garden taking on an air of decay. Malevolence hung thick from its gables and walls.

"How can we fight so many?" she asked.

Finn gave her a wan smile. "With a Jack's trick. A hob and the makings of a skillywoman, that would make them sit up and blink. But who would notice a pair of bogans in the company of a trow?"

"It'll never work," Kate said.

"It has so far."

"There's some that might know me in there," Gump said.

"Then you'll have to be convincing when you tell them of your change of heart," Finn said. "Are you with us?"

Gump nodded.

"Then let's get to it," the hob said.

Kate had the sudden urge to look in a mirror, just to be sure that her disguise really *was* working, but Finn had already set off towards the front of the house. When they crossed the street, two bogans were preceding a trow to the front door of the Tower. No one gave them a second glance until they entered the Tower itself and they were stopped by a black-bearded, duergar widdyman. He eyed Kate and Finn for a long moment, then turned to the trow.

"I didn't think to find you in our company again, Gump," he said.

The trow shrugged. "Times change, Greim. I've heard about the new boss. Word is, if you're not with him, then you're against him. I never liked to take sides, but this time it seems I have no choice."

"A pretty tale," Greim said. "And I might half-believe you, if it wasn't for the stink of skilly magic on your friends. I've learned to see through this trick."

Kate swallowed thickly, ready to bolt, but before she could decide which way to run, before the widdyman could call up an alarm or toss a spell, Gump hit the dwarf. He brought a meaty fist down on the top of Greim's head and the widdyman collapsed on the floor, sprawled out like a wet rag. Finn shot a quick glance down the hall to the kitchen, where they could hear the voices of other Unseelie creatures, but no one seemed to have noticed.

"Is he dead?" Kate asked.

Gump shook his head. "Though he deserves to be. He's an evil little creature, have no doubt of that."

"Up the stairs," Finn said. "Quickly!"

Kate took the lead. Gump followed, carrying the limp dwarf under one arm. It didn't seem wise to leave him where he could be discovered.

"We're just lucky this isn't a true Unseelie hall," Finn said, taking up the rear, "or our disguises would never have taken us even this far."

Kate nodded. Skilly spells didn't work in an Unseelie Hall.

"But how did he see through our disguises?" she asked.

Finn sighed. "You heard him yourself. He'd seen the trick before."

Seen the trick before, Kate repeated to herself, then she shivered. Seen it when they caught Jacky is what that had to mean.

Gump deposited Greim's limp form in Jacky's bedroom. The second floor was empty now. Looking out the window onto the park, they could see the Unseelie Host gathering in a motley array. Trolls and bogans, sluagh, hags and goblins. Bands of capering gullywudes. Spriggans who puffed themselves up to troll size, shrank again, then grew once more.

Kate turned away when she caught sight of their banner. The swan-man depicted on it reminded her too much of Jacky's friend Eilian.

There was no sign of the sidhe rade.

Kate turned to ask Finn about the fiaina when they all heard a shriek that came from the third floor. It dissolved into a long, aching moan that woke goosebumps on her arms.

"Oh, God," she said, white-faced. "That must be Jacky. The droichan's hurting her."

Gump nodded and started for the door, but Kate got there first. The sound of Jacky's moaning fired her worry to such an extent that she forgot to be afraid. She ran towards the stairs going up, but before she could take the first step, Gump caught hold of her arm and pulled her back.

"Wait," he said.

"We need a plan," Finn added. "We can't just rush in there against the droichan."

"But Jacky's probably dying—"

The moaning ceased abruptly and they heard a soft thump, like a body hitting the floor. Kate looked at Finn, then at Gump, a pleading in her eyes.

"We've got to do *something*."

Finn nodded. "Yes, but—"

Kate pulled herself free from Gump's grip and sprinted out of reach, up the stairs. She paused at the door to look back. Gump reached her side first, Finn, brow furiously wrinkled in thought, right behind him. They could hear voices—Jacky's and another's. The droichan's.

Relief ran through Kate. Jacky was still alive.

"When we go in," Finn whispered, "we split up immediately. No matter how strong the droichan is, he can't aim spells at three different moving figures."

"Then we crush him," Gump said.

He opened his big hands and then closed them into fists, a grim look on his face.

Finn shook his head. "We need his heart for that. No, the best thing would be to keep him off-balance. Throw him out the window perhaps — while he's concentrating on breaking his fall, we can try to escape."

"Or we could jump through the window," Kate said, remembering what Jacky had told them about its odd properties.

"That will still leave things as they are," Gump protested.

"Do *you* know where his heart is hidden?" Finn asked the trow.

Gump said nothing for a long moment, then slowly shook his head.

"This way we might win free to keep searching for it," the hob said.

Kate plucked at both their arms.

"We've got to go in now," she said, only just remembering to keep her voice pitched as low as theirs.

They could hear the sounds of a struggle from the other side of the door.

"What if there's more than just the droichan in there?" Finn wondered aloud.

But Gump was through with waiting. He bent low, put his shoulder to the door, and smashed it in. There was no more time for plans or second thoughts.

They went in, Kate darting to the right, Finn to the left, Gump charging straight through, rising to his full height once he was in the room. They saw Jacky pinned under the droichan in a corner of the room — the corner nearest to Kate. A moment's hesitation on their part was all the droichan needed.

"Can't spell you," he muttered to Jacky as he woke his shadow. "But what about your friends?"

Finn had it wrong. The droichan was quite able to throw more than a spell at a time. His shadow-creature lunged at Gump. An invisible force lifted Kate from her feet and slammed her against the bookcases. As he turned his attention on Finn, Jacky lunged from under him, throwing him off-balance.

The hob charged the droichan, but Colorc recovered quickly. He batted Jacky aside with one arm. Before Finn could reach him, the droichan's shadow-creature split into two, one pinning Gump to the floor, the other bowling the little hob over and trapping him as well.

"Don't even think of it," Colorc told Jacky as she pulled another wally-stane from its pouch.

But Jacky could only hear Kate's moaning from where she was pinned up against the bookcase. She could see Kate's wide-open eyes—only the whites showing, because they were rolled back in her head. Kate was staring into the void.

Jacky remembered that bleak place all too well. Kate was lost there. Trapped in its emptiness. Death, with its promise of the Summer Country, was far preferable to that. Death for herself, for Finn, for any of them, rather than letting even one of them spend eternity in that place.

She placed her will in the wally-stane and threw it, straight and true, across the room where it struck Kate and exploded into a shower of crystal dust. Kate's eyes rolled down, seeing this world once more. The invisible bonds holding her against the bookcase lost their power over her and she fell to the floor in a crumpled heap. Only then did Jacky turn back to the droichan.

Colorc towered over her, the fire in his eyes burning like a torched countryside. His cloak fell from his shoulders and pooled on the floor. The night skies outside the room went darker still. Thunder rumbled directly overhead. Rain exploded against the Tower's roof. Lightning seared across the sky in sheets of icy fire.

"This has gone too far," Colorc said.

His voice was quiet, almost conversational, but cold as a winter sky. He swept over Jacky, and before she could move, he'd grabbed the front of her shirt and hoisted her up, smacking her up against the wall again.

"Do you see your friends?" he said. "You've saved one, but my darkness will feed on the souls of the others. It will tear their bodies open and spill their entrails on the floor. It will suck the juices of their brains and make bracelets of their bones."

Jacky had hit her head on the wall when the droichan threw her against it. Sparks danced before her eyes. She found it hard to breathe with his hand pulling the throat of her shirt tight across her windpipe. But she could see the droichan's shadow-creatures crouched over Finn and Gump.

The side of the trow's throat was bleeding where the skin had already been broken. The shadow holding him was lapping at the blood with a black tongue while the trow struggled uselessly against the creature's superior strength. Finn was almost swallowed by the one on him. It lay across his body like a loathsome cloak, wet with the boggy reek of the sluagh. Kate was the only one not trapped, but she lay very still where she had fallen.

Colorc pulled Jacky from the wall and slammed her against it again. She tried to fight him, but his sheer strength was just too much for her. She clawed at his chest, tearing open his shirt, breaking the skin with her nails, but the droichan ignored her efforts. The unnatural storm continued to rage outside, counterpoint to the fires in his eyes.

"Give me what I want!" he shouted at her, spittle showering her face.

He pulled her back again, driving her against the wall with so much force that she thought she could feel her bones rattling against each other.

"Your friends will die," Colorc told her. "One by one, torn apart before your eyes, and then, then I'll take you apart with my own hands and feed your flesh to the night."

Thunder boomed, punctuating his words with an earth-shattering crack that shook the Tower to its foundations.

Jacky could hardly see the droichan now. Her eyes were blurred with tears of frustration and pain. She desperately needed air. She tried to focus on him, but she saw merely a blur.

There was the dark of his torn shirt, and the lighter hue of his skin. The red fire in his eyes. A gleam of brass or bronze hanging from his neck, hidden until she'd torn his shirt. The white gleam of his teeth as he drew back his lips, snarling at her.

He slammed her against the wall a fourth time, and then even those blurry sights were driven away by a new shower of dancing sparks.

"Give me the key!" the droichan roared, but his voice seemed to come from very far away now.

The scene was like something out of an old Hollywood western, Johnny thought as he and Mactire reached the park.

They entered off Bank Street, right near Billings Bridge. Spread in a long line along the bank of the river was the rade of the sidhe, ready for war as they had been when he and Jemi had called them up earlier tonight. If they were the Indians, then the Unseelie Host were the white-eyes. They were a disorganized swirl of creatures — bogans and gullywudes, trolls and goblins, things for which Johnny had no name.

"Jesus," he breathed as he and Mactire stopped to reconnoiter. "We haven't got a chance."

The Unseelie Host outnumbered the fiaina sidhe, three to one. Mactire frowned, also taking in their number.

"I hadn't thought there were so many left after the Jack destroyed their Court last year," he said. "But still. We have no choice. We must —"

The sound of someone calling Johnny's name made the wolf boy pause. They turned to see Henk running up to them. When he reached Johnny's side, he bent half over, clutching his side and breathing hard through his mouth.

"Henk. What're you doing here?"

Henk straightened slowly. "I wanted to see what you were up to . . . " His voice trailed off as he took in the scene before them. "Oh, Christ. Tell me I'm dreaming."

Touched by faerie, he could see into the Middle Kingdom now.

"You'd better go," Johnny said.

"No way. I'm staying right here with you."

"You don't know what you're getting into."

"I know enough," Henk replied. He pointed out Loireag and Dohinney Tuir near the center of the long line of sidhe. "Those two — they're the ones I met by the river when I was looking for you."

Johnny followed the line of Henk's vision, but his gaze went further to the small figure that the kelpie and hob were talking to.

"Jemi!" he cried.

Without looking to see what the others did, he ran along the line of sidhe to where she was.

She looked up at his approach, a faint welcoming smile appearing briefly on her lips before her features went grim once more. She was sitting astride a small shaggy pony and looked wet and bedraggled. Her hair was mostly plastered to her skull, except for the odd pink tuft near the back that was dry. As he got closer to her, a vague marshy smell came to his nostrils.

"What happened to you?" he asked.

"I had a swim in the canal."

She slipped from the back of the pony to give him a quick hug. Stepping back, she touched the back of her hand to his cheek.

"I'm so glad you're here, Johnny. I was afraid you wouldn't hear the call, but there was no time to go by your place. I just had to hope that you'd hear—that you'd understand what it meant and come."

"Well, I'm here. But Jesus, Jemi."

He turned to look at the Unseelie Host. They were jeering and catcalling the sidhe, but kept to their unruly ranks.

"This is going to be a slaughter," Johnny said.

Jemi shook her head. "Only if we don't kill the droichan."

"The what?"

"Droichan—it's a kind of gruagagh, but worse. Way worse. He's the one who's been behind all of what's been going on. I ran into him in Sandy Hill while I was fetching this."

She pulled the little bone flute pendant from under her shirt where it was hanging and showed it to him. Johnny felt a spark flicker inside himself at the sight of it. He put his hand in his pocket and closed his fingers about his fiddle charm. It was hot to the touch.

He tried to concentrate on what Jemi was telling him about the droichan—how his shadow could run free and kill people for him, how he was deathless, except he could be killed, but only if his heart was found first—but his attention kept wandering to the colour of her eyes, the line of her chin, the shape of her ear. He shook his head. There was no time for that kind of thing right now.

"I'm going into the Tower," she said, finishing up her explanation. "Johnny, will you lead the rade for me?"

Johnny shook his head again. "I'm going with you."

"But the rade needs a mortal to lead it—we'll be stronger then."

"I can't let you go in there alone."

"You don't think I can handle it?"

"I'm sure you can handle anything you set your mind to, Jemi. I just can't handle being out here and not knowing what's happening to you."

Jemi sighed, but before she could argue anymore, Henk stepped up.

"I'll do it," he said. "If it's the kind of thing that anyone can do, not just Johnny."

"You?" Jemi said, surprised to see him there. She'd only had eyes for Johnny.

Loireag moved closer. Henk flinched at the sight of her looming over him, but he stood his ground.

"Has this tadpole suddenly found teeth?" she asked, looking Henk over.

"Loireag," Tuir warned.

"Don't worry, Tuir. I'm saving my anger for the bogans. I just want to test the mettle of this tadpole, that's all." She turned her attention back to Henk. "Can you lead us against that?" she asked, pointing at the Unseelie Host. "Or will you run off with your tail between your legs halfway through the first charge?"

Johnny started to speak, but Jemi caught his arm and shook her head.

Henk's throat felt too tight. He swallowed, Adam's apple bobbing, and looked at the Host. He'd thought the sidhe had been his nightmares come to life, but he'd been wrong, he realized as he looked on the creatures of the Unseelie Court. He tried to imagine leading a charge against that monstrous, unholy crowd, and couldn't. But he knew that if he didn't, the dark would continue to haunt him for the rest of his life.

"I'm scared shitless," he said, looking back at the kelpie. She started to nod knowingly, until he added, "But I'll do it."

Their gazes met and held for long moments, then Loireag nodded.

"So be it," she said. "I think the Moon can ride you."

"Lend him your fiddle," Tuir said to Johnny.

"He can't," Jemi said. "He'll need that for where we're going."

"I can't play one anyway," Henk said. "My instrument's the concertina."

"Anglo or English?" Loireag asked.

Henk blinked. "Uh, English."

Loireag sent word up and down the line of the sidhe until a small hob trotted up on his pony and handed Henk an instrument. It was a beautiful old Wheatstone, its silver gleaming, its wood dark, its leather bellows worn but still strong.

"It was my father's," the hob said. "Play the Moon fierce in it."

Before Henk could thank him, the hob turned his mount and returned to his place in the ranks.

Henk hefted the instrument. "I'm not so sure I understand," he said. "We're going up against those things with music?"

"Oh, no," Tuir assured him. "The music's there to call up the rade and aim its strength like an arrow against our foes."

"Any particular music?" Henk asked.

"I think a march would do the trick," Jemi said. "Something fierce."

" 'O'Neill's Cavalcade'?" Johnny suggested.

"That would do," Jemi agreed.

"Okay," Henk said. "When do I start playing?"

"Now!" Loireag cried, but Jemi quickly shook her head.

"Wait for them to make the first move," she said. "If we haven't lost all our luck, Johnny and I will have put an end to the droichan and there'll be no need for this war. The Host will quickly lose heart without a chief to lead them."

"I want blood," Loireag said. "Someone has to pay for all we've lost."

"Tuir, please?" Jemi asked, turning to the hob. "Hold back until you've no other choice?"

"Different words from what you asked of us earlier tonight," the kelpie complained.

"I didn't know then what I know now," Jemi replied.

"If I've got to start it," Henk said, "I'll make sure we wait."

Loireag and Jemi both shot him looks, the one angry, the other grateful.

"Thank you," Jemi said.

Leaving her pony for Henk, she led Johnny past the ranked sidhe, back to Bank Street. From there they doubled up Riverdale, turning down Belmont to come up to the Tower by the front. There were few Unseelie creatures abroad now, most having gathered in the park to face the hosted sidhe.

"Have you got a plan?" Johnny asked as they crept near the Tower.

Jemi nodded. "But it means me going in and you staying out."

"I don't want that."

"Listen to me, Johnny. At least hear me out."

Reluctantly, Johnny did. When he heard what she had planned, he had to agree that he couldn't accompany her.

"But only if the front door's guarded," he said.

"That's a bargain."

And an easy one to keep, Jemi thought as they closed in on the Tower. She'd already spied bogans and a tall trollish figure in its doorway. They appeared to be looking for someone or something. She led Johnny quickly along until they were standing by the front of the Tower. Johnny looked up and shook his head.

"You can climb that?" he asked.

Jemi nodded.

"What are you—part monkey, too?"

"Just a Pook, Johnny—and a halfling at that."

"And you're sure the droichan's heart is in there?"

"I've met him," she explained again. "He's the kind that needs it close at hand—probably even on his person. Will you play the tune, Johnny?"

"Sure."

He opened his case and took out fiddle and bow. Tightening the frog until the bow's hairs were taut, he started to put the instrument under his chin, then paused.

"Jemi?"

She looked at him, then leaned close for a kiss.

"If we lose," she said softly, "I'll look for you in the Summer Country."

Johnny swallowed dryly. "Yeah. But we're not going to lose, right?"

"Right."

Fiddle under his chin, Johnny drew the bow across its strings and began to play the tune that Jemi had requested of him. It was an instrumental version of the traditional Breton folk song "Kimiad"—a sly music that fit into the sounds of the night so that the Unseelie Host would ignore it, but a music that would call down the Moon's strength for Jemi to borrow. She needed her own hands free for the climb.

"The Gruagagh had a window there, on the third floor," she'd told him. "A window through which he could see all of Kinrowan and some of the borderlands as well. It's there that the droichan will be. Like a spider in its web, hoping to catch a fly. But this fly will come in through the window, not by the door. I'll need that moment's edge, Johnny. I'll need the edge and the Moon's strength that your music will borrow for me. Luck in every note, liquid as her light, Johnny."

So he played the tune and called down the Moon as he could, watching with open-mouthed amazement as Jemi went up the side of the house, finding finger- and toeholds in between the bricks where there shouldn't have been any. He didn't know if the Moon was answering his call, but he felt a quickening inside him that had nothing to do with the rush of adrenaline that danger had called up in his body.

He could hear bagpipes in the music and harping, a hundred fiddles, and the sound of Jemi's own pipe. The music was a soaring chorus, but at the same time, it was filled with the sounds of leaf rustlings and wind, tree boughs groaning, houses settling, distant traffic.

"Don't let her be hurt," he whispered against the music that his bow drew from his grandfather's fiddle.

She had just reached the halfway point between the second and third floors when the sky suddenly went dark.

Christ, Johnny thought, forcing himself to concentrate on his music. I sure hope this isn't a sign from the Moon that she's got better things to do than help us.

Hard on the heels of the darkness, thunder boomed directly above him and the vast bank of clouds that had appeared to darken the sky loosed a downfall of rain. In moments, Johnny found it im-

possible to see more than a foot in front of himself. The wet hairs of
his bow slid against the strings and the music faltered, then died. He
tried to peer through the rain, up to where he'd last seen Jemi, but
his eyes filled with water faster than he could clear them. A sheet of
lightning tore across the sky. In that instant he saw that she had almost reached the third-floor windowsill that she'd been aiming for,
then the darkness fell again.

"Screw this," he said.

Fiddle and bow still in hand, he raced for the front door,
damn the consequences. He barely got into the hall when a
strange little creature that seemed to be made all of twigs ran up
to him. Johnny kicked at it and it fell to pieces as his boot connected with it. A grunt came from down the hall and a bogan
peered out of a room and spied him.

Johnny bolted up the stairs. Behind him, he could hear the
bogan scrabbling around the corner and starting up after him.

When the sky darkened and the rain hit, Jemi echoed Johnny's
thoughts, but for a different reason. The blast of rain very nearly
succeeded in knocking her from her precarious perch. For long moments it was all she could do to hold on, little say continue up the
side of the Tower.

But she refused to give in. Inside was her sister's murderer. Inside was a creature determined to drain Faerie of its luck and leave a
wasteland behind it as it moved on to yet another Court. Well, he
was going to be stopped, she vowed, and stopped here.

Squeezing her eyes shut against the downpour, she lifted a
hand, found a minuscule hold for it, and drew herself up another few
precious inches. One bare foot went up, found a hold, then the
other. She pulled herself carefully up, flung out a hand, and could
have kissed a bogan, for it closed on the windowsill she'd sought.

Cautiously, she went through the whole process with her feet
once more, first one, then the other. She started to pull herself the
rest of the way, moved too fast, and her hand started to slip. She did-
n't even think of what she did next. As the one hand slipped, she
concentrated on maintaining her balance, hugged the wall, and
caught a firmer grip with her other hand.

Then it too started to slip.

She tensed her hand and her grip held. A moment later she got her other hand into position and pulled herself the rest of the way up until she was crouched, wet and bedraggled, on the sill.

She peered down, trying to spot Johnny, but she couldn't see far enough. She listened for his music, but the rain drowned it out if he was still playing.

Oh, don't get brave and rush in after me, she prayed. Bad enough that one of us is probably going to die—don't you get hurt too, Johnny.

Then she turned her attention to the inside of the room. She'd moved with the utmost quiet—and had been helped by the downpour—so she wasn't surprised that no one inside had noticed her. Now that she was looking in, she understood why.

A trow and a hob were being held to the floor by a pair of the shadow-creatures that had pursued her. A young woman with curly hair lay by one wall, a book clutched in her hand. And then, as Jemi turned her head, she saw the droichan, slamming another woman against the wall.

Jemi wanted to help the woman the droichan was attacking, but she had to think first. Where would his heart be hidden? She'd get just the one try—if she was lucky—and no more. So where? On him, probably, but what would it look like? Would it be a ring, a charm, a pendant, a coin in his pocket, a button on his shirt, a thread in his cloak? Or would it be hidden somewhere in this room?

She looked around again, saw that the woman clutching the book was sitting up now, eyes wide as she saw Jemi perched outside the window. Jemi put a finger to her lips, but the woman merely opened her book and held it out so that Jemi could see the curious drawing on the page. When she shrugged her shoulders, the woman touched the drawing, then pointed at the droichan.

Jemi's teeth bared in a sudden grin.

Arn above, she thought as she swung into the room. She'd just been given the droichan's secret.

Henk sat uneasily on his borrowed pony. He had the concertina resting on one knee and he stroked the pony's shaggy mane while he stared across the park at the gathered Host of the Unseelie Court.

Nothing seemed real. At the same time, everything seemed more real than anything he'd ever experienced before.

"They make an awesome sight, don't they?" Dohinney Tuir said quietly, edging his own pony closer to Henk's.

Henk glanced briefly at him, then returned his attention to the Host.

"They're my night fears," he said. "I thought your friend the kelpie was one, but now that I can see those creatures, I know I was wrong. I've never really faced them before. I'm not always scared of them—hardly ever, really—but they still come back to me, just like that"—he snapped his fingers—"and when they do, they cripple me. Now that I know they're real . . . I'm not any less scared of them, but somehow it makes it easier to face them. To know that I wasn't crazy all those years."

"We might all die," Tuir said.

Henk nodded. "I know. But it beats getting run over by a truck. At least this means something."

"Does it?" Loireag asked, stepping closer to his left side.

She smiled as he glanced at her, but he wasn't sure if the bared teeth were mocking him, or if she just generally wore a sardonic air.

"To me it'll mean something," he said.

Before Loireag could reply, the sky went dark. Thunder cracked above them, impossibly close, and a sheet of rain engulfed the park, immediately drenching them. Lightning flickered like snakes' tongues through the dark.

"This is it," Loireag said. "They'll attack under cover of the rain."

Henk started to lift the concertina, wondering how he could play it in this kind of weather, but the little hob on the other side of him touched his arm. When Henk looked at him, Tuir shook his head.

"Not yet," he said. "This is some working of the droichan's— his rage manifesting itself in the weather. It means he's angry. Perhaps Jemi's reached him."

"He can cause this just by getting angry?" Henk asked.

"When you speak of droichan, you speak of power," the hob replied. "But they pay a price for such displays. They lose their souls, Henk. They lose the chance of all the lives that are to come.

And, in the end, they lose the green promise of the Region of the Summer Stars."

"Uh, right."

"They can live forever, unless their heart is destroyed. But destroy it, and they no longer exist—not on any plane of existence."

Loireag pawed at the ground with one hoof, the rain waking a dark sheen on her skin.

"I want his blood," she hissed into the night. "For all our kin that he slew. For Jenna. I want his blood."

"Patience," the hob said. His voice worked like a salve on her, reining in her anger. "You will get your desire all too soon."

Henk looked from one to the other, then shivered. He was soaked to the bone, cold and scared. He couldn't see the enemy anymore and that just made things worse. He thought of the creatures and the hellish banner unfurled above their ranks. The Host could be creeping up on them right now. They were already outnumbered.

His fingers touched the buttons of the concertina without pressing down on them, recalling the opening bars of "O'Neill's Cavalcade." Would the instrument still play in the rain? Would some enchantment make it work?

"How will we know when it's time?" he asked, his voice sounding weak and high-pitched to his ears.

"We'll know," the hob said grimly at his side. "Don't fret, Henk. We'll know."

"But what are they waiting for?"

Tuir shrugged. "The droichan's word? Some chief to lead them? I don't know. Perhaps they wait for courage."

"But they outnumber us three to one."

"To an Unseelie creature," Loireag said, "those are poor odds. They prefer the sure thing."

Henk shivered again and settled down to wait with the silent ranks of the sidhe. The kelpie might feel that the Host facing them was afraid, but he didn't have any such false hopes. He'd seen the creatures for himself. There was no way monsters like that could be scared of an army that was just a third of their own size.

"Christ, I hate waiting," he muttered.

Neither of his companions replied. He hunched his neck between his shoulders, uselessly trying to keep out the rain. He didn't know why he bothered. He was already as wet as it was humanly possible to get.

"Christ," he muttered again, then fell silent as well.

All he could do was wait.

Sixteen

When Jacky freed Kate from the machinations of Colorc's spell and brought her back from the void, some part of that empty place stayed inside her. Colorc's invisible grip lost its hold on her and she was dropped to the floor, but once freed, Kate's muscles were all slack and rubbery. She couldn't lift her head. She couldn't even open her eyes.

Memory of that empty place lodged inside her like a dark needle stuck straight through her heart. She wasn't relieved at her escape. She didn't feel anything, only a bleakness that was made worse by the sudden sensory overload as sound and smell and feeling all returned to her in a rush. She curled herself around Caraid, trying to escape it—memory of that place and the return of her senses—all to no avail.

She squeezed her eyes shut, willing her surroundings to disappear, but they flickered open almost of their own volition. Her nostrils stung with the reek of sluagh and other Unseelie creatures. Sound was worse. The sound of Jacky's struggle with the droichan. The whispering hiss and snick of the droichan's shadow-creatures. The rough rasp of a tongue against Gump's skin. Finn's moans.

But when she opened her eyes, she saw none of that. Her gaze settled on the window overlooking Kinrowan to see a wet, pink-haired figure balancing on its sill.

Slowly, Kate sat up. Her every bone and muscle ached at the movement, but she knew she had to help the newcomer. One look in the bedraggled figure's eyes told her that this was no creature of the droichan, nor one of the Unseelie Court. She opened Caraid to the page showing the curious image that she and Gump had found in that house in the Glebe, and showed it to the small woman in the window.

The woman shrugged, so Kate pointed at the drawing, then at the droichan. Understanding woke in the woman's eyes and she grinned fiercely, swinging down from the sill.

Kate leaned weakly against the wall, not really sure what the symbol meant to the woman, only that it meant something. That had to be enough, didn't it? But the void still fingered her heart, threatening to overcome her again with its empty bleakness.

The woman moved across the room towards the droichan, whose back was towards them. Kate watched her go. What did the symbol mean? What would the woman do? And suddenly Kate—fueled by the fear of what lay inside her, what the droichan had put inside her—felt that the knowledge she'd passed on wouldn't be enough. She got to her feet.

"No," she whispered to the woman.

Jemi froze at the sound of Kate's voice. The whispered word rang loud in her ears—too loud. It sounded above the tumult of the storm outside. The droichan paused, too, turning with Jacky still held upright by one arm. He saw the Pook.

"You," he said.

"My God!" Kate cried. "He's wearing it around his neck."

The droichan blanched. His free hand went to the medallion hanging from his throat, but he didn't move quickly enough. Jacky yanked what she saw as only a bright blur of metal on his chest and gave a sharp tug that broke it free of its chain. With what strength she had left, she tossed it towards Kate, but Jemi reached up and snatched it from the air.

The droichan threw Jacky aside and woke a spell. Invisible fingers plucked at Jemi's body and started to lift her into the air. And then Johnny came thundering up the last few stairs and burst into the room.

"Jesus Christ!" he said as he took in the scene.

His appearance distracted the droichan. It took only a fraction of a second for him to turn to see who it was, then return his attention to the Pook, but that was all the time Jemi had needed. She slipped free of his invisible grip with a sidhe sidestep—into the world of men, back into Faerie—and then she dropped the medallion onto the floor and ground it under her heel.

It had the look and feel of old gold, brassy and worn, but it was the droichan's heart and under the stamp of her heel it splattered as a human organ would have. The sting of its blood and bursting tissue burned the bottom of Jemi's foot and the floor hissed and smoked where the fragments landed. But Jemi could endure the pain. She had only to think of her sister and all those the droichan had killed. She had only to look at his anguished features.

A wail of despair left his mouth, then all the years he'd stolen fell upon him in a rush. His flesh grew lined, hard, brittle. It flaked and turned to dust. In moments, an empty sack of clothing fell to the hardwood floor in a shower of dust. The storm outside the Tower ceased as abruptly as it had begun.

Kate leaned back against the wall and slid weakly to the floor. The droichan's death had come too suddenly, looked too much like the last reel of an old B horror flick to seem true. Real beings, magical droichan or not, didn't just dissolve into dust, did they? But the sliver of the void was gone from her heart and while the blood still thundered in her veins, the realization hit home that the cause for all their terror was gone.

She looked slowly around. A strange young man with a fiddle and bow in one hand was crossing the room to hold the pink-haired woman. The shadow-creatures were gone and both Finn and Gump were sitting up, the trow clutching the side of his neck, blood leaking through his fingers. A bogan came barreling into the room, but Gump knocked it senseless with one blow of his free hand. Jacky lay against the wall where the droichan had thrown her, weakly trying to rise.

"Is . . . is it really over?" Kate asked.

The pink-haired woman shook her head.

"The droichan's gone," she said. "But there's still a war to be won."

The bogan Groot was the proud bearer of the Unseelie Court's standard. He held it aloft, grinning as it flapped in the wind, still grinning when the rain came and it clung wetly to its shaft.

Such a standard. A widdyman hob had stitched it over long nights, sewn every stitch widdershins. Such an unsainly emblem to lead them. And the droichan. He promised to be a better leader than any Big Man, hot damn. Kinrowan would bleed under their heels. But first there was the sidhe host to feed on.

He could see only their vague outline through the rain and wondered how long it would be before either Greim or the new boss himself would send word for the charge. He could already taste sidhe flesh. Just thinking of the toadsuckers made his mouth water.

"Come on, come on," a troll muttered beside him. "Spike 'em—what's taking so long?"

Groot nodded. Maybe he should lead the charge himself. He had the banner. The Host would follow. Wouldn't the boss reward him, hot damn, at the victory Groot would give him?

But then Groot frowned. Maybe not. The new boss demanded utter obedience—a hard thing for a bogan to buckle under—but he promised much to those who served him well. Human flesh, as well as Seelie. Though human flesh was luckless, it was sweet. Could he risk the boss's wrath?

"Whadaya think?" Lunt asked, joining him at the front of the Host.

"Think about what?" Groot asked the other bogan.

"Is Greim going to send the word, or did he run off and get spiked?"

"Don't talk like that," Groot warned. "Not unless you want to spend the rest of your life as a heap of shit."

"Bah!" Lunt spat in the muddying sod. "I think—"

Groot never got to hear what he thought. From the Tower behind them came a piercing wail, and then the storm suddenly stopped. The night seemed almost bright as the clouds vanished from above. Groot stared across the field at the long grim line of borderfolk, and an uncertain shiver went through him. It didn't matter that his own army outnumbered the sidhe three to one. It didn't matter that the Unseelie Host had a droichan leading them.

Something was wrong.

"What was that?" Lunt said.

"Guess the boss spiked that Jack," a voice said from the crowd.

"I'd like a bite of her myself," someone else added to a general laugh.

"I don't think that was it," Groot said. "There's a bad feeling in the air right now."

A moment later a shout came from the Tower.

"The boss is dead!"

Pandemonium broke loose in the unruly ranks of the Unseelie Host.

When the rain ceased, a stir of anticipation went through the long line of the waiting sidhe. They were wet and cold. Hands and backs were stiff from the unfamiliar weight of weapons and armour. It had been a long time since they'd gone to war. But with the rain gone now, they could see the ranks of their foe once more and backs straightened from slumped postures, weapons were readied again. Their gazes drifted from the Unseelie Host to the mortal who would lead them when the time was right.

Henk was uncomfortably aware of their attention. He could sense Loireag's tension beside him as she pawed the muddy ground. On his other side, Tuir sat glum on his small pony, knowing what was to come and regretting it. Mactire, resting in wolf-shape near the hooves of Henk's pony, rose to his feet.

"What are we waiting for?" Loireag demanded.

Henk stirred and glanced at her.

"It's not time yet," Tuir told her.

"Damn time and damn waiting," Loireag returned sharply. "I'm sick to death of them both."

Just then they heard the cry making the rounds of the Unseelie army. The droichan was dead.

"By the stag's own heart," Tuir murmured. "She did it." He turned to Henk, grinning. "Jemi did it!"

"Now let's finish the night's work," Loireag said.

"No need," the hob replied. "They'll disperse soon enough on their own."

Henk wanted to agree with Tuir, but he was looking at the house that they all called the Tower. Rising up from behind it—impossibly huge, at the wrong time in its cycle—was an enormous full moon. As he looked at it, something jumped inside Henk. Some part of him recognized that there was more to that orb than a dead asteroid floating in orbit around a blue-green planet. It was the wrong time of the night for that moon to rise. It shouldn't have been that full at this time of the month. So he knew that what he saw now was the Moon of Faerie.

And it was calling to him.

He touched the wet concertina on his lap and found that it was dry. He put his hands into both of its side straps. The Moon filled his sight, touched places inside him that he'd never known existed before. He wet his lips. He glanced at Loireag, urging him to play them to war, at Tuir, pleading for peace. Then at the Moon again.

It mourned the loss of its Pook.

It mourned the loss of so many of the borderfolk.

"Awake the music," Loireag hissed. "Send us to war."

"I beg you," Tuir said in the same breath. "Don't."

But Henk put his fingers to the buttons of his instrument and the music spilled forth.

Loireag gave a cry of joy. Tuir bent his head across his pony's neck in defeat. But the music Henk played was what neither of them had expected. He played the tune that the Moon woke in him, the music to call down her luck for the thirsty sidhe to drink, the liquid light of her luck that they'd been denied for so long.

As the music grew in strength, the Unseelie army began to moan. The bogan holding the unsainly banner with its crucified swan-man dropped the flag onto the muddy grass and fled. The whole of the Host broke their ranks and fled in all directions. Underfoot, radiating out from the Tower, grew a webwork of gleaming moonlight ribbons. The Tower was their center, like the center of a spider's web, and the moonroads spun out, through Kinrowan and out into the borderlands.

One by one, the fiaina sidhe dropped their weapons, and armour on the wet green grass. They looked to Henk. He stared at the swollen Moon that hung over the Jack's Tower, then dropped his gaze to the field before them. The Host was gone. Only the banner remained, trampled into the mud. The Moon spoke to him and gave him the secret pattern of its luck.

Still playing the music, Henk put his heels to the sides of his pony and led the sidhe out onto their rade.

The borderfolk fell in behind him as he took a moonroad that led away from the Tower, into the lands that were their own. They went, hobs and skinwalkers, a tall troll and waterfolk, little twigmen and tall willowy women, all the sidhe, until only Loireag and Tuir were left.

The hob looked at Loireag, but didn't speak. Loireag frowned. She tried to deny the tug and pull of the music and the Moon's rade, but she couldn't. At last she sighed and nodded to Tuir.

"This is the right way," she said. "We went back and forth, Jemi and I—first the one of us raising the banner, then the other—but it took a tadpole to stop the war."

She gazed after the last figures of the rade, almost lost from sight now.

"I'll still miss her," she added in a gruff voice.

"How could you not miss Jenna?" Tuir asked.

Tears brimmed in his eyes. He touched Loireag's shoulder, then touched heels to his pony and set off after the rade. Loireag waited a moment longer.

"Goodbye, Jenna," she whispered to that swollen Moon.

Then she took the shape of a dark horse and together the kelpie and hob joined the rade that Henk led through the borderlands in a pattern that the Moon had taught him when she moved inside him.

"You have faced your fears," Arn had told him as he first woke the music. "Now is the time to heal the scars they left behind. The night is for the strong and you have earned the right to take joy in its shadows."

As he led the winding column of the sidhe along a complicated pattern of moonroads, Henk understood what the Moon had meant. Whatever else this night left him, he would always look forward to the hours between dusk and dawn.

Jemi and Johnny stood at the window of the Tower's third-floor study and looked out over Kinrowan and its borderlands. It was Finn who had dissuaded the Pook from leading the sidhe into a charge against the Unseelie army.

"There'll be no need," he'd told her simply.

And, as they watched the Unseelie Host disperse in panic at the death of their leader and the waking of the Moon's music, as they saw Henk lead the sidhe away on the first rade the borderfolk had known for many a month, she had understood. So she stood by the window now, her arm around Johnny, his around her, and watched a quiet fall across Kinrowan.

In the room behind them, Bhruic's study had appeared once more between the four barren walls. The bogan that Gump had knocked down had woken and, after one look at the droichan's empty clothes, fled both the room and the Tower. Gump sat by the door, a bandage around his neck. Finn perched on the worktable, his legs swinging in the air. By the reading chairs, Jacky and Kate were sitting on the floor. They were both bruised and shaken, Jacky more so than Kate. They sat with their arms around each other, needing the comfort of their friendship to heal the fading memories of the void and everything that they'd so recently gone through.

It wasn't time to talk it through yet. It was just time to know that the other was there.

After a while, Jemi sighed and turned from the window.

Kate looked up. "When I warned you," she began. "When I said no . . ."

"I know," Jemi said. "The picture alone wouldn't have been enough. But the Moon was with us."

Finn nodded. "She has her own ways of dealing with droichan. I can see now that she used each one of us to do the task for her."

"Do you have a broom?" Jemi asked.

Kate nodded. "In the kitchen closet," she said, "If the bogans haven't eaten it. Why?"

"I thought I'd sweep up that mess," Jemi said, pointing with her chin at the heap of clothing and dust that lay in the middle of the room.

Seventeen

A month or so later, All Kindly Toes was playing a combination Halloween/farewell dance at the Glebe Community Centre. The four younger members of the band were finding that they needed more time for their university studies, Greg already had a new project lined up for the winter, and Jemi Pook had plans of her own. There was talk of re-forming in the spring—something similar had happened the previous autumn—but for now it was a time of playing their very best, because who knew when they'd all play together again? So the band was in fine form running through their favorites. "Shoo-de-poo-poo," "Mr. Big Stuff," "Love You Anyway," "B-A-B-Y," "Poison Ivy." . . . One tune followed the other, and the dance floor stayed packed.

Henk and Johnny were both there, Johnny standing on the sidelines, Henk dancing with Jacky or Kate, though more often the three of them danced together. Johnny just enjoyed watching them move and taking in the band—especially the pink-haired sax player who kept shooting him grins from the stage. When the long night finally wound down, the four of them helped the band pack up, collected Jemi, then they walked south down Bank Street to the Tower.

Gwi Kayleigh had returned from Ballymoresk in a day and a half, rather than the two she'd promised Finn, with a company of Seelie foresters in tow. She was relieved to find them all well and the threat over, though somewhat chagrined that she'd missed it all. She and the Laird's foresters were busy for a week or so, driving the last few Unseelie creatures from Kinrowan, but thereafter things settled down.

Once again it was possible to walk the streets of Kinrowan without spying a bogan or sluagh, though they all knew that wouldn't remain so. The Unseelie Court never changed. Sooner or later another boss would rise from their ranks, and they'd be dogging the folk of Kinrowan once more. But for now, it was quiet.

The damage to the Tower had been mended, though it was weeks before the boggy stench of sluagh and bogans was entirely erased. The trees in its yard snuggled close to its walls once more and the browning of its garden was due to the season now, rather than the presence of unsainly creatures.

When the five of them reached the Tower, Kate went to make tea for them all, while Jacky put on a Kate Bush record and they all made themselves comfortable. Just as Kate was bringing in the tea, Finn arrived, so she had to go back for another cup and dig up some donuts for the hob's sweet tooth.

"So you're really going?" Kate asked Jemi when they all had their tea.

The Pook nodded. "The sidhe have Henk to lead them on their rade and I never really wanted that anyway. I've lived most of my life outside of Faerie and I'm just as happy doing that."

"But looking for the Bucca?" Jacky asked. "That seems like it'll just take you deeper into Faerie."

"Maybe. But it's something I have to do." She touched a bone flute that hung in the hollow of her throat. "I want to ask him about these charms. Tell him about what happened to Jenna. And Johnny's coming with me, so what more could I want?"

"Jemi's promised to show me the fairer side of the borderlands on this trip," Johnny added. "And I want to learn more about what music can do in Faerie—how it fits in, and why."

Jemi grinned. "I'll make a Fiddle Wit out of him yet. Or if I don't, you can bet Salamon will."

"I almost wish I could go with you," Jacky said. "It sounds like it'll be fun." She shot Kate a quick glance. "If you should happen to run into Kerevan or Bhruic . . . "

"We'll give them all the news," Jemi said. "Shall I tell them you've got plans to become a skillywoman?"

Jacky laughed. "Not likely. I had three wally-stanes left after that night and I ended up wasting one trying to make myself a book like Kate's Caraid, only all my book does is tell me stories and try to play the odd trick on me. I guess I'm stuck being a Jack. But that's okay. Every Court needs one. Still you can tell them that Kate'll be a gruagagh before you know it."

"I've wondered about those wally-stanes," Henk said. "They seem . . . Well, I know if you've got a certain headset, *all* of Faerie seems impossible. But once you get into it, it begins to make a certain sense. Except for the wally-stanes. If they can do just about anything . . . ?"

"Hardly," Jacky said. "You should try using one."

"They're a rare magic," Finn explained, "and make for the basis of all those fairy tales of three wishes and the like. You won't find many these days, though. The nine that Jacky won from Kerevan are the first I've seen in a hundred years."

"Did you ever think of using one to wish for a hundred more wishes?" Henk asked.

Kate and Jacky laughed.

"God, no!" Jacky said. "Who knows what would happen if we did. They backfire enough as it is. If we tried that, they'd probably backfire a hundred times worse."

The record ended and Jacky replaced it with an Ian Tamblyn cassette.

"When will you be going?" she asked Jemi as she sat down again.

"Tonight." The Pook drank down what was left of her tea. "Now."

Johnny stood up with her. "We've our packs to collect and that's it. Thanks for letting me store Tom's stuff here. I couldn't think of a better place for those books."

"We collect books," Kate said.

"And hey," Jacky added. "We sure needed the furniture."

They said their goodbyes then, Henk leaving with Jemi Pook and Johnny. He was going to see them on their way as far as the Ottawa River. Finn left a little later, but not before reminding Kate to be on time for her skilly lessons.

When they were all gone, Jacky and Kate stood out in the back yard of the Tower and looked at the sky for a while.

"You don't think it was just the bone charms that brought Jemi and Johnny together, do you?" Jacky asked after a bit.

"What does it matter?" Kate replied. "They're happy enough now."

"Oh, I don't know. It'd just be nicer if it was only true love, that's all."

"God, you're such a romantic, Jacky."

"I guess." She turned to Kate. "We should go on a quest ourselves."

"What for?"

"Boyfriends."

"I take it back," Kate said. "You're not a romantic. You're just an incorrigible flirt."

Jacky gave her a slight punch on the arm, then sighed. "Maybe. But when you see something work the way it does for them, it kinda makes you want to have that for yourself, too—doesn't it?"

"Are you thinking of Eilian?"

Jacky nodded. "I'm not being very fair to him, am I? It's on-again, off-again, until neither of us knows what's going on. I keep getting afraid that one day I'll know for sure that he's the right one, but that by then it'll be too late. He'll have gotten himself married off to some Laird's daughter."

"So why don't you talk to him about it?"

"It's hard, Kate. My brain gets all tangled up and muddy when I try."

"Good things never come easy."

Jacky shook her head. "Trust you to come up with such an original thought."

She paused, looking as if she had more to say, but then stayed silent.

"But?" Kate prompted her.

Jacky gave her back a grin. "But I'll give it a try all the same."

"That's my Jacky," Kate said. "Ready to go in now?"

"Um-hmm."

Arm in arm, the two of them went back into the Tower to clean up the tea mugs and then to their respective beds. Above the gable peaks of the Tower, the Moon traveled west across the sky, and all of Kinrowan, and the Borderlands beyond, drank the bright luck of her light.